OF DREAMS AND ANGELS

OF DREAMS AND ANGELS

❖

JARED MORRISON

First Edition, 2021

Copyright © 2021 Jared Morrison

Copyright registered with the Canadian Intellectual Property Office.

All rights reserved under the Berne Convention for the Protection of Literary and Artistic Works.

No part of this book may be reproduced in any form or by any electronic or mechanical means, including information storage and retrieval systems, without permission in writing from the copyright owner, except by a reviewer, who may quote brief passages in a review.

This is a work of fiction. Names, characters, places, and incidents either are the product of the author's imagination or are used fictitiously. Any resemblance to actual events, locales, or persons, living or dead, is entirely coincidental.

www.jaredmorrison.ca

Cover design by Ashley Santoro
Book formatted for print and ebook by Phillip Gessert (gessertbooks.com)

For Erin
My real-life dream come true.

❖

And in memory of
Berit Karin Agasoster

CHAPTER 1
WHO BROKE *YOUR* HEART?

OCTOBER 1998

"TRUE LOVE NEVER fails."

Dawson regarded him for a moment, trying to get a read.

"Are you being serious right now?"

Joe burst into a laugh, threw his hands behind his head and leaned back in his chair. He kicked his feet up on the oak desk, a wide grin remaining on his face. Dawson shook his head and dropped into one of the high-armed leather seats normally reserved for clients.

"You are an unmitigated ass," he finally said. At this, another burst of laughter from Joe.

"Look, Dawson." Joe kicked his feet off the desk and leaned toward the younger man. "This is what—your second heartbreak this year? And at least the third since you started working for me?"

"What of it?"

"Well, that makes you either one of two things." Joe pushed any hint of mirth out of his expression and leveled his eyes at the junior associate.

"I can't wait to hear whatever this is," Dawson said.

"I'm being serious now," Joe returned.

"I don't doubt that."

"Either you're a slow learner, or a glutton for punishment." Normally in command of a stolid poker face due to the nature of his profession, Joe again broke composure and laughed. Dawson buried his face in his hands.

Joe stood and came around to take the other client seat beside Dawson. "Don't worry, I'm gonna go easy on you," he said, slapping a hand on the younger man's knee.

"Good. Because it's been an awful twenty-four hours, and I don't need you piling on."

"I know you don't. And all kidding aside, I know how you felt about Kerri. But do you mind if I tell you some other things I know, too?"

"Do I have a choice?" Dawson peeked an eye from between his fingers at his employer.

"No. But credit to you, at least you know that." Joe replaced the knee-slap with a clap on the back. "Here's the thing, young man—"

"You're not that much older than me. Twenty-five and thirty-seven don't exactly constitute a generation gap."

"Maybe not, but they do constitute a learning gap, when it comes to matters of the heart." Joe shifted in his chair, the groan of the cushion against the seatback releasing the scent of leather. This, to complement the oak, the paintings on the walls, and even the waterfall feature behind the desk—all designed to evoke the possibilities of proper financial planning. Not merely *getting* ahead, but staying there.

"I'll tell you what you need to do," Joe continued.

"And I know it's going to sound crass, or shallow, or whatever words you want to throw at it. I know it's going to deeply offend the sensibilities of your young, romantic heart." Joe reached over again and shook Dawson on the shoulder, trying to pull him out of the physical and emotional cradle into which he'd nestled.

"Again, I can't wait to hear this," the young associate muttered.

"You came in here—what was it, three years ago?—fresh off your degree, top of your class, and looking for work that would annihilate those student loans as quickly as you racked them up. We went for coffee. Then dinner. We worked out at the private club. Rode in the car I paid for with cash. A professional courting process, as it were, so I could get to know if you were a fit on this team, *and* to show you what's possible. And in the end, you said you wanted what I had, am I right?"

"Yes."

"Okay. Just recapping what you told me, seeing if it's still correct. And do you still want that?"

"Yes."

"Okay. Then answer me this: at any point in that process—whether when you ordered off menus with no prices, or when you took the wheel of a car where one of the tires cost more than that beater you were driving—do you remember seeing me with a woman? Do you remember me even *mentioning* a woman?"

"No."

"Exactly. Do you remember me telling you *how* I arrived at a place where I could tell you to order whatever you wanted, or drive my car around for a day, just to see how it felt?"

"Yes."

"What did I say?"

"You said 'A plan is not just a roadmap, it's a *decision*.' That the paper it's printed on is useless if you don't follow the path."

"I'll say it again: *exactly*. I don't get from the trailheads to the end of my hikes by suddenly veering off course and thrashing through the trees, or shucking my pack when it feels like a grind to carry. I don't bring on the next seven-figure client by deciding tax planning doesn't apply to them, just because it's tedious. And I sure don't order off the menu with no prices without knowing everything else has been taken care of, first." Joe loosened his tie and released the top button of his vest. Another grin spread across his face.

"You wanna know what love is, Dawson?"

Dawson turned his head to look at Joe. "Are you going to make me answer every single one of your rhetorical questions?"

"Part of the trade, and you know that. Never end a sentence in a conversation with someone you're trying to convert without asking a question. Ideally one where the only answer is '*yes*.'" Joe flashed the grin that had won more client conversions than anyone in the office could count anymore.

"Do you know what love is?" Joe asked again.

"What." Not so much a question as a grunt.

"'Love'—for most people, that is—is tossing out your dehydrated meals on the first day in the backcountry, deciding you can walk the rest of the trail on berries simply because they taste better. Love is deciding to pull money from your investments during a down-market to buy a shiny new—and depreciating, I might add—car, because as long as you have to get to and from work, you might as well look good doing it, right? Love is deciding that just because you've hit the big time in an income year, you don't need to budget anymore. You don't need to save, because it'll always be this good."

"I don't see how these metaphors fit."

"Maybe they don't—and maybe that makes them all the more appropriate, my young friend."

"Will you please stop calling me 'young'? It's ridiculous coming from you. Just because you're salty doesn't mean you're wiser."

"The point is that love *doesn't* fit. It *doesn't* make sense. It's irrational. I'm not saying it can't be beautiful. Some people, for reasons passing understanding, say that it is. But I am telling you—especially after three heartbreaks in three years—that if you want relationships in your life, they need to be part of the plan, just like everything else."

"Since when does anyone ever *plan* on falling in love?"

"Since time immemorial, probably. Matchmakers have existed since biblical times, at least."

"So now you're saying I should go see a matchmaker?"

"It probably couldn't hurt, based on your record. But no, that's not what I'm saying. I'm telling you relationships need to be strategized. Planned with bearish rates of return, and bullish inflation. The last time you got dumped—"

Dawson winced.

"Fine. The last time you got your heart smashed, by—what was her name, Julia? I can't remember. Doesn't matter. Anyway, you took at least a week off, and even when you came back you were far below capacity for at least a month."

A knock at the door, and Joe stood to take a printout of the day's closing market prices from his executive assistant. He glanced at the values. "Karen, can you call Stan Thibodeau, the new prospect, and find a polite way to tell him he either needs to get in here and christen the latrine, or else find another twenty years of life expectancy in which to keep working? He's missing tremendous opportunity here."

"Will do, Mr. Riley," she said, closing the door and returning to her cubicle outside Joe's office. Joe set the paper down and leaned against his desk.

"It doesn't matter to me, so much, if you're not producing—though you're an integral part of this practice, Dawson. What matters is that it goes against what *you* said you wanted out of life."

Dawson straightened up. "Career and cars and trips and security is not *all* that I said I wanted, Joe. I mean, what's the point in having all those things, if you don't have someone to share them with?"

"That would be a valid point if A: you had those things, and B: you'd held on to that someone to share them with."

Dawson crumpled in the seat once more.

"But at the moment," Joe continued, "you have neither. And based on the way these dump— excuse me, *breakups* set you back, you're definitely not going to get there."

"So what are you saying? I can be poor and in love, or wealthy and alone?"

Joe chuckled, and took his seat in the wingback chair behind the imposing bureau. "No. You're still missing it." He returned his feet to the corner of the desk, leaned back, and folded his hands over a stomach flat from endless miles on the trail. "And again, right now you're broke. Remember there's a difference between 'broke' and 'poor': the former a temporary condition, the latter a mindset. Right now you're broke and out of love, *and* you're alone."

"I am still in love."

"If you say so. I'll concede that point. Once more, however, I'll build off an earlier question: in all the time we've worked together, have you ever seen a woman in my life?"

"No."

"And do you think I'm a monk?"

"I don't know. You keep a better poker face about your private life than you do with a new prospect."

"And do you think I'm lonely?" Joe asked.

"I'll answer your infernal questions with one of my own: if you're normally notoriously private about the logistics of your life, how do you expect me to have any data on your emotional one?"

"Another point for Dawson. But the answer to both of my questions is 'No.'"

"Good for you."

"I'm not a cad, Dawson. I'm not spending weekends

packed into depraved clubs around town, plying women with drinks and flashing the vehicle logo on my keychain. Little as you may know about how I spend my time, you know it's not doing that."

"How would I know? Maybe all your pictures around here are just postcards from mountains and trails you think look impressive." Dawson bit down on his tongue.

"I'm going to let you in on a little secret—though based on how you're receiving the pearls I'm giving you here, you don't deserve it," Joe said, his million-watt smile back on display. "Are you ready?"

"Sure."

"Do you know why I have the life I have? Why it's 'Riley Private Wealth Management' on the letterhead, and not 'Metzger Wealth Management?'"

"Because you've been at this fifteen years longer than I have, and your last name sounds better than mine?"

"Both things are true, but no, wrong once again." Joe stood and walked to the closet between the office and his private washroom. He grabbed the three-button jacket matching his pinstripe vest and began pulling it on, not missing a beat in the conversation. "It's because *when I'm here, I'm here. And when I'm not, I'm not.*"

"I can't remember which school of Buddhism that's from—Zen or Yoda," Dawson said to Joe. And under his breath to himself, *"Shut up or you're gonna to get fired."*

Joe was undeterred. "This is in many ways a twenty-four-seven type of job, or at least in can be, in the beginning. I told you that when you started, when you said you wanted to build a practice like this one. But it's important that it's not all-encompassing. That you plan and build various side-accounts, if you like."

"This is sounding more salacious by the minute."

Joe re-fastened the button on his collar, straightened his tie perfectly without aid of a mirror. He sat down again in the vacant client chair.

"I've been in relationships, Dawson. Proper ones, despite whatever your misguided thoughts suggested. Beautiful, successful women; some with whom I even shared some of those things you spoke of before. But here was the key—and because you took umbrage with my last metaphor, let's try a different one. Like I said, when I'm here, I'm here. And when I'm not, I'm not. That doesn't mean you can't have someone in your life, it just means that it's important to keep that area as a module in your plan, and not the plan itself. There!—" Joe stood up. "That works—an island. You need to keep your relationships like an island in your life that you visit. The key is that *you* go to visit, so that if your little romantic beachside firepit becomes an inferno, it doesn't burn down the mainland. Understand?"

Dawson looked up at Joe. "Who hurt you, man?"

"I beg your pardon?"

"Who broke *your* heart?"

For an instant, years of practiced expressions—contingencies of body language built for any client concern or objection—fell away and were replaced by a look Dawson didn't recognize. The moment was shorter than the space between an inward and outward breath, however, and the look was gone.

"Nothing's broken here," Joe continued, the trademark smile back on display, "other than someone's bank balance after too many nights off wine-ing and dining in vain. Am I correct?"

"Take your questions and get outta here to wherever it is you go, and leave me alone with my dumped, broken heart," Dawson snapped back, extending a hand and mimicking Joe's smile. "Does that sound fair?"

Joe laughed, returned the handshake, and walked to the office door. He bid a good weekend to Dawson and Karen, and waved a hand at Janice, seated in the office adjacent to his.

"After all these years, I never know if he's off to another hike nearby, or the Redwoods in California, or the Appalachian Trail," Karen said, as Dawson came and stood beside her desk. "Did he mention whatever his next adventure is?"

Dawson shrugged. "He said something about an island."

CHAPTER 2
DREAMING

Of his "Non-Negotiable Success Factors," proper sleep hygiene was firmly in Joe's Top Five. Joe disputed the notion that to be successful, one needed to adopt an unrelenting entrepreneurial paradigm: back-to-back client meetings late into the evening. Phone calls and letters to follow. Scouring market prices well past the midnight hour. Rinse and repeat, starting no later than four in the morning. Seven days a week, eight would be preferable. To him, that was as absurd as a client attempting to achieve wealth without a plan.

If he was masterful with finding efficiencies in financial strategies, Joe adhered to the maxim of first being efficient himself. "I do more with four hours than most do with forty," he'd say. The Abe Lincoln quote, "Give me six hours to chop down a tree, and I will spend the first four sharpening the axe," was prominently displayed in his office, along with similar axioms by Tony Robbins and Jim Rohn.

When it came to rest and recovery, Joe applied the same discipline as he did with exercise and nutrition. No caffeine past noon. Consistent wake and sleep times. Blackout blinds for summer months where sunrise and sunset didn't line up with his day-timer. Air conditioning to ensure optimal temperatures for drawing him below consciousness between the hours of ten p.m. and five a.m.

As for whatever happened inside the body and brain during the hours he slept, Joe didn't know, nor did he care. He *did* know that whatever forces responsible for creating humankind had insisted on a sleep cycle accounting for one-third of the day. If that was necessary to squeeze more out of the remaining sixteen hours, far be it from him to balk at primal forces of nature.

If the trade-off for the hours spent between the sheets was occasional subconscious entertainment, so be it as well. Dreams, for Joe, were little more than musings of a drunk-tired consciousness. Nothing to read into, and certainly not worthy of analysis. What did it mean that he could never seem to turn on light switches or dial phones whilst in the company of Mr. Sandman? Nothing, no more significant than other nights when he had powers of flight. There had been little evidence suggesting he ought to extract meaning from the bizarre menageries of the night. There was no proof dreams ever meant anything.

Until he dreamt about her. Or more accurately, he dreamt *as* her.

Joe had only been under anesthesia once, for wisdom teeth extraction. As such, his sample size was small, but he did remember the dreamlike experience of coming to after surgery. The feeling of being in a haze for hours afterwards, yet knowing he was in fact conscious, he was in fact awake, in a world that had gone out of focus. The first dream was like that.

It felt as if he was looking through the eyes of someone else who was waking after anesthesia. It wasn't that *this* person was sedated, exactly, but more like Joe had been seated behind their eyes, trying to absorb what he was seeing while looking through glass that had been soaped-over. He was clearly in someone else's body, but he had no control over it.

Every time the person in charge of the body spoke, it was like a gong echoing within Joe's head. Though the voice sounded like English, Joe couldn't decipher the conversation he was hearing, as though the words had been tossed around in a raffle drum and then rearranged out of order. He couldn't tell if his inability to understand was because he was truly hearing gibberish, or if it was thanks to the overall sensory disorder. To add to the confusion, every movement from this body he was in provoked a feeling of swaying or spinning. Joe felt like he'd had orthodontic surgery on a boat.

Then there was the voice itself: unmistakably a woman's, but the tonality and dialect were unfamiliar. Joe's exhausted mind scanned the repository of voices he knew—mother, sisters, past lovers—but no lights of recognition flipped on. He searched further back. Was he dreaming through the eyes of an old relative? An aunt or grandmother? He was fairly certain this was no one he knew—he hadn't known anyone in his family with an accent similar to the one he was hearing.

He—or perhaps more accurately, she—appeared to be standing in a kitchen. The conversation he was hearing was between her and three children. Perhaps with another woman as well, but Joe couldn't see beyond the cloudy peripheral vision, nor could he will his host to turn her head. If the voice coming from this body was barely intelligible, those from the others sounded like the teachers from Charlie Brown cartoons. Joe didn't bother trying to sort out what they were saying in question or reply to the woman he was seeing through. It was enough to try and get his bearings, particularly while unable to direct her movements or what her eyes focused upon.

The children looked to be scattered in age between single-digits and the teen years. With progeny never part of his plan—and thereby usually becoming a sticking point in his relationships—Joe wasn't certain of the proper terms. Pre-teen? Tween? He tried to recall from infrequent visits with his nieces and nephews what the various ages even looked like, but they too—his memories, along with these dream-children—remained obscured and unfocused.

The scene itself appeared to be what any normal, school day morning might look like. Checking in on homework assignments, discussing logistics for that evening's extra-curricular activities, children adorning backpacks as though they were an irksome younger sibling vying for a piggyback. A coffee pot percolating, half-eaten bowls of cereal on the counter, a toaster ready to Jack-in-the-box its contents at any moment. It wasn't that Joe could specifically spot all these things with the fog-ringed eyes he was seeing with, but it was the feeling the dream offered. While he hadn't experienced this environment beyond his own childhood, it felt warm. It felt welcoming.

Yet confusion remained, and he strained to grapple

control over this body. In his own voice, Joe tried to blurt out, *"WH-WH-WH-HHH-OOOOO A-A-A-RRRRRRREE YUH-YUH-YUH-YOOOOUUUUU?"* and *"WH-WH-WH-WHEEERRRRR AM-AM-AM-AM IIIIIIIIIIIIIIIII?"* And perhaps most importantly, *"WH-WH-WH-WHOOOOOOOO AMMMM IIIIIIII-IIIIIII?"*

Every attempt to speak either produced no response from this woman's face, or a string of unrelated and incomprehensible words instead. Still, the others in the room appeared to understand whatever it was she did say, and replied in their dissonant melodies. The sounds in the room now felt magnified and deafening, as though he were underwater while fireworks cracked off above and a band played poolside.

The mounting cacophony instigated a feeling previously unfamiliar to Joe while dreaming: nausea. He felt that unmistakable and non-negotiable churning, and thought he might actually vomit. How, he couldn't imagine—*If I puke,* he thought, *will it be through this woman's body? Or will it just be a sensation like the rest, where she doesn't seem to feel it, but I do? Am I going to awake having booted all over my bed?*

Desperation came next: a frantic attempt to gain control and steer this foreign body towards a bathroom, sink, large salad bowl, anything. The body refused his commands and remained stationary at the kitchen island. If his host wasn't sweating and shaking, Joe knew he was, and couldn't comprehend how this human costume betrayed on the outside all the symptoms he felt internally.

His panic at a peak, he remembered thinking *thisisgon nabebadthisisgonnabeuglywhywon'tyoumovewhywon'tyouf indasinkwhatingodsnameishappeningthishastobeadreamb utwhywon'titstopitneedstostop*—and just as suddenly, Joe found himself in his own bed. His own room. Suspicion of a dream confirmed. Doused in sweat, and heaving uncontrollably.

The saving grace was a wastebasket he kept beside the bed. While he never wanted to accumulate trash in his bedroom—his sleep hygiene sanctuary—he wanted less to have something in need of disposal and nowhere to put it. In this moment of frantic, unplanned nonsense, Joe leaned over the side and evacuated half-digested bits of last night's dinner.

When that first wave passed, he made a lopsided dash to his ensuite in anticipation of a subsequent episode. Only a brief fit of gagging, coughing, and a half-cup of bile came with the next. This *real* world began to slow its spinning, while Joe began to get a handle on what just happened.

As he leaned one arm on the toilet reservoir, he realized his other arm was still holding the wastebasket. This prompted a wry smile; his mother always proclaimed the key to a clean home was in never wasting a trip to another room by not returning something that belonged there at the same time. Here he was, unconsciously adhering to that maxim, attempting to assert order on a disordered (and disgusting) situation. Joe dumped the remnants of dinner into the bowl, watched it join the rest of what his stomach rejected, and flushed.

He moved to the mirror to survey the damage, and

found his face reflecting the feel of the rest of his body: drenched in sweat, pale, cold and disoriented. Joe typically remembered fragments of his dreams, but the majority of these were nonsensical: some unconsciously stored memory of the day played out in a greater—or at least comically embellished—way while his body rested. Most of the time he found his dreams a nuisance, keeping his mind active on a peripheral level when he wanted silent and sublime reprieve from the demands of the day. He'd already lived his day once, he didn't need to experience it again featuring strange cameos by Spiderman or his boss from the golf cart cleaning job he had when he was fifteen.

The bizarre episode on this night was different than any previous excursion into the land of the subconscious. Not only had his dreams—even the rare nightmares—rarely affected his physiology, they'd never taken on such a real (if distorted) quality. There was always something—treehouse building with John from Head Office, for instance—within the dream to alert him of an unlikely situation, or the eventual return to wakefulness confirmed it. But here, now, standing in what he knew was his body and his home, he couldn't escape the feeling of having been transported—violently so.

He mulled this over while regarding his dilated pupils and clammy skin, feeling his heartbeat not only within his chest but pulsating at his neck and wrists. The voices of his internal committee—The Parliament, he'd dubbed them—were having a field day, engaging in full debate over the meaning (or lack of one) of this out-of-body, yet in-body experience.

In some long ago personal development seminar, Joe and fellow attendees had been told one of the pillars of self-mastery was recognizing, naming, and eventually claiming the disparate (and often discordant) voices within. He'd labeled two of the main internal political parties as "The Pragmatists" and "The Cynics," even assigning names to some of the individual voices that spoke for each. "Uncle Peter"—the namesake of a departed relative Joe recalled from childhood mostly for a soothing, wisdom-endowed baritone—was the appointed voice for The Pragmatists. It was Uncle Peter who spoke up now. *Hey, dreams are funny. They're not meant to make sense, or to make sense of. Wipe off your face, brush your teeth—stomach acid is murder on enamel— check the time, and if there's time, finish your sleep.* Joe obeyed these sensible commands; cleaned himself up, found it was one-thirty, and laid back down.

Yet sleep eluded him, and he found himself watching the numbers on the clock pulse from one minute to the next, eventually begging time to speed up so he could distract his mind with the demands of the day. Of all he couldn't sort through, what bothered him the most was why he felt bothered to begin with. It wasn't as though he'd dreamt of driving a vehicle that lost control, or had slipped off the edge of a skyscraper, or was bedside for a loved one's last moments.

He had been in a kitchen, for crying out loud. A perfunctory conversation between family members. The being-in-a-woman's-body thing was strange, but again, that wasn't what troubled him the most. Whatever it was that did—his mind couldn't put a name or description to it—continued to evade him, as did sleep. Until, classic to a night of interrupted slumber, he felt himself drifting off twenty minutes before his alarm stood ready to take him back to order, to consistency, to discipline, to *real*.

CHAPTER 3
PASSING OF THE SEASONS

F IVE A.M. WAKEUP, even on weekends. Even after those instances where a social or work function cut into his sleep window. Even when he'd apparently teleported across an ocean, to see through the eyes and move through the body of a woman he'd never met, forfeiting the time his own body ought to have been in repose.

Five a.m., but if anything—weekend or not—the sooner he could get on the trail, the sooner he'd clear his mind of whatever that had been. Whoever *she* had been.

Hiking was deliverance from whatever the week wrought, professional or otherwise. While Joe loathed the notion of fulfilling the stereotype of "working for the weekend," his diligence and discipline had afforded him freedom to pick up and go any weekend he chose, which was most. The mountains and trails offered a reprieve from the pressures and pursuits of the week, but mostly they offered a glimpse of a life that was *more*. They could "right size" Joe in a way few else things could—literally, mentally, and physically.

Once he was able to get past the tourist crowds near the front of the trailhead (who invariably turned back at the first signs of elevation or less manicured paths), Joe was left free to connect with that thing he dared not put a name to—lest he be duped in the end by anything resembling belief—but nevertheless had an inkling was there. At times he wondered if that was why he hiked in the first place: to connect with those dynamics of the universe—whatever it was that created the mountains and streams in a perfection independent of human touch—without ever having to admit they were acquainted.

But this, like every ephemeral dream up to that point, wasn't something Joe would have extended an abundance of thought. All the existential debate in the world made no difference to the mountains in front of him or the paths beneath his feet. Thought, or faith, or belief was good as far as they went, but philosophy wouldn't take his steps for him. Contemplation didn't assuage lost opportunity or regret. Action did.

It wasn't that he carried any conscious or pervading sense of disappointment with his life; he felt content, he felt organized, he was pleased most days with the life he'd designed and the progress he'd made. Yet at times the question would needle at the back of his mind: *Progressing toward what?* Maybe this was simply a rite of passage that came with one's late thirties; perhaps it was just an ironic good sense to question the sanity of one's choices, no matter their sensibility.

It was probably perfectly normal to wonder if there had been squandered time; if he should have followed improbable yet exciting childhood yearnings to go to space, write novels, become a movie star. Somewhere along the way the internal committee had taken over—

The Parliament began sitting in regular session—and voices purporting reason and practicality steered him toward the tangible, the controlled, the self-made. Joe watched family and friends forfeit their lives to paradigms of paying the mortgage and taxes on time, of contributing to employer-matched retirement accounts, of sitting on condo boards. He wondered if life in those circumstances hadn't regressed to consumerism in the name of lifestyle, and working merely to support whatever it took to keep up appearances.

He quietly observed as friends from school lived haphazardly, settling into lives of reactivity versus proactivity long before they were conscious of it. If awareness dared ever rear its head, it usually came in the form of tee times or poker nights masquerading for outlets to complain about wives they couldn't remember falling in love with. To vent about children they'd had out of obligation instead of love. To bemoan careers they never would have chosen if they'd known at twenty what they knew pushing forty. All this seemed in service of a dubious trade for cars and home theatres and recreational vehicles. For homes in which to house relationships they apparently couldn't stand, while working in careers for which they had no passion, to pay for lives they couldn't afford.

That wasn't Joe Riley. Life was far too demanding—too fickle, too finite—to be approached with improvisation and inaction. Planning was key, discipline was paramount. Consistency and execution were the corner and keystones of any well-ordered and well-lived life. "One shot," he was fond of saying to his clients, "one shot is all we get, so don't you think it's important to aim?" In moments of wondering what he might have missed, Joe would hear Uncle Peter proffer a comforting reminder that in every choice there is inherent sacrifice. That sacrifice was merely the cost of admission to the life one chose to design. One determined what cost was acceptable—making certain never to be a borrower nor lender in money, time or emotion—made the payment, and pursued the path.

If he privately lamented his solitude at times—in a lesser heard voice emanating from some rogue party that occasionally stole the microphone while parliament was in session—he'd rarely indulge beyond the initial, unasked-for thought. That voice was swiftly quieted by a coalition of the Realist and Cynic Parties who would say, "This is just what life is about. The biggest choice one will ever make is whether life happens *for* you, or *to* you." For Joe, it had become an enduring mantra that one's life was framed by deliberation, by action, by individual determination. Why leave things to chance? To the stars? Make your own universe. Live your own design. Those watchwords had served him well throughout his thirty-seven years, and while there hadn't been a complete absence of debris in the path, there was little reason to believe this creed wouldn't serve him well for the next forty or beyond.

He was the youngest advisor in his firm's history to reach nine-figures in assets under management. A sleek practice with less than one hundred clients. A team where the associates courted *him*, and not the other way around. Special dispensation to brand under his own name and private wealth banner. After expenses and overhead, there was passive income from his practice, used to fuel further passive income from investments and real estate.

He could make more money in a day without getting out of bed than many of his peers earned in a week—and yet there was no time wasted to sleep, no opportunities squandered to complacency. And certainly, no distraction in the way of a serially-broken heart as was the case with Dawson, or a debilitating, drawn-out divorce as experienced by their colleague, Janice.

Joe had been spared these encumbrances; the pain, mourning, and lost time that accompanied them. He'd laugh it off when family or friends peppered him with the "When are you going to settle down and enjoy your hard work?" questions, while they delighted in rides in his BMW, or regarding with awe the photographs from one backcountry excursion to the next. He *was* enjoying the work. He *was* settled, in his own way—married to the dopamine of discipline and achievement. The former fostered the latter, and the latter kept him free from shackles he saw constraining friends and family.

Yet from time to time that other, rogue voice would continue to needle at him.

This is just the way it is, he told himself. *There are people the world over far worse off, with honest-to-God problems that exceed the existential ones.* He was free. He was secure. He'd built something that was meaningful to him, even if it didn't completely fit the accepted traditions of society. He wanted for nearly nothing, and when he did, it was simply a matter of creating a plan to attain it. If the price for that was the occasional mental trip into the Forest of What Might Have Been, so be it. It was probably far better to wonder what might have come to pass from a place of security, than wonder what might have been while struggling to survive, or worse yet, feeling trapped by one's own life.

The mountains and the trails always worked to reframe the debate, however. Out here, none of those questions mattered. There was only the sense that somehow *this* was what was important. No matter what a person wound up doing to make a living—advisor, ad executive, astronaut, au pair—in the grand design none of it would be of any consequence. If the mountains themselves weren't eternal, then neither were the pedestrian pursuits of life.

It was a paradox that further exasperated Joe's ability to reconcile his choices, but this too was healed by the sojourns, grand or small, to places where humans hadn't made an imprint beyond the paths beneath his feet. It called to mind a sense of what was important once the minutiae and superficial had been stripped away: the need to eat, the need to sleep, the need to survive, and the need to move forward. Something about having to hike to where he would lay his head for the night, of constructing his own shelter, in creating his own heat for food—these things always brought him back to a sense of peace. A reminder that for all that could be questioned or go wrong in a given day, interaction, or relationship, this much of life could be conquered through these individual feats of survival, with none of it taken for granted.

For all the nights he fell asleep shivering from misjudging the weather and packing the wrong weight of sleeping bag, or bedraggled evenings when he couldn't get a fire started due to unexpected rain—rather than consternation, these small defeats usually came with a sense of peace, of humbling. *This* was what mattered. This was where life made sense. It was one thing to conquer the worlds of business or self-mastery—it was another to prove to himself he could not only survive against the elements, but thrive.

This reconnection with the fundamentals also went a long way to assuage the lack of connection he felt elsewhere. Even before the seminars on non-verbal communication or neuro-linguistic programming, Joe had always been a charmer—could get along and find a connection point with anyone—yet for most of his life he felt true relationship eluded him. Small talk, despite its place in his profession, was maddening. He had never been the guy who could pass the minutes at a social function talking about football scores or when the writ would drop on the next election. Even amongst other hikers and outdoor "enthusiasts," he was usually left wanting for conversation once initial talk of trails and gear was exhausted. If anything, he felt more frustrated by these surface bids for connection—after all, wasn't one of the main reasons for hiking found in the solitude, and the chance to be deliberately *anti*-social?

If small talk was tedious and wasteful, its opposite was equally daunting—if and when Joe was called upon to share details of his life. He was an expert listener; *that* was the part of his career he'd mastered long before he'd attended his first seminar or signed his first million-dollar client. When he'd interviewed with Summit Wealth nearly twenty years ago, the hardened and clichéd sales director asked Joe what he knew about closing clients. The young graduate pivoted and replied that he knew how to listen. How to hear pain points. How to respond with a word or an expression—or even a hand on a shoulder—that conferred understanding. Translated into compassion. Elicited connection—one-sided though it might be.

Maybe it had come from being the youngest in a family of three girls and a boy. Perhaps it was the years spent witnessing the serial entrepreneurialism of his parents—of fortunes won and lost, gambles made and profits squandered, of relationships pushed to their brink. He'd learned to watch, to listen, and ultimately, to empathize without patronizing. Most importantly, he'd learned to let listening be the extent of his connection to misery or compromise. He'd heard and observed the difficulties of others and drawn those pitfalls onto his own map of life. Learned where others strayed from the path, and how to keep his steps within the edges.

Dawson's question—*"Who broke your heart?"*—had thrown him, if only for a moment. There had certainly been encounters along the way that had threatened to derail the plan. A stolen glance, a profound impromptu conversation with a stranger. Some of these progressed into those islands he'd permit himself to visit, after that quiet voice of "what if" became persistent. Yet these little holidays rarely led to more than unnecessary complication or distraction, and often had the side effect of forcing a (misguided, he was certain) sense of loneliness every time the isle turned to ashes. They left him with the pervading sense—if not fear—that in the end, he was still truly, irrevocably, alone. Perhaps *meant* to be on his own. A completely independent entity, in practice and spirit.

He knew the whispers of friends and family, of women who had drawn close to the flame—and most certainly those who had been burned by it—wondering why he wouldn't commit. Conspiracy theories proliferated as to what might be wrong with him. For those untouched by the fire—especially in this age range where many long-term relationships crumbled, where many a divorcée reentered the dating pool—there was no shortage of suitors keen for his affections. Yet for the supposedly lucky few who cracked past the outer shell, Joe remained as unreachable as ever. They often left their time with him even more baffled about the man he was, what made him tick, or for whom he was searching.

For Joe, he ended those dalliances more disillusioned than before, viewing couple-hood as nothing more than two people indulging their biological and emotional needs for a time, and in the end, ultimately compromising one another. There were too many layers, too much complexity—though he endeavoured to be clear about who he was and what he wanted from the start. Most relationships seemed to amount to little more than a protracted game of who could compel vulnerability from their partner without relinquishing too much of their own heart. A disillusioned friend once said "The person who cares less in a relationship is the one with the upper hand," and Joe had experienced little evidence in his liaisons to suggest this wasn't true. One person always fell harder than the other, and that was the one who got hurt. It was dangerous to be that person. Vulnerability was a trap.

There was a part of him that loathed this reflex of his mind when it came to relationships; he knew some corner of his fortified heart longed to believe these things weren't true. Just as he subscribed to the mantra of "Map your life, follow the path, enjoy the destination," when it came to business and achievement, in a distant life he'd attempted a similar paradigm when it came to love. "Make a list of the qualities you want in another person, find them, date, move in together. Propose, marry, make a family, live happily ever after." For a time, he began that journey only to watch the plan fall to pieces after he'd bent his knee.

Rachel had been a good girl—sweet, trusting, and honorable—but even at twenty-three carried enough pain and patterning (they both did) to lead Joe to the realization one is never dating just the one human being. *We're in relationship with everyone who ever held sway over that person. We're not just seeing the woman or man,* he'd think, *we're dating their mother and father, brothers and sisters, and every single person who has held their heart—for better or worse—up to that point.* Rachel was beautiful, wickedly intelligent, studious and ambitious. But in their mutual inexperience of knowing—if anyone ever could—the necessary ingredients and recipe for a successful relationship, they had done untold damage to one another's hearts. Rachel had long ago moved on—literally, had moved across the country—but Joe's heart had not.

Not from a feeling of yearning for her, but in the

scars that remained. Their dissolving relationship made its final death gasp in the form of Rachel's announcement she was going to pursue her graduate degree at McGill, which might as well have been half the world away in the universe of a young relationship. Citing her scholarships, she professed the need to focus on nothing but school, saying she couldn't afford any distractions. Joe had taken his mortally wounded heart and dealt with it as an animal deals with illness or injury. Alone. He wasn't about to fight for someone who viewed his heart and love as a "distraction," though cognitively—and later with the quality of wisdom only ever extracted from looking back—he knew that's not what she meant. At least not entirely.

She was hurting too, and in the coded language of "needing to focus" and "can't have distractions" was likely saying, "You and I, in all our fallibility, occupy all my thoughts and emotions. I want us to work, but I can't carry this pain at the same time I'm trying to build my life." In that last moment, he had seen her off at the airport along with her parents. After his ne'er-to-be in-laws stepped away, she handed him back the engagement ring adorned with a tiny rock, the one he'd scrimped for with serving jobs squeezed in between his own undergraduate hours.

After she'd quietly whispered in his ear "I know you loved me, and please know I truly loved you, but maybe love is having the courage to do the hard thing when things are impossibly hard," Joe had taken his pain and gone underground. In doing so, he vowed he would never be that open again, he would never be the one who cared more, or shown their cards first.

Joe was certain a therapist—to say nothing of Dawson from work—would have a field day if he ever coughed up that information. That is, should he ever require therapy that the mountains and trails couldn't offer. He knew, in that pivotal moment of donning his armour, that he had likely sacrificed untold gifts, passions, growth and connection. But he also knew he had successfully never been hurt like that again. Not even close.

He had resolved to build his life without compromise, without pain, without that maddening dance of who should go first or who was more involved or who was feeling what or who was doing whom. If the cost was ruminating every now and again on lost connection, that was a cost he could bear. What he couldn't bear again was a heart shattered as it had been that rainy morning on the departures level. No reward was worth that price.

As was the usual effect of hiking, Joe realized he'd been musing on these things for the better part of several hours, while the endless shades of green, orange, and red of the fall foliage passed with every step. Though the breeze carried traces of the bitter cold that would envelop this part of the world in the coming months, this was his favourite time of year to hike. Snow had begun to cap the highest peaks again, returning the mountains to that sense of majesty the summer meltdown robbed. The trees blanketing the hillside looked like an ocean on gentle fire. Metaphors danced in Joe's head about the passing of the seasons; how life can be at its most beautiful during times of endings. That in order to rebuild, for a time life must go dark, cold, and quiet.

He reached his destination for the night: a beautiful

treed-in stretch along a slow moving but talkative river. He would always walk as far as needed to find that perfect backdrop, although fifteen minutes into the mountains that was almost anywhere. A place he could raise his tent along water, whether one of the emerald glacial lakes found at these elevations, or one of the incomparably beautiful rivers Joe sensed were more alive than other moving bodies of water. Streams teeming with life, carrying endless stories of nature's secrets. A world untainted by man. Life unfettered by obligation, desire or heartbreak. Life at its purest, simplicity in survival.

There were few things closer to perfection than opening a tent flap to see and listen to the narration of a flowing river, set against mountainside in every direction. What stories existed in those hills? What kind of eyes might be on him now, as he sat beside his inapposite tent and gear? Part of the joy was in knowing he would never know. Part of the bliss was the knowledge that out here, he was just a temporary part of the backdrop, of a wild community where his stature was reduced. Far from being just a man among men, he was a creature among many, and certainly not the most powerful. These brief, but frequent sojourns did more to charge Joe's batteries than any new client, acquisition or investment—and certainly any romantic entanglement—ever had, nor could he imagine ever would.

Joe built his fire and went to that most sublime of places—being active in tasks necessary for survival. He wasn't about to freeze or starve anytime soon, yet sat with the knowledge that if he wanted heat, he needed to create it himself. If he wanted a warm dinner, that subsequent action was reliant on the first. Sure, he had a stove to heat a dehydrated meal if necessary, but that would cheapen the experience of relying on the elements. Relying on his own abilities. Action, set to the soundtrack of nature. The consistent, indiscernible—yet somehow entirely understandable—language of water and woods.

He listened to the discussion of leaves in trees as the wind nudged them toward the denouement of their little lives. He heard their chatter of resistance as they tried to stay aloft for a day or two longer. There were occasional sounds of fallen branches snapping from the footfalls of animals Joe couldn't see. Echoes of stifled arguments between squirrels and chipmunks fighting for wares to last the frozen months ahead. A few remaining birds offering last-minute travel tips to their kin as they squeezed out the last habitable Canadian autumn moments, as had Joe.

This was perfection. This was life at its essence. Whatever mattered during business hours faded out of existence here. No matter how pressing anything ever seemed in that fabricated hamster-wheel of being, all of it was carried away by the wind in these woods. There were no deadlines to meet, no traffic to contend with, no Black Friday deals to queue for, no can't-miss-TV moments. No broken hearts to mend, no dreams to decipher. There was just *this*: food, heat, shelter, the elements, the animals, and peace in his thoughts. Peace in his heart.

Joe leaned back in his portable chair with a steaming bowl of food in his hands, the fire at his feet, and a book in his lap. He watched as the last lines of sun slowly crept down to the tops of the west-facing peaks, and satin suede drapes of stars revealed themselves. From his downtown condo he rarely saw the cosmos. As cities do, his had expanded at a relentless pace, and the light pollution made stargazing next to impossible. Not here. It was like having a view of an entirely random but intentionally beautiful Christmas display. The stars and moon created a bright and natural night-light that mixed with the interminable and pure blackness, something the city and its sodium lamps could never duplicate. Even this moon- and starlight felt restorative, in counterbalance to the way the city light was draining.

It was only around seven in the evening, but "hiker's midnight" was setting in. Joe read until he could no longer discern words on the page, then tilted his head back to rejuvenate at the sight of his private, celestial backdrop. He sat in quiet meditation on nothing and everything. Every concern faded away now, any lingering stream of thought merged with the darkened stream beyond his feet. The dancing of orange and red flames framed his hiking boots, the sway of shadow-cloaked trees encircled him, the silhouetted mountaintops were blanketed by an ocean of stars. When the fire burned down to its slow-dancing waves of blue heat, he finally, and reluctantly, covered them with the forest floor and retreated to his tent.

Breathing in the cool mountain air, Joe fell into a deep and dreamless sleep.

CHAPTER 4
FEELING

Tuesday night. The remainder of the weekend and start to this week passed as they usually did: prosaic and predictable. A return from his twenty-four hour oasis in the backcountry, and back to the machine early Monday morning. The dream of last Friday night had faded altogether from Joe's thoughts. It had to have been a bizarre, one-off anomaly, and though he had double-bagged the wastebasket beside his bed in case of emergency, he hadn't needed it.

Yet on this night, within moments of slowly lowering from one level of consciousness to another, he at first felt the black, and then everything was impossibly bright. He was thrust back into that feeling of nauseating disorientation, and he instantly knew he was once again looking through someone's eyes. *Her* eyes.

They were in an office building this time. Although he—*she,* rather—was sitting behind a desk within a glassed-in office, the rest of the space was clearly designed to be open concept. Joe could see rows of workstations intended to look tasteful and modern, all crammed together and adjacent to floor-to-ceiling windows overlooking a city.

Although Joe only knew from movies, this dream office had the feel of a media workplace—a newspaper or magazine, perhaps. There was a steady hum punctuated by ringing phones, clacking keyboards, and chatter volleyed from one workstation to another. He could sense the body he was in—while it felt tired, somehow—was invigorated just by being in the room, drinking up the charge of energy floating through the space.

He could see a mess of paper scattered across the prefab desk at which she sat. Sticky notes were affixed to anything and everything: computer monitor, landline phone, a bulletin board adorned with newspaper clippings. Innumerable lights flashed on the telephone—messages waiting, calls on hold, other calls active. The phones in the bullpen never seemed to stop ringing.

He could sense her stress; this felt like an environment where the action never really subsided, perhaps even after-hours, yet at once he could feel how it energized her. He didn't know *how* he knew this, but felt it as acutely as any of the sensations within his own body.

He was grateful she was sitting; it helped somewhat with the disorientation. He found it difficult to track with her eyes. Since this wasn't his own head or body, it mirrored the feeling of watching slides of a presentation being changed before he could glimpse what was on the screen. He'd want to look to the left—to spy a piece of paper with a letterhead on it, say—and she would turn her head in the opposite direction toward the computer monitor. Though he strained to see what was displayed on the screen, it remained too blurry to discern through this ethereal dream-fog.

Someone approached the door of her office. When this newcomer began speaking, the aural distortion from the last dream returned. Joe could hear their voice—once again thought he detected an accent—but whatever the words were, these came through incredibly muddled. It was like trying to listen to a conversation in an adjacent room by putting an ear to the heating ducts. When his host replied, the next sensation was overwhelming, like hearing someone talk into a microphone that had been turned up far too loud.

Joe felt himself trying to recoil. He attempted to close his own eyes but couldn't, any more than he was able to turn her head or move her hands. It was like having his eyelids taped open; the only reprieve was when she blinked. Even this offered little relief—if anything, having someone else in charge of the blinking only added to the disjointed and jarring feelings.

The person standing at the doorway uttered another muffled-trumpet comment, and Joe's head—the one he was sitting in, anyway—replied with an indiscernible but full blast reply. As she spoke, Joe's host looked down to jot a note on yet another sticky paper. She affixed this one to a paper-clipped printout sitting among the splayed stacks of correspondence.

The blurry colleague turned and left, satisfied with the unintelligible discourse. The Head (as Joe was coming to think of it) turned back to the computer monitor, and looked at what might have been email. She sifted through messages he couldn't make out and scrolled at a rate he couldn't keep up with.

The nausea he'd experienced the other night returned,

and he felt the urge to beg the Head and Body to remain still, if only for a moment, so the sensation of spinning fluid in *his* brain might stop. Barring that, he wanted to plead with her to locate a wastebasket, if for no other reason than to protect the array of paper on the desk. Oblivious to his entreaties, she continued with the email triage. She clicked and dragged with unrelenting speed, provoking flashes from the screen that only added to his nausea.

He could feel so much, yet not quite feel any of it. There were his own sensations: the queasiness, the sense of sweat on his own face and underarms. Joe's brain sent messages to his hands to reach up and dab what he was certain would be a damp forehead, and for a moment thought he'd been successful when she raised an arm, but this reached behind her and massaged the back of her neck instead.

Maybe this is what it feels like to be paralyzed, he heard himself think through the mounting clamor.

Then there were the sensations he could feel through *her* body: muted, as one's sense of touch might feel when a local anesthetic wore off. Numb and tingly, but nonetheless there.

Finished with the email triage, she appeared to lock her computer, and stood up. That put him over. Whether the rest of Joe was paralyzed within this body or not, the vomit was certain to be real and non-negotiable. With every ounce of concentration he possessed, Joe tried to will her to the nearest bathroom or sink. Where either might be, he had no idea, but like any human hit with the sudden need to expel matter from one end or the other, his radar for a bathroom was instantly activated.

Yet her legs moved casually, indifferently. If anything, he felt her mouth forming a smile as she walked by the workstations outside her office, offering more microphone-blast greetings to the new faces they passed. Joe had a sickening sense he was going to vomit in his own mouth, and possibly choke when no mouth was there to open. His gag reflex activated, unrestrained.

Mercifully, this deactivated the paralysis, and he felt his actual body bolt upright. His hand flew to his mouth, holding back last night's dinner of salmon, brown rice and kale. Joe scrambled to reach over the side of his bed, and had a brief moment of gratitude for the double-bagging of the bin a few nights before. When the first wave passed, he tossed aside his sweat-soaked sheets and ran to the ensuite. In the glare of the bathroom light, he watched the rest of his dinner eject, chased by stomach bile for an extra dose of discomfort.

His muscles and nervous system finally relaxed, informing him the second wave was done. Joe braced his arms on the vanity and drew his gaze to the mirror. He was covered in sweat, his hair matted and drenched in strands that curled against his forehead. His normally tan complexion was pallid, save for splotches of red in his cheeks and ears. His eyes were racooned by stress and sleeplessness; the whites lined with rivulets of bright red from straining against the upchucking.

What is this? What is going on? He'd never been one to experience recurring dreams. Perhaps the odd scenario repeated here and there in terms of location, people, or background, but not a movie-esque reboot of an exact situation. Nor was that what he had just witnessed, exactly—everything about tonight's vision differed from the week before. Everything except the perception of being in a foreign body. *Her* body. That much, he felt certain of: whomever this was, it had been the same woman.

Unaware of the time, he walked himself through another middle of the night cleanup. All the while, a thought nagged at him. This seemed like a real person. It appeared to be a real workplace. It had been real-time somewhere, in some specific place in the world, just as the previous vision had occurred in what looked like a veritable house. The woman's colleagues, although hazy, were as three-dimensional as the children from the last dream. They looked to be as real as the T-shirt that clung to his sweat-soaked torso, which he now peeled off as he turned on the shower.

There would be no sleep the rest of the night, regardless of the time. He was too wired, too confused—too nervous, perhaps—to slip back into slumber. Maybe that would be the key for resting the following night anyway—exhaustion—and a deep sleep might find him quickly. Hopefully, one that didn't result in a dead-hour shower, cleanup, and costume change.

CHAPTER 5
CONNECTION POINTS

WIRED THOUGH HE may have felt after being awoken at what turned out to be quarter of three, Joe now sailed along the currents of second, fifth, and what eventually felt like eighth and ninth winds as the workday dragged on. He'd resorted to a cup of coffee before leaving the house—an even rarer occurrence than recurring dreams—and on several occasions he found himself in the office kitchen where Karen brewed refreshments for clients.

It wasn't just regular exhaustion he felt. It was a mental fatigue that comes from thinking too much on a subject one knows should be inconsequential, or easily solvable, or even more easily dismissed—yet the mind refuses to let go. The only saving grace as it related to the work Joe wasn't but should have been doing was the planned downtime his team took on Wednesdays, between client-heavy Tuesdays and Thursdays.

He ought to have been catching up on letters, or the email correspondence that was lately taking up more of their time, or reviewing markets and client portfolios. Instead, countless minutes—and now a stacking of hours—had been lost to looking at the mountains framing his office windows, wandering the halls to get his blood flowing, or standing at the coffee pot he rarely poured from.

On one of these sojourns, Janice wandered into the kitchen and joined him at the urn.

"Afternoon, Joe." Though Janice's voice was consistently housed in a lower register, even when she was excited, it shattered the silence in a way that was jarring to his exhausted mind.

"Hey, Janice, good afternoon. How's your day going?"

"Same as usual. Fighting with Head Office on every little thing. You'd think they'd prefer we spend all our time on paperwork, or compliance, or continuing ed, rather than working with clients. It's as though they think we have nothing better to do." She took a breath, cleared her throat and feigned a smile, turning her top lip into a thin line. "I shouldn't have gotten going there. Let's change the subject. Big plans for the weekend?"

"Not sure yet."

Despite asking, Janice hadn't expected a detailed answer. For as outgoing as Joe could be, she'd learned early he was a closed book with his personal life, as much as he was when it came to client confidentiality. Still, she always tried. "My sister and her husband are pulling their fifth wheel up to the lake, and invited me and the boys," she proffered, attempting one of the connection points they ostensibly shared. "I think I'll go, even if we have to tent instead of cramming into the trailer. You never know this time of year when the last decent weekend will be."

"Ahh, yes, the days are still warm, but the nights can

drop to freezing in a hurry." Joe's mouth voiced the words for him, but his thoughts drifted back to the subject that wouldn't leave him alone. *What were those accents? English? Australian? South African? One of those?*

Janice attempted to run with the benign discussion on Canadian autumn weather and late-season camping. Joe heard her speak; innumerable client meetings had made him adept at listening while his mind ran in the background. For a moment, Joe paused the unceasing dream narrative to wonder about Janice herself. They had worked together for the better part of the last decade; Janice had at one time run her own practice before merging with his. Though she exceeded him in both tenure and age, by her mid-forties she'd cited exhaustion from donning the multiple hats required for running a solo practice. Joe, in less than ten years, had amassed a book of business that dwarfed what Janice had built in over twice that time.

Rather than the thinly-veiled kudos he was accustomed to receiving from other senior advisors—green not from dollars but from one of the famed sins—Janice had approached him with the stern-yet-sturdy, no-B.S. tack she took with clients. Despite his reasonable proficiency with numbers and planning, Joe had always needed to work at it. Janice, by comparison, had an innate, data-driven mind. He knew it, and she knew it. Yet far from disparaging him, Janice simply said, "We both know your magic is with the face-to-face, and mine is with the facts and figures." Joe couldn't argue the point. When she went on to express her desire to focus more on building the plans than building a practice, he'd hired her on the spot.

Yet in spite of all the years since, it struck him now how little they knew about one another. He was aware of her divorce a few years earlier, not because she'd worn the demise of a marriage the way Dawson wore any matter of the heart. Joe might never have known at all, except for the handful of times she'd quietly asked him to witness documents he knew had nothing to do with their work. When Joe had looked up at her before affixing his signature that first time, she'd merely said, "Even some of the best projections don't always work out."

Practical and pragmatic though she was, Joe wondered what Janice dreamt about. Spreadsheets, likely, but still he pondered what theories she might hold regarding the ethereal. He considered blurting out, "Do you think dreams mean anything?" in the midst of the latest bend in conversational stream toward fire bans and boat inspections. Before his mouth could let loose the non sequitur, Joe thought better of it.

These third-party—or whatever they are—dreams really are messing with you, aren't they? one of Joe's internal committee members said. While he couldn't shake the discomfort of the visions pervading more than a passing thought, he had even greater difficulty letting go of what had happened, or why.

"Joe? Are you all right?"

"Hmm?"

"You're here, but you look like you're far away. And if you don't mind me saying it, you look like you're carrying some luggage underneath your eyes as well. Late night?"

"Something like that."

Knowing she was unlikely to get anything further, Janice headed back to her Excel files. Joe remained lost in his thoughts.

CHAPTER 6

EVIDENCE OF EVERYTHING AND CLARITY ON NOTHING

Though it was painfully slow and tied up one of the office lines, Joe clicked on the connection to the Internet and waited as sounds from the modem pinged off the walls. Aside from email, he hadn't much tried his hand at the World Wide Web—wasn't even certain where to begin, other than the Netscape Navigator icon Karen had told him to click on if he ever wanted to visit cyberspace. He'd heard that if one had a discerning eye, the 'Net could be a trove of information. "The Superhighway," people called it.

He had the feeling he was about to get creamed by a semitruck on the freeway.

Proponents of the Internet hailed its democractic nature: unfettered access to unfiltered information. With every new "weblog" Joe stumbled upon—after waiting for the pages to load line by line—he agreed it might be unfettered and unfiltered, but deemed it equally untrustworthy. There were few references and many suspect sources. Most of what he read amounted to little more than someone's opinion, these as ubiquitous as the saying went about nether regions. *One day they'll figure all this out*, he thought. *Information will be curated and streamlined, checked and balanced by the people themselves. It will probably be as difficult to spread misinformation on the Internet as it currently is to log onto it.*

Before long, his search history was littered with words like "recurring" and "meaning" and "lucid," and eventually, the rabbit holes of "astral projection," "out of body experience," and "past lives." Most of this Wonderland reading amounted to exactly that: a cheshire cat disguised as a white rabbit. Joe was reading articles or clicking "related" links more for the wry amusement of it, confirming his burgeoning belief that on the Web, one could find evidence for anything but clarity on nothing.

Yet he continued to test various search engine queries, trying to find the right sequence of words that would lead to a plausible explanation. He'd landed on a story that related brain trauma to purported out of body experiences, and hadn't noticed the figure at his door. Karen waited with the poise of a quintessential executive assistant: knowing how to make her presence felt without being intrusive. When she quietly began shuffling the trade reports and mail correspondence, the sound of something other than his racing-yet-exhausted thoughts startled Joe back to the present moment. He had an instant to consider he was becoming practiced at being in one world, then suddenly jerked back to another. At least this shift hadn't brought his last meal up with it.

"Pardon me, Karen, I didn't see you walk up."

"Not a problem, Mr. Riley," she said. After nearly a decade of Karen as his EA, Joe had never grown accustomed to "Mister," but had stopped insisting on being called his given name after around the third year. Though clients and colleagues might be deceived by Karen's matronly appearance, Joe knew better: she could be as willful and tenacious as any top producer in the office. He wasn't going to win the fight about standing on ceremony, as with countless other situations where her steady hand called him to a higher standard. He'd truly struck gold when a thirty-year colleague retired, stranding Karen, who at the time still had a good couple of decades remaining.

"I have today's reports and correspondence, as well as that section of tax code you asked for," she continued.

"Great, thank you," Joe said, turning his attention back to the screen as she placed the collated pile on the corner of his desk.

"I don't mean to intrude, but are you okay?" Karen asked. "You don't look well... as though you haven't slept in a week."

Joe pulled his attention from the monitor, his head turning before his eyes released their hold on a new article concerning sleep aids. "Thank you, Karen, but I'm all right. And it's not quite a week of sleeplessness, but I was up part of last night with stomach issues," Joe replied. *Hmm,* he heard a voice say from within. *Is that right, Joe?*

She raised her arms, crossed them in front of her face in a hex symbol. "I'll keep my distance, then. My daughter is pregnant and paranoid about germs, and I've been looking after their eldest while her husband gets the nursery ready. Even though I'm on speed dial for babysitting, I'm barely allowed to go near her unless I sign an affidavit stating I've fully decontaminated. Except she's also highly sensitive to scents—"

As another link opened a page about sleep apnea, Joe realized he couldn't remember the names of Karen's children. Names were another facet he'd needed to work at with diligence. When it came to faces he was always able to place someone, but within moments of an introduction—at least in the early years—their name would fly entirely out of his mind. He'd employed many of the tricks: saying the name three times in early conversation, or constructing rhymes (for internal use only, never aloud). He'd become proficient, and now awed clients with his ability to recall the handles of relatives, pets, or even the names of their children's coaches or professors. Yet here he sat, unable to remember if Karen had two daughters, or one and a son, and certainly couldn't call to mind how many grandchildren she had.

"Mr. Riley?" The sound of his name yanked him back. Joe realized he hadn't a clue how long Karen had continued talking while he clicked three levels deeper into the pharmacology of sleeping pills. This was also new: losing people in conversation. Distracted and discomfited though he might feel, Joe still had his limits and wanted to maintain decorum. He hit the power switch on the monitor and heard the cathode-ray tubes pop off.

"I apologize again, Karen. It was just a long night, and I haven't slept well a couple of times now in the past week, so I'm in a bit of a fog. I was trying to see what the Internet might hold for information on a couple companies, but between the sleep deprivation and dial-up connection it's taking all kinds of time."

"Why don't you give me the names of the companies and I'll compile the information for you? Or if you need an analysis, I can hand it off to Janice or Dawson," she offered. "I can also clear your calendar for the rest of the week, if you'd like. Have you tried valerian root or melatonin? I've heard they work quite well. My father was an insomniac for years and said they worked wonders." Karen looked down and rearranged the remaining papers in her hands. "It's also perfectly normal for most people to take a sick day, once in awhile."

"Thank you, Karen, but I'll handle this one directly. No need to change the schedule, and thank you for the recommendations. And I'll take a sick day whenever arrives the day that *you* do, Karen. But I appreciate it, and I appreciate you." He flashed the smile, affected a relaxed posture. Enough cracks had shown today; it was time to put the game face back on.

"Very well, Joe," she said, with a trace of her own smile. Though Karen was largely immune to his charms, she wasn't impervious. She wagged a finger he was certain her family had been on the receiving end of more than once. "But if you're still unwell tomorrow morning, you call me first thing and I'll take care of it."

"Sounds great. If they made them better than you out there, Karen, I don't think I could believe it."

"Oh, enough now!" Another trace of a smile, and she turned toward her workstation.

"Karen?"

"Yes?"

"Have you ever had lucid dreams?"

Woah there. Roger, Joe's moniker for the chair of The Cynic Party—named for a chronically miserable college roommate—was speaking up.

She turned, looked him over slowly. "As in when you're aware you're dreaming?"

Change the subject, Roger warned. Joe paused, considered his words. "I suppose so. Or where you've felt like a dream was entirely real."

Or don't, Roger chimed again. *And instead of tip-toeing around the line of reason, why don't you leap right over it.*

Karen appeared to consider her own response. "I'm afraid I'm not quite certain what you mean. Are you talking about déjà vu—that sort of thing?"

Before Roger or any of the other standing committees could weigh in, Joe straightened up in his chair and reached for the reports Karen had placed on the desk. He attempted a chuckle. "*I'm* not sure what I mean. I'm certain it's just a product of feeling under the weather. I took some Gravol last night for the nausea and had some strange mind-theatre after. I'm sure that's all it was."

Lying now, are we? Uncle Peter and Roger spoke in tandem. Joe began sifting through the papers, wanting to close the door on this conversation he'd opened.

Karen produced a tight-lipped smile and nodded, appearing to want out of the discussion as well. She closed his door and returned to her desk.

Her departure prompted reflection on a subject Joe contemplated often: the happily ignorant. Not that Karen was even close to uninformed or unaware—for as little as he could summon about her personal life (*And a bit of a trend there too, perhaps?* Peter and Roger chorused), she embodied the phrase "still waters run deep." Yet for whatever consideration she gave to the existential, her demeanor never showed it.

There seemed to be entire camps of people unencumbered by the larger questions. Folks who never appeared plagued by late-night What-Ifs. Joe was certain their contentment was born of either an unwillingness or inability to consider subjects of greater magnitude than what television shows would be watched that night, where the big vacation would be taken this year, or at the most consternating level, if the investment should be in stocks or bonds. And as it pertained to unwillingness or inability, Joe wagered it was the latter. His internal Roger may have had a hand in spurring that bet.

Yet as horrible as these thoughts might have sounded aloud, Joe's judgments were coupled with earnest admiration: he wished, often, that he needn't overthink every single little thing that came his way. In an external world where Joe found solace in systems and streamlining, he wished he could do the same with his internal one. He could feel the call of the mountains again. Would this coming weekend be too cold? He turned his monitor back on to see if he could search the weather, only to find the dial-up had disconnected.

Maybe he *should* take a sick day, he thought.

CHAPTER 7
CONSTITUTIONAL OBJECTIONS

D ECIDING TO LEAVE the ambiguity of the World Wide Web on the other end of wherever that phone line dialed into, Joe attempted to bury himself in work. That lasted for less than an hour, when he became aware he'd read the same paragraph on insurance policies and tax law no less than a dozen times, without absorbing a word.

Aware of his militaristic approach to sleep hygiene, his colleagues rarely saw him with bags under his eyes, let alone an unfocused demeanor. When Joe popped his head into Dawson's office and mentioned taking an afternoon to convalesce, the associate was tempted to go see a doctor himself, lest Joe be carrying a resurgence of the plague. It could be the only explanation as to why his RoboCop of a boss was leaving early due to professed health reasons.

Joe felt languid and aimless, walking about on a Wednesday afternoon before the rest of the downtown core broke free for the evening. It felt as if part of his physiology had been misaligned, as though half of his body ought to be in another dimension altogether. He wrote this feeling off as simply from being out of the office during business hours. He kept looking at his Rolex, calling to mind a memory of his earliest days with the wealth management firm. He'd been out on a lunch with a successful senior associate; though Joe hadn't the money in his pockets then that he took for granted now, he had asked the experienced advisor if he could treat him to a meal in order to pick his brain.

Fresh from a lifelong paradigm of school bells and timetables and punching in and out, Joe had looked at his watch throughout the meal. Though he'd hoped to receive an unlocked vault of wisdom between mouthfuls of Thai, the only advice Joe would later remember came as a result of his attention to time. "Never lose that habit," the older man had said, pointing at Joe's then-Timex. "Nobody is going to chase you, here. You can sink or swim, being your own boss, and the temptation is always to take an extra half-hour here, leave a half-hour early there. But if you remember to still treat it like an employee-employer relationship—in that you're an employee to your own success—and if you keep an eye on the time, you'll be okay." Joe had kept disciplined hours ever since.

It felt foreign and incompatible walking the sidewalks while the workday was still in motion. He had essentially slept-walked to his car after departing the office, and had climbed in without a destination. He hadn't wanted to go home, nor was he in any mood to go to the gym, yet felt a need to be upright and active. Getting the blood flowing would certainly be an antidote for the listlessness and brain fog. He pulled his car over beside a downtown park several blocks away from his condo. It wasn't quite the mountains, or even a stretch of forest, but it was out of doors and hopefully imbued with enough of nature's restorative properties to get his head back on straight.

They're only dreams, Uncle Peter said repeatedly, as though purring a mantra. *Sure, they're by far the weirdest you've ever had, but they don't have to mean anything.* As with the first dream, Joe was bothered by the idea of being bothered to begin with. This was messing too much with the order of things. Interfering with control. Joe had always dismissed those who were ruled by their emotions. Feelings were as unpredictable as Canadian weather, and he was not about to be governed by something as fleeting as an emotion, or ephemeral as a dream. Yet here he was, in the middle of the afternoon on a Wednesday, playing hooky from work and trying to sort out his mind. An actual stomach flu or the plague might be preferable to this.

The downtown park, while beautiful with its cultivated trees, curated streams and manicured lawns, only provided a couple square kilometres of terrain to traverse. Before long, Joe meandered along storefronts in the retail district surrounding the park. Shopping was another activity he abhorred; he longed for the day when he could avoid the activity altogether and have everything—from Christmas presents to groceries—delivered to his door. It was a time and money waster, with shops specifically designed to help people part with their money (*And their self-respect,* Roger chimed in), faster than if one could simply adhere to a list and order only those items they required. Window-shopping seemed to Joe the greatest waste of all—why look at wares he either didn't need, or hadn't formulated a strategy to buy?

Despite his constitutional objections, he felt his tired eyes drawn to each shop window he passed. A music store here, a lighting store there. A natural foods market, a bookshop. Cafés interspersed among the mostly upmarket and vintage stores.

All the while, much as he tried, he couldn't eliminate the thought of *her*. *Who was she?* Someone from his past? He couldn't think of anyone he'd known who worked in media. Was she someone he went to college with? She was certainly not anyone he had ever dated; while her speech in both dreams had been indecipherable, there was the accent. British? Australian? He'd heard it both from her and the apparent colleagues she interacted with last night.

What does it even matter? She doesn't exist. If she does—if she's someone you've met somewhere along the way—it still doesn't matter. Dreams don't mean anything, and if you decide they do you might as well start watching Miss Cleo at night and Oprah during the day, and go get your aura read and chakras aligned while you're at it. Get yourself healthy, man. Go to the gym. Have a meal. Go to bed early. Let this go.

As he passed another shop window, his vision hooked on the last thing his mind desired to see right then, but something his eyes and tormented spirit couldn't ignore. Standing amongst salt lamps, crystals, and other elemental paraphernalia was a book on astral projection. Joe felt himself shaking his head, yet feeling like a moth to a flame. He took a step back from the display window to take in whatever this going concern was.

A throwback to an earlier time of retail, this hole-in-the-wall was nestled between sleek purveyors of imported coffee and modern art. Whereas the other shops featured crisp signage, motion-activated doors and attractive lighting, "Kemp's Books & Wares" had a hand-painted sign above the wooden door and latticed display window. Although quaint, the entire storefront looked like it hadn't been updated since the grand opening. Thirty years ago, according to the sign: Est. 1968.

The door frame and window casing had chipped away over time, and the proprietor had clearly decided what wasn't wholly broken didn't require even temporary fixing. The original coat of royal blue adorning the wooden surfaces had faded while it absorbed nature's colouring, brought about by three decades of springs, summers, autumns and winters. Untold pairs of hands had cupped the windowpanes to peer into the cavernous confines within. Endless shoulders had pushed against the plate glass of the door, while arms were otherwise engaged holding purchases from adjacent stores. Other shops that had either evolved with the time, or been replacement products of it, while this relic—a "destination location" for whom, Joe had no idea—had apparently survived thirty spins around the sun.

Against his better judgment—to say nothing of his dignity—Joe reached for the tarnished brass doorknob.

CHAPTER 8
IDEAS WORTH REMEMBERING

THE DOOR GROANED as it opened. Decades of expansion and contraction had warped it against its frame, and the jamb offered its own greeting to potential patrons. A bell jingled above, and with this sound Joe spotted a long-haired cat—who appeared as old as the shop itself—scurry from one side to the other. A symphony of smells greeted him; a menagerie of old books and yellowed newspapers, incense and tea. The dusted-over scent of a room where the furniture might well be fused into the floors or walls, unmoved for ages.

These were comforting smells, reminiscent of his grandparents' homes. The aroma from an ever-present kettle. The smell of varnish on scuffed yet welcoming wooden floors. Potpourri in the living room. Old Spice in the bathroom. These were scents of reflection, just as certain songs become the soundtrack of moments passed. While Kemp's, with its timeworn shelves and eclectic goods, didn't exactly remind him of his forebears' houses in content—his grandparents epitomizing 1950's conservatism—it did remind him in feel.

Joe surveyed the shelves, spotting more books on the

supernatural, and certain he wouldn't find a novel for his next airplane flight here. Incense burners. More oddly-shaped lighting. Much as the wares this purveyor was peddling were as foreign to Joe's sensibilities as poetry to a pauper, this place somehow had the feeling of safety. Familiarity. Wisdom. Answers, perhaps.

"Oh," a voice croaked from behind a large, solid oak counter that seemed to run the length of the store. It looked more like a barroom fixture than a point of sale for retail goods. Like the shelves, it was covered with more knick-knacks than Joe could absorb or put names to. "Well hello there, friend. Welcome. You look lost." The voice was as weathered as the hardwood floors that creaked beneath Joe's feet.

Between more displays of books like The Alchemist (fiction after all) and the Bhagavad Gita, hookah pipes and prayer flags, Joe couldn't spot from whence the voice originated. He heard slow shuffling of what sounded like slippers on the hardwood. He half expected Gandalf or Merlin to greet him.

"What brings you in today, young man?" the voice said, now closer to Joe's right. "I'm afraid for as long as I've lived here, I'm not great with directions."

As Joe turned toward the sound, he locked eyes with the cat that had darted across the shop when he'd opened the door. A mangy thing with intelligent eyes, sitting proudly now on the countertop. This neither surprised nor frightened him—it was consistent with the way this day was shaping up overall. After dreaming through the eyes of a woman, speaking with a cat didn't seem that outlandish.

An age-spotted and marble-knuckled hand appeared above the crown of the feline's head and gave it a scratch. Joe saw a face to match the hand emerge from behind a stack of what could have been first edition Dickensian works, by the look of their weathered hardcovers. It wasn't Gandalf or Merlin, exactly—there was no pointed beard, nor cape or conical hat. This gentleman looked more like an adult-sized troll with a friendly disposition. Rimless spectacles rested above the tip of a bony nose. The glasses were positioned in such a way that their wearer had to tilt his head down in order to look up, and tilt up in order to read down. Behind the eyewear were small but keen glacier-blue eyes.

"No, no," Joe finally coughed up as the eyes studied him carefully. "I'm not lost, exactly. Well, actually, maybe I am." He laughed. "I don't really know today, to tell you the truth." He chuckled again, but there was no humour in it.

"Ahh, my son, well as our great sage Tolkien said, 'Not all who wander are lost.' Maybe today you're just a wanderer." This was followed by a wink and a smile. This character reminded Joe a bit of his paternal grandfather, and the feeling he'd had as a child that there was no answer beyond Grandpa's reach, no break that couldn't be mended. Just as Granddad's smile conferred safety and understanding, so too did the grin of this stranger.

Despite the warmth, Joe felt his challenge with small talk flaring. Client meetings were one thing, but stumbling into a store hocking Fisher-Price spirituality left him wanting for words. He thought of the girl he'd dated in college who put crystals in her bra to ward off negative energies. She would have felt at home here. Joe decidedly did not. The best he was able to offer the elfish gentleman was an awkward smile.

"Pardon me for saying this," the elder man said, "but you look troubled. And you definitely don't look like the type of customer I normally get through the doors."

"To tell you the truth I am—troubled, that is—but I'm having a hard time putting my finger on why. And yes," he laughed, "I'm probably not your typical demographic. I really don't believe," Joe said while waving a hand around, "in any of this sort of stuff."

The proprietor laughed. "And what's 'this sort of stuff?'"

"You know, the mystical. The fantastical."

"And what do those things mean to you?"

"Well, I don't know. I'm not sure." Joe cleared his throat, unconsciously adopting his meeting voice. "Doesn't it ever strike you as funny that if people spent even half the time on improving the tangible world around us—the things we can see, hear, smell, touch and taste, to say nothing of human relationships—as they do on all this, that things would be a lot better off out there?" Joe paused. "Wow. That was an unexpected wave of verbal vomit. I apologize."

Another warm chuckle. "Not at all. It does strike me as funny, but it also strikes me that if people do stop investing in this 'stuff,' I better find another way of putting food on my plate." He extended a bony hand. "William Hollings, proprietor."

"Joe Riley... Cynic, apparently." At this they shared a

laugh. "You aren't the original 'Kemp,' of 'Kemp's Books and Wares'?"

"Nope, that was an old, dear friend. She was definitely the one more interested in all of this. Always trying to touch the divine through literature, or the elements, or even through chemistry—much to the chagrin of our families. They aimed so deliberately to have us follow in their footsteps of medicine and science, and right up until she passed, I did." He stroked the chin that seemed in competition with the nose as to which could jut out further. "But funny enough, at the end, she was the only one that left something to hold onto: this place. We had all been too busy with career and material aspirations to give much in the way of relationships or posterity.

"I was her executor, and came in ten years ago with the lawyers and accountants, expecting to be tied up for months unraveling whatever mystical mess was here." William waved a hand toward the stock-in-trade. "But as I began going through the inventory, I felt like I was getting to know my friend for the first time. There was more there than I ever realized. And I don't just mean more *stuff*." He paused, lost in recollection of a time and place nowhere near.

William pulled his eyes back to Joe and cleared his throat. "I guess it made me sad I hadn't tried harder to make sure we hadn't— that we didn't... lose touch, I suppose, while she was here. It made me appreciate the work she did, whereas that whole time I was supposedly the healer." He straightened up, though it did little to increase his stature. "Then I started to hear from some of the people who frequented this place she built; how it helped them get closer to whatever it was they sought. And I thought, 'If I shut this down...'" William abruptly stopped, then beamed warmth from his grin again. "Now look who has a case of the verbal vomit. You're not contagious, are you?"

"Not at all, I hope. Go on, please. I'm interested."

"I just started to think 'If I close this place, what does that say about life? About her life? About mine? That what we do ceases to matter the moment we take our last breath?' It's funny, as a physician, faced with literal questions of life and death, I never gave much thought to any of that. One would think I might have, but life and death became... so transactional. It was either a problem for me to solve, or a condition for the patient to accept. I never paused to consider the implications beyond that. Maybe I was scared. I don't know."

"Scared of what?"

William paused before answering. "Scared of the futility of all of it, maybe? Of what I might find, or think—or viscerally know—if I did stop to consider it? It's no secret that many doctors have a bit of the 'god complex.' Someone comes to us unwell in some way or another, and we diagnose, we write a solution on a little pad, and enough times in a day that process leads to a micro-cure, for that day anyway. Everything we do relates back to a quantifiable process somehow—the mechanisms of physiology, the pathology of disease—and so a lot of the time we can trick ourselves into believing we have answers. And when things go right enough of the time, we can really start believing we have *all* the answers."

William reached up to scratch an open plain of spotted scalp. "But in our gut, we know we're only one patient away from having our illusions disrupted. Of being reminded we're still fallible, after all, no matter the thousands of hours spent hunched over textbooks or in labs or writing dissertations. That's not good evidence for a healer to have, or be reminded of: that in the end, if the universe, or God, or whatever machinations exist behind all we can see, hear, touch, smell and taste, as you spoke about... If whatever that thing is decides this one's not going to go according to the treatment plan... Well, then, no matter how much the science says it should, there's nothing we can actually do about it.

"Self-honesty can be one of the most powerful assets a human being can have, but not if you're a doctor, son. And your patients don't want that, either."

"Wow. Yeah I suppose if my doctor ever said something like that to me, I'd be asking for a referral to someone else."

"Exactly. At any rate, after Ms. Kemp's cancer took her in that autumn of eighty-eight, despite my attempts at throwing everything I had into fixing her, I found myself considering the existential questions for the first time. What does it mean? Why are we here? What's after this? Before this? Why are we doing what we're doing?

"Whatever intent I may have had in becoming a physician, I couldn't recall anymore. I know I wanted to feel like I was doing some good, that I was improving quality of life, providing hope, giving clarity. But when so much of what you do is tied up in your ego, and in that whispering-but-lingering thought that you might be omnipotent—not *The* God, but godlike, in ways—and then you're reminded that you're not, well..." He trailed off, lost again in some recollection evident on his face, but indiscernible to Joe.

The cat had displaced itself from the counter and took Joe by surprise when it weaved a figure-eight through his legs. He reached down to give it a scratch. "But may I ask...?"

His voice startled William back from whatever memory had pulled him through space and time. "Of course. I rarely speak of this, but whatever verbal virus you're carrying was not only infectious, it apparently mutated as it hit me. Might as well let it run its course," he chuckled again.

"It's just... I don't know. What makes a man like you—a man of science, so to speak—let the pendulum swing all the way into running a place like this? Is guilt that powerful?" Joe nearly threw a hand over his mouth after this latest projectile left his lips. "I apologize, again."

"And again, not at all. Believe me, I was the last person I thought would ever patronize a place like this, let alone stand behind its counter. I don't know if it was guilt. I'm sure that was an element of it. Perhaps guilt, crossed with a midlife crisis, crossed with a metaphysical one. I just knew that if I shuttered the doors, then that was the end of my best friend, unceremoniously and undeservedly." Another pause, as Joe stood transfixed.

"I don't know... maybe even then my motives were selfish. I needed her life to matter more than that. I needed there to be meaning in the loss. And I needed to know my place in all this. If I couldn't save her with my science, prescriptions, and therapies, and if all this—" William dramatically waved his arm around in a good-natured imitation of Joe, "hadn't saved her either... well, I guess I wanted answers. If there was a God—whose powers and plan clearly superseded my own—I wanted to have some words. And I knew I wasn't going to find that in my lab coat between swabs for strep and prostate exams." He laughed again. "So I guess I decided to become a double-agent, and insert myself behind enemy lines."

Another chuckle. "But in truth, my young friend Joe, I don't know that I ever considered it to that depth at that time. I maybe knew the part about not wanting to close up the shop—and by extension, her life—but a lot of the considerations were in fact more... practical.

"This may be hard to believe, especially by the sight of this place, but after I had the accountants go through the books—and then take a hard look at mine—this place turned a profit more consistently than my medical practice did. The overhead was miraculously low, between a legacy lease and inventory procured on the cheap. It's amazing what one can find between classified ads, flea markets, and estate sales. And while we don't exactly have the foot traffic of Walmart or Starbucks, the customers are very dedicated."

William walked to the edge of the counter, raised a wood divider, and joined Joe on the shop floor. "I was quite astonished—if not impressed—at how savvy my friend had been with the place. I wish I could have said the same for my practice. The only saving grace was selling it during an economic upswing after I made the decision to take over this dust-bucket full time."

William cleared his throat. "But that is certainly more than enough about me. So tell me, Joe Riley, what is it that you do, and more importantly, what is it that's troubling you?"

"Uh.... Well, the first part is easy, I suppose. I have a private wealth management practice."

"Ahh. That explains the cufflinks and tailoring, and deer-in-the-headlights look," William replied with a broad grin.

"I suppose. But it's been a good career. A good life, helping people. Some sacrifices, but it's meaningful work."

"Hmm."

"Hmm?"

"Sounds like you don't believe the words coming out of your own mouth."

Joe's lines about his profession had become rote so long ago that he couldn't remember the last time he'd considered them. He certainly couldn't recall anyone ever questioning their veracity.

"No, no," he stumbled, "it's a good career, really. It's important. People need a plan—something better than relying on pensions or governments for benefits that may or may not be there. I've often said that the second-best feeling in the world is telling folks they're able to retire, and handing them their first retirement paycheque. The *best* feeling in the world has to be *receiving* that news and cheque. I'm inferring, of course, but I'll be there one day as well."

Joe checked the time, looked toward the display window and the foot traffic increasing outside. "Aside from that, I wanted the freedom and flexibility—an illusion though that can sometimes be—of running my own business. I also wanted a long-term career and stability, something recession-proof. Everyone has to stop working eventually, whether they want to or not, and they need a plan, whether they know it or not." He was back on solid footing, an elevator-pitch he'd given countless times. "So I designed this path as much as possible. I don't hold with those who jump from one career to another based on impulse, or 'chasing their dreams.' I don't chase anything. I design it, I map it out, and then I go and get it."

"Well those are lovely—if not packaged—answers, to be sure," William said. "Sounds like maybe we ought to arrange a meeting. Eventually my knees and back won't want me in this place, even if I want to be."

Joe smiled. The words hardly ever failed him.

William smiled back. "But what did you *want* to do?"

"Pardon?"

"You've just told me about what you thought you *should* do. What did you want to be, before questions of 'ought' and 'should' entered into the decision? Don't give me the practiced answer, either. Give me the real one."

"Well I— I... don't know." Joe paused. "I can't really remember."

"Hmm."

At this one, Joe laughed. "Hmmmmm?"

"Just hmm-ing at the idea that some ideas are worth remembering. Worth looking back on. And sometimes worth pursuing."

"Is this *you* speaking, or are you channelling your friend?"

"Ha! I'm no medium, that's for certain. Never seen a ghost, certainly never heard from or spoken to one. I guess it's just been my experience that we only get one shot at life, and more and more these days I wonder whether 'ought' or 'should' fit anywhere in that. I wonder if practicality ought have anything to do with it at all."

One shot. Joe's mantra, though turned on its head.

"That sounds awfully reckless for a man of science," Joe countered.

"I loved science. Still do. I'm human, and I believe we're all driven by a need to comprehend, to make sense of this planet and life we've been thrust into. Science and mathematics are beautiful mechanisms to provide context for so much of what we see and experience. But it's also been my experience that when one lives long enough, there's a significant collection of experiences we can't explain. Which then casts doubt on what we thought was already summed up neatly in our little boxes and paradigms. At some point the discernible answers fail, and then what?" William scooped up the cat, ran a hand through the matted fur as the three of them looked toward the street.

"And then I guess there are the larger questions of, 'How much of this do I *want* to be easily explainable?" William continued. "How much of this do I *want* to fall into tidy parameters? How comfortable am I with the idea everything I ever see or do can be summed up in an equation?"

William set down the cat and walked toward one of

the sagging bookshelves, thumbing through the titles. "Or do I want to allow room for an experience capable of transcending boundaries? Of a life with feelings and experiences that are more than what can be explained away by physiological responses of my nervous system? Science has always been to a certain extent about possibility, yes, but it's also about *disproving*, about ruling out. And when it comes to the soul, even as a man of science I don't know that I'm comfortable limiting. I don't want to rule anything out."

"While I didn't know her—or you, for that matter, until now—I wonder if more of your friend rubbed off on you than you realize." Joe had opted for an amiable tone, but William's eyes momentarily lost their twinkle. The lines along his brow and mouth creased.

"I only wish more of her had."

"Shoot." Joe looked at his feet. "I'm sorry. I really don't know what's come over me the last few days. I need some sleep."

William returned from the shelves to Joe. "And again, my young friend, I will tell you to pay no mind. Sometimes—not often, but in rare, shooting-star moments—conversations with strangers can be fertile ground for honesty. It can sometimes be easier to open up—it can be easier to be honestly honest—with someone we're unfamiliar with, as opposed to a person with whom we know their pain points, their insecurities, their touchpoints."

William put a hand on Joe's shoulder. "I'm grateful for this conversation today. I like thinking about—and talking about—my friend. It keeps her alive, just as this store you've wandered into does." William paused. "But once again, let us return to you, Mr. Riley. And if it sounds better," the twinkle and laugh lines were back, "you can tell the 'good doctor' what brings you into the office today."

"Well... I've been dreaming."

CHAPTER 9

SEEING

THIS TIME, THE feeling was like being propelled up to the surface of the ocean with sudden violence.

The last thing Joe remembered was fighting to stay awake while reading "Man's Search for Meaning"—one of William's parting gifts, along with another book on dreams by the Dalai Lama. Joe had finally left when the older man began closing shop, their conversation having stretched the better part of two hours. Joe had promised a full financial plan—whether the retired doctor became a client or not—in exchange for the de facto therapy and philosophy session.

Now he was suddenly in a shower, but knew all at once that *he* wasn't. The water wasn't hitting *him*, exactly—there was a muted sensation of water on skin, but the feeling was closer to being beneath an umbrella and placing one's hand against the canvas. He was startled, at first trying to avoid the deluge, and was met by that all-too-familiar feeling of being unable to move this body. Straining against the feeling of paralysis, he heard his mind say *Okay, here we go again*.

Quicker to grasp the lucidity of the situation, and attempting calm instead of fighting whatever this new scenario was, Joe tried to get his bearings. It was a bright, spacious bathroom filled with nearly blinding white fixtures, in contrast to the ubiquitous dark marble in his condo. The shower The Body stood in was a corner unit, abutted against a wide jet tub. Joe had never been a bath man, viewing lying in a tub as a waste of time, but this looked as inviting a soaker as one might find. It was adorned with an almost decorative motif: soaps that looked like seashells and starfish, candles along the ledges, and a frosted picture window above.

This room had the feel of a sanctuary, a place away from demands of a busy work and family life. He wanted to crane the neck to take in more of the space, but her head angled mostly toward the ceiling as she rinsed her hair. Joe couldn't help noticing how long this took in comparison to washing his closely-cropped coiffure.

Despite the steam, Joe could see clearer this time. The edges of his (her?) vision still had that soaped-over quality, but the front of their sight was starting to lose that just-got-off-the-merry-go-round effect, and he could track with her movements a little better. Granted, she was standing relatively still, and there was no accompanying conversation like before. *I guess we'll see what happens when she* really *starts moving*, he thought.

As though on cue, she turned in a half-step to shut off the water, then rotated again to open the shower door and reach for a towel. A momentary pause for morality entered Joe's mind, wondering if he should avert or close his eyes should she look down while drying her body—but as before, he could do neither: his eyes seemed peeled, all movements involuntary. He was spared of the dilemma as one towel was swiftly wrapped around the length of her body, and another just as deftly wrapped around her hair. Joe had always admired the quiet grace the fairer sex brought to even the most pedestrian of actions, like putting up hair.

So far, so good, he thought, on the movement front. There was yet to be an attack of nausea, although she hadn't moved in any drastic fashion. *We're about to find out, though.*

She stepped toward the vanity, and though he had the lingering feeling of being strapped into the kind of robotic exoskeletons he'd seen in movies, it wasn't nearly as jarring as the last event. He wondered if he wasn't getting used to this odd, third-party tracking; this sensation of observing through a helmet camera. The feeling of acclimation was met with anticipation: Joe realized that—barring an abrupt end to the dream—he was possibly about to see her for the first time.

He could feel the breath in his own chest hitch as she approached the mirror. He wondered if his body back home did the same, or if it was a psychosomatic trick. Just as quickly, he felt a twinge of dismay as he saw the mirror was steamed over, and he could only discern the outline of her head and body.

Her eyes looked directly at the clouded reflection for a moment, and then she leaned her arms against the edge of the countertop. She lowered her gaze, and he felt her inhale deeply. This seemed appropriate; in another physical parallel, his heart had quickened. Deep breaths felt like the correct response. He wondered if she could feel it too: his heart, in an unconscious body laying—metres?

kilometres? oceans away?—beating with anticipation. Did her heart register an echo?

She turned away from the sink and Joe felt another pang of disappointment. It was bad enough being robbed of what used to be dependable and restorative sleep, exchanged for this crazy carnival ride of physiology and psychology. But the inability to manoeuvre was now coupled with what felt like a maddening slow-reveal on a reality show.

I have no desire to solve a mystery in my sleep, he thought. He had no desire to solve mysteries ever; didn't enjoy reading or watching thrillers, feeling he had no talent for investigation. *So if you're not going to show me who you are, would you at least let me sleep? I probably need to be up in a few hours, and I don't have time to watch someone else get ready for work when I need to do that in no time myself.*

She opened a door opposite the sink and Joe saw a walk-in closet. She reached to her right and grabbed a hand towel, and for the first time, Joe had a feeling of direct sensation. He could feel the plush cotton in his (her?) hands as she turned back toward the mirror. She opened another door perpendicular to the sink, presumably to let steam out of the bathroom. In the adjacent room, Joe glanced a bed with blankets and sheets tossed from a night of sleep. *At least one of us is getting some rest*, he thought.

She faced the mirror once more, and again steadied herself against the countertop. She lowered her eyes, reached a hand up behind her head and adjusted the towel. She paused to draw another breath. *She feels it too,* Joe thought. *She doesn't know what it is any more than I do, but she feels something.*

After another slow inhale, she looked back to the mirror and used the hand towel to wipe away the mist. With her arm extended, Joe had the sensation of trying to peer past someone in a crowd, trying in vain to move his head left or right as her arm moved in slow circles. Her hand blocked the reflection within the labyrinth of water droplets left behind by the towel. She pulled her hand from the mirror but just as quickly leaned back on both arms, lowering her head to take in another breath.

Look up, please. I need to know who you are. I need to see you.

At the edge of her inhalation she held the air for a moment, and as she stared at the sink, began to say something aloud. At first, Joe had the sensation of a bell being rung, but this too had diminished in severity from the previous episodes—perhaps because he was getting used to this too, perhaps because she had spoken barely above a whisper. For the first time, he was able to discern what she said:

"Just take this a day at a time."

He couldn't sense what this meant; thought it might refer to any number of things. What registered was not so much the words as the voice that had spoken them. It was beautiful. It was calm. Strained, perhaps, but sweet. Joe, who had once nearly broken up with a woman because her phone voice reminded him of a distressed cat, paid attention to this more than he would have preferred. Like becoming conscious of one's breathing, it was a difficult quality to ignore once noticed.

But this voice was music. Soft and enchanting melody.
And then she looked up.

CHAPTER 10
RUNNING IN PLACE

For one of the only times in his career, Joe Riley called in sick. After the vision of her abruptly ended, Joe's clock told him it was only quarter of two in the morning. While he fought to fall back under—if not for the salubrious properties of slumber and more in the unadmitted hope of seeing her again—his nervous system was too piqued.

He couldn't get her out of his head.

Even though he had been in *her* head.

You know what I mean, he thought.

She had been a vision. Years later, Joe couldn't have said what made that first glance so extraordinary—a woman wrapped in towels and fresh from the shower, barely glimpsed through the mist on the mirror. In his dating exploits following Rachel, Joe hadn't exactly sought substance in his partners, and wasn't secretive or shameful about his superficiality. But something about *her*—devoid of makeup, heels, or fancy dress—caught his heart in his throat.

Her striking, light green eyes, which glowed with a translucence that reminded him of the glacial lakes along his hikes. Her dark hair—glimpsed only briefly as she pulled the towel away from her head—that cascaded over her shoulders as she shook it free. The contrast between the lightness of her irises and deep brown of her hair only accentuated those eyes even more. Eyes that seemed to hypnotize him in that fleeting moment, before he was violently—and for no discernible reason—yanked from sleep.

At least there wasn't vomiting or near heart-palpitations this time, he thought. If his nervous system was running hot, it was from his urgency in trying to get back to the dream. Back to her.

That was no dream though. No invented spectre of my unconscious mind. I'm sure of it.

And then:

You're losing it.

Sleep failed to greet him the remainder of those long, early morning hours where a minute felt like three, and an hour a short lifetime. By five, he ceased fighting; arose and went to his rarely used television, knowing he was too foggy and distracted to try reading. By seven, he called Karen to avail the offer to clear his schedule, but not before asking her to call William Hollings at Kemp's Books & Wares. He asked her to set up an appointment and begin the onboarding process with the erstwhile doctor. Joe assured his executive assistant he would see his own physician if his "condition" worsened, and would manage some of the workflow from home.

"Catching up from home" or "meeting at client's house" were typically alibis for sleeping late and taking in episodes of The Price is Right or other daytime drivel. Joe usually scoffed at these common refrains when he heard them from other advisors. Yet today, he didn't know if he would be much better.

This had to be an anomaly. It had only been three dreams—and yes, in less than a week—but three did not a condition make. The best minds of the world had sought to understand the subconscious, often with scant progress. It was downright weird at times, and that's all there was to it. Joe was likely exasperating the issue by paying it too much heed.

The worse you make it, the worse you're gonna make it, he thought, trying to force his mind into not thinking about the thing it refused to stop thinking about. *Look. Stay awake today, go for a hard, impossible-to-be-distracted-from workout early afternoon, lay off the caffeine, and hit the hay when it gets dark. You're so exhausted you'll probably be out instantly and sleep the night through, too deep to dream. And as dreams go, I'm sure you'll never see her again.*

And then:

But I want to see her again.

Enough! he thought. Joe had little patience for people who indulged their feelings, especially to the extent of letting their days and commitments be affected. And yet, here he was on a workday, watching Bob Barker whilst in his pyjamas. Feeling like his eyes were pushed out from their sockets. Watching his thoughts drift undirected or on a maddening loop. The outer edges of his brain felt like they were padded by the exhaustion, dulled from forming complete thoughts. Yet one thought prevailed.

William from the bookstore had remained largely mum on the subject of Joe's dreams, despite their marathon conversation. Joe sensed amused intrigue on William's part, watching this young man—who clearly preferred order, sense, linear and binary thinking—struggle with an experience that defied explanation. William mostly listened to Joe's recounting of the physiological reactions, the vivid feelings, the sense of paralysis. He offered little more than occasional "hmms" and "that's interestings" in response.

Yet there *had* to be an explanation somewhere, didn't there? William had been holding out on him, he was sure of it. Perhaps all that time surrounded by old books and crystals and star charts had dampened his medical mind, but surely he knew of dream-related conditions and their ability to affect heightened emotional and physical responses? Hell, every teenage boy knew about that.

Surely there were others who had dreamt in the body and mind of a different, invented human being? This must be some manifestation of a baser level of his consciousness. But then, the implications of such weren't something Joe was keen to pay much mind to. What did this say about him? Did he want to be a woman? He'd never considered this before; never dressed in drag even as a joke, or felt a longing to live in another skin altogether. He had always thought—at least until now—that he was perfectly comfortable in his own.

And what of the thing she'd said? *Just take this a day at a time.* What did that refer to? Wasn't that an Alcoholics Anonymous saying? Was it a message? If this was merely a conjuring of Joe's subconscious, what was he trying to tell himself? A day at a time for what?

The image of her face remained vivid, knotting his

stomach every time it came to mind. *You really* are *losing it,* he kept saying to himself, as though repetition of the idea would cancel recurrent thoughts of her, the dreams, the exhaustion, the maddening loop in his mind.

An hour later, divorced from hope of sleep or halting the freight train of his thoughts, Joe dressed for the gym. Second to the mountains it was usually a cure-all, yet even here he went through the motions listlessly, losing track of reps and sets. He wasn't about to suffer the indignity of shirking work for even a day longer, however, and plunked down the dumbbells and made his way to the treadmill. He loathed running, but in lieu of snow-capped peaks and heart-pounding ascents, this struck him as the next best thing.

Joe tried to outrun the visions of the night, getting nowhere.

CHAPTER 11
WONDERING

The impromptu five mile run did, for a time, have the effect Joe hoped for. It also provided plenty of unintended effects on his knees, shins, and what felt like every bit of connective tissue between his hips and toes. Despite the shock to his system and a limp that would last the following day and a half, he did manage to sleep soundly from seven p.m. onwards.

This time, she didn't come to him until nearly the dawn.

It appeared to be a school pick-up or drop-off lane. Joe could see that he (she? they? we? What *were* they, at this point?) was seated behind the wheel of a vehicle. And at first, his hearing was assaulted by clangor worse than the previous encounters combined.

He wanted to writhe his head back and forth and close his eyes to the skull-rattling noise. He thanked the universe that at least she wasn't moving. He thought he had begun to acclimate to the visions, but perhaps not.

She was looking toward a brick schoolhouse, as children with backpacks and pigtails and soccer uniforms and neon sneakers piled out the doors and across the school lawn. Her eyes shifted to the rearview mirror while she ran fingers through the back of that dark hair, and Joe spotted her speaking on a cell phone. That, at least, explained the reason for the renewed discordance.

And for a moment, Joe was once more entranced with the eyes that had inadvertently locked with his. Transfixed by their gaze, which drowned out the erratic cathedral bells ringing in his head. He wished the limited reflection in the mirror would expand to the rest of her face. The one that had caught him so unexpectedly the night before.

She shifted her sight back to the schoolyard, clearly scanning for a specific child, or children, perhaps. The rapid shifting of her pupils compounded with the phone conversation to leave him feeling as though a fissure was opening along the crown of his head. He strained once more to close his eyes, and only realized after the noise from the call abated that his vision had gone black. For a moment he thought the dream had ended, and expected to see his darkened bedroom upon opening his eyes. Instead, he could hear the sound of schoolyard shrieks and laughter.

And then the voice, gentle but hurried—"Oh honey, Mummy is running behind!"—shocked his eyes into opening.

He was still there, still sitting behind the wheel of the vehicle, the open eyes continuing the rapid scan of the playground. He squeezed again—darkness. This was new.

The pervasive sense of paralysis from previous dreams no longer felt so non-negotiable. Was it possible he had some measure of control? If not control, then separation, at least? He sent the signal from his brain to slowly open his eyelids once more, and now found his host's sight directed toward a young girl with a wide, toothy grin, running to the passenger door.

He blinked once more for good measure. Momentary darkness. This was a start, at least. Of what, he couldn't say; Joe was certain nothing was guaranteed in this dreamworld. Just because he could close the internal curtains on the bizarre human-eye window that opened on this woman's life now, didn't mean he'd be able to next time. Should there *be* a next time.

The young girl running toward the vehicle threw open the back door and bounded in. She fastened the seat belt without taking off her backpack, comically bulging the shoulder-belt as though she was Quasimodo. The voice said, "Ahh honey, you still have your rucksack on!"

Definitely an English accent. Joe could make out the words clearly now. It sounded not unlike how his own voice reverberated within his head, just heightened, as one might sound with a sinus cold or after ears had popped on an airplane.

The young girl giggled and handily removed the pack while keeping the lap belt on, as though performing a magician's trick. The woman laughed as well, turned to face the road, and moved out of the pick-up lane. "I have to stop by the office, honey, before we pick up your brother."

"That's okay Mummy! Sarah gave me her Toy Story colouring book because she got a new one for her birthday, and there are still lots of pages to do! I'll colour a picture for you."

"Oh honey, I love you so much! How did I get such a brilliant daughter?"

"I am pretty brilliant, Mummy!" This elicited laughs from both.

The woman tapped the steering wheel with both hands, struggling to navigate the after-school traffic. Her eyes darted around, possibly looking for unaware children hopping between the parked cars. Her vision moved with a rapidity that was once more disorienting and threatened to bring on a wave of nausea for Joe. His ability to close his eyes continued, much to his relief, without any apparent effect on her—a good thing, with the car in motion.

He wondered, with this new capability, if he could perhaps strain against her field of vision and direct his own gaze around. Perhaps capture details of the surrounding area. The name of the school, maybe. A street sign. Despite his concentration, he could no more direct her eyes than her head, arms, or legs. He would have to settle for this newfound victory: the ability to grant himself respite from the eye movements, and hopefully keep his chicken-quinoa-pepper dinner moving in the right direction.

"Mummy?"

"Yes honey?"

"I got my school pictures today. Do you want to see?"

"I can't wait to see them! Once we stop, I'll have a look."

The girl rummaged through her bag, and Joe could hear the crunching of paper and cellophane. Out of the periphery of the woman's eyes he saw an envelope thrust forward. The vehicle reached a stoplight, and the woman turned to take the blue and clear package. A toothy grin set against a plush grey background looked up from the folder.

"Oh my love, you are just about the most amazing thing I have ever seen!" the woman said.

"I *was* pretty cute that day." More laughter from both.

Closing his eyes turned out to be a particular mercy as it related to contending with traffic. He'd given no previous thought to how quickly and frequently the gaze of a driver shifts: mirror, windshield, dash, mirror, side mirror, horizon, car in opposing lane (and for the first time, he realized—unsurprisingly—that the cars were on the 'wrong' side of the road), back to mirror, glance at daughter in backseat, front view, side mirror again. All within the space of less than a few seconds.

Much as he wanted to look for landmarks, he couldn't keep his eyes open for more than a moment without a feeling of vertigo. It was like watching someone else flip pages of a book, or channels on a television before one's eyes had a moment to catch up. She wasn't looking around beyond the immediate demands of the road anyway, and what Joe could observe didn't trigger any semblance of recognition.

"Mummy?"

"Yes honey?"

"When I'm older I'm going to work with you."

"Oh really? And what are you going to do there?"

"I'm going to write the news articles." Joe—with his eyes closed again to focus on the conversation—was amused by the accent from the tiny voice. The way he could hear the 'w' in 'write' and 'news,' and how 'articles' came out as 'ahhticles.'

"But I'm only going to write about things that make people happy," the girl continued.

"What sorts of things, darling?"

"You know, favourite bake shops or the best places to get a new puppy or stories about my best friends."

The woman smiled broadly. Joe could feel the sensation of it; tightening around the cheekbones and crinkling around the eyes—the latter of which he could see in the mirror as she looked back at her daughter.

"Well that's lovely, Ainsley." *Some intelligence!* Joe thought. "I'm sure people would love to read about your friends."

"I *know* they would, Mummy! Sarah knows all the best jokes, and Jillian reads all the time so she knows so many facts! She told me about the pyramids today."

"That's amazing, honey." Another quick glance at the rearview mirror, but this time Joe could see and sense more strain behind her eyes.

She maneuvered the vehicle through more residential traffic, as the girl in the backseat began to sing an off-key tune that was unfamiliar to Joe. He once more closed his eyes against the motion and sat in darkness, feeling both the vehicular momentum and the head and arm movements of the woman.

"Is it a big story, Mummy?" The singing abruptly stopped and the voice from the back—sounding as though one of The Chipmunks had been infused with an English accent—called out.

"Is what a big story, honey?"

"The thing we have to go to the office for before we pick up Jackson."

"It could be, baby. I need to meet with one of the reporters to discuss their sources."

"How did they get hurt?"

"Hmm?"

"What happened to the reporter? How did they get hurt?"

"What on earth do you mean, sweetie? They're not hurt."

"But you said they have sore-ses!"

A pause, and then a burst of laughter that shocked Joe's eyes open. He kept them open long enough to spot their progression from the residential area onto a causeway, headed towards what appeared to be a city centre full of high-rise buildings. If he wasn't mistaken, and while he had never been there, was that…

"Mummy what's so funny?!" the tiny voice protested from the backseat. Defiant and angry against the perceived slight at what Ainsley clearly believed to be a very reporter-like question.

Before Joe could absorb more of the approaching landscape to suss out the growing landmarks, the eyes darted back to the mirror. "I'm sorry, honey. That was a great question. Arthur isn't hurt, he's perfectly lovely. A 'source,' or 'sources' means someone who is providing one of our reporters with information for a story. We call them a 'source'—s-o-u-r-c-e—but I can understand how it sounds like 'sores'—s-o-r-e-s!"

She turned her head to glance directly at Ainsley. "But I can assure you, they are definitely painful to deal with at times!" This was followed by another laugh as her head whipped back around to watch the road. Joe had to quickly go dark again to stop the spinning.

"Oh. Well I thought it was an important question, Mummy." The big indignity remained in the little voice.

"It was a *very* important question. And if you want to write news articles when you grow up, important questions are your most important tool. I love the way your mind works, baby."

Silence, for a moment, apart from the hum of rubber on the road. The feeling of the vehicle's vibration, something Joe hardly ever noticed in his own car, in his own body. He debated whether to attempt another opening of his eyes.

"Ainsley?"

"Yes Mummy?"

"I sure missed your face today."

"Well now you'll never have to miss it, because you have a picture."

At this, even Joe felt the urge to laugh. What his body did or didn't do, he had no idea, but the woman's body laughed in kind. "Oh I just love you, so much!" she said.

"I love you too! Mummy, what time are we..."

For a halting second, nothing. Joe strained to hear the rest of whatever the child was about to say and heard the blast of a car horn instead, mixed with the *WEANNH-WEANNH-WEANNH* sound of an alarm. In the split-second before he opened his eyes he was certain the car had collided with another vehicle. Though the feeling of momentum abruptly stopped, there hadn't been a violent lurch forward, and Joe could sense the entire orientation of his body was different. His eyes shot open.

No collision, just his room, with daylight forming a rectangular halo around his blackout curtains. It wasn't an alarm he'd heard, but his cell phone vibrating on the surface of his bedside table. For the first time he could ever recall, he hadn't set a wake-up time on his clock, which now displayed nine-thirty.

Ignoring the phone, he threw back his blankets and found he was once again drenched in sweat. *Why does this have to be a side effect of the dreams? I'm all for clean sheets, but laundering a set every other day is becoming tiresome*, he thought. He went to the ensuite, flipped on the shower, and stood at the mirror while the water warmed.

"What *is* this?" he said aloud. "Why is this still happening?"

I need this to stop. I need sleep. I need to get back to routine, to normal.

Don't forget the part about starting to talk to yourself, Roger spoke up.

It occurred to him he was about to lodge another first in his career: showing up late. He might be the boss, but his usual punctuality couldn't have been a detriment to the morale of the team.

He scrambled out from the ensuite toward his phone, thinking he ought to call Karen with this earth-shattering news. He saw it had been her—or at least someone from the office—who'd awakened him by phoning. His trembling fingers selected the missed call and hit Send. *Man, you're really discombobulated by all this,* Roger said.

Though he couldn't see him, Joe wondered if Uncle Peter wasn't nodding along with The Cynic's representative.

Karen picked up with her standard "Thank you for calling Riley Private Wealth Management," and breathed an audible sigh of relief upon hearing Joe's voice. Despite the prior sick day, she'd expected him today after he'd given the go-ahead for a meeting with William Hollings, MD. Joe told her a half-truth about his stomach continuing to bother him, and while she threatened to rebook today's client—and all of next week's, if need be—Joe said he would be at his desk within the hour.

As he closed the cell phone and sat on the edge of the bed, part of Joe's mind reminded him the shower was still running, wasting valuable warm water—a needless expense on next month's utility bill. It may have only amounted to pennies, but as Joe would say to his clients, "If you mind the pennies, the dollars will take care of themselves."

The confusion of being transported time zones—not to mention the change of *body* to go along with the time—the late wakeup, the overall disruption to his routines... These were beginning to form discernible cracks in the preferred order of things.

Joe remained on the edge of the bed, trying to get his bearings, attempting to slow his thoughts.

Pennies down the literal drain it would be, for the moment.

CHAPTER 12
LET'S RULE OUT THE IMPOSSIBLE

Joe scrambled into the office a few minutes past ten-thirty. He'd foregone a tie, along with shaving, to reduce the tardiness to some degree. The private washroom beside his office had a shower and standing wardrobe; Joe would remedy his lapses in appearance once he'd prepped for the meeting with William.

Karen busied herself around Joe's desk, preparing a new client package and asking benign, work-related questions. Dawson also wandered up to the doorway, keeping his distance. By the time Janice began hovering, Joe assured all of them he was fine, it was nothing contagious. He hoped.

By eleven-thirty he had prepped for William, caught up on the previous day's correspondence, shaved and adorned a tie. Dr. Hollings wouldn't be arriving for another four and a half hours; William had requested a late appointment so he could keep the store open until the college student who worked the evenings arrived. Joe looked at the computer monitor sitting dormant and wondered if he should attempt the World 'Wild' Web again.

He was desperate for answers, or even *an answer*. He tried to grasp onto something—anything—that would explain whatever was happening, but his mind was too exhausted to make connections on its own. Numerically, he'd just had a full night of sleep, yes. More than that, even, with the missed alarm. Yet with each occurrence he felt increasingly drained from the activity of the dream, the feeling of being transported, the reactions of his nervous system, and the mental fatigue from the looping thoughts that followed.

"Well, first, let's rule out the impossible," he whispered to the windows and the mountains beyond. Before he could begin the process of elimination, Roger volunteered his input: *Oh this is wonderful... apparently talking aloud to yourself is becoming a thing.*

This isn't a real person, he thought, and hoped Karen hadn't heard him from beyond the doorway. *It's impossible she's real. Yes, she looks—and feels, in whatever this feeling is—the same each time, but my brain is the source. My subconscious. When I have hiking dreams it's usually the same trails I see, and yet not exactly any trail I've actually wandered—more like a composite of routes. This must be the same. She's a composite of every woman I've ever known, or every woman I've been with, or the ones I hope to be with. That's it. She is not real. She* can't *be real.*

But you've never known a Brit, came an interrupting thought. It wasn't Uncle Peter or Roger; this voice was newer.

Doesn't matter. Get it out of your head RIGHT NOW that this is anyone who actually exists. You're going to drive yourself mad, if we're not on the road to that already. There is a rational answer for this, you just don't know what it is. This is probably rooted in biology somehow.

He glanced at his watch: twelve-thirty. He wondered if his family physician's office would accommodate a walk-in, and was about to ask Karen to make the appointment before thinking better of it. Though she loathed when he messed with the schedule or made work-hour appointments without informing her, Joe had no desire to have her relay half-truths concerning why he wanted to see his doctor. He got up and closed the door, and made the call from his cell phone.

After the clinic confirmed they could squeeze him in, Joe stepped out, telling Karen he hadn't packed his lunch and would be back later. *When are you going to stop with the little white lies, Joseph?* Uncle Peter asked.

"When these dreams stop messing with my life," he answered aloud, on the way to the parkade.

CHAPTER 13
GOD AND SCIENCE

JOE HAD NEVER discussed anything psychological with Brian Murray, MD. The bulk of their relationship had been limited to recurring bouts of tonsillitis during Joe's childhood, and an annual physical since he attained the age of majority. His youth notwithstanding, Joe surmised this was almost a point of pride for Dr. Murray, regarding Joe as a rare success story of the apple-a-day variety.

Nonetheless, every visit, every concern was met with equal gravity in this now antiquated strip mall that had housed the clinic for decades. What Murray brought in focus to his patients was forsaken when it came to décor: the pictures on the walls of the examination rooms hadn't changed since Joe was a toddler. He could remember looking at the same images of jellybeans and bunny rabbits as a child, enrapt with their colours and glossy finishes. He had a moment to wonder what little Joe would think of his grownup counterpart, before turning his attention to what he would say to the doctor.

Dr. Murray burst into the examination room as he always did: with high energy and a wide smile, underscored by an air of solemnity. Joe had never been able

OF DREAMS AND ANGELS

to imagine any wild college years for Brian Murray; he looked as though he'd worn the same side-part and glasses since kindergarten. He was amiable, yet unwaveringly professional and well-read concerning any ailment Joe had ever asked about. Apart from one conversation where he shocked Joe by saying "I don't think God and science need to be mutually exclusive," (and Joe sorely wished he could recall the context for that comment now), Dr. Murray had been a textbook man, appealing to Joe's sensibilities. In part, that's why he was here: Murray would have the answers.

"How are we today, Mr. Riley? Long time, no see," came the greeting as Murray took his seat on the revolving black stool. He plunked Joe's file—thick from nearly forty years of appointments—on the desk opposite the examination table.

"Not too bad, Dr. Murray, and you?"

"Doing excellent, young man, doing excellent. What brings you in today?"

"I'm having a bit of trouble with my sleep."

"Hmm... okay." Murray wheeled his stool over to Joe, pulling the penlight from his lab coat and shining it into Joe's eyes. "When did it start? Trouble falling asleep, or staying asleep?"

"Falling asleep is usually no problem; I guess it's the staying asleep part. Started about a week ago," Joe said between blinks, as the penlight momentarily left white-yellow auras in his field of sight. He could see in his peripheral vision Murray making notes in the file.

"Okay, and what happened a week ago? Any lifestyle changes? Changes in diet?"

"Nothing I can think of. You know me; I'm a bit of a stickler for routine."

Murray erupted in his surprisingly hearty laughter. "A *bit? A* bit *of a stickler?* Joseph, while I don't see you much more often than once a year, I know that since the time you potty trained you've done *every*thing on time since. You're as regular as crabgrass in summer."

Joe let loose his own, restrained laughter. "I suppose you're correct about that." It felt good to laugh.

"More caffeine than usual these days? Anything like that?" Murray continued his examination as he spoke, variously taking Joe's temperature and pulse, and listening to breaths through a stethoscope between questions and answers. He was like a seasoned magician sliding through tricks before the audience perceived any movement.

"Well I guess that's a bit of a catch-twenty-two. I *have* deviated from routine a bit and had the odd cup of coffee past noon, but only on those days where I've been exhausted *because* of the interruptions. But still nothing past about two p.m."

"Hmm. That's likely not helping the issue, if you're not used to having it in your system that late in the day. But tell me about these 'interruptions,' as you called them."

"Um... okay. Well," he paused, straining to look Murray in the eye. "I've been having dreams."

Murray started laughing. "From the way you gave me that shifty glance and embarrassed tone just now, I might have thought this was twenty-five years ago and I was speaking with a pimply-faced Joey Riley, who'd just dreamt of his junior high crush."

Joe returned this with a stifled laugh. The command

he felt in most conversations was once again absent in this one. "It's just that this is going to sound... a little bit strange."

"Son, in forty-two years of practice, there isn't much I *haven't* heard. Try it on me."

"Okay, well, they *are* about a woman, but *not* in that way, if that's what you're thinking. I'm a little old for that now, I would think."

"Not impossible by any means, but yes, I would agree. Someone you know?"

"No. That's the thing. I've racked my brain and I don't think it's anyone I've ever met. She's English, for starters. Or British. Something like that."

Murray waited a moment to see if Joe would elaborate, and when he didn't, offered a smile. "Okay—so tell me what is so jarring about a dream with a British woman. Was it Margaret Thatcher, taking you to task over fiscal ideology?"

Joe offered a distracted smile. He could see his dream woman's face as he thought about it. "Nothing like that, no. If anything, the overall settings have been.... unremarkable, really. Everyday kind of stuff."

Murray wrote more of his physician's scratch in Joe's file. "All right, and how many dreams have you had? Is this every night?"

"About four. Not every night, no."

Murray whacked below Joe's knees with the little rubber hammer, producing the intended kicks. "So tell me about the part where the dreams affect your sleep. It doesn't sound like they're nightmares, so far."

"Yeah... so, here's the weird part," Joe began.

"Go on."

"I'm not just dreaming *of* her, I'm dreaming *as* her."

Murray cocked a greying eyebrow. "Explain."

"I see through her eyes. I'm in her body. And that's what the jarring part of it is. When I had the first couple, it was so disorienting that it became nauseating, and I've even vomited after a couple of them. I see through her eyes but I can't control her movements, so every time she takes a turn, it's unexpected for me and results in dizziness and queasiness. I wake up suddenly, covered in sweat, feeling like I'm about to lose my dinner."

Dr. Murray put down his tools of trade and gave Joe a look. "Well, I said before there isn't much I haven't heard, but congratulations, your story is starting to veer into that territory."

Joe laughed. "I'm not looking to set any precedents here; I just want to get back to unbroken sleep."

Murray sat back down on his stool and jotted more notes. "Any other unusual occurrences in your waking hours? Headaches, seeing spots, hearing issues—anything like that?"

"Nothing other than a case of prolific yawning."

"And any emotional disturbances as of late? Relationship issues, family issues, work issues?"

"Nothing there either, Doc. I'd have to *have* relationships in order to have issues," he laughed.

Murray ignored this, and motioned for Joe to sit back down in the chair beside the desk. "So if you had to summarize, no changes to your daily life, diet, physical or mental well-being lately?"

"Apart from the dreams? Not really."

The doctor stopped writing and turned to face Joe, folding his hands in his lap. "As I said, Master Joey—" *What is it with adults who knew you as a child, that they can never really see you beyond that?* thought Joe. "I've seen and heard a lot in over four decades of family practice. I *have* heard of third-party dreaming, I guess one would call it, but not necessarily to the extent where it affects the patient physiologically. Those types of dreams are usually of the nightmare variety. These sound a little more prosaic than that."

"That's almost the maddening part of it—if I'm going to be woken up violently and toss my cookies, I'd prefer to have a good story to go along with it," Joe said.

"Despite my experience I'm also no dream expert, nor do I really know who is."

"I didn't come looking for interpretation, I just want to get back to full nights of sleep."

"Don't we all," Murray said with a wink.

While Joe hadn't made the appointment with a preconceived expectation of how his lifelong physician would solve the issue—nor did he care much for remedies of an unnatural variety—part of him had hoped Dr. Murray would wave his magic wand and conjure a spell via his prescription pad. This wasn't the proffered potion, however. Joe knew the good doctor eschewed a rush to chemical remedies as much as he did.

Joe was sent on his way with more congenial smiles and a recommendation to up the consistency of his sleep hygiene. Eliminate caffeine in the afternoons; even better if he could rid himself of the habit entirely. Regular bed and wake time. Perhaps a warm shower and hot tea with chamomile an hour before bed. Joe did leave the office with prescription paper in hand, but this was merely a note of recommended doses for valerian and melatonin (Karen would approve) if he couldn't restore his sleep cycle hours with the other remedies.

What I really wanted was a prescription to end the dreams, Joe thought. *Are there any remedies that do that?*

CHAPTER 14
KNOWING

His eyes shot open and the light was momentarily blinding. Sitting on an examination table in what looked like a doctor's office again, but not Murray's. The décor was entirely different—impersonal and modern. He went to turn his head for a further scan of the room, and there was that feeling again: paralysis. *Away we go,* he thought.

Accompanied by a second thought: *But I did hope I would see you again.*

He'd crashed soon after getting home from his office and the meeting with William. The older man had asked about the dreams; if there had been more, with any new discoveries. Joe had wanted to tell him—and could tell William wasn't buying it when Joe sailed past the question—but felt he owed the older gentleman a proper first appointment and review of his portfolio. Though William hadn't overstated the bookstore operating at a modest profit, based on his personal holdings he also hadn't overstated keeping it open for emotional reasons. He certainly didn't need the income.

The meeting had drained Joe of any remaining reserves. He'd no sooner tossed his suit on the side of the bed—another crack in the veneer—before he'd fallen asleep. Now here he was, ostensibly awake again.

She appeared to be alone. Arms leaned against the examination table, legs extending out from a hospital smock and crossed in front of her. She was variously looking at the floor and back to the three walls in view, these adorned with posters of common conditions and musculoskeletal diagrams. She reached a hand up and touched the back of her head—a sensation as palpable as if she'd run her hands through *his* hair—then looked back down toward the floor. She was tapping her fingers against the padding of the table. Another thought: *No ring.*

There was a gentle rap on the door to the right, and the handle turned. A woman in glasses and white lab coat opened it, made eye contact with Joe's woman (he still had no idea how to refer to her), and smiled.

"Good afternoon Claire, nice to see you again," the doc said as she walked into the examination room. *Ahh, finally! Claire. It's beautiful. Perfect, somehow. And some intelligence I can actually use.*

Use for what? Going further down this rabbit hole? Roger piped up.

He felt the sides of Claire's face raise in a smile, and felt that now-familiar reverberation within their skull with her reply. "Thank you, Dr. Lewiston, nice to see you too."

I need a pad and a pen, Joe thought.

"So, you're here on follow up from our last appointment, I would imagine?" the doctor said, shifting her glasses toward the point of her nose to read the papers at the top of the file. While Claire looked at the physician,

Joe strained to peer at the paperwork, hoping to gather any additional new information—a last name, perhaps. Before he could glimpse anything, she looked once more at her knees.

"Yes, hoping no news was good news," Claire said.

"Absolutely. If there had been any concerns, I would have called you in sooner. I'm pleased with your bloodwork and other vitals; things are looking good." Dr. Lewiston stood up and walked over to Claire, beginning a physical overview mirroring what Joe experienced earlier in the day. "How have the last weeks been?" she asked, palpating Claire's throat. Though this touch didn't feel as direct as Claire's own, Joe could pick it up all the same, as if through several layers of clothing.

"Good. Tiring. Long. Work has been—well, work—and the kids are in full swing with school and extracurriculars, so it's made for some really long days."

"How are the children doing?"

Joe felt Claire's smile once again at the cheekbones. "They're wonderful. Ainsley is loving the routine of full days at school—or shall I say full days with her friends; let's not kid about priorities there. Holly is getting used to the idea of having to do some schoolwork *after* school. And Jackson is..." The smile left Claire's face. "Well, he's Jack. I don't know how much of his moods are legitimate—I shouldn't say that, *all* his feelings are legitimate—I just mean to say I don't know how much of what I see has to do with what's going on for him, and how much is just typical moody teenager." The smile returned. "It's my first time raising a young man, and a fifteen-year-old young man, at that."

"Of course," Lewiston said, moving fluidly as Dr. Murray had that afternoon, from pen light to blood pressure cuff to the nose-and-ear tool (*Whatever that thing is called*, Joe thought), and still maintaining an easy conversation with her patient. "With our first, everything feels new—everything *is* new—and if you're like me, you're convinced everything *you* do is wrong, and you're scarring them for life."

They shared a laugh. "Absolutely!" Claire said, brightened. "It's been hard enough with David gone and doing this on my own, to have any faith I'm doing anything right. And with Jack, everything has *always* been new, always been the first time, so I feel like everything is trial and error. I never seem to know if the decision was right until after the fact. And only if there's no calamity." They both laughed again. "And even in the absence of calamity, the most confidence I ever seem to feel is that I dodged a bullet for the moment."

Dr. Lewiston made eye contact with Claire, and being only inches away from her face, Joe thought he might have been discovered. He felt like an intruder spying from behind a tree. A flash of guilt flared next, and his mind shouted (and were it not for the immobility of this strapped-in, front-row-seat predicament, his mouth would have hollered along with it), *I'm not doing this on purpose! I never asked to be here!*

"Have you been journaling?" the doctor asked.

"Not as often as I should, but a little more lately, I suppose."

Dr. Lewiston searched Claire's eyes for another moment. To Joe, it felt like an eternity. Finally, the doctor smiled. She took a seat beside Claire and laid her physician's tools aside. "And how are things on *that* front?" she said, adopting a gentler tone.

"What front?"

"The David front."

"Oh. Well." Joe could feel Claire stiffen. "It's fine. These are his decisions, you know that."

"I do know, Claire, but I also know these things are never easy at the best of times, let alone under the circumstances."

"Well, to his credit he actually acted with some balls—the ones that were getting him into trouble anyway."

"I know, darling, but the timing—"

"Is there ever good timing for something like this? Would it have been easier without everything that's been happening, when the kids were grown, when we were retired? Probably, but then there would have been all those years—if years were what was left—wasted, in a marriage he didn't want to be in, and this undercurrent of pain prolonged. It's better this way." Claire turned to face the door. Anxious, Joe could feel, to be done with this conversation and appointment.

He could feel a hand now on her left shoulder. "Claire. Claire, look at me."

Her head turned. "I was your friend, first, before I was your doctor," Jacquie said. "And so sometimes I still cross that line—where I hate what he's done, and I hate the effect it's had on you, and on those beautiful children—and I can't help it when it creeps into our conversation. I know that's not why you're here today. I also know you're handling it well, painful though it is. But sometimes I wonder if you're handling it a little *too* well."

"What does that mean?" Joe felt clear irritation now.

"It means I think it's not a bad thing if you let yourself feel this a little bit. All of it, not just what concerns David. Since things have stabilized you've thrown yourself headlong into this juggling act with work and the children, and while it seems to be helping—or at least not harming—I worry that at some point it's all going to pile up like a big, brick wall you're going to run into headfirst."

"Jacquie, I'm fine." She stood up, grabbing a pair of jeans that had been tossed on a nearby chair. Joe felt a quick wave of vertigo as her body moved. Her head snapped back in the doctor's direction. "I assume the physical examination is over—if not the emotional one—and I can get dressed now? It's bloody freezing in here."

"Yes, Claire, you can get dressed," the doctor said, looking down toward her folded hands. "But if you won't listen to me as your friend, then listen to me while—for the moment—I'm still your doctor."

Claire whipped around to face the physician, putting her hands on her hips. Joe had to momentarily close his eyes against the centrifugal motion. "What do you mean, 'while I'm still your doctor'? What is that supposed to mean?"

"It means that you can't carry on like this forever, and I won't stand idly by forever. We've talked about this—that things are fine at the moment, but I can't watch you run yourself into the ground in an effort to stay distracted. I won't watch you do that."

"Oh what, so you'll walk away too? That's fine, I'm used to that."

"My god, Claire, how did we run so far off the track in the last three minutes?"

"You brought it up, not me."

Dr. Lewiston stood, extended her arms and touched Claire on both shoulders. "I love you, okay? That's it. That's all this is. And it's incredibly hard to know what to say at times, and I'm going to say the wrong thing plenty of times. But I hope you know whatever does spill from my mouth is motivated by love. Always has been, always will be." Joe could feel Claire's crossed arms loosen slightly.

"And I probably didn't mean what I said, just now," Jacquie continued. "We've had one another through thick and thin since primary school, and that's not about to change. It's just hard to watch someone you love suffer. I want to turn this pen and prescription pad into a magic wand and take all of it away."

Joe felt Claire's tension release entirely. He had a moment to think, *If these are still just dreams, they're becoming clearer than my waking hours lately.* Followed by, *If? If they're just dreams?*

That thought was interrupted by her voice, which called him back like music every time, "I know, Jacquie. And I love you too." He felt her finish slipping on her jeans, moving to finish dressing up top, underneath the hospital gown.

"It appears you need to go—or that you want to go, at least," the doctor said softly. "We didn't really get a chance to discuss your checkup."

"You said 'no news is good news,' didn't you?"

"No, *you* said that, but you weren't incorrect. I said that I was pleased with where things are at. But we should still get together and review everything a little more formally—but perhaps in an informal setting? This pen might not be a magic wand, but dinner and a bottle of wine might be the perfect spell for an evening, at least?"

Claire halted her movements toward the door and smiled. "Okay. Yes. I would like that."

"May I cross the physician-patient line and hug you?"

"As you said, you were—and are—my friend before my doctor. So yes, I would like that too."

They embraced, and the sensation was both startling and comforting to Joe, less muted than any previous feeling he'd experienced in her body. He almost felt himself trying to squeeze back in return. *This trip to Crazytown has either been incredibly short, or I'm flooring the accelerator,* he thought. Roger made it clear he didn't disagree.

The women let go, and for another moment the doctor held Claire by the shoulders and searched her eyes. Joe was again taken with the instinct to hide, though he had no idea how or why. Jacquie smiled once more, her expression seeming to say, *I want to believe you're okay, and I am here for you, but I know deep down you're hurting.* She held the gaze a moment too long, spiking Joe's flight instinct again, and he could feel the tension return in Claire's body. Dr. Lewiston let go, and started toward the door.

He felt Claire let go of a breath she'd been holding, as she turned to watch her friend leave. As the door closed, Joe's vision went black.

CHAPTER 15
REAL OR IMAGINED SCENARIOS

THE DREAMS CAME every night now. Or she came to him. He went to her? Joe still lacked the language to describe any of this—though he had no intention of sharing his experience beyond his doctor and William.

Any passive, dreamless sleep he managed to achieve was still largely restless. He'd lay his head down most nights on schedule, still desperately clinging to the hope that structure would somehow solve this—and yet he'd lie there in anticipation of seeing her. While most visions remained calm and uneventful on a surface level, every night there was something new: some new piece of information, some new part of her soul.

There were the three children: Ainsley, aged six, Holly, aged twelve, and Jackson (or Jack, as he was often called), fifteen. David was the father who sometime in the last few years (from what Joe could glean) finally walked out after years of serial infidelity. This latest and last time with one of Claire's oldest friends, Miranda, which served as the ultimate betrayal.

When the affairs had been limited to the "skanks on

the road"—Claire's sister's oft-used description, to Claire's chagrin anytime the children might be in earshot—there was some sense of being able to summon the courage necessary to continue the marriage in the name of the kids. These were circumstantial and one-off dalliances resulting from David's frequent business trips, rather than full-on relationships. This was what Claire was forced to tell herself, at least; the best she could conjure anytime she'd look at the faces of her children while contemplating throwing their lives into upheaval.

But then there had been Miranda, right under Claire's nose, right in her face, and most likely (though she stopped short of demanding confirmation) right in Claire's own bed. When David finally copped to the affair after mounting, impossible-to-ignore evidence, the admission of—or at least use of the word—"love" had been the hardest to hear of all. Claire and David's ardour had admittedly faded not long after Jackson arrived; they had been young, in the throes of starting careers and family. They mutually allowed their relationship to slide to fourth or fifth on the priorities list, if it even ranked that high much of the time, yet no such retrospective assuaged the pain of hearing that word directed toward someone else. Someone new. And yet entirely familiar.

The "coming clean" session consequently tainted the waters of everything from the previous years. David's progressive insistence at inviting Miranda, her husband Louis, and their children over for dinners and games on weekends. Family trips taken together. Most notably, the trips. Louis had the same adventurous streak as Claire when it came to visiting the jungles of Peru, or engaging in marathon, sixteen-hour sessions at Disneyland Paris with kids in tow. In contrast, David and Miranda always (Claire realized with hindsight) made a case for staying on the resort, sometimes with one or more of the children.

It had been impossible, after the fallout, for Claire not to scour memories and timelines for real or imagined scenarios: had David and Miranda sent the kids to the pool while they retreated to one of the bedrooms? Had any of the children been wise to what happened? Had they ever seen anything? Had they witnessed an embrace that held just a moment too long, and simply been unaware of what they had seen? These unanswered questions assailed Claire with a sense of guilt, unwarranted though she knew it was.

The resulting dissolution and blending of families devastated like a fault line splitting the ground in two, shattering and separating everything in its path. That was perhaps the biggest indignity of them all: the in-her-face reminder every time Claire picked up her kids from her former best friend's home, every second weekend. The ten metres between the curb and their doorstep always felt like a marathon through mud.

She had nearly insisted, in the prolonged and acrimonious dissolution, that David be made to pick up and drop off exclusively from her home. Yet as often occurred in the legal dismantling of broken hearts, for every crenellation constructed by one side, the opposing army brought a weapon of equal measure to bear. Warranted, or not. Relative, or not. Reasonable, or most certainly, not. It occurred to Claire that most actions in this societally managed deconstruction of love were rarely warranted, rarely relative, and certainly far from reasonable. The invocation of the rule of law usually meant things had progressed in a far from reasonable way.

When he later reflected on that season of dreams, Joe wasn't able to say how he knew these things, exactly. He hadn't witnessed almost any of it firsthand. He couldn't even come close to reading Claire's conscious thoughts, despite residing behind her eyes. Yet he *felt* the thoughts, somehow, felt the emotions, sensed the memories. It was much the same as he could feel his own instincts, impulses or emotions, without necessarily having corresponding, clear thoughts to accompany them.

She seldom spoke of the things he learned in the midnight hours she came to him, especially if the children were around. Yet pictures would somehow form amongst his own thoughts, where he could see the Peruvian resort, or late-night fights with David while he still occupied their home. These memories (or pictures, or sensations—whatever they were) stayed with him even after the dreams ended. They might as well have been his own recollections, but closer to the memory of seeing a stage production. Actors, live in front of him, playing out a rehearsed scene. But these were no performers, these weren't scripted moments. This was quite possibly someone's real life, with Joe an audience member for a show he'd never paid admission to see.

Despite her pain, which was ever-present and carried like an unwelcome weight strapped around her heart, he also knew she felt composed—and even content—most of the time. It couldn't be called anything resembling joy or even active happiness, but for whatever she couldn't escape in her heart, she found shelter from in the hearts of her children, whom she clearly adored. Her career, too, which Joe could sense invigorated her as little else could.

After the past two weeks of these nightly visits, there was still much Joe hadn't been able to ascertain. He now slept with a book and pen on the nightstand, ready to write down any new details the moment he woke. He knew she worked at some sort of media company, surmising she held an editorial or producer-type position. He hadn't seen anything clearly enough to confirm this; there had been flashes of letterhead, business cards, and even an email signature, but he strained against her field of vision to read them without success. As usual, anything Claire's eyes weren't directly looking upon remained blurred and out of focus.

She wasn't a boots-on-the-ground reporter, that much he knew. Those actors were the ones that continually made their way to her office to run this or that idea by her, or to discuss another source or potential interview. They were the ones who called after-hours, where she would deftly handle the real or perceived emergency while never taking her attention from Jack, Holly, and Ainsley. She was never (or at least Joe hadn't seen anything to suggest this) at the scene of some breaking story—though he sensed she longed to be.

Joe wondered if the day job wasn't also a convenient—and much needed—shot of distraction and adrenaline. There were only two scenarios where he couldn't sense her pervasive anxiety or feeling of loss: at work, or at play with the children. Even with the kids, however, there were unsolicited moments of uncertainty. Was she raising them well? What would become of them? What counter-influences were they exposed to every second weekend? How was that bizarre situation—a shared home with former playmates turned step-siblings—affecting their young psyches?

Joe knew Claire struggled with doubt and grief over that aspect the most. He knew that *she* knew it was irrational to feel a sense of guilt over a situation she hadn't played a part—at least an overt one—in creating. He knew it kept her awake some nights, wondering what she could have done differently. Or had this always been in the cards?

She'd had surface knowledge of David's history before they were formally introduced in college, his reputation preceding him. But with the naïveté of youth, those indiscretions were written off as 'boys being boys,' and even carried some dubious charm—part of the composite of David's Big Man On Campus charisma. That seemed to be part of the package with boys like David; the campus equivalents of Jack Kennedy or Warren Beatty. Claire tried to tell herself that when the most popular boy at college takes an interest, the improprieties were just a norm to be accepted, and she—for a time, anyway—adhered to that age-old fallacy that the "right girl" would set him straight.

Yet she still wondered now if she could have loved him more. Post-graduation, she launched into her career as he had launched into his, both trying to make names for themselves. Then the children began arriving, and she'd pivoted to the years-long cycle of loving a toddler off the ground followed by a frenzied return to work, trying to regain footing she worried she might have lost during her absence. She hadn't been overly affectionate in either words or touch in those early years, she knew that, and for the longest time it wasn't from a lack of love—it was simply from a lack of time, and energy. David hadn't appeared overly bothered (though in retrospect, also a clue), and had cheerfully gone about his evening duties as a father on the nights when he wasn't away for work. (Of that, for as much as Joe could sense, he hadn't been able to confirm where or how David made his living.)

Whenever she'd had doubts about their marriage—before the infidelity became overt and pronounced—she'd comforted herself with the notion that this was just what happened in all marriages: couples became busy with careers and children and extended families and buying homes and vehicles and car-seats and cribs, and somehow, someday, they would catch up on all the intimacy that waned from the early days of spontaneous romance and cancelled plans and afternoons in bed. One day they would recapture that, one day they would reconnect. But they never did.

The worst part for Claire about a failed marriage was the grieving process. The lack of rationality and rollercoaster of feelings. Claire simply wanted to be able to hate David; hate him for the betrayal, the lack of love, the death of their intimacy and sacred trust… but all at once she couldn't. What she hated more than him was the part of her that still held on, that still questioned what might have been different, if they might have survived somehow, if she could have loved him better, why he didn't love her enough.

She longed for the clean emotional break, freedom from equal parts grieving, loathing, and longing. Simple detest would have been easier; predictable, dependable, practical. Yet there she was, every second Sunday, making that dreaded walk from curb to door—shrouded and surrounded by opposing armies of dichotomous feelings she couldn't reconcile. *That* was the worst part.

Her sister, Audrey (who Joe later realized was the figure he couldn't quite see in that first dream), had been an oasis and a lifeline. Shortly after David moved out, Audrey moved herself in, knowing better than Claire what Claire needed. Audrey quickly and quietly assumed her role as point guard, knowing if she was in the home, David wouldn't be. She was four years younger than Claire and had yet to marry or start a family. She'd also chosen career (in this case, fledgling artist) over long-term relationships, but seemed imbued with an innate knowledge (if not cynicism) of the dynamics of male-female couplings. She had terrific instincts for the patterns and paradigms that came with love and loss, and knew there would come inevitable moments of post-breakup weakness between David and Claire. Despite David's fledgling infatuation with Miranda, Audrey knew he would come knocking again at some point, and he most certainly had.

The "Maybe We Made a Mistake" talk occurred on a Friday evening a few months after the fallout. David had come to collect the children for his fortnightly weekend, inviting himself in and talking Claire into a glass of wine "to give the kids time to gather their belongings." The children were already prepared, Claire always ensuring their bags were packed on Friday mornings, not wanting to prolong the exchange at the door. And yet sometimes, simultaneously and paradoxically, wanting to draw out the minutes.

Despite their readiness, David sent the three children off again on a ridiculous errand to collect ice skates, beanies, and mitts for a supposed excursion Claire was almost certain wouldn't take place. Two-thirds of a glass of wine later, Claire could hear herself agreeing to a "movie night in" with the five of them, "for old times' sake," and had nearly started the popcorn maker when Audrey emerged from her suite above the car park.

Audrey would have normally stood guard during these hand-offs, but David had arrived twenty minutes early while she was still in the bath. The rustling of kitchen wares, and the sound of kids rummaging through boxes in the car park alerted her to something amiss. She appeared in the kitchen, towel wrapped around her hair, and robe painted against her skin as it soaked up water she hadn't had time to dry. She stood beside the island, arms folded across her chest, daggers shooting from her eyes as David—glass of wine in hand and Cheshire-cat smile across his face—stood beside Claire. She held a bowl in one hand and a bag of popcorn kernels in the other, an initial smile on her face, too.

Audrey said not a word, simply regarded them both. David cut the silence after setting his goblet down—smile and colour draining from his face—saying, "On second thought, we should probably run. I just realized we're low on groceries and should stop at the market before it closes." Audrey responded with a glare that seemed to say, *Yes you should. You better leave, and you better do it now.*

There had also been a physical toll for Claire at some point. Joe could sense (but not quite grab) other memories of a leave of absence from work, and frequent doctor and therapist visits. Then had come the requisite rebuilding phase—or at least a reinvention of the exterior self if the mind, soul, and heart took longer to catch up. Yoga. Meditation. A running group, for a time. All whilst continuing to put the children first. It didn't matter what the theories said, the metaphors casually tossed about (by people who rarely seemed to have firsthand knowledge) saying, "Put the life-mask first on yourself before applying it to a loved one." Any parent knew this sensible theory never made sense to the instincts amid acute danger. The children were always to be protected first. Overcoming that impulse—even with the rational knowledge that if she didn't take care of herself, it might eventually become impossible to care for the children—was like trying to stop a freight train by grabbing onto the last coupling and digging one's heels in.

Claire had been determined that no matter the pain, no matter the cost, Jack, Holly, and Ainsley's suffering—or at least their immediate trauma caused by the separation—would stop then and there. If that meant the gym at five a.m. and yoga at nine p.m., when Claire was already exhausted by ten-hour days (that never really stopped, even after she stepped out of the office), so be it. She would spare their tiny and tender hearts in any way she could. In that first year of crisis, the compulsion to protect them from further pain became more vital than the air she breathed.

Audrey had been a lifesaver in that regard, too. While Claire made sure she returned home from her morning workout in time to wake her darlings up, Audrey worked in tandem to have breakfast ready downstairs. Later in the day, she'd have dinner in progress when everyone arrived home. She assisted with endless pick-ups and drop-offs at school, whenever Claire couldn't do it herself.

Audrey for a time had even done the biweekly pick-up from David and Miranda's. Unable to conceal her disdain, however, this effort to be helpful ended up causing just as much harm. The children could clearly see and read it, and Claire eventually stepped back in to shoulder that indignity.

No matter her vacillating level of loathing, Claire recalled what one of the therapists had said: children forever see (if unconsciously) half of themselves in one parent, half in the other. When one parent is harmed or insulted, the children interpret it as a lack or failure in themselves as well. Thus, after a blissful few weeks of not seeing David face-to-face, Claire had grit her teeth and concealed the wrenching in her stomach and stabbing in her heart. She told herself it only amounted to perhaps ten minutes of interaction every fourteen days, but it still felt like a small eternity each time.

In addition to the disruption of his sleeping hours, Joe's first half hour of the day was now dedicated to adding these details to his journal. *A Chronicle of Insan-*

ity, was the way he felt about it most of the time. *When they finally come to lock me up, I'll have handed them their entire case right here—a full-on biography of a family that doesn't exist. One that haunts me every night not via the closets or under the bed, but between my ears and behind my eyes.*

Yet the compulsion to write, document, and map out Claire's history and connections was too strong to ignore. The visions now felt as real as any waking experience; the muted, soaped-over sensations had dissipated. Claire's voice was no longer even a tinny echo in the head they shared. Sometimes the dreams were short, truncated scenes: at the dinner table while the kids laughed and teased one another, or standing in Audrey's doorway where Joe would catch only a fragment (but often a telling one) of dialogue between the sisters. Other nights, the visions were all-encompassing, teleporting him to Claire's life the moment after he closed the drapes on his own.

Joe had no idea what he aimed to do with the information he was collecting, other than to answer an instinct that overwhelmed him. His latest attempt to find solace was in asking for a referral to a psychologist from Dr. Murray. That hadn't been an easy conversation, not because of the physician's response, but from Joe's ever-increasing concern at his own mental health. Joe had remained vague during the request, saying only that the recurrent nature of the visions and the disruptions to his sleep made him wonder if he hadn't accumulated unresolved baggage from an unprocessed event. Rather than take to the Yellow Pages, he told the doctor he'd have greater confidence in a referral. Dr. Murray agreed amiably, responding as though this was a request for X-rays or blood work. His only comment had been that the therapist's office would follow up with Joe within a couple weeks.

In the meantime, Joe laid his head down every night with an equal mix of apprehension and excitement. What would tonight's vision hold? Would there be new information? A new revelation? Or would it be another mundane, literal walk in the park? Children playing, sun shining, but little in the way of useful clues? *Clues for what?* the Cynic Party would pipe up. *That you're hanging on by an increasingly fraying thread?*

The arguments between his inner political parties were becoming perhaps the most maddening aspect. Joe felt it would be easier if his psyche would simply acquiesce in one direction or the other. *Let's just drop the whole thing now, knowing it's ridiculous, implausible, and irrational,* he'd think, *or let's tip over all the way into belief.*

That internal third voice, the one that had traditionally spoken far less than the Pragmatist or Cynic parties, was piping up more often. This voice sounded like no influence Joe had ever known, and thus he'd never assigned a proper noun to it. While it was quieter than the bombastic smarminess of Roger, or even the soothing reassurance of Uncle Peter, it spoke in equally compelling tones: *There has to be a reason for this. Do you truly believe—do you truly* want *to believe—that it means nothing? That the hours of sleep lost to the visions, and the lost waking hours to thoughts of the visions, have no purpose?*

And then, it would offer the thought Joe was too fearful to devote conscious attention to. A thought becoming incessantly louder:

What if she is real?

He couldn't escape the idea that potential, actual life—a whole universe of people in complete detail—was coming to him nightly. People he'd never met, who didn't resemble any individuals he'd ever known, other than in the most surface of traits. Why would his subconscious do that? Why would it write a consistent and progressive novel, night after night, without varying detail?

It wasn't as though one night Claire would have blonde hair and blue eyes, then back to brown and turquoise the next. The house never changed. Audrey, Jackson, Holly, Ainsley—they never changed in appearance either. Most of the dreams Joe could recall from his life prior to Claire barely managed to stay consistent from start to end, let alone in recurrence. These visions felt legitimate. It almost seemed a disservice to call them dreams. They were windows, into people and lives that felt real. *She* felt real.

And then, the ultimate, inadmissible thought:

You want *her to be real.*

And:

What if she is? What are you going to do then?

That idea was simply too disconcerting for Joe to consider.

CHAPTER 16
SECRET SANCTUARY

THE PSYCHOLOGIST'S OFFICE wasn't what Joe would have imagined. His occasional forays into prime time television suggested the archetype of a sterile room with a chaise longue wasn't the way of modern therapy anyway. This room was homey, very much a working office as well as a therapy room. Shelves and stacks of academic volumes sat behind a mahogany desk, all of it neatly organized. Beautiful but placid paintings adorned the other three walls. Joe was certain these were chosen with painstaking care, as neutral as possible to placate whatever neuroses entered the room. Nothing red, nothing antagonizing. *Nothing to remind anyone of anything,* he thought.

A window to his left overlooked a beautiful and apparently unused green space; Joe was confident this too had been a selling feature for the PhD when she had chosen the office. Calm. Soothing. Showing the beauty and tranquility of life. The literal changing of the seasons, which he was sure made its way into more than one therapeutic conversation. A diffuser sat on a corner table positioned beside a plant, filling the room with the scent of eucalyptus or tea-tree oil—he wasn't sure which. *One of those new-agey scents, anyway,* Roger opined. *Either way, covering all the bases.*

Why all the judgment, all the predetermination? Uncle Peter interjected. *We haven't spoken more than twenty words with this woman, and already there's all kinds of assumptions about how this is going to go.*

The psychologist had seen Joe into the office and was now getting them coffees for the session. He sat in a serenely comfortable plush armchair, continuing his survey of the surroundings. *It's not quite a chaise longue,* he thought, *but I could get comfortable enough to nod off in this thing. Then again, these days I feel like I could nod off anywhere.*

"Here you are, Mr. Riley, two sugars and a cream," she said from behind him, handing over the mug.

"Thank you, Dr. Henderson." She sat down in another armchair angled a few feet to his left, rather than taking station behind the desk.

"Oh no, please, call me Jill. Certainly, it took a few years to add those initials after my name, but being called 'doctor' just reminds me of all those late-night hours, lack of sleep, dissertations, and ramen noodles," she said with a smile. *Everything intended to disarm,* came the thought. Followed by: *Can you committee heads just take a breather for the next hour, please?*

"All right, well, as long as you agree to call me Joe," he said in return. "Not even my dad is Mr. Riley. My grandfather was, maybe."

"What is your father called?"

"Dad. Ben, to others. Dad, to me." *We're starting in on the 'tell me about your father stuff' already?* Then the opposing thought: *Oh for crying out loud. Stop it! Just listen. Get to the root of this, whatever that looks like.*

She had already shifted gears. "Well it's a pleasure to meet you, Joe. I look forward to our sessions together. Dr. Murray said in his referral that you're having difficulty sleeping, and the two of you have worked to rule out physical factors?"

"That's correct." He felt tentative, cautious. He may have asked for the appointment, but it felt risky to just come right out with everything.

"Well I've read the referral, Joe, but why don't you tell me everything in your own words."

Dammit. "Okay. Well, I guess it—the problems sleeping—started about four weeks ago." He paused. *I don't know why I'm going to make you yank this out of me, but nevertheless, I am.*

"Okay, and how would you describe the nature of those problems?"

"I started having recurring dreams that often violently wake me up, and disrupt the rest of the night's sleep, whatever is left. And if they don't wake me up, they're so lucid they're taxing, leaving me exhausted even after a full night of 'sleep.'" He used air-quotes on the last.

"When you say recurring, is it the same dream every night, then?" Her pen had begun working with speed, but she seemed never to lose eye contact.

"No." He took a long breath in. *What did you think was going to happen, exactly? Did you think you were going to dance around this? Guess we're on the crazy-train already, might as well pick her up and take her along for a stop.* "They're about the same person."

She smiled. "And who is that?"

"It's a woman." He broke the unnerving eye contact and looked down at his hands.

Jill leaned forward, seeming to reach out and touch Joe without actually making connection. "Joe, I know from your referral and the intake form you filled out that talking to someone like me is new for you. And maybe I ought to have said this at the start, but I want to make a couple of things clear." Her voice was gentle, soothing. Almost reminded him of Claire's, without the accent. He looked up. "Everything we ever discuss here is entirely confidential," she continued, "unless I determine you're a danger to yourself or others. That's the first thing. The second," there came that disarming smile again, "is that there's not much to keep confidential—or to begin unpacking and working on—if you're not willing to be open.

"I'm only ever a guide, Joe. This is your path; you do the walking. Once we've assessed the terrain, then a lot of the time—not always, but often—I'm able to say 'Oh, I believe I've seen this trail before, walked it with another friend. Here's a map, to help us.' But if the person in your position just stands still, it's awfully difficult to get through the forest."

He released a stifled chuckle. "Did Dr. Murray tell you I like to hike?"

"He didn't tell me much of anything other than you asked to see a therapist for sleep disturbances, and that you're otherwise physically healthy. I just like metaphors; they make it easy to relate."

"Well, that one was right on the money. Hit my home-away-from-home." They both smiled. "Okay. I apologize. I'm just nervous. Nothing like this has ever happened to me, and I'm confused, and—" He paused. "Well, a little frightened."

"Frightened of what?"

"I've always been of the mind there's a rational explanation for everything. And I mean *everything*. Even phenomena I can't understand or describe. My inability to explain something probably just means I don't have the language for it, or the view I have is limited based on my own experience."

He motioned to a watercolour of a lake and forest scene. "Like looking at a spot on that painting through a straw. If the circle of my view was fixed on the lake—if I suddenly awoke and that's all I could see—it would likely be confusing. Especially if my body senses I'm *not* in water. All I can see is the blue, but that doesn't mean that's all there is." He smiled. "There. How's that for a metaphor?"

"Not bad," she smiled back.

"My point, which I'm sure you picked up without me needing to belabor it, is that just because one doesn't have all the details doesn't mean an absence of a perfectly reasonable explanation. In this case, I'm *not* in water; I'm sitting in a chair, looking at a *painting* of a lake. A painting that only comprises part of a larger wall, which itself is part of a larger room. In fact," he could tell he was trying to sound articulate, overcompensating to sound reasonable, "the actual, real outdoors is in the opposite direction." He motioned to the window overlooking the greenspace. "And there's no water to be found anywhere."

He adjusted in the chair, fidgeted with the buttons on his suit jacket. "So I guess that's how I've looked at things for pretty much as long as I can remember. I never believed in ghosts or the paranormal. Sure, I had the requisite periods during childhood where I thought there were monsters lurking in the shadows of my bedroom. But instead of staying scared, I got curious and started reading about the properties of light and dark, the way light refracts, how our eyes perceive shadows. And at five years old, instead of demanding a night-light, I just knew it was the way the elm tree in our yard blended with the curtains on my window, and cast a shadow on the opposing wall from the streetlight outside. That was it. Nothing to be afraid of. A perfectly reasonable explanation."

"I get that," the psychologist said. "I appreciate that. An admirable view for a five-year-old to take. But you still haven't told me," she adjusted the glasses on her face with one hand while continuing to write with the other, all while never breaking eye contact with Joe, "what you're frightened of."

"Um." He looked back down, fiddled with a thread that was coming loose on one of the buttons. "I mean, I *know* there has to be an explanation for this. I just haven't been able to figure it out on my own. That's why I'm here."

"Are you afraid there is no explanation? One that fits with your view of the world, in any case?"

Answer carefully, one of the committee members said. Joe took a long pause. "Maybe. I don't know."

"Tell me more about the dreams themselves. Tell me about the woman."

All aboard! his mind shouted. He recounted the information he'd given Dr. Murray, how Claire (while omitting her name) was nobody he'd ever met, how she apparently lived in England though he'd never been there, how she and her family never changed. And how he always saw the world through her eyes.

"So you're the woman in the dreams?"

"No. No. Not exactly."

"Joe," that gentle leaning forward again. "These questions I ask, I can assure you are devoid of judgment. I'm just trying to get a complete picture. There's no judgment, no shame, no inference, anything. Just questions, at face value."

"I don't know how to describe or explain this," Joe continued. "I don't think I'm *becoming* a woman in these dreams. She isn't me. I'm not her. I'm just seeing through her eyes. She has a whole life that has nothing to do with mine. In fact, it's the opposite." As the words started pouring, his need to preemptively defend rose up once more. "I suppose one could argue that's an aspect of why I'm having the dreams in the first place: her life is almost everything mine isn't. The opposite gender. The UK. Kids. Divorced. Chaotic."

"You've seen all this detail in the—how many dreams has it been now?"

"Yes, I have. I've lost count, exactly, but it's probably in the neighbourhood of a couple dozen now. At first, I'd have one every two, three, or four days. Now it's every night."

"How do you know she's divorced, as an example? Give me a scenario of a typical dream." Jill adjusted in her seat, leaning forward. This time not out of practiced concern, Joe thought, but genuine curiosity.

"Okay. So last night, as an example, I 'woke' in the dream—that's what it feels like, that I suddenly 'wake,' but in the dreamworld, in *her* world. She was at what looked like a soccer practice for one of her daughters, Ainsley."

"You know her children's names?"

"Uh... yep. Yes, I do." He stared down at his hands once more.

"What are they?"

"Jackson, Holly, and Ainsley. Jackson is the eldest, a boy. He's fifteen—though I'm not entirely sure. I haven't seen birth certificates or IDs or anything like that. Holly is around eleven or twelve, and if I had to guess, Ainsley is around six."

"And the woman? Do you know her name too?"

"Yes."

"Joe..."

"I'm sorry, it's just that as I'm saying all this, I *know* how crazy it sounds. It feels crazy for me to say it, even though I'm the one experiencing it. I can't imagine what it sounds like to hear it."

"First of all, Joe, I don't hold with the word 'crazy.' We all experience what we experience, and we get ourselves into trouble when we decide there's a continuum, that there's a relative scale. Let's forget about all that for now. This is happening to you. You're experiencing it. So let's just agree to do some fact finding, and to do so without judgment. As I told you, I'm not judging what you're saying, but it's apparent *you* are judging it. Do you think you could let that go, even for a little while?"

"I'll try."

"Good. What is the woman's name?"

It took him a moment to bring the word forward. "Claire." It felt like divulging a secret sanctuary, though he couldn't understand why. *'Claire,'* in whatever shape and form she was, was what had driven him here. The thing that had blown up his life, as he had understood it all these years.

"And what does Claire look like? You said she's the same in every dream?"

He could feel the colour rising in his cheeks. *Oh great, this too. What am I, talking about my high school crush? Get yourself together, man.* "She's about five-foot-seven, auburn hair, likes long walks on the beach." He grinned.

"Why do you think you feel defensive right now, Joe?"

Good one, he thought. *Not accusatory—in tone, at least—just threw it out there.* "I really don't know. You have to understand what my life was before. Everything has always been according to plan. Which is not to say there haven't been surprises or deviations, but we've just always been a family—and I've always been a man—who held with controlling the things we can control. Bumps in the night are not ghosts. Dreams are not soothsayers. And talking to psychologists..."

Jill allowed the pause to hang in the room, inflating like an overstretched balloon until rupture was inevitable.

"...talking to psychologists is just not something we do," he finally continued. "Don't get me wrong, we aren't a 'sweep it under the rug' family either, but we're a 'hold onto what's real' one. Don't waste time delving into and inventing meaning, for that which is meaningless."

"Do you think what you're experiencing is meaningless?"

This *part is stereotypical—answering every statement with a question,* he thought. "I think I just want to figure out what short-circuited in my brain recently, for whatever reason. Whatever happened to cause these... disruptions... and do whatever work is required to eliminate them, so I can get back to sleep."

"A moment ago, you said 'hold onto what's real.' But this is real for you, Joe."

"Sure, the fact that I'm dreaming and having my sleep interrupted is. But not the content of the dream. And any meaning I choose to give it is simply that—a choice, and completely arbitrary."

"So if we're operating under that premise—that the dream content is imagined, that the event is only as meaningful as the meaning you assign it—then why don't you want to tell me what Claire looks like?" Hearing someone else say her name provoked a pang in his stomach.

"Um... well... Okay. I was joking before, about her height—about everything, obviously. I don't know for certain how tall she is—"

"You're not describing someone for a police report here, just tell me what you see," Jill said, with a recurrence of the gentle smile.

"Well, she's—" He could feel the colour rising in his face again, and the words, this time, coming in a torrent he wasn't going to be able to dam in time. "She's beautiful.

She has this beautiful, dark brown hair that flows past her shoulders, and these eyes... eyes that are haunting, in the most beautiful way. They're the colour of a calm sea, first thing in the morning before the wind and the waves hit. I only ever get to see her when she passes by a mirror, but those eyes catch my breath every time."

Good God. Now you've gone and done it, Roger chirped. *Maybe I will go on that sabbatical you've been asking me to.*

"Joe?"

He raised his elbow to the arm of the chair, propped his chin on his fist and looked out the window. Wishing he was out there rather than in here. He had a moment to rue that the weather was beginning to turn, that many of the trails he loved would soon be closed for the season.

"Joe."

"Yes?"

"Joe, would you look at me, please?"

He slowly turned his head, met the therapist's eyes for a moment, then looked down.

"I can sense how challenging this is for you to speak about," she began, "and as I said before, I also sense how laced with judgment your own words are against you. But do you mind if I observe something for a moment, with the caveat we're just getting to know you, and just starting in on this process?"

"Sure. I've said enough already, so I'd be happy if you talked for a bit."

"Despite whatever meaning you've assigned to what you're experiencing, when you described her just now, that's the first time today I've heard you speak with any level of passion, or even emotion, that wasn't laced with judgment. For a moment, if this had been just a casual conversation at a social gathering, I would have thought you were speaking about the love of your life."

She leaned forward again, coming into Joe's downcast field of vision as if to call his eyes back up. "I *know* you aren't, but it was almost refreshing and encouraging to hear you speak with that quality, rather than that of cynicism and skepticism. Is there anything else you feel that way about?"

He turned to face the window again. "Out *there*."

CHAPTER 17
ROUTINE DISRUPTION

Although he tried to remain engaged in their conversation, that instinct of self-preservation continued to dominate Joe's responses to the psychologist's questions. Despite his efforts, he felt himself become more and more evasive. The doctor certainly felt it too, and in the verbal equivalent of throwing up her hands she finally brought the session to a delicate end, as if guiding a 747 with a novice pilot and full payload to a skittish landing.

Joe let slip that he was documenting the dream details in a book, and she encouraged him to bring it for their next session. They would go over "relevant background" as well as "present details" and "future course." They set a date two weeks out to meet again, but Joe had a good idea he wouldn't be there.

"It's just too insane to talk about, but I know I'm not crazy," he said aloud on the drive home. "Says the guy talking to himself," he laughed, while glancing in the rearview mirror, which led to another of the endless strings of thought about Claire. Mirrors always reminded him now of her face.

So what are you gonna do, Joey? one of the Parliamentarians asked. *Be consumed by this and* not *talk to anyone? Try to drug-up again in the hopes you don't dream about her?* He had tried that particular strategy about a week prior: bought an over-the-counter sleep aid for the first time in his life, hoping it would knock him out so thoroughly that his sleep might be dreamless.

The experiment produced the effect of bringing on sleep quickly (which hadn't really been the issue anyway), yet a vision still came. Joe had felt foggy—drunk, even—and the disorientation effect that had diminished over the previous weeks returned with full force. He nearly vomited himself awake again, then spent the dead-time hours of the night unable to fall back asleep, but feeling groggy and nauseated. He'd tossed the pills the following morning, having known even before the suspect trial run that it wouldn't be a long-term solution.

But what is talking *about it going to do, anyway? How is that going to help? What, short of a prefrontal lobotomy, is going to stop my subconscious from doing whatever it's doing the moment I slip below sleep?*

And then:

But do you still, really believe, that this is only *your subconscious?*

Joe hadn't been to church, beyond Christmas and sometimes Easter with his parents, since he was a teenager. While his parents had never overtly discussed their beliefs with Joe or his sisters, church had always seemed a perfunctory duty in nearly every family of that generation. It was simply what one did come Sunday morning, and nobody ever appeared to question or suggest doing otherwise. Nor was religion rammed down his throat; it was just an accepted practice in that particular time, like writing cheques or making collect-calls home while in college.

There had come a point in his teens where Joe heard one of those inner voices ask if he actually believed the stories he heard on Sunday mornings. He believed in the principles, sure, but the rest struck him as little more than allegory. Yet so many of the adults he knew insisted the Bible was literal—that these events actually occurred— and that was where Joe departed. His need to hold onto reason and the explainable made him feel like the path of religion was akin to walking into an overgrown wood without a map and blindly accepting that that was the way, when there were clear paths all around.

Despite those misgivings, was this a spiritual thing? He nearly cringed every time that thought began flirting with his imagination, and the internal parties would roar, *What, like a burning bush? The angel Gabriel? Comeon, Joe. God—whatever or whomever that is—hasn't said boo to you for thirty-seven years. He has people like the Pope advocating for him twenty-four-seven. Do you really think he's gonna choose* you *to talk to?*

I am so, so, so *losing it.*

Who would know? Whom could he talk to? The internet was a bust. His family doc wasn't going to be much help beyond maybe capitulating on pharmaceutical sleep remedies, but if Joe's recent experience was any indication, that was just an invitation for greater physical discomfort to accompany the mental one. The psychologist? She was nice enough, understanding enough, but Joe had the sense it was going to wind up all Freudian and somehow about one or both of his parents.

One of his colleagues? Absolutely not. It was bad enough his Ironman demeanor had begun to show cracks. Indiscernible to anyone else, maybe, but the pride he'd carried all these years—the unfaltering discipline with his own life and plan in tandem with those of his clients—was eroding. He needn't offer further fodder by explaining the bags under his eyes, or the listlessness he'd felt when it came to stock prices or earnings reports or changes to the tax code.

His parents? Sisters? No. It wouldn't be close to accurate for Joe to self-apply the word "misfit," nor would his relatives have used it as a descriptor for the baby of the family. Yet he hadn't exactly followed tradition, and in that way he was as close as the Rileys came to a black sheep. His mother still clung to the hope he would eventually "meet a nice girl," even bringing up Rachel from time to time. Though his commentary on Joe's romantic life was far less, his father once lamented it appeared their family would only ever include sons-in-law. Neither parent was exactly the ideal candidate with whom to discuss his love life, to say nothing of a literal dream woman.

His sisters were busy with their marriages, careers, and Joe's many nieces and nephews. While he'd always had good relationships with the three of them, for him to appear out of the blue and ask for a serious conversation—in which the subject matter was seeing through a woman's eyes—well, he didn't need that particular headache nor amateur psychoanalysis.

Psychology, spirituality, and family aside, there had

been the unofficial sessions with William Hollings. It had become a running joke that when the next appointment was booked to discuss insurance or taxes or estate planning, those subjects were largely nominal. William had been delighted to learn that if he never earned another dollar of new income, yet managed to live to one hundred and twenty five, he still wouldn't run out of money. Joe had encountered this before, with some of his higher-net worth clients: a lifetime of saving hadn't necessarily translated to an understanding of feasibility or success. William hadn't been the first millionaire to ask Joe if he'd "be okay."

Upon learning he would be just fine, the retired doc delighted even more (and seemed to hold greater interest) in discussing Joe's nocturnal life. Though their meetings hadn't come any closer to formulating answers than Joe's other pursuits, it was of some comfort having *someone* familiar to talk to, even if that person was a recent stranger-turned-client.

William never once appeared skeptical nor questioning of Joe's soundness of mind—even if the younger man continued to wonder himself—and instead approached the issue with genuine curiosity in his hybrid scientist-metaphysicist way. While Joe still exhibited occasional reticence in an effort to maintain *some* semblance of the advisor-client line, once the office door closed William's face would spread in a cheek-splitting grin, followed by, "So? What did you try this time? Another doctor? Meditation? Chat room?" Having someone to debrief with was like having someone light a candle in a cave: Joe still couldn't see where he'd come from or where he was going, but Doc Holling's legitimate interest shone at least a flickering light on where Joe found himself for now.

Along with journaling the content of the dreams, he'd taken William's suggestion to note everything that had led up to them—everything he could recall, at least. Had there been a change in his routine? Doubtful, he knew, but *something* must have led to this. Some alteration, somewhere. He'd read through the Dalai Lama book William had given him, wherein the Tibetan discussed dreams with philosophers and scientists. One of the contributors suggested that dreaming was merely the consciousness sorting out images and emotions seen and felt during the day. If that was true, where was the genesis in this case? There *had* to be someone in his life, or some event that had instigated this, and perhaps now it was self-perpetuating.

He had somehow thought himself into this—consciously or not—and therefore he could think himself out.

And yet:

You don't want *to think yourself out, do you Joe? You look forward to seeing her, as much or more than anything you look forward to in a given day. You maintain this internal game—this façade of disturbance—during your waking hours, but the truth is you can't wait to get to sleep. Can't wait to see whatever it will be tonight. Learning something new. Stealing another glimpse. Sensing her heart.*

That quiet, fledgling internal party certainly had more to say, these days.

"I've got to get away," Joe said aloud.

Maybe that was the ticket. It was the wrong time of

year for it, but perhaps a complete disruption of routine would reset all this. His camping trip weeks before yielded at least a temporary lull; he'd slept dreamlessly while breathing in the forest air. He'd have to get far away from here now that the snow had set in, but a trip to the California coast wouldn't be out of the question. And maybe, just what the doctor ordered.

Months earlier, he'd begun doing research on a plan to hike the Pacific Crest Trail in the year 2000: commemorate the new millennium by accomplishing a lifelong goal. Perhaps he could take a "scouting trip" now, spend a couple weeks racking up some miles while getting a snapshot of what he could expect during the six-month retreat. He could get his head right, and there was no better way than days on the trail, nights back in nature.

What if she does *leave you, though? What does* that *mean?*

Oh shuddup already, would you? This conjuring of your imagination needs to stop. Look how much time you've lost to this, in just a few short weeks. She needs to go. I need to go on.

That night, she came to him again. That night, he also began to fall.

CHAPTER 18
FALLING

THE DREAM FELT endless, lasting from the moment Joe closed his eyes at dusk to the moment he woke at dawn. Her office. A yoga studio. Time with the kids. A chilly walk in the park by her house.

Apart from the continued lack of control over any action, her body might as well have been his. He could feel the way the wind chilled her cheekbones on the walk. The moisture of her breath through the scarf she'd wrapped around her neck and face. The touch of her hand when she raised it behind her head and tucked her hair under her hat. The way her feet seemed to take hours to warm up afterward (in contrast to his own, size-eleven furnaces he stuck out of the covers at night). How she kept wiggling her toes to induce circulation, and barring that, kept them as close as possible to the heater under her desk.

A member of her reporting staff had approached Claire's office during the workday. They were compiling a story involving some sort of local scandal, and as usual, needed to bounce the content past Claire. Joe tried to grasp what he could of the conversation, thinking if he could just grab *some* identifying detail—a full name, location, whatever it might be—it might provide a link to ultimately determine if Claire shared the same world he did. Yet for as clearly as Joe could hear and feel in most dreams now, it was still a challenge to maintain focus on conversations or other details.

Not only did he have Claire's sensations to contend with, he still had his own—his own thoughts, his own center of focus—mingling with hers. He'd be scanning the outer reaches of her vision for an identifying element when she'd suddenly shift her gaze. He'd be listening for some detail when Claire would speak or move, interrupting his concentration. At times he realized she'd had entire conversations where he hadn't registered a word, either distracted by what was at the edge of her sight, or by some peripheral part of her being, like cold toes.

From what Joe could discern from this workday conversation, there was scandal afoot relating to mismanagement of money and an affair on the part of an executive at a local company. The affair had led to the information leaking. "We need to proceed delicately," Claire had said. "Yes, we are—above all things—committed to the pursuit of truth, and we are not in the business of protecting reputations of those vain enough to believe they were impervious to scrutiny or consequences." Joe loved watching her mind and words at work. Loved hearing the way she processed information and the world around her.

"But I want us to remember there are families involved here," she continued. "Ripple effects in the community. So while we will follow where the truth leads us, before you write any sentence in any article about this, I want you to ask yourself: is this part of the story? Does this inform the community in a better way? Or is this just a salacious detail that—while it might arouse a reader—is not part of the overall picture? If I'm his wife—who, as far as we still know, was an unwitting victim in this—do I need to read about this or that sensational detail? Is the community served by knowing?"

"But Claire—" the staffer in the doorway began.

"Jamie, you know me. You know the path I was on before I... chose the path that led me here. You know where I saw myself going. I know this is exciting for all of us. I know we want to be as hard-hitting as The Guardian, and I also know this doesn't happen around here very often." Claire stood up, and Joe worried he'd lose pieces of the conversation in the shuffle.

"But at the end of the day I think we need to always have an honest look at *why* we might want to go to press with a particular piece of information. Does it serve the greater good? Or if by withholding, that line of reasoning could be misconstrued as 'serving the interests of those in power,' then simply, does it serve the truth? Does it serve as legitimate news? Mr. Anderson's proclivities, outside of those that led to the loose lips sinking the ship—get that smile off your face," Claire halted, though she began laughing as well. That beautiful, musical sound that occasionally veered into a full-on belly laugh that Joe could not only feel, but had come to adore. It was infectious, and any time she was audibly amused it aroused an internal, paralyzed, sleeping laugh in him as well. He often wondered what that looked like from the outside—had even thought of buying a camera to view footage of him sleeping. Did he move in the night? There was little evidence in the morning he ever did; usually woke in the same spot he'd fallen asleep, bedding still relatively composed.

Joe craved more of her laughter; it filled some reservoir of dormant feeling whenever he heard it. For the moment, her amusement subsided. "You get what I'm saying," Claire continued. "I don't care if we hear that he was into this or that, unless again, it serves the public trust. Yes, we need to know what led to dozens in the community suddenly out of work, and we know the dominoes began falling when he started free-wheeling with his paramour. But beyond that—and I don't give a damn if The Star eventually gets interested in this story and pays that floozie a million dollars for every spicy detail in order to sell more of their rag. We will not do that here, okay? So don't come to me with that, unless it's a pertinent detail that informs how this community wound up in the state it's in. Understood?"

Just as her laughter fueled his soul in vessels he hadn't known were empty, the strength of her resolve fueled him as well. He knew its impetus was of integrity—an earnest desire to serve, from the outlet she was in possession of. He knew her own experience with infidelity factored in somewhere—it must have—but he could sense her decisions would have been the same, with or without her personal lens. He admired her all the more because of it.

The yoga had taken place after work; Audrey must have offered to pick up the kids, as Joe had an intuition this was an unexpected respite. Claire stepped into a beautiful, spacious studio with all the expected accoutrements—candles, prayer flags, warm and soothing colours on the walls, wise old Buddhas looking on from their lotus positions, a faint smell of incense.

This was among the newer and enhanced sensations Joe had become aware of: he could catch certain smells and even tastes from time to time—dinner on the stove, the smell of the city in downtown traffic, the perfume Claire wore. Of the latter, it was a scent light and flowery, never over-the-top as with anything else about Claire's life. Consistently modest, yet naturally beautiful. Joe had even caught himself during a recent stop at the drugstore picking up women's samplers and breathing them in, wondering if he could find her brand, before being interrupted by a clerk and leaving in embarrassment when he realized what he was doing.

Claire's shoulders eased as she passed over the threshold of the yoga studio; Joe could intuit this place had become a true oasis. It was as though the rest of the time she walked with an adapted heaviness, a weight of cumulative hurt and responsibility and challenge and sadness. A weight mitigated at times by purpose—her love of curating stories for her community, or the presence and joy she felt with her children.

Yet it was all wrapped up in a pervasive pain; wounds that had never quite healed right. Broken pieces never set properly which had morphed into misshapen new forms. Forms that struggled to bear the same—and often increased—weight of before. Rather than an arm or leg, the casualties had been her heart and spirit. Never restored to what they were previously; grown around and into those wounds and scars.

Here, if only for an hour, that compensation and heaviness faded. She even walked differently: shoulders back, head higher, breathing deeper. He felt her tension gradually release from the moment she kicked off her shoes and unrolled her mat, and felt it leave altogether as she progressed through the various poses.

She was so relaxed, so... reconnected, that Joe thought he might fall asleep (*How would* that *work*, he wondered), but sought to stay present as she reached the zenith of presence with herself. He could feel everything now: every muscle, every bead of sweat that formed along her hairline. The way her ponytail brushed along her upper back as she moved from pose to pose (he knew none of the terms; heard "cat cow" and was struck by an amusing visual of a magnificently obese housecat mooing in a field). The way her cells seemed to tense—though deliberately, in this closed world of the studio—and relax, as she'd lean into the next movement.

He felt every emotion, and while her exact thoughts wouldn't yield, he could feel the essence that was Claire. He could feel her bruised heart that had somehow survived its pain, to beat rhythmically and stoically on. Strong. Peaceful. Pained, but determined.

At the end of the session there was a meditation. Despite the physicality of the past forty-five minutes, the meditation brought its own form of exertion, a spiritual concentration. He was surprised by the effort of all of it, having assumed yoga to be "lazy man's stretching." He'd been proven indisputably wrong this last hour, feeling drained as though he had done the work himself.

He could feel this meditation period was where Claire's heart and mind really went to work. He also felt a darkness he hadn't noticed before. It was as though she called forth every moment of pain, disappointment, despair, and uncertainty toward a black hole within her core. For a moment, Joe became so discomfited he almost fought to escape the dream, much as he sought to be with her these days—admittance of that fact or not.

Despite his discomfort, he sensed the conjuring of this sphere of pain was intentional, as though to actively combat it. While the instructor quietly talked them through a meditation on presence and release, he felt Claire begin to direct every bit of positivity, every feeling of hope and security and serenity toward this internal vacuity. When Joe thought she couldn't have inhaled deeper or relaxed further, he felt himself transcend as well—into his own lost moments, his own longings, his own gratitude for the good fortune of his life.

He was on the brink of rare tears—the compounding of Claire's emotions with his was almost too much to bear—when he was yanked back to awareness by the overhead lights of the studio turning on. He had travelled so far inward in this dreamworld voyage of intertwined emotional spectrum that he hadn't heard the end of the meditation. He hadn't felt her move, and realized his eyes had remained closed even after Claire's had opened. She was already up and rolling her mat, another one of the burgeoning yogis walking over to visit.

"I just love the savasana at the end, don't you, Claire?" the woman said. Her brightly patterned blue, orange, and yellow leggings were as striking as the bouffant-styled ginger hair. In stark contrast to the UK-range of accents Joe had become accustomed to hearing (though he still hadn't a clue on dialects or which regions those corresponded to), he heard a thick, Southern-US intonation that might have been charming at other times, but jolting in this scenario.

"I do; I have to watch myself so that I don't drift off to sleep," Claire replied.

"Me too, honey. How you doin these days?"

"I'm well, Lucille, how are you?"

"Just lovely. Walter's on the road again so I've been entertaining the ladies at our place nearly every night. I would love it if you came out one of these evenings! We crack a bottle of rosé, play cards, and talk about life and love, honey." Lucille managed to keep her mat held under one arm while fishing in the purse tucked under the other for what finally emerged as lipstick. She somehow applied this while squeezing both purse and mat under her arms, and carrying on the conversation with Claire.

"Oh, thank you, Lucille. You know I would love to; it's just a challenge most nights with the kids and their activities, with work, and this whole balancing act that is life." Claire finished gathering her things and stood. Joe was momentarily woozy from the sudden shift in gravity, after having fallen into that state of sublime surrender.

"Well honey, part of *balance* is taking care of *you*, and not just by twisting yourself up into a pretzel in these flow classes. Lord love me if I ever manage to successfully flow myself into mermaid pose." Joe immediately liked this woman. Despite the bouffant and heavy makeup there was no pretense about her, which was all the more remarkable in the midst of a yoga studio somewhere in the United Kingdom.

Or somewhere in your subconscious, Roger reminded him. *In dreams,* nothing *is out of place.*

Would you shut up and let me pay attention? Claire is saying something.

"—suppose you're right. I don't know when I can commit to an exact date yet, but I will commit to making sure it happens sometime in the next few weeks. How's that?"

"Well it's better than a kick in the behind!" Joe had one of his soundless, internal laughs at the 'ba-hind' pronunciation. "My sweet Claire, I'm gonna hold you to that."

"Good as gold," Claire replied.

"I know you are, sweetheart." Lucille winked, putting a hand on Claire's shoulder while deftly handling the mat and bag. Joe felt the warmth of the connection. Lucille's touch lingered for a moment, as she searched Claire's eyes. He felt that twinge of self-consciousness, the fear returning that he might be discovered. He resisted the urge to look away (not that he ever could) and kept his sight (such as it was) on Lucille.

She could sense something, he felt, knew things perhaps about Claire. He guessed it was the divorce and possibly the infidelity. Over the course of the dreams it seemed to be a topic nobody in Claire's life spoke of (other than Audrey, almost to a fault), but one in which they maintained an awareness and respectful silence. Still, when one looked at another human being as directly as

Lucille looked at Claire now, the quiet pain always disclosed itself. The eyes never lied.

The women parted and Claire made her way to her car, then to her home. Joe was beginning to recognize some of the routes—knew when she had turned into her neighbourhood off the main thoroughfares, and recognized the houses on her street. She drove in quiet contemplation, a carryover perhaps of the—was it 'savannah-nah'?—from the yoga, while a cello concerto played quietly from the CD player.

He kept his gaze with hers—as always, with no say in the matter—but longed for moments when she would glance in the rearview mirror. *Why are you hurting, Claire? I can feel it, but I can't access it. Help me see it. Help me to know you. Help me carry some of it for you, if I can.*

And then:

How many days do you think you have left before the men in white coats come for you? This can't go on forever and end well, Joseph.

Shut up. At least let me be present to whatever it is, for whatever it's worth.

Joe knew the obvious reasons for her pain, but after nearly three years apart from David and with a reasonably settled routine, it felt like there was something more. Was it the children? He knew she worried for them as any parent—or so he assumed, at any rate—would, but was there something deeper with one of them, something he hadn't seen or heard yet?

Was it Audrey? Their parents, perhaps? Nothing in the dreams had pointed in any of those directions; Joe realized he knew nothing of her family outside of her sister, or where or what they had come from. He realized there was still so much he didn't know about the person in whose soul he resided through the midnight hours.

Yeah, what you really need is to take your dream-girl out on a dream-date, Joey, half The Parliament laid in. *Ask her twenty questions over a candlelit dream-dinner at a dream five-star restaurant. How would that work, you think? She sits at one end of the table, and you get her to put a mirror on the opposite chair? She asks and answers the questions herself?*

The quieter voice interjected. *Let me be here, with her.*

Joey, you're falling for someone who doesn't exist. Even Uncle Peter spoke up now.

Claire pulled the car into her driveway, and paused for a series of slow breaths after putting the vehicle in park. The car shuddered as she turned the ignition off; he felt her body shiver as well. She pulled the sun visor down and opened the mirror there, giving Joe one of those glimpses he hoped for. The hair along the sides of her face was slightly matted from the workout sweat, and she slowly moved these strands away from her face before moving her hand to massage her neck.

"The only meaning this has is the meaning you give it," she whispered.

Another cryptic mantra, like "take this a day at a time." *Where are you hurting, Claire? What is the part of the pain you won't let me—won't let anyone, even yourself—see?*

She took the key from the ignition and left the vehicle, making her way up the footpath. The air against her face was crisp, mixing with lingering beads of sweat and sending a chill through their body. Yellow light spilled from the windows framing the front door, and for a moment Joe caught another reflection in one of the panes. Claire's face was bathed in the warm glow. She was already smiling.

She opened the door, and the sound of "Mummy!" called out. Joe heard the *whap-whap-whap-whap* of little bare feet running on hardwood, and Ainsley appeared with her curls and grin. She ran toward Claire and leaped from what looked like an impossible distance, yet Claire caught her easily, pushed back only half a step.

"I love you, Mummy. You were gone *for-ever*!"

"I love you too, sweetheart." Claire closed her eyes, soaking in the embrace. When they opened again, Joe was looking at his bedroom.

Time to face my own day, I guess.

CHAPTER 19
DESIGN BY COMMITTEE

Joe's team looked at him as though he'd just sprouted a second nose when he announced he was taking two weeks off at the beginning of December. The time away itself was benign—the rest of the team would be in the office, waiting to take their days off at Christmas and New Year's—and it was a slow time of year besides. Yet the out-of-character behaviour was beginning to stack.

"Joe, I know I shouldn't ask this—" Janice had followed him from the boardroom to his office after the team meeting. "But is everything okay?"

Joe flopped into his wingback chair. He hadn't even tried to conceal the maps and guidebooks on his desk. "Yes, of course. Why do you ask?"

"Just friendly concern, I guess." Janice pushed the thick black frames of her glasses up the bridge of her nose, meeting the matching thick eyebrows above. "You've just been a little... different, lately," she continued. "Not in a bad way, necessarily, but I just wanted to make sure you're all right. Again, I don't mean to pry."

Despite his preference for privacy and the undeviating

discretion of his team, Joe deduced that if they were willing to ask *him* about his state, they might have already asked one another about it. He decided that providing a morsel of fodder was preferable to having them invent their own reasons for his increasing erraticism and sudden time off.

"I haven't been sleeping well for weeks, and the effect is sort of... compounding. I just thought I'd try a hard-reset and get away for a couple weeks. Hike it off, so to speak, somewhere warm."

"Where are you headed?"

"I haven't completely worked that out yet. California, probably. A stretch of the Pacific Crest Trail, most likely."

"You could do worse," she said. "If you're not sleeping well after that, I don't know what will do it for you."

Joe smiled.

Janice feigned a smile in return, fidgeted with one of the lapels on her jacket, and finally pursed her lips with an accompanying head nod before returning to her own office.

Joe shuffled through the maps and weather printouts. *Two weeks,* he thought. *Two weeks of planning, then two weeks away.* He hoped the suddenness of the trip and the planning it required might be enough to busy his mind away from thoughts of her. He hoped to then walk himself to exhaustion out on the trail. Maybe by the time he was done, the dreams might be, too.

You'd miss her, though, came the thought.

Oh for crying out loud, came another.

If nothing else, maybe I can walk you *and your committees out of my head.*

'Is everything okay?' Janice had asked. Joe had assured her it was, but for the first time in thirty-seven years, he no longer knew.

CHAPTER 20
I SEE YOU

THE FOLLOWING TWO weeks kept Joe busy enough to rarely afford time for meandering thought. The visions of Claire, however, as though sensing they were under attack from distraction, maintained their intensity: Joe continued to be with her from the moment his head hit the pillow to the moment his alarm sounded. He knew he was technically sleeping, or at least away from consciousness of his normal day, but his mind had no feeling of pause or restoration. It was as though he was held prisoner by his own physiology; a strange, unceasing onslaught to mirror the 24-hour-a-day cable news channels proliferating television.

The days consisted of rising—later and later these days—and using his first waking hour to gain enough momentum and energy (specifically, an avalanche of caffeine) to rouse his clouded mind and get to the office. An unintended, perhaps positive consequence of his obliterated routine was the outflow of productivity in those first few hours of office time: Joe would quite often accomplish by late morning as much as he would have in an entire day weeks before, when life still possessed the appearance of normalcy.

He needed the rest of the day for planning: lunchtime trips to Mountain Equipment Co-op for supplies, afternoons and evenings for research and preparation. Two weeks wasn't the longest period of time for a hike by any means, but planning was still key: estimating where he would be every three or four days, and figuring out where to ship himself resupply packages in order to lighten the load.

He was aiming for twenty miles per day; ambitious, perhaps, considering it had been weeks since he last laced up his boots. Yet he wanted to cover as much ground as time would allow; as many steps as it took to step back into his life as he'd known it before. He would accept however many blisters the trail produced, if it meant even a few nights of pure rest. A part of him did wonder what might happen if he lost her completely. Then one of the committee members would say, *Lose whom, exactly? Enough is enough, Joe.*

Enough *was* enough. He could read all the books or internet discussion forums he could find, or attend all the counselling sessions for which he was willing to fork over the money. He *had* appeared for his next session with Dr. Henderson, overwhelmed with guilt at the thought of a no-show. As he'd predicted, she'd gone digging on a lot of backstory he felt was irrelevant, and for his part, he'd remained cagey in providing further details about Claire or the latest dreams. He knew it was a lose-lose situation; he simply wanted the psychologist to provide a quick remedy, without him needing to provide more detail than absolutely necessary.

All the background in the world did nothing to affect

what really mattered: taking the next step in front of him. He'd hiked enough literal trails to know it didn't matter what the mind thought or feared or hoped or knew about the obstacles ahead. It didn't matter if it dreaded the downslope or the next elevation gain. The only course was the next literal step, the next foothold. Psychotherapy felt like standing along a ridgeline, equal points from trailhead and summit, and just staring at the map for hours alternately considering the point of origin and the destination. That's great information, sure, but did nothing to move him to where he needed to be.

'Where,' in this scenario, was a return to normal. A return to plan. Chat-sessions focused on his relationship with his parents were not going to accomplish that. The trails, the trees, an ocean to his right or left… those things just might. At all rates, it would be money better spent than what he was throwing away on therapy sessions or literature or over-the-counter sleep aids.

There had even been a dubious attempt at a session with a Medium. The hiking store Joe frequented was nestled in a busy commercial area downtown; on an afternoon when he couldn't find parking nearby he'd finally located a spot several blocks south. During his walk over he saw a tiny window he'd never noticed before, alight with a Vegas-abundance of neon. The shop purported seeing, communicating, readings, and finally—Joe's irresistible mot-de-jour as of late—answers. Though he'd resisted the pull of the paranormal at first glance, the draw was too strong on the return trip to his car. On at least one front, he couldn't argue: the price. Fifteen dollars for a fifteen-minute reading. *I've wasted more than that sometimes on unplanned meals*, came the thought.

That ended up being all it took to make him jaywalk through afternoon traffic and open the metal-framed door for a meeting with Sondra, the Medium.

A bell sounded over the doorway, and Joe was greeted by a shop not that dissimilar from Kemp's a few weeks before. This establishment was less about tangible goods for sale, however, and more the solution-promising, making-sense-of-the-madness type. Sondra was hocking hope for the seekers in life, and Joe was once again overcome with myriad prejudices. The internal cynic suggested those who normally walked through the door were likely of the cat-lady variety, looking to connect with lost loved ones, or lost love, period.

The shop was small and simple; half a commercial bay nestled between Starbucks and a printing company. The waiting room held two 70's-style upholstered chairs set against a wall painted crimson red. A well-worn leather couch sat against the opposite wall, this a deep purple accented with hand-painted gold swirls and designs. A third wall toward the back of the shop—this one painted a sunny yellow—housed a single doorway, upon which was painted "Reading Room." Joe was almost disappointed it wasn't an open frame adorned with a beaded curtain.

As he was picturing this, the door of the Reading Room opened. A stout woman with long, curly brown hair and deep lines in her face appeared, draped in a shawl and leading with a smile that was impossible not to reciprocate.

"Good afternoon, young man. Are you here for a reading?"

Joe cleared his throat, felt colour rise in his face. "Uh... yes, I suppose I am."

"Wonderful. I'm just with another client, but we'll probably be finished in a few minutes, if you don't mind waiting." Her voice was raspy. Vocal cords layered by the smoke of a hundred thousand cigarettes, Joe assumed.

"I don't mind, thank you," he said. *There's still time to get the hell out of Dodge, should you decide to come to your senses*, Roger opined.

"Great! I'll be with you shortly, Mr..."

"Uh.... Riley. Joe Riley. But please, call me Joe."

"Very well, Joe. I'm Sondra. Looking forward to our chat." She returned to her reading in progress.

You can't just cut and run, the quiet voice said. Roger followed with, *Yeah, she could be relying on that fifteen bucks for her dinner. And shouldn't she have known your name, if she's a psychic? You might as well pull out that ten-and-fiver and light them on fire with one of the four hundred candles in here.* Then Uncle Peter: *What on God's green earth is the matter with you?*

Attempting to ignore the debate, Joe continued his inventory of the shop. A small counter with an ancient cash register stood in front of the neon-lit picture window. Two glass display cases flanked the counter, these filled with tarot cards, beads, essential oils and incense. A bookshelf ran along the maroon wall Joe sat against; he stood to survey the collection for sale. Philosophy, communicating with spirits, astrology, religion, aligning one's chakras. *All the answers in a six- by three-foot shelf,* Roger offered. *Laugh it up all you want, Chuckles, but we walked in here all on our own,* Uncle Peter replied. *She didn't call or beg us to come in.*

The Reading Room door popped open, startling him from his thoughts. A young woman with reddened eyes emerged, spotted Joe, and averted her gaze. She was followed by Sondra, who walked the client to the front counter. In hushed tones, they continued whatever discussion had begun in the room while Sondra rang up their session. *Not without a few add-ons from the display cases,* Roger observed.

To the soundtrack of dings and springs from the cash register, Sondra and the departing client concluded their conversation. The medium came around the counter and wrapped the smaller woman in a hug, with Sondra placing her hands on the sides of the woman's face as they released. She met the client's eyes with kindness in her own, and a smile that creased her face in a thousand wrinkles.

Before The Cynic Party could offer commentary, Joe felt a twinge of—was it envy? longing?—and instead sat quietly, observing the exchange. Understanding the true value of the fifteen dollars that had just changed hands: someone to say "I've got you. I see you. I understand you." A sentiment, he considered, possibly more valuable than any scientific explanation or well-drawn map.

The woman departed the shop and Sondra turned to Joe, clasping her hands in front of her maroon and bejeweled shawl. She smiled again. Joe couldn't help but smile back.

"Well, young man? Shall we step into my office, so to speak?"

Here goes nothing, one of the committee members said. "Sure," was all his actual voice could muster.

The room was as brightly coloured as the rest of the shop. Celestial patterns were hand-painted along one wall in the same gold as the adjacent room; these were set against a dark blue backdrop. The wall behind the medium—where the seeker of secrets would face—was adorned in a simple green, presumably to evoke calm. *This place is just as deliberate about its colours as the head-shrinker's office*, he thought. A plain wood table sat in the center of the room, with a chair on either side. Decks of cards were piled along one edge of the tabletop. Lit candles ran along the opposite side. Sondra motioned to one of the chairs and Joe eased onto it as though there were pushpins spread along its surface.

"So what brings you in today, young man? I don't believe we've ever met before, and unless I'm mistaken, I would guess this is your first time at something like this?" That smile spread from ear to ear again.

"Is it that obvious? Or are you able to read my mind?" he asked with a half chuckle.

"The former, darling. I can't read your thoughts any more than you can read mine or anyone else's."

You'd be surprised, was Joe's first thought. *But thank goodness you can't*, was the second. "I see. But yes, you're correct. I have no idea how this works."

"Well, it can work in a couple of ways. If you like, you can tell me a bit about why you're here. If you're concerned that will prejudice anything I say, I can do a couple

OF DREAMS AND ANGELS

of readings—your palm, or we can use the deck," she said, motioning to the stacked cards.

"Let's start with a reading, I guess. I'm interested to hear what you pick up, without me saying anything."

"Okay darling, give me your hands."

He eased them above the table.

"It's okay, Joe, I'm not going to latch onto them like a cobra," she laughed, the charms and jewels on her necklace clinking together as she did. Joe's shoulders loosened and he let his hands be wrapped into hers.

"Before we begin, I'd like us both to take in three deep breaths," she said, closing her eyes. After regarding her for a moment, Joe followed suit and inhaled, though his eyes remained open.

Following the breaths, Sondra lifted her head and scanned his palms. She closed her hands around his and shut her eyes once more. "You're incredibly tense, Joe. Don't worry, I'm not here to steal state secrets. This is all about listening. So why don't you listen with me."

He capitulated, feeling the sting of dryness as his eyelids closed. He saw Claire's face, immediately. This had become the norm, it seemed, anytime he turned off from the exterior world—though in his waking hours it wasn't the dream reflections he witnessed through her eyes at night. This was more of an imprint; a shadow visage one might see behind their eyelids after looking at a bright object.

Sondra continued holding his hands but shifted her grip here and there, making "hmm" and "mmm" and "okay" sounds with each movement. Joe cocked one eye open and saw her deep in a trance-like state, gently rocking back and forth, variously moving her head up, down, and to the side. It was as though she truly conversed with ethereal beings in the room (*Or perhaps outside*, he thought, *way outside*). He closed his eyes again.

"You feel very, very lost, Joe," she said, the sound of her voice shocking him out of his own meditative state he'd slipped into.

Sondra opened her eyes and met his. "I could sense your skepticism the moment I laid eyes on you—and that's perfectly all right. It doesn't matter if *you* believe, Joe, so much as if you're willing to believe that *I* believe. But in any case, I'll word all of this gently."

She let go of his hands. "So much of a 'reading' involves listening, as I said before, and reading energies. Yours is blocked, somewhere, somehow. It's like you've deliberately shrouded it in a cloak, so that nobody—maybe even yourself included—can take a look. Does that sound about right?"

He had to concede that much. "That's not far off the mark."

"I can tell you don't want to cough up too much in the way of information—skeptics never do—so let's see how close I am to the bullseye in other ways."

She took his hands again and closed her eyes. Joe kept his open this time, regarding her closely. "Something has disrupted your normally ordered life. Severely disrupted it."

She 'hmm'd and 'mmm'd some more, gently swaying back and forth in her chair. "Nobody has died—recently, anyway. And this isn't a lost love—exactly," she trailed off, eyes still closed.

"Hmm," she finally said again.

Joe sat for a moment, locked on her face, where she was still in the midst of seeing with her eyes closed. The urge overwhelmed him. "Hmm?"

"Hmmm... but there is.... someone." She frowned.

He let the silence build, hoping she would elaborate. She continued to frown, her head lowered.

"Someone how?" he finally asked.

She opened her eyes and looked in his, her irises dancing between his pupils. "This is different," she finally said.

"Different?"

"There is someone there, there is someone who is with you, but it's not like the—how do I word this..."

She smiled again, tried to mollify her expression. "Normally when I sense someone this strongly, it's a family member. A dearly departed. But with you, it's different... somehow." She closed her eyes as she said this, as though peering deeper into whatever she saw behind that veil. She sat for an interminable amount of time without saying anything, and Joe began to shift in his chair.

Her eyes reopened, this time glassy and working to pull focus. "I'm not sure what to make of all this," she said, her mouth drawing down at the corners. "This has a different feel, a different energy from what I'm used to reading." Her eyes searched his. Joe remained silent.

She reached forward to take his hands again. The smile returned. "Do you want to tell me what's going on in your life, Joe? I mean no offense, honey, but you look like you could use a friend."

He took in a breath. "I don't know," he said, pulling one of his hands back and running it through his hair.

"I don't know, Sondra. I mean no offense in return—you seem nice enough, caring enough—but I'm really in uncharted territory here too, on so many fronts."

She reached back, took his hand once more. *Not afraid of intimacy, this one*, he thought.

"It's been my long experience, Joe, that quite often it's easier for people to discuss uncharted territory with someone they don't know. So in that spirit, I'm offering my services. And this part of the session," she said, rising from her chair, "is on the house." She shuffled out into the adjacent room and switched the OPEN sign on the door to its counterpart, and turned the lock.

As she sat back down, Joe's eyes darted between hers, the tabletop, the walls on either side. Finally, they landed on hers again, and he let out an audible breath.

"Well, there is someone," he said.

"That's *very* apparent, yes."

"But she's not a dearly beloved, recently deceased, or recently departed."

"I got that too, yes."

"In fact, I have no idea who—or what—she is."

"Okay..."

"Other than a wildly detailed and imaginative conjuring of my subconscious, that is." His eyes darted from hers, and he fidgeted with the buttons on his shirt.

"Go on, Joe, it's okay."

"I get to the point where I'm almost ready to talk about it—where I feel *compelled* to talk about it—but as soon as it nears my lips, every internal voice starts screaming, '*You can't let this out! Do you have any idea how crazy this sounds?*'"

She let out a small laugh. "Joseph, do you have any idea the kinds of things I hear, sense, and say in this room? You'd have to drop quite a doozy to shock me in my shorts." These little sprinkles of patois were bringing more involuntary smiles to Joe's face.

"All right, well, here goes nothing," he said, taking in another long breath. He paused, while the internal committees issued their grievances.

"Joe, really, it's okay. Just say it, whatever it is."

"I dream..." The button he'd been toying with relieved itself from duty from his shirt. "I dream about a woman."

Sondra waited for him to elaborate. When he didn't, she tried "Okay... well on the scale of 'normal-to-batshit,' that's fairly benign, Joe."

"No, I know that, but as you sensed, there's something different about this."

"Okay, go on." Sondra had settled into her duty of coaxing him forward.

Joe, for his part, eventually settled into releasing the story. Various committee members made certain to remind him how insane it all sounded, but he spoke over them, and their agitated voices were slowly replaced by a feeling of relief. Freedom in finally releasing—in an unvarnished capacity—what had plagued his waking and sleeping hours these past weeks.

There was something easier about telling this particular stranger, in this particularly strange environment. When it had been his physician or psychologist, his internal guard had redoubled even though the answers he tried to tell himself he wanted might be rooted in something resembling science.

But here he sat, with this odd woman and her little idioms, her ornate shawl and pervasive scent of patchouli, and he felt palpable relief at the idea this might be another person who understood. He knew now why the last patron had hugged Sondra before leaving.

She absorbed the story intently, with the skill of someone practiced in the art of hearing human beings for the things they actually said. She didn't appear to be listening merely for subtext (though she was equally skilled in that, Joe thought) as it might relate to some textbook pathology or psychological paradigm.

When he finished, she regarded him awhile longer, and said, "I don't know what it is that's happened with you, Joe. I believe deeply that there is meaning in our dreams, and I suppose we could say your visions of Claire mean any number of things. But I guess what I really want to ask, is..." Her voice trailed off, as her irises danced back and forth between Joe's.

"Yes?" He shuffled in his chair, broke her gaze and looked back at his hands.

"Do you believe she's real?"

He'd known the question was coming, yet despite the unceasing internal commentary, he hadn't formulated an answer. To have pre-packaged a response would have been to allow himself to consciously consider the question. Though it had danced along the edges since the earliest dreams, it had seemed too outlandish, too unreasonable.

"Joe?" Sondra broke his micro-meditation, as he'd sat twisting his palms and fingers together in every conceivable contortion.

"Ahm." He cleared his throat; the sound foreign, as though he'd swallowed gravel.

She reached across the table once more, tugged the sleeve of his right arm to bring his hand above the table. She clasped it in the warmth of hers. "It's okay, honey. It really is. Do you believe she's real?" she asked again.

"I guess— I don't know— I think…"

His mind raced for a combination of words that might somehow feel right leaving his lips, but any sort of syntax continued to elude him.

"*SPIT IT OUT! FIRST THING THAT COMES TO MIND!*" She said this suddenly, forcefully, trying to release whatever words had dammed up at the edge of his mouth.

"*YES SOMETIMES I WONDER IF SHE IS!*"

He'd startled himself, and felt colour rising in his cheeks as he searched her eyes for any hint of offense. There was none.

"And do you *want* her to be real? Just answer, Joe— only two possible words could have come to your mind as I asked that, so say the first one you heard. *GO! SAY IT NOW!*"

"*YES!*" He paused, pulled his hands back and settled them in his lap, where he also settled his gaze. "Yes. I don't know why. But part of me hopes she is."

"Tell me about the part of you that hopes that."

Damn, he thought, *she's better than the psychologist was*. He supposed that in this line of work, one would need to excel at reading people, in order to offer believable readings.

"It's just— I don't know. If she's real, then it means…"

he paused, but continued before she offered the prod he knew would come anyway. "It would mean there's some reason for this sudden madness in my life lately. I have no idea what that reason is. I have no idea how—if it's true, that is, that she's really out there somewhere—how it's even possible. But it would at least mean there's an *explanation*, even if I have no clue what that is."

"What do you *hope* the explanation is?"

He laughed. "Well, that I'm not losing it, for one. Although I really don't know what the proverbial 'they' would have to say—let alone her, if she's out there, if we ever met—about a guy claiming to have dreamt about a woman he's never met, but exists nonetheless..."

Sondra once again picked up her cue to coax him forward. "What else, aside from 'not losing it?'"

Joe looked up at Sondra, smiled a half-smile, then looked back down again. He was about to speak, then laughed again.

"I really don't know, Sondra. She seems like a beautiful woman. I don't just mean in the face—although she certainly is that—but on a deeper level. As I mentioned, it's not that I can hear her thoughts exactly, but I can *feel* her thoughts. I can *feel* the essence of who she is, as much as I can feel my own. It's like a knowing at the level of the soul, and there's something beautiful there." He fidgeted again, waiting for a rebuttal that never came.

"There's pain, too," he continued. "Deep pain, but when that's stripped away there's this beautifully strong, courageous woman. A wonderful mother. A committed worker, someone engaged in their passion. A loving sister. A kind friend. A human being carrying the weight of the world on her shoulders, but doing it so beautifully, and with such grace."

He glanced up, did a double-take when he saw the Medium smiling. He preemptively laughed at himself. "Good lord. Listen to me, singing platitudes about a figment of my subconscious imagination. I'd be grinning too, listening to that."

"That's not why I was smiling, Joe." She leaned forward, shrinking the distance between them. "Do you really believe that? The figment-of-the-imagination part?"

He sat for a moment holding her gaze, then broke it to stand and began pacing the small room. "I just— I don't know what I believe. I think about what it means if I am *just* dreaming this. If that's all this is. Just this nightly onslaught of the most vivid, lucid, recurrent dreams imaginable. What does it mean if that's all this is? What does that mean for what's happening with me? How did it start? How do I fix it?"

He stopped his pacing, leaned his arms against the top of the chair, looking—not without a measure of effort—directly at Sondra. "But then... what does it mean if I'm *not* just dreaming this? What does it mean if she's out there?"

"What do you think it means?"

He started laughing again. "You oughta charge more than fifteen dollars for fifteen minutes, let alone *pro bono*, if that's still what this is. I paid a hundred-and-fifty a session to a headshrinker, and she didn't even come close to getting me to talk about all this."

"I'm not getting you to do anything, Joe. I'm merely

providing a door for you that I think you maybe wanted to walk through anyway."

"What does that mean?"

She laughed, setting off another percussive symphony from her necklace. "Now we're trading on the meaning of things. It simply means that there are some things we carry around with us, that are just begging to be set free. You've been carrying this for awhile, unsure of how—or even if—you could let it free, but you clearly needed to. Even if you haven't always wanted to."

She adjusted the beads on her necklace. "So tell me, what do *you* think it means, if she *is* out there?"

He let out another stifled laugh, circled back around to the front of the chair and sat. "I'll hazard a guess, but I definitely want to hear *your* thoughts when I'm done. I thought people came here to get answers from *you*, not to figure it out themselves."

"Oh, Joe, honey—the answers are almost *always* within, and very rarely without. Like I said before, I'm more of the door-opener. But yes, I can hazard a guess too, after you've risked your own."

He took another long breath in. "Well... I guess... if I *try* to think about this analytically—which always seems ridiculous, on some level—I do ask myself, '*Why would I get these visions of her life*?' Putting aside *where* they come from, or from whom, or even the why on a deeper level... Why would an ordinary guy like me, have these dreams of someone I've never met, who lives in a place I've never been? What purpose is that meant to serve?"

"And what have you come up with?"

"Well... doesn't it mean—uhm..." He cleared his throat, looked at Sondra, almost hoped for a prompt this time.

She merely held his gaze until discomfort forced the rest.

"Doesn't it mean I'm supposed to maybe try and find her?" Joe asked.

"Are you asking me? Or is that rhetorical?"

"Ha. I guess a bit of both." He shifted in his chair, brought his eyes down again. *I can't believe I just said that out loud. I can't believe I've said* any *of this out loud.*

"Do *you* think you're supposed to find her?"

Full laughter left his lungs now. "Are you sure you weren't in the head-shrinking field before this? Because you definitely sound like one now."

"Just showing the doorways, Joe. Turning the handles, if I have to. Comeon honey, work with me here." She gave him a wink.

His eyes wandered around the room, as though one of the corners or colours or designs would provide an answer.

"Joe? Do you believe you're supposed to find her? Don't think. Just answer," Sondra said.

"I think if I presuppose that for a minute—'that' being that she's out there—and put aside all other conjecture for a minute..." He paused. "If I operate under the premise she's out there, then yes. Simply yes."

He felt his chest relax, his shoulders loosen, the moment he'd said it. "I mean, what else could be the reason—the immediate one, anyway—for it? I can't logic my way into it, offer a reasonable and palatable notion of *why* I'm supposed to find her, or what's supposed to happen if I do, or how any of it plays out... but I can't logic my way into any other reason for the dreams, either."

Sondra continued to listen, waiting to see what her client might see for himself.

"What am I supposed to do, just continue having these visions of another, real-life human being, and that's it? That's all?" Joe continued. "Just carry on with the dreams, seeing through her eyes in the greatest privacy invasion of all time, and *not* do anything about it?"

He brought his focus back to the table, back to Sondra. Another small, covering-for-nerves laugh left him again. "Okay. That's enough out of me. Please. I'm dying to know what *you* think. This is about as vulnerable as I've ever been with another human being in my life—a stranger, at that—so please don't leave me hanging."

"And," he smiled warmly, reached across the table and grabbed her hands this time, "not another answering-a-question-with-a-question, please."

Sondra laughed. "Well honey, as I said earlier, I don't quite know what's happening with you. I've heard many different things in this room; felt many different things. Folks often have dreams where their dearly departed visit them while they sleep. Dreams of ex-boyfriends or wanna-be lovers. I've even heard of people dreaming through the eyes of another. But this is the first time," she patted the top of his hands, "that someone has told me they're dreaming this vividly, and regularly, of someone they don't know. Someone who could be out there."

She adjusted in her seat, toyed with her necklace. "What do I think? Well, before I answer that, I do need

OF DREAMS AND ANGELS

to ask you another question, honey, even though you asked me not to." She laughed again, her eyes fixed on his in that stare that nearly caused him to squirm each time.

"Okay, go ahead."

"Do you think that this life—and the things we see and can explain—is what there is? Is *all* there is?"

"Up to this point of my life, yes, that's all I've ever held with."

"You struck me as that kinda fella, Joe. And that's okay. Plenty of folks feel the same. I ask you only because you need to understand that my answer—to what I think might be going on here—is from the perspective of a woman who deals all day long with the unexplainable. I didn't walk through these doors and set up shop because I had an 'A-to-Zee' childhood, if you catch my meaning. So to me, it's less of a question of whether her being out there is a possibility, and more whether or not *you* will accept that possibility."

"So you think she's somewhere out there, then."

"Honey, based on everything I've seen, heard, and experienced in my fifty-nine years, I think there's *less* of a possibility she *doesn't* exist compared to the probability that she's out there."

"And what makes you say that? Aside from your experience?"

"Well, here's the part where I need you to—at least for a moment—suspend your notions of how the world operates. Can you agree to do that for me?"

Joe nodded and she leaned forward, lowering the pitch of her voice as though divulging classified information. "Joe, the universe is *always* trying to communicate with us. Always. Sometimes it whispers, and sometimes it eventually has to beat us over the head with something."

She let loose another gregarious, full-bellied laugh. "And I think in your case, it knew it was going to have to smack you sideways!"

Her laughter was infectious, and he eventually let loose as well. "I suppose you're right. That's about the *only* way it could get my attention."

Sondra continued her assessment. "I'm open to the idea—because being truly open doesn't mean just looking for evidence of things I hope are true, but the opposite as well... I'm open to the idea that these are *just* dreams. But to finally answer your question, my dear, I don't believe for a moment that's what this is. Something, somewhere, is trying to get your attention. And if she's out there, that same something probably wouldn't have—as you said before—invaded your sleep like this, unless it wanted you to know her. To find her.

"The reason for *that* part of the journey, of course," she leaned back in her chair, picked a piece of lint off her shawl, gravity inflecting her tone, "remains to be seen."

"Do you have any thought as to what that is? Even speculation? I mean, you're a psychic, aren't you?"

"Of course I do, honey." The smile returned. "But I'm gonna hold onto that one."

"What? No! Let's turn the billable clock back on here. I want your professional, psychic opinion." At the last, Joe burst into laughter. Sondra returned it with her own.

"Believe it or not, Joseph, there is an element of discretion in this job. Not leading people *too* much. Something tells me *why* you're supposed to find her, but that same something tells me you need to figure that part out on your own."

"Ahh come on," Joe said, leaning back in his chair, crossing his arms over his chest. He looked past the doorway to the street outside. Daylight had faded to dark since he'd arrived.

"So you actually haven't told me anything about my future, then. You held my hands, held quiet congress with some spirits, maybe... I volunteered a *ton* of information, and when the moment of truth arrives, you balk."

He paused, returning his eyes to hers. He expected to see offense, but there was still none he could discern. "I apologize, Sondra. I feel like I haven't slept in weeks, and it's led to a lot of distraction, and a little bit of irritability. I'm normally a lot more measured than this."

She leaned forward again, reached for his hands. Her signature move, apparently. "It's okay, honey. Maybe it's time your life became a little *un*-measured.

"I'll return to what I said earlier, Joe. I'm merely somewhat of a tour guide. I can help you see where the doors may be, but I'm not meant to walk through them for you, or anyone else. You asked me what I think, and on that front, I think it's worth finding out if Claire is out there. What do you have to lose?"

"My dignity?"

"Well, you don't have to run around with it printed on a T-shirt, darlin. But I can tell you this much—and this much I knew before I had your hands in mine, or heard the words you were longing to say—I can tell you're going to regret it if you don't."

CHAPTER 21
PAY ATTENTION

THE FRIDAY EVENING before Joe's flight to Southern California, he reviewed all manner of checklists: one for gear and supplies, another for his condo, last-minute client concerns and investment trades. A check-in with a neighbour who'd agreed to pop in every few days to water the plants, make sure a tap wasn't dripping or the fridge door popped open.

Joe was exhausted; the last couple weeks taxed him as never before. Trip planning. Winding up at work. And the unceasing, round-the-clock consciousness—his own, and Claire's—that pervaded every thought, every action.

I'll walk you away... That had become a mantra of sorts, whenever the feeling of overwhelm became too much. That, and his lists: when the exhaustion, confusion, and running background commentary of her felt unrelenting, he'd circle back to that incantation and onto the next checkbox. It was often enough to keep the momentum going, rather than sitting in the pervasive paralysis of questioning, wondering, despairing, hoping. All these irreconcilable thoughts and emotions, slowly driving him mad.

After his "reading" from Sondra, the merry-go-round

intensified. He'd given serious thought to trying to locate Claire, but after reexamining his journal and replaying all he could recall from the dreams, he knew the information he had was vague at best. What was he going to do—fly to a city of seven million, in a country of nearly *fifty* million—armed with a first name and physical description? He'd rifled through the pages of his notebook wondering if he'd jotted some revealing clue about her neighbourhood or job. Nothing. No logos. No obvious landmarks.

He realized that if someone was dreaming through *his* eyes, perhaps the particulars of his daily life wouldn't be as obvious as the details he took for granted. He never walked by the main entrance of his work with the clear signage; he used a private door instead. He parked underground at both the office and home. *How easy would I be to find?* he wondered. *If Claire started dreaming about 'Joe the Canadian,' would my daily life reveal enough clues to find me?*

After losing a few days to this cycle of thought, he'd called William back into the office, ostensibly to talk about Long Term Care insurance. "Life has really come full circle," William mused, before Joe danced around the idea of what it would take to find her. Far from attempting to dissuade, William seconded the psychic's assertions. If he couldn't positively say whether or not Claire was out there, he did believe Joe would regret not trying to find out.

"Her career is the best clue you have," William suggested. "I suppose that's the most obvious starting point: you could research the daily papers." Joe replied wondering how many publications there were in London itself, let alone England or the entire UK. William shrugged his shoulders as if to say, *It's a better idea than thumbing through the White Pages, isn't it?*

If the older man appeared keen on donning the Sherlock Holmes hat, Joe remained unconvinced. When William gently suggested Joe's internal voices of doubt and ridicule might be running the show, the younger man steered the conversation back to insurance.

"Which are you more afraid of?" William asked. "How you think it looks, if you go looking for her? Or how you'll feel if you don't find her?"

Joe dodged the question outright, claiming the need to end the meeting for another client coming in. Whether Claire existed or not, both men knew the alleged client didn't.

I'll walk this away—and for a moment he'd feel as Claire did in her yoga classes, when the instructor would repeat their universal mantra: *Come back to the breath.*

Good lord. He felt like he needed a month of deep inhalations, if nothing else.

Lists checked, calls made, fridge and garbage emptied, pack stowed by the door. Joe arranged his passport, airline ticket, and US cash on the kitchen table. *You're afraid to go to sleep,* he thought, looking at the clock. It was nine p.m. His flight was at seven, meaning he'd need to be at the airport by five, equating to a wake-up at four. *You're afraid that even with multiple alarms, she'll come in and keep you in her world, and then you'll never get out of this one.*

In thirty-six hours, everything will make sense again.

The plan was to fly into Encinitas, where there was

a trailhead for the PCT on the outskirts of town. He'd booked a cheap hotel room for the first night, knowing with the early flight he'd (hopefully) be tired enough for lights-out by eight, or even seven p.m. He would be up and making his way to the trailhead by first light Sunday morning. If she came to him during that last night in civilization, so be it. It wouldn't matter. The mere thought of being back in the warmth, back in the hills, back with the elements—that was enough to instill some peace of mind. If she stayed with him on the trail... well, he figured he would figure that out with nothing but endless miles to walk, and the silence to sort it through.

He lay down and immediately felt the pre-trip adrenaline coursing through his veins. *Maybe I won't sleep anyway, despite my best laid plans.* He set two alarms on his bedside clock: one at four, another at 4:10. He brought his cell phone into the bedroom as well, setting its alarms for 4:05, 4:15 and 4:20. He hoped it wouldn't come to that.

What on earth makes you think that even twenty miles a day is going to suddenly eradicate this?

Now that he was supine, his checklists complete, the Parliament saw a perfect opportunity to strike up debate. He looked over at his night table, at the infamous journal. His dream log, or a diary of a none-too-lengthy descent into madness, depending on which committee member weighed in whenever he picked up the pen.

Maybe I ought to pack this too, just in case, he thought.

Yeah, if nothing else it'll make for good fuel for your campfires, a committee member answered.

He wasn't certain what time he finally drifted off—his

last glance at the clock told him it was quarter past one—but as with all nights he went from the foggy, incoherent state between wakefulness and slumber to sudden brightness, sudden clarity.

She was standing in the bathroom again, a now familiar milieu, adorned in her white housecoat with a towel wrapped around wet hair. He knew it instantly: she had been crying. He felt the urge to reach out, wrap her in his arms and say *Whatever this is, we'll get through it.*

His internal committee had a field day with that one.

She was leaning against the counter again, tears slowly leaving her eyes, dropping to the porcelain below. It wasn't anything close to a sobbing cry; though he had 'walked into' the middle of the moment, Joe knew that immediately.

He knew Claire's demeanor didn't permit outright breaks in composure; it was a quiet pain that haunted her deeper thoughts. Whatever those thoughts might have been, Joe still didn't have access to. Much as her bathroom was an oasis at times, it was also where myriad distractions of work and play often abandoned her, leaving her open and vulnerable to whatever lingered underneath. *I know that feeling,* Joe thought.

She looked up into the mirror, and as it always did Joe's heart hitched in his chest. Her beauty was always arresting, and because he spent so much time seeing from behind her eyes, he'd often forget how striking it was to look into them. She reached behind her head, pulled at the towel wrapped around her hair. She shook out curls that landed around her shoulders. Joe knew she straightened her hair most days, but when it was freshly washed

OF DREAMS AND ANGELS

her dark strands were naturally curly. He knew she was beautiful, either way.

Whenever Joe's thoughts drifted in this direction, Roger of The Cynic Party usually delighted in goading him. This time all he said was, *Well, at least if we have to be plagued by a figment of your imagination, you made her easy on the eyes. I won't go into whatever it means to be attracted to something you made up—*

Shut up. She's hurting. Pay attention.

Claire began applying the various creams and powders of the daytime uniform, while Joe tried to feel for anything resembling a discernible thought, an available clue.

I wish you could talk to me, tell me about that pain you carry. Is it David? Has he done something to drive the knife deeper? Is it just you, just life? Trying to wear too many hats and juggle too many pins? I wish you could talk to me, Claire. Maybe I couldn't fix it, but I would sure love to try.

Beauty and grace in everything she ever did, including pain. He loved her quiet dignity, the understated way she handled every scene he'd ever witnessed. Her life was much more spontaneous, eclectic and unstructured than his. He supposed with three kids, a fast-paced deadline-driven career, a home, and a broken heart, life was bound to its own clock rather than any plastic one. Yet she still handled it all with a deftness he admired. The more chaotic it became, the more she seemed to meet it with strength and resolve. He was starting to love that about her.

Watch it, one of the voices said.
Go away, Joe responded.

That's probably a correct assertion, Joseph—going away is what's about to happen to all of us if you keep this up.

Just shut up, would you?

She put down a brush and raised her hands to her face, gently rubbing at her temples, closing her eyes. Her touch brought goosebumps—or at least the feeling—to his skin, and butterflies to his stomach. Every time.

She opened her eyes, and reached toward a tray at the corner of the sink where she put her bracelets at night. Charms from her children or sister (and many moons ago from David, before his conditional attention span moved to the next conquest). The bracelet made gentle rattle sounds as she fastened the clasp around her wrist—her hand feeling for a moment like it was on Joe's. The gooseflesh returned to a sleeping body an ocean away.

Claire raised a hand to her face once more, dabbed a tear that lingered along the lower lid of her eye, forcing it into a drop that moved from the lash to the tip of her finger. Joe felt it there too, felt an instinct to kiss it away, yet was unable to move as always. Instead, she wiped it away in a slow circle between her thumb and forefinger, and returned the hand to her cheek.

While he knew he'd have no more ability to move her hand than he did to remove the tear, he closed his eyes, directing every swirling ion of whatever energy existed between them into that left hand, hoping she might feel it. *I've got you, Claire. Whatever this is, for some reason I'm here, and I've got you.*

And before any of the party members could shout their way in:

I won't let you go.

CHAPTER 22

ANSWERS IN ALL THE RIGHT PLACES

Is it possible to start falling for someone, whom as far as you know, could be a chemical imbalance in your own head?

This was among the babel of thoughts that assailed Joe's mind as he sat in the rear seat of the cab shuttling him to the airport. He hadn't needed to worry about his alarms, or the vision overrunning into a missed flight. After that attempt to make connection with Claire, the Sandman hadn't allowed him to see if he'd been successful. The dream had ended right there, and the clock told him it was quarter past three.

Great. Two whole hours of 'sleep.' That oughta help my mental state as I go through Customs. What am I going to tell the officer? "Yes sir, I'm off to hike the PCT so I can throw one of my multiple personalities off a cliff, before I can fall in love with her."

Maybe you ought to just stick with the first part of that sentence, Joey. That's plenty.

At the last minute he'd grabbed the journal, rationalizing that for as much as the plan was to walk himself dreamless, he didn't want to be privy to some telling detail in the night, only to forget it as the morning tide swept over the dreamscape. Beyond this thought, he hadn't permitted himself to consider what he would do if this hare-brained plan of walking two hundred miles in two weeks didn't work. What if the dreams never stopped? How many more journals would he fill?

The cabbie was mercifully quiet throughout the twenty minute drive. Other than a healthy grunt after attempting to lift Joe's bag into the trunk—Joe handling that courtesy after observing the pack was nearly the size of the man—all the driver had said was, "Which airline?" as they pulled into the Departures level.

Joe walked into the International flights area, finding a screen to locate his gate. The airport was quiet even at this peak hour, and he made his way to the check-in desk with hardly a lineup. A woman at the counter called him up.

"Good morning, sir, and where are you headed today?"

Joe doffed his massive pack onto the belt, knowing it would exceed the weight allowance and he'd be asked to dole out an additional fee. He handed his passport to the rep. "San Diego." He was out of practice with a pack this loaded. The walk from the cab to the counter had been enough to leave his quads burning, and his shoulders feeling semi-dislocated.

"Oh, that will be lovely this time of year. Yes, Mr. Riley, we have your flight confirmation here, and will get you all set with the check-in. Are you aware that your pack..."

She continued with the formalities, Joe listening and

responding with the ear and words of someone at half-attention. His exhausted thoughts began racing again. Somewhere between the departures screen and the check-in desk, the Parliament had launched a raucous debate after his eyes drifted from the San Diego departure line to the one for London-Heathrow.

Don't even think about it, the cynic had said.

This is insane, Uncle Peter added, breaking with his trademark diplomacy.

You need to know, said the quiet one.

That same, whispering voice that had pushed him through the doors of Kemp's and Sondra's. The one that told him to start the journal. Who tried to connect his hand with hers in the last dream.

What if she's out there? What if you never try? What if you just keep living this life of pre-planned routes and you never, even once, try your own, true path?

The other voices intensified their shouts, firing barbs like *You've never even been to London. You don't even know if she is in London. Right now you're like the tourist who hears 'I'm from Canada' and says, 'Oh you must know my cousin, he's Canadian!' England may not be the geographical size of this country, or even this province, but it isn't exactly a small town with one stoplight. How do you know it's even England? It could be Wales, or Ireland, or one of those places—that's how vast your knowledge of dialects is.*

The airline rep continued her would-you-like-a-window-seat-or-aisle banter, while the dissonance in Joe's mind persisted. He nodded and delivered monosyllabic replies in all the right places.

Then, in the midst of questions about dietary restrictions or would-you-like-to-upgrade-at-the-low-low-price-of-almost-fifty-percent-of-your-airfare-just-to-get-another he heard this exit from his lips:

"What time is the flight to Heathrow today?"

He'd stopped her mid-sentence, and for a moment the practiced smile faltered and her head cocked to the side, like a confused puppy. "I'm sorry?"

"London. England."

She slowly pulled her stare from Joe's expressionless face to the keyboard, and began clacking away. "Uh, well, Mr. Riley, I'm not sure. Do you have a family member or friend taking that flight?"

"No."

"Oh, okay." Her lips pursed, forming a thin line. "There's one at 8:55 a.m. with a stopover in Montreal, and another red-eye tonight at eleven."

"What would be involved in switching this flight to that one? The one this morning?"

"Uh, well, Mr. Riley, that's an entirely different destination. You're going to California, to—by the looks of it—hike, am I right?"

"There's been a change of plans." *Please don't try to talk me out of this. I have enough of that going on between my ears.*

"Well, there would be an administrative fee to change the flight, as well as the difference in fare..."

"Okay. But it's possible to switch?"

"Technically yes, but between the admin fee and the fare increase, and depending on when you were returning— Would you be coming back on the same date?"

"Yes. Yes to all of it. Whatever it is, make the change,

please." His heart was pounding in his ears, the committee members deafening with their cries. He tried drowning them out.

Just get me through this check-in, get me through security, get me through the gates, and get me on the flight. Please, before these guys can change my mind.

And then:

What the hell *are you going to do when you get there?*

CHAPTER 23
STARTING POINTS

THE PLANE HAD been airborne nearly an hour when Joe's heartbeat finally slowed to something resembling a resting rate. The jostle through security and to the gate had thankfully demanded most of his attention, keeping the members of Parliament to a dull roar.

The conflicting opinions were endless, ranging from comforting to condemning to rationalizing to lamenting.

If nothing else, you're going to finally see London and England.

Yeah, in the middle of December. It's probably as cold or colder than it is here.

What are you gonna do? Hike your pack along the Thames? Looking for dark-haired women with translucent eyes? Asking around for Claire, ye-of-unknown last name?

You have some basic information. It's not entirely impossible to build upon.

You also have nothing resembling a salient idea of what you're doing with your life anymore, Joseph.

There was the journal. He'd hastily retrieved it from a pocket in his massive pack before checking the bag; it was the only carryon he'd brought for either leg of flights that would deliver him across the pond Sunday morning, UK time.

He had no idea where Heathrow was in relation to the city. No idea where he was going to stay, or where he would begin searching first. No idea of where Claire lived relative to London, either.

No idea if she, or the suburb you've seen her in, even exist on a map of the imagination, let alone a real one.

Okay you've more than made your points. But we're here now. We're in the air. Might as well start making a plan based on the information we do have, whether it's ludicrous or not. You plotted a route for the literal wilderness of the PCT—plotted many a backcountry excursion where you'd never set foot before—so just do that here. Start somewhere.

With a few nonchalant questions to one of the flight attendants (Joe didn't want to press, and thus come off entirely clueless regarding his final destination), he worked out that Heathrow was only a quick train ride to downtown London. Joe presumed he'd be wildly jet-lagged by the time they landed, between the spotty sleep the night before, and the seven hour time difference. By his internal clock—fractious though it had been, of late—it would be one a.m. to his body when he arrived. His plan for the first day became locating a hotel he could immediately check into. If he could find a place that would take him for a morning check-in, even if that meant paying another night, he'd try to catch a few hours of sleep. Then find a library, or some kind of information centre.

Let's review the information we do *have,* he thought, opening the journal. He had a moment of gratitude for the less than full flight in this pre-Christmas time period. No wandering eyes to peer toward his tray table and the Journal of Dubious Intent.

Looking for a woman named Claire. Last name unknown. Three children. Possibly a suburb of London. *Possibly a suburb of anywhere,* one of the representatives chided. *Possibly a suburb of nowhere, other than your rapidly declining sanity,* another goaded. Joe ordered a whiskey. Rarely more than a social drinker, this seemed like an occasion for it. Maybe he could get the voices to slow, or at least slur, and perhaps a bit of booze would temper the fluctuating arc of anxiety he was feeling. A glance out the plane window, or another announcement from the cockpit would set it off. Stark reminders of where he was and what he was doing, and the committee members would go once more into overdrive.

YOU'RE FLYING TO LONDON, ENGLAND, TO CHASE FIGMENTS OF A DREAMWORLD. WHAT HAS COME OVER YOU, JOSEPH?

A drink might help. Only one, however—he was afraid of what might happen if he dozed off. What if Claire came to him immediately, as she almost always did these days? What did that look like from the outside? What would the flight attendants observe? It could be nothing. Could be anything. Whatever it was or wasn't, he didn't want to find out.

The journal helped somewhat to ground him; sticking to the "facts" forced the other thoughts to the sidelines. Employed at a newspaper. Sister named Audrey, an artist. Ex-husband named David, possibly also in media. A recent story on a company shutdown and the improprieties of its owner. This was good intelligence, should even a fraction of it turn out to be true.

He'd never managed to capture much in the way of landmarks from wherever she did reside. It seemed like a suburb, but there was no Tower Bridge or Buckingham Palace that ever showed in any of the visions. That didn't mean it *wasn't* London—how often did he ever walk or drive by the landmarks in *his* city?—but Joe knew he couldn't be sure.

He'd start at a library, combing through whatever dailies he could find, searching for reporting and editorial staff. Looking for Claire or David, although of the latter he hadn't any definitive clues. Of David's current lover (and Claire's ex-best friend) Miranda, Joe hardly knew anything beyond the affair, thus not providing much in the way of leads there either.

If the names on the bylines yielded little, he could search the society and announcement pages (if those were still a thing—Joe hadn't a clue), starting with the present. He knew from a conversation between Claire and Audrey that David had floated a test-balloon with the kids about making his situation with Miranda official. The discussion had sent the two younger children reeling. It was one thing for Daddy to be living with Auntie Miranda, provided that's all it was. Somehow, that kept the eternal dream of every child from a broken home alive: that Mummy and Daddy would one day reconcile, the home reunited under one roof once more. When David mentioned his plans to the children over ice cream (a deliberate ploy) on one of his custodial weekends, Holly had burst into tears, followed by Ainsley. Jackson had eventually walked out of the room, processing whatever his reaction was in private.

Lousy as that situation was, on a logistical front it could yield breakthrough information. Not only would a marriage announcement confirm Claire's existence by proxy, it might lead to an actual date and location where Joe could find her. If David did work at a media company, Joe couldn't imagine they'd shy away from news of a wedding for one of their own.

It may have been a stretch, but it was a straw for Joe to hold onto, anyway.

If the infidelity-turned-nuptials road didn't lead anywhere, he would work backwards, starting with the children. The thought immediately overwhelmed him; he'd only the faintest estimates of their ages, let alone birthdates—and still, no last names. *This might have been easier in an age when people still addressed others by their surnames,* he thought. Birth announcements on the children were undoubtedly needles in endless haystacks.

He took another sip of his airline-sized shot of whiskey and thought, *But it's still something. These are starting points. Stick to what we know, what is possible, and don't focus on the endless roads or possible dead ends.* He had to believe that *something* would lead *somewhere.*

He'd booked his return from London for the same Saturday as the flight he should have been taking from Bakersfield, California. What, exactly, was he going to do in the two weeks between now and then? Pour over microfilm day after day at the library? How long would he even tell the front desk at the hotel he'd need a room for?

People are spontaneous all the time, Joey. You're just normally not one of them.

He took another sip. He'd only lowered the small drink about halfway, but already it was making him fuzzy. He would order a coffee instead. If the conflicting voices of doubt and encouragement were apt to continue, he might as well fuel them on with caffeine rather than risk slipping across time and space in view of dozens of other souls.

He smiled ruefully as he put the glass down, the whiskey calling to mind a supposed recovery slogan he must have heard in a movie or television show, and one that felt appropriate now: one day at a time. Then a flash of memory of the first time he'd seen her face, in the bathroom mirror, when she'd said that very thing. A brief pause for thought: was she an alcoholic? No. He'd never seen any evidence of that; the occasional glass of wine with Audrey, which Claire rarely finished.

I wonder what she meant by that, he thought, recalling a dream that had been wonderful for him, but clearly a moment of pain for her.

Whatever it had been, or meant, here he was, without a plan or certain outcome for the first time in longer than he could remember. *You'll disembark the plane. Collect your pack. Find the train. Find a hotel, hopefully. There must be hundreds in downtown London. Sleep for a bit. Then begin your search.*

CHAPTER 24
THE MOMENTS BEFORE THE MOMENT

IT HAD BEEN difficult to keep awake on the connecting red-eye to London. After the stopover in Montreal they had departed at seven p.m., and the crew dimmed the cabin lights only a couple of hours in. Joe's new row companion had promptly made a makeshift bed between her aisle seat and the unoccupied middle chair between them, making him wary about turning on the overhead light to read the novel he'd picked up during the layover.

His healthy fear of whatever his dream-voyages might look like from the outside kept him awake, despite the mounting fatigue. After he'd burned through a couple of the movie options, he finally flicked on the lamp somewhere over the moonlit Atlantic, in an attempt to get lost in the latest Stephen King thriller. His seatmate hadn't stirred. *At least one of us appears to be getting rest, even if she had to bend herself into a pretzel to do it.*

A lifetime and several coffees later, he felt the plane shift into its descent. Adrenaline seized him as the capital city came into view through the clouds; he peered out his window looking for landmarks he'd only seen in films. The Thames glinted against the pale sun, and he was able to pick out Big Ben and the Palace of Westminster.

Everything else was foreign to his eyes. In a planned trip he would have done the appropriate research, bought a Lonely Planet book, discovered the best side of the plane in which to sit for arrivals, the best hotel in proximity to all the sights. His unfamiliarity with nearly everything in this strange city only served to underscore the feeling of impulsiveness and futility.

The plane touched down and Joe straightened in his seat. *Whatever this is going to be, it begins now. Maybe these are the moments* before *the moment.*

CHAPTER 25
INANITY AND IMPROBABILITY

After attempting to decipher a street atlas called "London A-Z," Joe had thrown up his hands and hired a town car from the airport instead. He'd asked the driver, Gene, to take him to the heart of downtown and find a "comfortable" hotel that might take a morning check-in.

The hotel was all too happy to take Joe's impromptu reservation, at what he was certain was a marked-up rate. The trade-off was a beautiful space in a beautiful building, just minutes away from the Thames and parliament buildings. He'd reserved the room for a tentative three nights, having no idea where he might be within the haystack at that time, searching for a needle that might not even exist.

With the exchange rate, the three-night stay was already going to cost more than Joe's entire budget for the PCT; yet another dig at his sensibilities when they'd swiped his rarely-used credit card through the imprinter. *Does this constitute an emergency-fund emergency? A mental one, perhaps?* Roger, apparently, wasn't too jetlagged to natter an occasional comment.

The elevator doors opened on the eighth floor and Joe hauled his pack to the room written on the cardboard key folder. The suite, for what it was worth, held some semblance of "getting what you paid for": an inviting king bed in a separate room off a generous living area, with floor-to-ceiling windows that overlooked the river. Under different circumstances he might have appreciated the view and amenities, even with the notorious London fog bringing a low ceiling over the horizon. At the present moment, every sight served merely to underscore the inanity and improbability of where he was, and why.

It would have been a couple hours past midnight in California right now. He should have been asleep (whatever that meant these days) in a motel a fraction of the price. A few hours from setting foot on a famed trail he'd wanted to hike for longer than he could remember. Instead, it was ten a.m. in sleet-filled London, as Joe stared out the window at pedestrians bundled in massive coats and scarves. A mini-bottle from the minibar in his hand (he hadn't bothered to fix a glass with ice), and his sense of sanity loosening from his grasp.

He couldn't remember the last time he had earnestly prayed—he'd mouth the words during those semi-annual visits to his parent's parish—but now seemed as good a time as any. *If you're out there, I think I need some help. Help me make sense of what's happening, of why I'm here. Or have mercy and send the men with the white coats so I can stop wondering what's going on and what I should do.*

He lobbed the tiny bottle into the waste bin as though making a free-throw shot, and decided to down another shooter for good measure before pulling the blackout blinds across the windows. Later on he hadn't known if it was the alcohol or the exhaustion, but after falling into the bed fully clothed, he'd disappeared deep into sleep.

For the first time in weeks, she wasn't there.

CHAPTER 26
CHASING SNOWFLAKES IN A STORM

HE AWOKE NEARLY eighteen hours later, disoriented and unsure of where he was, or where he'd been. After weeks of the dreams it felt strange to have slept through the night (and day). Even when Claire was in some unfamiliar milieu, there was a feeling of familiarity simply in being with her. Throughout the entire Sunday that he'd just slept away there had been nothing, only darkness.

He stumbled out of bed toward a sliver of arc lamp peering through the curtain. Joe opened it to the dormant street below. *Oh right. None of this was a dream—in the exact sense of the word. You're in England. That actually happened.*

He checked the clock beside the bed and it showed quarter past four. Based on when he'd fallen asleep and the current time of year, that could have meant four in the afternoon. The streets were too deserted, however.

For a moment, he felt grateful for the first uninterrupted sleep he'd had in weeks. He felt groggy, from both the marathon slumber session and time change, but all at once quenched, as though he'd taken the first swallow of water after a long walk through desert climes. His circadian rhythm was utterly destroyed—it would be nine p.m. back home right now—but it had been in disarray regardless, for longer than he cared to remember.

She wasn't there, though. What on earth is that *supposed to mean?*

He showered and dressed. It would be hours before the city awoke, and he certainly hadn't packed for walking aimlessly in winter temperatures. He made a mental plan to find an early breakfast, and then with the aid of the concierge map out the hours to come. Locating a library seemed the best, most logical first step. From there... well, that was the part he still hadn't a clue, and where the internal committee attempted to resume its assault.

Library. Breakfast first, get his bearings, then the library. As he donned what thermal layers he had brought for the hike, he kept repeating that mantra. He couldn't afford even a moment's pause to reflect whether his efforts would bear fruit. Let alone why she hadn't come to him during sleep, now that he was here.

He ate breakfast in the hotel, grabbing that morning's copy of The Guardian to see if her name (or even David's) popped up anywhere. *You know, you could have done this from home—there are shops that carry international papers, and likely the libraries too—and saved yourself a few thousand bucks or whatever this insane diversion is going to cost.*

Thanks for mentioning it, Roger. I wasn't feeling ambivalent enough about this as it was.

She's here somewhere, that other voice said. *I can feel it.*

The paper yielded no results, and picking at his English breakfast only dragged time out to a quarter of seven. After inquiring at the concierge about the library location and hours, Joe layered up further and decided to tour past some of the iconic landmarks near the hotel.

The walking helped; sightseeing offered a brief lull from his thoughts and mission. Even the weather was proving tepid, the sun beginning to emerge and dissipate some of the fog. He strolled past the Palace of Westminster and Westminster Abbey, knowing embarrassingly little about either but recollecting hearing the latter was a resting place for poets and kings. Surely many among them had sought the improbable in their lives? Chased instinct, as opposed to reason?

He continued with the directions given by the concierge, making his way past 10 Downing Street and along St. James's Park. For a moment he felt awash in the history of this place, and reflected it would be nice to visit under more ideal circumstances—better weather, and not chasing at a snowflake in a storm.

He arrived at the steps of the London Library and made his way inside the fabled space, just as its curators were opening the doors. He asked for the reference section, where he would find current and archived newspapers, and was directed to The Reading Room. It occurred to Joe he should have loaded up on coffee as one of the librarians plunked a stack of current dailies in front of him. This pile alone would take hours to comb through, to say nothing of the endless microfilm.

This is too much. Too ridiculous. Go back to the hotel, call the airline, and whatever it costs just book your way to San Diego. You might even get there by tonight with the time difference, and you'll have only lost two days and forty miles of hiking. You're just going to drive yourself even more mad than you already have by staying here.

And then:

She's in there somewhere. I know it. I feel it as strongly as anything I've ever felt in my life.

CHAPTER 27
ONLY ONE FROM MILLIONS

Hours passed like minutes as Joe poured over every sheet of every paper, blackening his fingers with the ink of a thousand pages. He'd even succumbed to asking the librarian for a magnifying glass, both for his increasingly tired eyes and to augment the chance her name might jump out at him.

Nothing. The occasional 'Claire' in the impossible sheets and innumerable words, but never in the spot of a reporter or editor. When her name did appear—stopping his heart for a moment each time—it was always in some item that couldn't possibly be related to her. A senior citizen's obituary. A married spouse. A different nationality. He made notes and took photocopies anyway, in case he was left at the end of this preliminary search without anything definitive and had to comb back through what initially seemed like unrelated or disparate information.

He'd been certain her name would eventually show amongst the editorial staff in one of the publications, but not a single paper yielded anything—many copped for "from the editor" sections cloaked in relative anonymity. The pages that did list writing, editing, and publishing credits drew a blank. He wondered if perhaps she wrote under a pen name. Did that happen in newspapers? Maybe, but wasn't that more for 'Dear Abby' type columns? Did Claire even write, ever? It occurred to him he hadn't directly witnessed this.

There were various Davids amongst reporting staff, but no pictures; nothing to definitively identify her ex-husband. Newspapers rarely ran byline biographies of their writers, and Joe doubted if many would elect for "serial philanderer" as a leading qualifier. He noted the names and titles anyway, should it help to later narrow the overwhelmingly large net he'd been forced to cast.

He looked for stories of local scandal featuring improprieties by the chief executive. Joe quickly discovered this was either too common to make big headlines, particularly when weighed against the appetite for royal scandal, or the information he had was too nondescript. He'd written down the last name he'd heard in that specific discussion—Anderson—but once more, nothing popped out.

Claire's surname would have felt like a gilded piece of information; he'd at least be able to focus on phone books rather than papers. As Joe sat in the immense, gorgeous library (a slight consolation, that), the awareness of the little he knew threatened to overwhelm. The vastness and history of the library only served to underscore that fact. Hundreds of millions of words surrounded him, and precious few would be the one word he was looking for: Claire. Fewer still would be *his* Claire. Perhaps none at all.

After he'd scanned through the various dailies the

library received from across the UK, he'd turned to the microform machines. It was already two in the afternoon, and aside from a trip to the loo to wash the ink staining his hands, he hadn't moved from the table at which he'd taken up residence. His stomach protested with hunger but his adrenaline—combined with the need for validation—overruled and kept him at the search.

He began on the microfilm as he had with the papers, starting with London and combing his way outward—geographically, and then back through time. He was possessed with the idea he'd eventually see her name call to him from a writing credit, like a desert island castaway frantically waving at a search plane. Yet every turn of the dial, each eye-exhausting focus on the negative images, offered nothing absolute.

The Cynic and Uncle Peter increased their volume, but the third voice also continued its gentle nudging: *She'll be here. You will find her. She found you, and there had to be a reason for it.*

Afternoon began drifting into early December evening, the light through the windows casting long shadows from the shelves across the research tables. The library was soon aglow in muted lamplight, as other seekers poured over their volumes or machines. Joe found himself wondering what the man to his right, face alight by the boxy machine, was hoping to find. *Is it your dream love too?* The Cynic piped up. Joe rubbed his eyes and turned back to his own screen.

At points throughout the day, friendly (and very proper, Joe thought) librarians would gently put a hand on one of his shoulders and ask if he needed anything.

OF DREAMS AND ANGELS

Aside from requests for the next date ranges for the volumes he poured over, he hadn't come out and divulged what he was looking for. One librarian had directly asked, proudly proffering their collective investigative prowess. He'd choked out a half-formed lie about general research of trends in the UK over the past decade. She'd asked if those were related to any specific industry or area—fashion or the monarchy, by example—and he'd smiled awkwardly, saying he was just "enjoying soaking in British culture." The librarian responded with a combination of polite smile and undisguised frown, as if to say, "You could never possibly understand, my dear."

A final tap on the shoulder came at quarter of eight, whispering that the library would be closing shortly. Could they make any photocopies for him, or even provide a guest library card to check out reference material? Joe sighed and declined, saying he'd most likely be back in the morning.

He gathered his only personal effect—the journal, where he'd made scattered notes on the Claires or Davids he'd come across—and looked at it with something bordering on loathing: it was becoming a physical reminder of the fruitlessness of this journey. The wind outside whipped his face as he walked, doing little to assuage the feeling of futility. The humid air was quick to chill him in contrast to the dry cold of the Canadian Rockies, and he only made it a couple of blocks before calling a cab. The hiker in him balked at the sloth—Roger also happily piling on about the hemorrhaging of cash—but Joe needed a win, even if that was a short escape from frozen cheekbones.

He arrived at the hotel and elected for an overpriced meal from the gift shop, consisting of a bag of crisps, chocolate bar, and soda. He had no appetite, though his stomach waged protests for some level of sustenance beyond coffee. He'd purchased what he thought he could choke down in small bites, just to quiet at least one of the voices assailing everything about this misadventure.

His eyes were strained. His back had begun barking at him sometime in the afternoon, no matter how he adjusted in seats that hadn't been constructed for comfort. Strictly utilitarian, for the Renegades of Research that occupied them. *At least those people probably have some kind of verifiable aim they're working towards. The peccadillos of the Royal Family. The Great Fire. Rebuilding after The Blitz. I have first names. No actual proof of anything other than weeks of compromised sleep. And a mounting charge card bill.*

Joe tossed his half-eaten Snickers into the wastebasket he'd moved from the corner of the room to the side of the bed. He lay down and closed his eyes as a child will do when they believe it will make them invisible from that which has overwhelmed them. When he opened them next, proof of his reality stared him brightly in the face: he was still here, still in London. Tuesday morning's light greeted him through windows he'd failed to drape the night before.

He'd fallen asleep in his clothes, and once more slept the night through in the black. Claire wasn't just missing from the millions of words he'd poured through the day before, she was now missing from his vision, too.

CHAPTER 28
DID YOU FIND WHAT YOU WERE LOOKING FOR

JOE RESUMED HIS post at the research table with that day's papers. The librarians welcomed him back with a smile, offering assistance once more. He declined with a smile in return—his on the embarrassed side.

More pages. More stories. More names. More nothing. Nothing resembling a lead, some proof of life, some road to her. It was as though every word he read was another flake of snow landing on and around him, while he stood waist-deep in an avalanche of his own making. Eventually he'd be gently suffocated, unless he could find the proper noun belonging to the proper person, which might become a rope with which to pull himself out of this mess.

Sunlight produced its pale and ashen beams through the tall library windows, the shadows creeping along the room as the day wore on. Joe finished the daily papers within a couple hours, and had moved back to the microfilm. Hundreds of slides. Thousands, maybe. He couldn't tell, didn't know, didn't want to know.

Despite the tedium, he still felt one committee member driving him on. *You will find her. She's here. Somehow, in some way, you'll find her. She'll find you.*

Twelve hours later, those hopes were dampened once more; another hand on his shoulder alerted him to the closeness of closing. The librarian asked again if he'd found what he was looking for, if they could be of aid somehow.

"Not yet, but I guess that's the essence of searching, isn't it?" he replied, handing back a couple of magazines he'd tried and gathering his notebook. He hadn't written anything in it today.

CHAPTER 29
GLIMMER OF HOPE

THE WEATHER ON Wednesday proved slightly milder, nearing almost ten degrees, the sun threatening to cut through overcast skies. Joe decided to tour the city a bit more.

He'd also—against the advice of his inner critics—extended his hotel stay to the end of the week. *If we're gonna be here, let's be here. We're here already. Might as well try to enjoy it.*

He purchased a "hop on, hop off" ticket for one of the famed double-decker buses, indulging his inner child by going to the second level and sitting at the front. There were stops at the Tower of London, Tower Bridge, St. Paul's Cathedral, and even Shakespeare's Globe.

Though he winced every time he signed for his credit card at another unplanned attraction, some part of him relaxed with the day's deviation. He'd always liked studying history, believing there were equally compelling—if not better—stories in the history of humankind, compared to anything in a work of fiction. The distraction from his original quest in this fabled land was a welcomed one, and as he listened to guides speak of kings and queens and legends of lore, for fleeting moments he forgot the mythical turn of his own life.

As another afternoon quickly collided with evening, he boarded a bus that would drop him at the library. He'd wanted to check the off-chance that Tuesday's editions would offer some glimmer of hope. They offered none. The librarians smiled sympathetically as he returned the stack, as if to say, "If you'd just tell us what you're looking for, we'll find it for you."

But how does one find what dreams are made of? he thought.

When Joe returned to the hotel, he made a phone call.

CHAPTER 30
CUTTING INFINITY IN HALF

It hadn't been his intent—he'd just needed to vent to *someone*—yet before Joe could process what was happening, William was hanging up the phone to arrange the red-eye to London.

"Think of it this way," the older man said over Joe's protests, "even if the haystacks are endless, at least you'll be cutting infinity in half."

Joe insisted that his call hadn't been to solicit help—on the scale of a client flying overseas to search for what might only be a figment, no less. He'd merely wanted to decompress, commiserate with someone at the improbability of life taking this latest turn. William had replied with, "I think we both know the client-line was crossed by each of us, ages ago. This was always about my interest in you and Claire, and about you having an external voice to compensate for the ones that chide you from within. And let's be clear on another point," he added, "if I might not believe *you* took this turn, it doesn't mean I don't believe it's a turn worth taking."

Joe could concede that much: to hear someone else use her name, as though she were an actual person, went a long way in diminishing the onslaught of doubt from every other turn. Before Joe could object further, William ended the call by saying he needed to dig out the Yellow Pages for his travel agent.

It would be around eleven the following morning when Doc Hollings arrived. After the older man called back confirming his overnight flight, Joe arranged for Gene—the driver of a few days prior who'd given Joe his card—to collect him at the hotel the following morning, in order to meet William at the airport. In his guilt, Joe also booked a room for the erstwhile doctor-turned-accomplice, before they'd have the chance to argue about it.

I'll be spending an entire day recalibrating my own financial plan when I get back, came the thought. *Well, maybe then you can write this off as a business expense. Researching the financial cost of losing your mind, and gifting a client accommodations to watch you do it.*

If William wasn't too jet-lagged, the plan was to "hit the stacks"—as William called it—at the library after dropping his bags at the hotel. Whether his biorhythm was disturbed or not, Dr. Hollings didn't show it upon arrival, his eyes looking as alive as ever.

Before they'd had the chance to discuss strategy, William plunked a phone directory down on the desk at the library. "Have you tried calling?"

"Calling whom? You know I don't know her last name."

"The papers. Calling their receptionists and asking for Claire."

It wasn't any worse than Joe's own ideas, though the

thought of connecting with a live voice and saying Claire's name aloud raised his heart rate and made his skin tingle.

"What do I say?" Joe asked, a lump like a ball of paper forming in his throat, drying out his mouth.

"Just ask if they have a Claire that works there, and if there happens to be more than one, say you think she's in the reporting or editorial departments."

"What if they ask for a last name?"

"Just be honest. Say you don't know."

"What if they ask who *I am?*"

"I'm not a reporter, but I've seen many played on TV," William winked, "and I'm sure they get calls all the time from sources who don't want to identify themselves—if a receptionist even bothered to ask."

"What do I do if *she* answers?"

"You're overthinking this, Joe. Just make the calls. You've cold-called before in your profession, haven't you? You'll figure it out."

"I always had a script when I did."

"Joseph," William said, sitting down in the chair beside him, putting an age-spotted hand on the younger man's. "You keep trying to plan around this thing. To strategize your way in or out of it." He patted Joe's hand. "Make the calls. You'll know what to say if you find her."

The paper ball swelled in Joe's throat. Something about dialing the phone raised an immediacy and reality to the situation. He could be talking to her within minutes. Why hadn't he thought of this? *You would have talked yourself out of it anyway,* Roger said, before adding,

But the old guy is right. If she's there, you'll know what to do.

If the internal committees were getting on board, maybe it *was* time to "screw courage to the sticking place," as Shakespeare's line had doubtless been uttered countless times in this city.

Joe told one of the librarians they *could* finally help him, by directing him to the nearest phone.

CHAPTER 31
COURAGE TO THE STICKING PLACE

"I'LL CONCEDE IT was a good idea in theory," Joe said, dropping the directory back on the desk. "But in practice, it left a little to be desired."

"What happened?" William straightened up at the table he was hunched over, his face bathed in yellow lamplight. Joe reckoned the jetlag was catching up.

"The usual reaction was, 'Do you have any idea how many people work here?' When I tried to narrow it down to the reporting side, I was still usually hit with 'Which division?' or 'What department?'" Joe plunked into the seat beside William. "Apparently answering 'The News Department' was neither helpful nor amusing."

"Well, it was a thought, anyway." William rubbed his brow, the arms of his glasses wrapped around his fingers.

"I did have one bite, however."

William straightened, replacing the glasses on his face. "Oh? What happened?" Energy and intrigue had returned to his voice.

"I must have been at least a dozen calls in—funny when you think about there only being a handful of newspapers where we're from. I opened with my usual 'I know this is a shot in the dark, but do you have a Claire who works—', and before I could finish, I heard a 'Hold please' and a ringtone. I nearly fell over."

"And then?" William was wide awake now.

"This scratchy, irritated voice came on saying 'Payroll.' I sat there for a moment, paralyzed, and she was about to hang up when I said 'Is this Claire?'"

"And?"

"She said, 'Yes it is, hon, what's it to you?'"

"It wasn't *your* Claire."

"Nope. I knew it from the moment she said more than one word. After hearing Claire's voice up close and personal all this time, I'd have known it in a second."

"What did you say to this one?"

"I did ask—just to be sure—if she ever worked on the news side. Between what I'm certain were drags from a cigarette she said, 'The only reporting I've done around here, hon, is how much money other people are making that I'm not.'"

"Ahh. That's too bad. Worth a shot, though."

"She did offer to meet with me, however."

"Oh?"

"Yep, said 'You sound like a handsome devil, what's your name?'"

William roared, prompting several head turns from other patrons, accompanied by the requisite shushing. "Did you take her up on it?"

"I'm not that desperate, yet."

CHAPTER 32
ENOUGH IS ENOUGH

THE REMAINDER OF the week progressed much as it began, even with William's help. Joe settled into a routine, which was comforting at least. Wake by seven. Breakfast and coffee in the hotel restaurant. Over to the library for opening at eight-thirty. Through the dailies by ten. Onto the archives, to resume where they'd left off the day before.

Lunch at a nearby sandwich shop sometime around twelve-thirty. Afternoon tea around four (*When in London, after all*). Crushing defeat and dejection around seven-forty-five. Back to the hotel. Dinner with William to debrief. Sleep. No sign of Claire.

In some measure of relief, the nights were restorative, at least. Uninterrupted and dreamless. Not even the garden-variety nonsense of BMX bike rides with long-dead Prime Ministers, or flying like a comic book hero. Black. Nothing. Just the closing of fatigued eyes somewhere around nine p.m., the switching off of an overworked mind, and complete darkness until his new-natural rhythm woke him the following morning.

He had no idea what to make of that.

While he welcomed the pure rest that had eluded him for weeks, it hadn't rectified the floundering confidence in this wildly irresponsible mission. By Friday afternoon—when he and William had little to report to one another apart from further discoveries of Palace intrigue—Joe had called the airline to change their return flights from Saturday, the twelfth, to this Sunday, the sixth. "I'm sorry you came all this way for nothing," he'd said to William.

"I could be doing nothing at home, or I could be doing nothing in London, young man. I'm perfectly happy with the latter," William replied.

He'd even convinced Joe to accompany him to the West End that evening, saying, "What could be more appropriate than theatre in London on a Friday night?" Despite the younger man's pleas to hit the bed early and return to that place of unthinking, un-debating unconsciousness, William assured him the diversion would do just as much to improve his state. "Though we'll aim for a comedy instead of tragedy, yes?" he'd winked.

They agreed to seeing the show that evening, a bit of a sleep-in the following morning, and taking in some sights the remainder of Saturday. William seemed delighted to be anywhere that wasn't the bookstore or the long-ago hospital hallways; they'd negotiated on the wake-up time as though Joe was bargaining with a child about Christmas morning.

They'd forego the newspapers altogether tomorrow. William only faintly suggested a quick stop by the library as they set the itinerary for the day. He could read the answer in Joe's eyes. Enough was enough.

Maybe Joe would drive to the west coast once he was back in Canada, in search of warmer weather and day hikes. Maybe he'd simply go back to work. He hadn't a clue, anymore.

There had been such conviction from that whispering inner voice; the belief the sudden itinerary change at the airport would bear fruit. In reality, it had been little more than fanciful flight. Every minute now was choked with an unforgiving thought: he had indulged all he'd ever rebuffed since that morning on the departures level with Rachel. He'd become no better than those college friends who chased desires in lieu of deliberation, or the patrons of Kemp's and Sondra's who longed for quick answers on the shelves or in the rooms. Enough *was* enough; he would go home, and he would carry on. That was the *true* English spirit, wasn't it?

When he handed the stack of papers back to the librarians at teatime on Friday, Joe felt another sense that had eluded him for weeks: relief. There was something about shutting down the search that calmed all the internal voices, even the quiet one.

It seemed that voice had grown weary as well. Eternally chasing sunsets, only to have the horizon eventually, and inevitably, go dark.

CHAPTER 33
GHOSTS IN THE THEATRE

Joe hadn't packed anything remotely resembling London theatre apparel, and as such indulged the library staff's eternal willingness to be of assistance. By the look on their faces, his enquiry left them disappointed: directions to the nearest menswear store.

A pressed pair of trousers and button-down shirt seemed in order, and a peppy clerk at Selfridges was all too happy to oblige. As was Joe's charge card. The internal member representing the subcommittee for budgets and prudence had apparently gone quiet as well, in blithe surrender.

Joe walked back to the hotel to take another shower, washing the ink of a forest's worth of paper from his hands, and the scent of the library—hundreds of years of collated dreams and pain—from his skin. He was ready to be done with London. He needed something to plan, to look forward to, to take his mind away from the last few weeks. A proper, extended hike of the PCT. Perhaps he'd take a full four weeks away in February or March when the Canadian winter was firmly entrenched, the days short and the nights long. That time of year where it became easy to believe the sun would never shine bright and bold again. That was the ticket. Have something big to look forward to now, instead of passing away the hours for some imperceptible date long into the future.

Maybe he'd even try dating again. Seriously, this time.

Good lord, one of the committee members spoke up, *you sound like a person who was just broken up with, trying to move on.*

Joe supposed parts of that weren't entirely untrue.

He cut the tags from his new duds and dressed, the show starting in less than two hours. He ordered room service—again, at this point, why not—and ate while scanning channels on the TV, something he rarely did in hotels. He flipped through everything and watched nothing in particular, some part of him wondering if this too was just another guise, another last-ditch hope for something that might point him to her. As he dabbed the remnants of fish and chips away with a napkin, he knew she wasn't to be found on the screen, either. She wasn't to be found anywhere. Maybe again in dreams, someday. Part of him hoped that might be true. Most of him did not.

He met William in the lobby at seven and they began their walk to the West End. William wanted to arrive early to tour the building and absorb a bit of the history. During the walk he delivered a soliloquy on milieus where imagination came to life while surrounded by tangible history. Joe thought the tangible was probably good to hold onto, right about now.

The theatre was vast, and although full with fellow patrons the gentlemen made their way along the wood-paneled corridors, pausing to read various posters and playbills from productions past. Joe admired the high, painted ceiling of the mezzanine, adorned with various accoutrements and a requisite but beautiful chandelier made with what looked like a thousand pieces of crystal, refracting simulated starlight all around.

The hotel concierge had lined them up with prime seating on the main level, yet William bounded with childlike fascination to the second and third balconies, wanting to view the stage from various angles. Joe had never been one of the drama geeks in grade school, nor had he cared much for theatre. He didn't dislike it either, merely felt indifferent. But here, in this place, he had to concede something about it felt magical. Historical. Art, in its home, in its essence. Being here felt good for his worn out mind and soul, the latter having gone quiet out of something resembling regret.

The "fifteen minutes to curtain" call came over the tannoy, and while William continued to explore, Joe headed to the lineup for drink service in the mezzanine. As he stood in the queue he continued to look around, soaking in the wonder of this place. He was tired, yes, but for the first time in days he felt content. Enjoyment, even. All was not lost, perhaps, and William had been right. He was in London, England, taking in a theatre show on a Friday night.

If he could, for a moment—or better yet, the next three hours—forget the circumstances that brought him here, it was far from a bad way to spend one's time. While the committee members had barked and balked for myriad reasons like operating without a plan and without a budget, he'd at least had the time, the ability, and the resources for this to be possible. And for the first time in more than just days—weeks, perhaps—he felt something resembling gratitude. He felt himself smiling.

Two away from the front of the queue, Joe shifted his gaze to a display beside the bar. There were various handbills for upcoming productions and events both at the theatre and surrounding area.

And there she was.

Not Claire. Audrey.

Audrey Evans, sculptor, with an exhibit on Saturday, December 5TH at 7 p.m., at the Tate Gallery.

Evans? Could that be their last name? Joe's mind rifled through the archive of his dream memories. Had he seen something—anything—that might confirm that? No, he would have made a definitive mental note if he had. Nevertheless, how many Audrey's could there be in England that were professional artists? *Could be thousands, mate,* a sarcastic voice from the committee offered.

His memory flashed at least half a dozen snapshots of Audrey walking into the main house from her studio above the car park, dried plaster up her arms and dotting her clothes. *How many could there be?*

He'd never overheard a discussion regarding Audrey's career specifically, nor seen evidence to indicate her art was more than an avocation. Yet it felt implicit that there wasn't some full time corporate vocation, either. Part of Audrey's relocation to Claire's had been contingent on her flexibility: she was most of the time freely available to help with the children, with pick-ups and meals and bedtimes, and whenever Claire needed downtime.

Joe's skin had broken out in gooseflesh, his heart in his

throat and his breathing shallow. It was just a name, but it was as close to spotting someone familiar in a sea of strange faces as he'd felt in ages. He felt a hand tap him on the shoulder. He half expected to turn and see Audrey—or the heavens willing, Claire—standing behind him, somehow knowing who he was, too. William's bright blue eyes met him instead.

"You look like you've just seen a ghost," William said.

"Not quite, but possibly much better."

He had no idea later how he'd sat through three hours of theatre; his mind raced at breakneck speed the entire time. William was equally fidgety, whispering in the manner of old men with "hushed" tones louder than the regular speech of most. The older man's rhetorical questions in combination with Joe's thoughts formed an unanswerable loop: Could it be? Had they truly found a needle amongst the stacks? Would this lead him to her? What if it was just a complete, unrelated coincidence? What if Claire was at the gallery? What would he say to her? Would she look the same in real life as she had in his dreams? What would happen next?

Above all, Joe was possessed with one, overwhelming thought: he couldn't wait for it to be twenty-four hours later.

Though the temperature had dropped several degrees and a light wind blew the wet, fluffy snow of London around him, Joe had happily chosen to walk back to the hotel after the show. Citing age and the weather, William opted for a cab despite the excitement. They'd agreed to reconvene in the morning over breakfast.

Joe needed to move, to indulge the surge of adrenaline

and dopamine. *This must be how a mariner feels after spotting land since time out of mind. Something. Something to sail toward.* It may not prove to be the land he was searching for, but it was an islet to place his feet upon, at least for awhile.

Joe didn't sleep a wink that night.

CHAPTER 34
AFTER COMING THIS FAR

AT NO POINT during the sleepless night or following day did the soundtrack cease. Joe tried to temper his hopes, tried to tell himself it could still be a coincidence, could still be a dead-end.

Yet what if it wasn't?

At breakfast with William, where neither man did more than push their bangers and eggs around their plates, they discussed returning to the library in lieu of sightseeing, now that they had a surname. Though he knew it eschewed logic, Joe tossed out a half-formed excuse about not wanting to waste another day and miss out on the sights should their new canvassing turn up nothing. In truth, he couldn't bear the thought of another rejection via a piece of paper. After coming this far, he wanted to see the show—and possibly her—for himself. In person, with his own eyes.

They followed through with their original plan, taking part in guided tours of Buckingham Palace, Westminster Abbey and the Parliament buildings, as arranged by the hotel's concierge. Joe viewed the sights much the same as he'd watched the stage production the night before—his eyes seeing it all, but registering little. Seven p.m. seemed an eternity away.

By early afternoon, the ghost of exhaustion had crept up behind both shoulders. Though their tours hadn't finished, Joe determined it was worth attempting a power nap to defragment his brain and ease the red from his eyes. Better to get two or three hours of sleep than to power through, fueled solely on an erratic supply of adrenaline.

He left William to soak in the remaining factoids of Her Majesty's Kingdom. The older man hadn't fared much better with his attention span, but he'd at least slept. Joe gave William one of the key cards to his room, telling the good doctor to "throw a bucket of water on me if you have to, even if it looks like I'm having the best dream of my life."

CHAPTER 35
THE NEXT STEP

Some part of Joe's physiology managed to creep below the line of sleep, and he dozed for a couple hours. Another level of his mind continued to run, however, and while it wasn't like the activity he experienced when he was with Claire, the looping thoughts never completely faded. The only evidence Joe had of slumber was the sudden shift of the clock to four p.m. By the time William called over to his room, Joe had showered and dressed for the evening.

Tickets! Did they need tickets? In the race of his mind and heart, it hadn't occurred to him until now. He'd never been to an art exhibit in his life, and had no idea how these affairs functioned. Was it invite-only? No, couldn't be. Why would they advertise it with a handbill if it was?

What kind of silent torture would that be—arriving at the doors, and denied admittance? What if, after an ocean and continent away, he came within steps of seeing a link to the woman—if not the woman herself—that had taken over his waking and dreaming hours, only to not know for certain?

What would he do—sit outside and watch for people coming and going, see if he could spot Audrey? How would he even know, if it was a different Audrey altogether? What if his dreamscapes were more like a filtered lens, and though the sisters might appear close to what he'd seen, weren't exact captures? Similar to how some people weren't photogenic, and bore little resemblance from pictures to their actual look in real life?

What if because she was the artist, Audrey never even used the main doors? What if there was some side or back entrance? He couldn't be in two places at once—the irony of that thought not lost on him—so would William need to stand guard while Joe scouted around? William wouldn't even know for certain who he was looking for; all he had was Joe's description. How big was this building, anyway?

Joe's mind continued this assault as he paced his room, chomping on a room service sandwich, when William knocked on the door. Before the older man made it past the threshold, Joe began unleashing the torrent of questions dammed up in his mind.

William put up a hand.

"Already took care of it. The concierge."

A gentleman by the name of Edward at the front desk wasn't familiar with the show or artist, but he was familiar with the locale and was quite pleased (or at least sounded that way, William surmised, with the "very good, sirs" and "it's a pleasures" peppered into the discussion) to make enquiries into admission. If need be, Edward would attempt to pull strings after years of cultivating relationships in the arts scene.

After a couple of phone calls, the concierge informed William that the exhibit had been by guest list only (it had been advertised, yes, but the list had closed two days prior), however he was able to work his magic and get the Canadians on the registry.

"Did the venue ask why, or who we are?" Joe asked.

"Not that I know of. All the concierge said was that he'd known the front office 'chap,' having gone to 'primary school' with him, and they were happy to indulge the favour. Then he added that he was certain we would enjoy the show, as 'Ms. Evans apparently has quite the reputation as a rising star in the visual arts world.'"

She—or more accurately, someone she might be related to—has been the entirety of the stars in mine, Joe thought. He thanked William for the guest list work, and second-guessed himself for not trading up the Queen's residence for his seat at the library. If not to find information on Audrey, then at least on sculpting and visual arts. If someone asked his opinion on a particular piece—were they even called pieces?—he'd have no idea how to respond. William confessed equally little knowledge.

In the nervous system overdrive from excitement and sleeplessness, little of this had occurred to Joe prior to now. His thoughts had been almost exclusive to the possibility that tonight, he might look in her eyes directly and truly for the first time. The thought of this, and the feelings accompanying it, had been enough to curtail much in the way of logic or planning.

And the biggest question of all: if he saw Claire, what would he say?

Hi, you've never met me, but I know you. I've dreamt of you almost every night for the last six weeks. I know your children's names. I know what you do for work, even if I don't know exactly where that is. I know your sister here. I know about David's affair.

Good lord.

For all the hours you were awake last night, Joseph, you would think you'd have spent more time on this.

He tried to comfort himself with the notion that the possibility of finding her had still seemed too ineffable, too unlikely. He hadn't allowed himself to chart a course as it related to talking to her, as it seemed too laughable. It opened the door for those voices of ridicule to chime in. Despite their regular assault at the castle walls, he'd quietly known the ticket to getting this far had been looking only at the next, single step. Up to now, that had been the search, uncertain and fruitless though it was.

Now the next, single step, might be the most improbable conversation of his life.

No.

Uncle Peter had spoken up this time, Joe sensed not in scorn, but with his steadying and reassuring tones.

The next, single step, is out of this room. Down to the lobby. Then to the end of the block. Each, single step at a time, until you're at the studio doors.

And then, if she's there, try to have faith that whatever fate brought her to you—which then brought you here, and you to her—will give you the words you need.

He kneeled to tie a lace that had undone, stood, and stepped to the door.

CHAPTER 36
PIVOTAL MOMENTS

Joe felt like he could hardly breathe.

The men elected for another "hackney carriage" cab ride over to the venue—if for no other reason than William's enjoyment at saying the name with a butchered accent. Wet snow had continued to fall throughout the day, and Joe didn't want to arrive sopping wet, like a dog at a doorway. This was going to be bizarre enough as is, he needn't be disheveled on top of it.

They provided their names at the venue door, and per Edward's promise were let in without incident. A server in a sleek black gown handed them glasses of champagne while another porter took their coats.

The foyer opened on a grand, beautiful room—part ballroom, part warehouse hybrid. It was lit throughout by incandescent bulbs, creating the appearance of a starlit night. Gorgeous looking people with coiffured hair and formal wear mingled in twos and threes, chatting in hushed tones as though this were a classier version of the library.

Jazz mixed with classical music over hidden speakers throughout. Half-walls adorned with paintings and portraits were everywhere, standing at haphazard (but clearly deliberate) forty-five-degree angles. Between them stood large sculptures set upon white marble blocks. Sculptures of what, Joe hadn't a clue, but the mode of both the pieces and place carried the essence of high art. He could recognize that much. He felt entirely out of his element.

They began to walk the room, feigning interest in various pieces (there were no labels or placards under any of them, further exasperating Joe's ability to have even some semblance of what he was looking at), while making a survey of the people. Earlier in the day, William had repeatedly asked Joe for physical descriptions of Claire and Audrey. Joe offered his best, but beyond cursory details of hair and eye colour, approximations of height and build, he was as lousy at describing their appearance as he was coming up with what he might say to either of them.

The room seemed to twist and turn in endless stretches, and between the half-walls and dim lighting Joe couldn't make out faces from a distance. They'd have to approach each group in order to pull focus.

There were at least a couple hundred people here, and based on Joe's inadequate description, several whom William thought might be a match. After the fourth instance of William's loud whispering of *"Hey, is that her?"* and conspicuous finger-pointing, Joe respectfully replied that he would assume the scouting duties. William was to do recon on the sculptures instead, gathering any intelligence on the artist, the pieces themselves, and what the two of them might say if asked their opinions.

Joe covered about half of the room, with no recognition of anyone. No familiar faces, just polite head-nods and curt smiles from people he assumed could pick up the reek of his outsider scent. As disappointment coupled with anxiety began to mount, he heard a tap on a microphone, followed by a gentleman clearing his throat.

"Ahm, yes." *Thunk-thunk,* as the source of the voice tapped the mic again for good measure. "Is this thing on? Ahh! Yes it is. Good evening everyone."

Joe couldn't pinpoint the source of the sound, with the overhead speakers making it ubiquitous. He saw the assembled groups turn their attention to an area three-quarters along the length of the room, past a set of appetizer tables along the left-hand side. William was nowhere to be seen.

Joe needed to step past some of the half-walls to gain purchase on a better sightline. There was a small white stage flanked by black curtain stands, and when the attendees gathered round they created a half-circle several rows deep. The best he could manage without breaking groups apart was along the back row. His head was on a swivel, scanning the faces within view while attempting to remain nonchalant. There were still several in profile that he couldn't discern and far more facing away from him. Of those he could see, none were familiar.

"Good evening everyone, and thank you for coming out to this wonderful exhibit tonight," the man on the stage said. He stood solo, wearing what looked like a tuxedo dropped one step below formal to give it an artistic, fashionable flair. It was almost garish—certainly nothing Joe would ever wear—but this sprightly man with his round glasses and thinning but deliberately spiked, working-with-what-you-got hair, pulled it off with élan.

"I am so very pleased, and so very humbled," he continued, "to welcome you here tonight. This is the third exhibit by someone who is not only one of the most naturally talented artists I've had the pleasure of working with, but an absolute lovely human being as well."

Joe's head continued its periscope movement, focused on the area near the stage. The Audrey headlining the bill was obviously here somewhere, but she was either not Claire's Audrey—if she was among the women Joe could spot flanking the stage—or she was still out of sight.

"For those of you who don't know me, my name is Miles Colborne, and I am Audrey's agent. Right before she ran to the loo—three shows in and she still hasn't mastered those butterflies—" he said with a wink, to scattered laughter, "—she informed me that if I spouted plaudits before she stood up here, she'd have my head afterwards. You know Audrey." More laughs.

"But since she's still behind the curtain and not up here to actually remove it from my shoulders, I'm going to do what I'm best at: denying my artist's wishes." That answered the question of where the artist was.

He went on about Audrey's natural talent and emerging success in the London art scene, while Joe's mind and vision raced. His stomach had begun to knot (an unpleasant feeling mixed with the champagne), and his heart pounded as though it had relocated just south of his Adam's apple. While his eyes darted in every direction, his heart beat with the knowledge that whenever this little man on stage finished his lauding (*And would you please, kindly, shut the hell up,* Joe thought), everything hinged on whoever appeared from behind the curtain stands. Joe's sanity. The past six weeks. The weeks to come.

If he'd ever had a pivotal moment like this before, Joe couldn't recall it now.

"...and so before you all pull out your chequebooks and begin freely dispensing those vast sums I know you want to part with for this one-of-a-kind, stunning, and moving work you see before you," Miles continued with the wink-and-a-handshake demeanor, "please take some time to let Audrey know how you feel about her work with your *words*, as well. She's a beautiful—if irascible—soul, and I know she wants to thank each and every one of you for being here.

"Ladies and gentlemen, it is with my fondest and fervent love that I ask you to please join me in welcoming our marquee artist of the evening, Audrey Evans."

The applause rose.

Joe's heart stopped.

It was probably only a matter of seconds while Joe followed the heads of the crowd turning to a slice of curtain that began flapping frantically, as a pale hand wrestled with the opening. A fraction of a moment, but for Joe another lifetime expired, waiting to see the face connected to that arm.

At first it was all dress and hair and stumbles that emerged, while the crowd gently laughed at the curtain mishap. The artist belonging to the body regained her footing but continued to wobble a bit on the heels. While her back remained turned to the crowd she smoothed out the dress that looked as foreign to its wearer as the pumps.

From behind, the hair colour was a match, at least. The auburn strands normally thrown into a top-knot, shooting off in spikes this way and that, now sat straightened in what looked like a tamed but elegantly styled lion's mane. She remained with her back turned only a moment, gathering composure. The world foreclosed on another eternity, punctuated by the percussion of Joe's heart. That sound was all he could hear.

She made a quarter-turn, and stepped up on the stage.

It was her.

It was Audrey. *The* Audrey.

Joe made an abrupt turn, doubled-over from the clenched knot in his stomach, and bolted to the washroom.

CHAPTER 37
THERE'S A LADY WAITING

"Are you all right, mate?" came an echo off the bathroom walls, about thirty seconds after Joe had evacuated the room service sandwich from earlier.

He was still hunched over, one hand supporting his stomach, the other outstretched against the wall behind the toilet. "Uhhh... yeah, thanks. Think I ate some bad shrimp earlier at dinner."

Laughter came from outside the stall. "Well at least it wasn't the art! Although I hope Audrey didn't see you dash off as she took the stage."

Joe wiped his mouth with tissue paper and flushed his overpriced, unbudgeted sandwich down the drain. He re-tucked his shirt into his trousers, and attempted to straighten himself without the aid of a mirror before emerging and greeting the source of the voice. Whoever it was clearly hadn't stepped out of the washroom yet, in an apparent act of benevolence toward a stranger. Joe unclacked the stall lock and stepped out.

It was David. *The* David.

For a moment, Joe thought he was going to faint. Another potential first in his life.

"I'd shake your hand, but I don't know where it's been, or what it's been covered in just recently!" David clapped Joe on the back instead. "Just wanted to make sure you were fit, my friend. You ran off in a hurry."

David was smiling. Charming. Handsomer than Joe remembered, which made him wonder if by seeing through Claire's eyes, he'd also seen people as *she* saw them—with accumulated emotion, colour and history. Joe could see how David had easily used these powers of charisma and allure for less than honourable purposes.

"I'm David," he offered, another clap on Joe's shoulder this time. "You going to pull through, ol' chap? Or do I need to call the men in white coats? The ambulance kind, anyway."

That's not too far off the mark, Joe thought. "I'm good, thank you. I'm sure it was just a bad piece of food from dinner, and I'll probably be fine now that it's out."

Having still not glanced a mirror, and with David running supposedly magnanimous interference, Joe had no idea how he looked. Either post-projectile, or in response to this man with whom he'd had an entire (if arm's length) history already. A less than pleasant one at that, having felt the wash of Claire's pain at the sight—or even mention of—David. Why was he here?

"You don't sound like you're from around these parts, my good man." David waited for Joe's reply, the Kennedy-esque grin on full display.

"Canada. I'm Canadian."

"Well, a pleasure to meet you, Mr. Canada. Though it's regrettable it couldn't have been in a better setting. Or with the benefit of a breath mint," this latter statement accompanied by a wink. "Once you wash your hands, I'll shake one of them. David Bradley."

"Joe Riley." He stepped to the sink, saw his pallid skin and hairline matted with sweat, eyes bloodshot from the force of vomiting and lack of sleep. *That's wonderful. I'm possibly meeting the literal woman of my dreams, and I look like I've just walked out of a jungle after contracting malaria.* He washed his hands.

"What brings you to Her Majesty's Kingdom, Joe Riley?" David stood with a drink in one hand, the other in a pocket of a tieless suit. Looking like an Abercrombie & Fitch model, even with his relaxed posture.

The better question is What are you *doing here?* Joe thought, but proffered the quickest thing that came to mind. "I wanted to take a quick trip somewhere I'd never been, and my travel agent was able to get an excellent deal on London."

It occurred to Joe that no one, whether at the hotel, library, or any of the sights he'd visited, had asked him this question. In the myriad hours lost to unrelenting thought, he hadn't prepared a response to this either. He dried his hands and shook one of David's. Firm grip. Confident. Used as part of the charm package, Joe was certain, in encounters romantic or otherwise.

"I have no doubt about that, coming in the meek and murky doldrums of early December. What are you doing here at Audrey's show?"

Joe ought to have known this was coming as well, but stammered over a hastily-formed reply. "It was— just something recommended by the hotel concierge. Took in a theatre show last night, thought I'd take in some art tonight."

"Ahh, well that's lovely. A man of culture!" David flashed that impeccable grin once more, clapped Joe—beginning to pique his irritation—again on the shoulder. "Well Mr. Riley, enjoy the art, and enjoy London! Now that I know you're not hemorrhaging or going cardiac on us, if you'll excuse me I ought to get back. *There's a lady waiting,*" he said, leaning in with a wink, as though conferring a secret among men.

Which lady? Miranda? Claire? Perhaps he simply meant Audrey, on stage now, giving a speech Joe could hear only in muffled tones through the bathroom walls. Or did David mean another woman altogether, his latest conquest?

"Nice to meet you," Joe offered in return, and watched him leave.

He returned his gaze to the mirror. "Good lord," he hushed at the reflection. "This is not good." He dabbed at his face with one of the cloths from the bathroom counter, and fished a piece of gum from his pockets.

"This is absolutely wild."

Was it possible he was dreaming this, too? If so, it was by far the most lucid he'd ever had. Based on the past weeks, that was another feat of improbability. His thoughts turned to lying down earlier that afternoon—was there a chance he'd not actually awoken, and this was all just an incredibly vivid illusion created by his subconscious? A hope of how things *might* be once he set foot through the gallery doors?

It would be weird to dream up David, he thought. But

then again, weirdness was the essence of most dreams. After these last weeks, feasibility ought to have been the last expectation.

That vomiting had *to have been real. The snow on my face as we left the hotel. The cab driver. William. The emcee for this thing. David. Audrey. Did my mind really conjure all this?* For however improbable this moment, this place—these people—might be, it seemed equally impossible he was still lying in the hotel bed, snoring away the afternoon or evening.

He took another evaluating glance in the mirror, dabbed the remaining sweat away from his brow and fixed the matted hair. *A splash of water probably wouldn't hurt,* he thought.

The cool flow from the tap shocked and refreshed his hands and face. *If I* am *dreaming this—this water, these drops I feel falling along the sides of my face... this knot in my stomach... the beating of my heart... If I am...*

He shook his head at his reflection. This whole thing was already one for the books. This particular scene was the most outlandish chapter yet. Should someone actually call for the asylum, Joe was prepared to acquiesce.

But while we're here, may as well see what happens next...

CHAPTER 38
I THINK YOU DROPPED THIS

WHEN HE EMERGED back into the main room, Audrey appeared to be at the tail end of her speech. She was as charismatic as David, but with a complete absence of manipulation—her charm was on the awkward and endearing side. Joe missed most of what she said, even as he slowly made his way (trying, at least, for discretion following his bathroom sprint) back to the assembled crowd. He'd lost William somewhere in the group, nor could he spot David.

Audrey was thanking her agent, the venue, and a litany of names Joe didn't recognize. He was waiting to hear only one.

Either he'd missed it, or she hadn't said. He joined the rest of the attendees in their applause. *I haven't the first clue what this type of art is called—but this entire situation is surreal.*

And then:

What do we do next?

The crowd began disbursing, some queueing to speak with Audrey or Miles. Others headed to the refreshment tables. The pockets of socialization reassembled; wait staff hovered about to quench a thirst or satisfy a nibble while animated conversations recommenced. Some admired the sculptures, some the paintings on the walls. Some reached out for friends or colleagues with whom they hadn't yet spoken.

Joe searched for only one.

He considered approaching Audrey, but was once more paralyzed by the thought of what he might say to her. He knew he'd stick out like a sore thumb between the accent, the mad-scientist look, and the inability to speak cogently about art whilst at an art show. He'd keep it in his back pocket; if he didn't see Claire, then he'd somehow find a way to speak with Audrey. Hopefully he'd think of something to say.

Claire. The thought of her knotted his stomach tighter than even before. If the entirety of supper hadn't already departed, he thought another trip to the loo might have followed. Mercifully, the knot merely tugged and that was the end of it. For the moment.

If he didn't know what he might say to Audrey, then *what on earth* was he going to say to Claire?

David. Was David the open—if dubious—door? He was clearly the extroverted type and wouldn't shun conversation with a stranger, especially since they'd bonded over a potential health crisis.

A potential mental *health crisis,* The Cynic Party spoke up.

For the love of God—Uncle Peter and the quiet one spoke in tandem—*even* now *you won't shut up? We're here, this appears to be—well, whatever it is, it's happening, right now—and you still have to throw your two cents in?*

I'm not the one who decided to show up here, let alone without a plan, Roger replied.

The knot pulled even tighter.

Joe meandered, feigning interest in various exhibits, keeping an eye above the sculptures and along the half-walls.

Why do you have to pre-plan anything to say, anyway? he thought. If she was here, why couldn't he just approach and make conversation, like a normal human being? Strangers do that all the time. *You've done it all the time, in the name of business.*

And then, Uncle Peter's reminder: *Have faith that whatever brought you here will also bring you the words.*

He felt a tap on his shoulder, and heard a voice say, "Excuse me? I think you dropped this."

He *knew* that voice.

His stomach knotted so tight he thought his abdomen might wring itself free from his body.

His breath momentarily disappeared, and came back in sudden and shallow wisps.

And his heart? For the first time in his life, it leapt.

CHAPTER 39
IN THE SPACE BETWEEN THE WORDS

HE TURNED SLOWLY, as though every minute of his thirty-seven years, every facet of his world to that point, all pivoted in that moment.

He also felt an element of fear; somehow he'd turn and it wouldn't be her—despite the voice—just another stranger in the crowd.

Perhaps his subconscious would levy the ultimate cruelty: if he moved too fast, maybe he would awaken. Discover this had all, in fact, been the most elaborate dream yet.

He didn't wake up. She wasn't a stranger. To him, at least. And this was indeed a new beginning.

Later, in endless daydreams when he'd return to this time, he'd wonder if there'd been cameras (there must have been, in an art gallery) that captured the moment. Captured The Day that Changed Everything. Logged the expression on his face. Was his mouth ajar? Did he look like a madman? Had he retained any semblance of cool or verve? Unlikely, but that hadn't mattered.

It was Claire. Standing directly in front of him, engaging with him, looking in his eyes. This wasn't a dream; he wasn't about to wake and find her lost to the ether once more.

Later on, he would also think there ought to be better words for moments that change a life.

She was smiling. She was beautiful. She'd arrested his heart, stopped it from beating somehow, and yet it coursed his body with a flow and feeling he hadn't felt in longer than he could remember. Perhaps ever. She was speaking, and beneath his shock something alerted him to the sound, and his hearing flooded in mid-sentence:

"...if I ask, are you okay?" There was gentle laughter underscoring that beautiful voice. At least she was smiling and not repelled, he'd think later. "You look as though you've just seen a ghost."

Some compensatory mechanism stepped in and helped gather his wits, allowing him to form the first words he ever said to her: "Bad shrimp, I think."

"Oh my, from here?" she said, her smile replaced by a frown.

Joe cleared his throat, feeling his awareness flood fully back to the situation. "No, no. Not at all. My hotel, I think. I'm starting to feel better, believe it or not."

"Well thank goodness." The frown departed as quick as it had come.

What a gorgeous smile, he thought. It occurred to him he'd never really seen it directly. Sometimes he'd see the crinkles at the corners of her eyes in the rearview mirror when she was driving with the kids, but rarely in full-on reflections. How often do people smile at themselves in the mirror? It threatened to steal his oxygen and heartbeat once more.

"The way you dashed to the loo..." Now she began to laugh, couldn't seem to help herself. "I thought 'this man either really hates art, or he's catching something on the rebound.'" She was really going now. "I'm so sorry! Pardon the expression, and pardon the laugh."

It was the easiest absolution of Joe's life. After endless nights and lost hours, a real ocean and a sea of newspapers, wonder and panic and uncertainty... this was music.

He started to laugh too—couldn't help the infectiousness of it—and looked down for a moment, shuffling his feet. "You saw that, did you? My frantic sprint?"

"I did. I was standing just to the right of you, so it was difficult not to take notice. And when you spun around and bent over," she said, raising her hand, "this fell from your pockets."

She was holding up the little cardboard folder that held his hotel room key. He'd put his ID and charge card in there as well, so he wouldn't need to cart around his entire wallet. He must have dislodged it when putting his coat-check ticket in his pocket.

"Oh! Well, thank you. I might have had a bit of trouble trying to manage without some of that. My driver's license and credit card are in there."

"We certainly wouldn't want that, Mister..." She smiled that brilliant smile once more, and extended a hand.

"Joe. Joe Riley."

"Hello, Joe. Oh! That's fun to say. I've never really

known a Joe, now that I think about it. I'm Claire. Claire Langdon."

We've got a mess of last names here, he thought. Even if he had found something within the reams of newspaper he'd poured through, the connections wouldn't have been obvious. *I wonder what the story is there.*

We've time enough to find out now, the quiet voice replied.

He reached out to accept her hand, feeling both the warmth of hers within his, and the tingle that ran through his arm as they made contact. In reply to her introduction he'd wanted to say, *I know. Well, the first half, anyway.* Instead, he elected for "It's so very nice to meet you, Claire." He'd nearly slipped a "finally" in there.

"I almost followed you into the loo with your billfold but held back, lest that look completely scandalous. That, and I saw my ex-husband rush in after you with that hero act of his." Though the words were biting, Joe didn't detect malice in her tone.

"You're here with your ex?" Though his stomach was still in a partial knot, Joe spied around for another glass of champagne, as he could feel the words starting to become cotton in his mouth.

"No, heaven's no. Audrey, the artist, is my sister. David and I were married for quite a few years, so they're acquainted, obviously. And for reasons passing understanding, one evening while he picked up the children she mentioned her show, and offered the polite invite we never thought he'd accept. But here he is." She looked to the side and down a bit, the corners of her smile momentarily softening. She looked back at Joe and the smile returned. "But that's not at all just-met-a-stranger-conversation—and you sound like you're a stranger to these parts as well, Mr. Riley."

This was the ultimate, surreal moment. Having a conversation with someone he'd just met, but in possession of these details already. While he hadn't known the specifics of why David was here, what Claire divulged hadn't surprised Joe in the least.

How was he supposed to respond to any of this? The internal ridicule threatened to return from the lack of preparation for this pivotal conversation, yet it had just seemed too improbable. Too outlandish.

Still, he hadn't woken, hadn't rolled over to discover he was in his condo, facing another day at the office. Here he was, in London, in the flesh. Claire standing before him. Waiting for him to take up his cue in the conversation.

"Uhh... yes! This isn't my usual neighbourhood. What gave that away?" he said. Claire smiled, causing another skip in his heart. The missing beats were at an all-time deficit. "I'm from Canada."

"Oh! Lovely. I love Canada. Whereabouts?"

"Near the Rocky Mountains."

"Like Banff? That sort of area?"

"Yes! You know it?"

"I do! After my first year of uni I took a year off, so I was one of the many tourists you find working the shoppes in the Canadian National Parks. In between a million hikes, I worked at one of the campgrounds near Lake Louise. I haven't been back in almost—well, I suppose it's almost been twenty years now, which feels outrageous to say—but I absolutely adored it there."

She'd said the magic words, and their conversation fell into an easy, familiar rhythm. Time evaporated, as they stood in the middle of the gallery like rocks in a stream. Thoughts of what to say or how to react fell from Joe's mind; he was taken with the rare feeling of conversation as a river instead of an obstacle course.

When talk turned to her children or career, he'd heard the muted shouts of The Cynic still trying to get a word in, like a vanquished candidate decrying election results in spite of a landslide. While Roger trumpeted feeble claims of deception, Joe listened to Claire as if hearing all of this for the first time. In a way, he was.

It turned out she worked at a newsmagazine called *Unvarnished,* as a managing editor. It was an upstart publication, formed only a year earlier in the aftermath of Princess Diana's death. The magazine's founders were spurred by the same intent of many publications in their infancy: an earnest desire to deliver the news independently, without spin and corporate interests, or thoughts of market share and ad buys.

The sentiment appeared reflected by its initial circulation—the inaugural issue reached a respectable twenty thousand souls, without celebrity nudes or exposés on drug dependence. The purported ideals of the readership didn't last, however, and within six months the monthly magazine had already shifted to quarterly. "It turns out being above reproach may be good for the soul, but not so good for the corporate wallet," Claire explained, the twinge of sadness in her eyes betraying her smile. It seemed no matter how much the general public claimed their desire for facts and objectivity, when it came time to grab a magazine off the rack, it proved difficult *not* to reach for the latest dish on Charles and Camilla, Robbie Williams or the Spice Girls.

Despite the independence and uncertainty of the publication, it heralded a personal autonomy for Claire: prior to *Unvarnished,* she and David both worked at The Guardian. When his reporting career didn't amount to much (one too many filing deadlines missed while he was busy wooing an interview subject), David had moved to their advertising department, filling column inches in the Classifieds rather than the news section.

With more time spent on maternity leave than the front lines, most of Claire's tenure involved researching and editing for reporters rather than in the action. Though she longed to be on the ground, editing had at least kept her close to home, available for football matches or school concerts. When word spread of former colleagues launching *Unvarnished,* Claire viewed the opportunity as the best of all worlds: a fresh start and a clean break.

She told Joe about her salad days and ambition to take on the coveted role of investigative reporter. While her early trajectory pointed in that direction (editors had been keen on her style *and* substance), marriage and children and support of her ex-husband's floundering career had curtailed upward movement. She'd been happy to make the sacrifice, and spoke glowingly—as Joe knew she would—of her children. She told him how there was always the idea that once the kids were old enough, she might take back up the path she'd begun. It seemed less and less likely these days, with life holding to its own design.

Joe nearly felt as he often did when listening to his parents or grandparents, hearing stories for the umpteenth time but endeavouring to listen with fresh ears. He was, truly, hearing her speak of children, career, and marriage for the first time in her words, but he had felt the essence of so many of these things for weeks. Yet even if he *had* heard it all from her before, he would have remained captive; he would have listened to her read the London directory.

As Claire spoke, he also felt a sense of relief as she filled in details he hadn't been able to see or find in the dreams. Although he'd half-heartedly sifted through a half-dozen magazines on the second day at the library, he'd been so certain it was a newspaper that he'd allowed confirmation bias to cloud his search. Yet who knew if *Unvarnished* was substantial enough for inclusion in the library catalogue alongside *Radio Times* and *Vogue?* Even knowledge of Audrey's last name would have been of little use, with Claire explaining her younger sister had taken their mother's maiden name in tribute to the woman who was once a fledgling artist in her own right, but hadn't pursued her dream beyond a tiny attic space in their childhood home. Where Katherine Evans hadn't made a career of her talent for sculpture, Audrey had taken up the moulds (and the gift, Claire asserted, professing her own inability to create anything aesthetic even with Plasticine).

Even if I'd settled in the Reading Room for a year, I

might never have found you, he thought. *And yet here you are, as real as the air I breathe. A real-life, literal dream come true. Still, if William hadn't insisted on the theatre, I might never have been standing here.* Where was William, anyway?

"Joseph, I see you've found a friend," came the familiar voice over his shoulder.

Right on cue, Joe thought. *It's as though something is going above and beyond to drive home the point that I ought to stop questioning everything, stop trying to engineer all of it.*

"Uh, yes, William. I have. William, this is Claire. Claire Langdon," Joe said.

"M'lady," William said, taking her hand and offering a slight bow. "It's a pleasure to fi— It's a pleasure to make your acquaintance."

Joe fumbled through the remainder of the introductions, unsure of how to describe either person to the other. After a disjointed explanation of his financial planning practice and how William was a dear client (if omitting the part about being a recent one), the elder gentleman came to the rescue with his usual disarming candor.

"I'd been telling Joe here about never having been to Europe. I really lucked out when he took me on as a client, as not only is he an amazing financial planner, he's also quite the backpacker and thus an excellent *travel* planner—always keeping an eye out for deals. We got talking about a mutual interest in seeing the United Kingdom, and next thing I know, here we are."

Before Claire had a chance to respond, another voice piped up from behind Joe.

"Ahh and what's this—I see everyone's getting a chance to meet the Mad Dasher!" Joe watched Claire's expression sour. He recognized the voice, too.

"I would ask if you two know each other, but I would doubt that, since our Man from Canada has just arrived—and spent half the night in the loo," David said.

"And I would introduce my new friends to you, David, but I know you've already met Joe. Just as I know your bounds of gallantry only extend so far," Claire said, her tone adopting that terseness Joe had only ever heard in interactions with her ex. The *'my new friends'* comment, however, set a butterfly within his stomach in flight.

"Indeed we have. Joe, nice to see you again, looking marginally better than earlier. And aren't you an interesting looking chap! David Bradley," he said, extending a hand to William. "Claire, darling, I wonder if we might have a word."

"Not now, David," Claire said with a thin smile. While the forced civility hadn't dimmed her radiance, Joe thought, the smile was still fraught with the pain of a long history, a denouement of betrayal, and this embarrassing interruption now. The warmth Joe felt from the new friend comment a moment ago—and the tingles from the entire conversation leading up to this—was replaced with a pang. Even from the outside, Joe had become attuned to her pain.

"It's about the children," David attempted.

Sure it is, Joe thought. *It's really about your ex-wife*

having any life beyond you. He kept quiet, however. For now.

"If it truly is, David, then it's certainly important enough to have a proper conversation at the proper time, isn't it? And right now is not that," Claire said. Joe felt the strength he'd come to know as much or more than her pain, and remembered she didn't need him to speak up. She could handle David just fine on her own.

"It will only take a moment."

"Then we will take a moment some other time." She returned her attention, and her smile, back to Joe.

"Claire—"

"David!" A new voice from behind.

"Audrey." David's tone changed from half-charm, half-desperation, to full-dejection. Not to be entirely outdone, he quickly shifted gears to the man-of-the-match routine Joe experienced earlier in the washroom. "Absolutely lovely show. Brilliant work! I am so proud and delighted for you."

"Oh shut it, David, you've never cared a lick for my work or anyone else's, so let's agree not to pretend you do now, shall we?" *There* was the Audrey that Joe had known up to now, stage fright eradicated and candor back in full force. "Claire," a smile bloomed on Audrey's face, "why don't you introduce me to your friends." She extended a hand to Joe.

Claire introduced the Canadians, and the four of them also fell into effortless conversation. Audrey's interference gambit effectively made David the odd man out, both in energy and literal position: she had inserted herself in front of him, walling off the intrusion between Joe and Claire.

Joe watched David from the corner of his eye, seeing the exasperation and calculation on how to handle the affront. Before any spinning wheels locked into place, Audrey shot a glance over her shoulder and said, "Say hi to Miranda for me."

David pretended to recognize someone a few parties over and surrendered in that direction. For the moment, at least.

Joe knew Audrey shared the awareness that her big sister could well defend herself, but he also knew that when it came to love, one showed up to haul the bricks anyway. He'd had an appreciation for Claire's de facto bodyguard and her sardonic demeanor early in the dreams, but his fondness was instantly confirmed in that moment.

In all the occasions Joe later longed for a time machine, of all the scenes he wished to revisit, this was paramount among them. He could never remember exactly what the four of them spoke of, few things beyond the pleasantries of a first conversation, but he remembered the laughter. The ease of discourse. The way Claire's eyes locked on his when either of them were speaking, staring intently as though this was the only conversation in the world. How sometimes, in the space between the words, she'd become just slightly self-conscious of the shared gaze, and for a moment would direct her eyes downward. He remembered how some kind of energetic superhighway had opened in the space between them, and how for a time, the rest of the world ceased to exist.

Far from being third-wheels, Audrey and William

enhanced this exchange, directing them around conversational roadblocks. The younger sister knew Claire would never talk herself up; she was far too self-effacing for that. Audrey assumed that role with her own brand of subtlety—which wasn't much, truth be told.

Joe reflected that on a night where hers was the name on the bill, they spoke about Audrey the least. When conversation sojourned in that direction, Joe elected for honesty (though the committee had a small discussion on the irony of that), and professed less-than-novice experience with the visual arts. Audrey handled this with grace, saying, "The beautiful thing about art is you need not have studied it to know whether you like what you see. You either do or you don't. Even more beautifully, you're fully permitted to feel either way." She also added with a laugh, "But I do hope you like it, at least." Joe said he did, very much, and that was also the truth.

For his part, William assumed the role of countering Joe's sudden modesty and inhibition. The older man was adept at jumping in at just the right moment. He knew when to insert a subtle accolade concerning his newfound friend. He knew how to leave space when the man and woman with colour in their cheeks and intrigue in their eyes needed a mutual breath, or a shared glance all their own. He engaged Audrey in side conversation whenever Joe and Claire disappeared once more along their own path of discourse.

Apart from the moment where William leaned over while the women debated appetizers and whispered *"Unbelievable,"* in Joe's ear, every minute, every word of the conversation was perfect. As was William's descriptor, unsubtle though it was. When the sisters returned their attention upon hearing the false-hushed word, William covered immediately, if dubiously. "Refillable," he said. "I wonder if we'd all like a refill, and ladies, permit me to find whatever it is you'd like for food and drink."

Audrey used the moment to excuse herself, feigning the need to schmooze the other attendees. And, Joe thought, perhaps run further interference on David, who had hovered at times on the periphery. With a smile, Audrey said she hoped enough pens would ink enough cheques that they wouldn't require the lorries to move any pieces back to her studio.

"Joe," Audrey said, extending a hand once more, "it was so very nice to have met you. I do hope we see you again before you return to Canada." As she stepped away, William professed his need to get back to the hotel, as these "late nights in London have kept me up long enough to nearly match my bedtime back home." William bid goodnight to Claire, and before Joe could interject, their tiny universe comprised only two.

Of his return home, Joe fibbed in the heat of the moment. He heard the words spill from his mouth before he could consider them: he claimed he was still in town for another week—many places yet to visit, naturally. He'd thought about possibly heading up to Scotland or over to Ireland. The words poured from a source Joe didn't exactly recognize, driven by a desire to prolong the moment. To see her again, beyond dreams.

You and William have a flight about ten hours from now. An expiring hotel reservation. A budget for an initial two weeks that was blown in about twenty-four hours. Where does this go, Joe? How does this work?

And then:

When are you going to tell her how you really *know her? How are you going to tell her?*

These thoughts—not exactly The Cynic, though Roger was more than happy to yell from his banishment to the back benches—threatened to distract from this perfect moment. The magic of a first conversation. The exchange of the unseen, but undeniably felt. The start, of something.

"...so is your itinerary set? Are you heading north on a specific day, or....?" he heard Claire say, her eyes searching his. He pulled focus from dissenting thoughts and back to her.

"I don't really know, to be honest. Been kind of taking it day by day since I arrived, seeing where the winds take me."

"I know all about that," she said with half an eye roll, looking to some distant point in the land of thought. "Well, Joe, it has been so nice to speak with you. Despite my profession, I'm actually painfully shy when it's not a work environment, and it's rather unlike me to strike up such a detailed conversation with a complete stranger. I ought to take a look around and see some of my sister's art before I leave for the night. I told the sitter I'd be back by ten."

She extended a hand, her mouth and face forming an expression Joe hadn't seen yet: a half, shy smile. Eyes that tried to hold his, but would dart away. Colour that rose in her cheeks. "I am glad you dropped your billfold, however," she added.

He took her hand in his, a fire blazing from their touch up through his arm.

"I am too, Claire." And before he had time to think about what he was saying, "I am so glad you were actually here."

Her expression changed to a lopsided grin and raised eyebrow. "That I'm actually here?"

He looked down and let go an embarrassed laugh. "Sorry. My mouth is working faster than my brain tonight, it seems. I just meant I'm glad of an unexpected encounter, with a certain someone even more beautiful than the art."

The words surprised him as much as Claire. The colour that had risen in her face a moment before went into full bloom.

"Thank you, Joe," she said quietly, glancing down. She looked back to him; they shared a smile and a spark a moment longer. "Well. I should—" she motioned over her shoulder, somewhere in the direction of Audrey.

"Right. Have a good night, Claire."

She turned to step away.

WHAT ARE YOU DOING?? a cacophony of voices bellowed.

"Claire?"

She turned back. "Yes, Joe?"

"I know this is a bit forward, but we're on a limited timeline. Would you like to have dinner with me, sometime before I go?"

The colour that had begun to fade flushed back, and

her smile broke out into a full grin before her gaze momentarily touched the floor again. Every movement, every flush, every half or full smile, endearing her to him even more. She looked up, eyes meeting his, stopping his breath and heart once more.

"I would like that very much, Joe."

CHAPTER 40
PANCAKES SEEMED IN ORDER

He couldn't remember walking back to the hotel. Couldn't really recall anything after Claire had turned and—reluctantly, it looked like; hesitantly, he hoped—walked away from him at the gallery. In whatever had come next, his mind was too occupied with replaying the entire scene over and over. A loop he was—for once, lately—happy to indulge.

She'd given him her number, writing it on the back of the folder from the hotel. That little piece of cardboard, worth more to him now than all his assets combined.

They'd left off with a promise to call the following day to work out details of dinner. In the meantime, he had his own logistics to tend to, not the least of which was rearranging flights again for the eventual return home. All of a sudden, that return—even re-extended by a week—was far too soon.

He'd stopped at William's room and lightly tapped the door. The old man was bright eyed as though it was midday, his cobalt-blue irises dancing with questions before Joe even began speaking.

Joe recounted the rest of his conversation with Claire,

finishing the story by producing the cardboard folder with her name and number written in beautiful cursive. It occurred to him as he showed it to William that he produced it less as proof of the exchange, and more as a reminder of the proof of her existence.

William listened wide-eyed, peppering more *"Unbelievables"* and *"Astoundings"* into the mostly one-sided conversation. At the end he'd said, "I ought to write a book about this someday—with permission from the two of you, of course."

For a moment this recalled the pin that was increasingly needling at Joe's mind: not only the circumstances that brought him to Claire, but how and when he would broach the subject with her. Their conversation tonight had been so effortless, so dissipating of time, that in the throes of her laughter and sparkle from her beautiful eyes he'd nearly forgotten everything of his life leading to that moment.

William supplied the coup de grâce with those thoughts, however, changing subjects to the return flight home. He told Joe he would keep with the itinerary and board the morning flight home, while Joe made arrangements to prolong whatever time the universe afforded this encounter. Before laying down in his own room, Joe phoned Gene and booked transportation to the airport for his unlikely companion.

Exhaustion took him not long after he laid his head on the hotel pillow, yet on this night, for a time he tried fighting sleep. Unless he was going to see her again in dreams, which hadn't occurred since setting foot on London soil, he wanted to keep view of her in his thoughts before sleep grabbed hold.

When his breathing and pulse finally slowed in the darkness, he took another moment to wonder at the improbability of it all. Far from questioning his sanity, he now marveled at whatever it had been that brought him here. Brought her to him in the first place in those sleeping hours, and then him to this place. And finally, her—with that tap on his shoulder—to him. This was no longer a dream. No more a question of whether she was a conjuring of his subconscious, a composite of people he knew.

She was as real as the beating of his heart in this moment. A pulse that felt new, as though his heart had only just formed in his chest and began coursing for the first time. He'd looked in her eyes. Touched her hand in a moment he'd been certain would overwhelm the circuits in the gallery and burst out the lights. Just as he hadn't wanted to let go of her hand, he didn't want to let go of this moment.

In the morning a call from the front desk greeted him at seven. He vaguely recalled stopping at the hotel lobby after floating back from the gallery, some prudent part of his brain requesting the wake-up call at the same time he'd extended his stay another week. The hotel was once again happy to oblige on all fronts, particularly the part where they swiped his charge card once more.

The wake-up request was to ensure he made his own outbound call to the airline, and hopefully, avoid another exorbitant fee to change a flight he ought to have been boarding about then. Despite the cost, even the internal subcommittee on budgeting and finance remained largely without protest. The best it mustered was, *Well, perhaps this is part of what all these years of savings have been for. Maybe this qualifies, now.*

He felt too excited to eat, but after a shower resumed his post in the hotel restaurant for the customary high-protein breakfast. This morning, however, pancakes seemed in order. Whipped cream. Highly irresponsible quantities of syrup. Never, in the entirety of his life, had Joe been an "eat for feeling, eat for fun" type, but on this morning—when even the sun cut through the London fog—he wanted every sensation, every taste, every touch, to somehow mirror what he felt inside. Hard-boiled eggs and overcooked bacon simply wouldn't be up to standard.

Above every other thought was the anticipation of when he could call her. He wasn't sure what the "rules" were—what his bachelor friends would say was the accepted norm—but he knew he didn't care. This situation was unlike any other. (Which, for a moment caused him to wonder if anyone else in the history of the world had met under these circumstances.) Whatever "normal" standards were typically in effect, they wouldn't apply here.

He would call her this afternoon. Leave the morning with her children uninterrupted. Then, sometime around when lunch was being cleaned up, he'd dial the numbers on the card. Wait for the ringtone he knew would upend his nervous system. The hours between this breakfast and that phone call felt like a lifetime away.

He passed the rest of the morning walking along the

Thames. The sun painted the streets with a vibrant yellow uncommon this time of year, carrying some warmth when the breezes subsided. Even the wind wasn't cutting, and it seemed to Joe like everything about this Sunday morning was designed to reflect the moment.

It felt like the universe had coloured this day, these last twelve hours, especially for him. He knew he might have the look of a madman, swaying along cobbled walkways with half a grin and a starry look in his eyes. At best, perhaps the look of a man who celebrated the night through to the dawn. That wasn't altogether far from the truth.

He saw more sights, wandered into more attractions and museums. As before, he retained little of what his eyes and ears took in. Earlier in the week his vision and accompanying senses were clouded by remonstrances of his purpose here. Now his senses were seized once more, but not with questions of why, or where, or how. They were held ransom by the memory of the sight of her. Her face, captured in that half smile. Those beautiful, emerald eyes that would hold his for a moment, look away, and hold them again.

She went with him everywhere that morning, as she had these so many weeks. Except now, he knew where she was beyond the will of dreams and angels.

She was at the end of that phone number, handwritten under her name on the billfold he kept pulling from his pocket. He must have looked at it a hundred times.

CHAPTER 41
WORKING WITHOUT A PLAN

Somehow, the self-appointed hour of one o'clock arrived. *Why is time so relative?* Joe thought. *Why did it take a generation for this morning to pass, and only a blink when I was with her last night?* Big Ben, in view of his hotel window, felt no relativity at all; merely droned on from one minute to the next with unrelenting rhythm.

For human beings, and the human heart, Joe mused, it was an entirely different experience. With shaking hands and a pounding heart, Joe dialed the numbers on the folder.

The phone rang with that *dool-dool* ringtone of European phone lines, and in this tiny space, another era passed. Decades, it occurred to Joe—it must have been decades since he'd felt this way, been this nervous.

"Hello?" a woman's voice greeted him. In the background he heard the din of clattering dishes, a babel of voices. Though one word had been spoken, he knew this wasn't Claire. For a moment his heart palpitated with fear he'd dialed a wrong digit, or worse yet, she'd written it down incorrectly, or worst of all, perhaps she'd conned him, written down the wrong number altogether.

Maybe the energy he'd felt, the ease and flow of their conversation... had it been one-way? Had she just been overly polite, seeing this disheveled traveler lose his dinner, and taken pity on him? That wasn't possible, was it? She had agreed to go out, hadn't she?

The voice on the phone repeated. "Hello? Is someone there?"

He cleared his throat. "Yes, pardon me. I'm looking for Claire—Claire Langdon?"

"Joe!" The voice immediately perked up. His senses recalibrated with the realization it was likely Claire's sister who had answered.

"Audrey?"

"Yes! How lovely you've called. Thank you again for coming last night. I hope you enjoyed yourself."

"And I hope it was a smashing success," Joe said. He'd only been here a week, but it seemed the parlance was beginning to rub off.

"It was; I'm overwhelmed, really. Only two of the pieces didn't go, but there are interested parties I'm just waiting to hear back from." Audrey cleared her throat. "But you didn't call round to talk about my art, I'm sure, gentleman though you are. I'll fetch Claire for you."

His heart faltered a beat yet once more. "Thank you, Audrey. A pleasure to speak with you again."

The handset was placed down and clanked off a surface, followed by more background noise. Joe heard Audrey's muffled tones say something unintelligible, followed by a pause, then a different voice (presumably

Claire's) answer. He heard steps grow louder as someone approached the phone.

There was time enough for another wave of thoughts to crash through: *What if it's Audrey coming back to the phone? What if Claire said "Not now," or "I only agreed to dinner on the spur of the moment," or a thousand different variations?* The phone rattled from displacement of whatever surface it laid upon and being maneuvered in a human hand.

"Joe?" He wasn't sure whose voice it was.

"Yes?"

"Hi." The voice was warm. Smiling. And now, though only two words had been spoken, he knew it as well as he knew his own. A smile came over his own face.

"Hello, Claire."

"Did you enjoy the rest of your evening? I presume you made it back to your hotel all right?"

If she was nervous, it wasn't coming through in her tone. He hoped he might manage the same.

"I did. Just went back and slept, got up and did some more sightseeing this morning." If there was a certain way to sound cool, nonchalant, Joe wasn't sure if he was even in the vicinity of it. Some voice from the past cropped up in his mind and said, 'When in doubt, just ask questions.'

"How about you? Everything okay with your children and the babysitter?"

She laughed and went on to describe a situation involving an attempted whipped cream and pudding creation by the sitter and Ainsley, who had gone a little overboard with the cream and mixer. They'd succeeded only in creating a spackled kitchen outside the mixing bowl, and butter within it. "There was a good hour of cleanup where the sitter made a valiant effort, but at one a.m. Audrey and I were still finding globs on light fixtures and underneath cupboards. Life of a parent, I suppose."

Joe winced at this, for reasons he wasn't certain. He'd never consciously regretted his choice when it came to parenthood, yet her comment struck a pang. Unable to see his expression, Claire carried on as though their conversation the night before hadn't ended.

He listened to her speak as all-too-familiar internal dialogues ran along. How was he going to ask her? Where was he going to take her? When would they go, if her answer was still yes? Once more he cursed himself for a lack of planning; in all the minutes between last night's hour and this one, he hadn't worked out his approach. In all the years of nursing heartbreak and dating more for companionship than connection, he'd never needed to think any of this through. There had been endless setups by friends and family; excruciating double-dates where the arrangements were handled by someone else.

Joe had shown up to these matchmaking attempts all but entirely disengaged. They were merely to buy a bit of space between the "When are you going to settle down" talks, and temporarily alleviate fears he would become some tinfoil-hat wearing miser, alone in old age. He'd never needed to consider what to say to his "dates," as he'd never placed an ounce of investment in these setups. Suddenly, the pressure of that—the distant stranger that was vulnerability—threatened to overwhelm.

"Joe? Are you still there?" Claire's voice wavered.

"Yes, of course." He realized he hadn't registered the

last of what she'd said. Something about the whipped cream shenanigans continuing this morning when Ainsley flopped into Claire's bed, hair reeking of soured cream.

"I'm sorry," Claire said. "When I get nervous—which isn't often, but I'm not immune—I start prattling on."

"Not at all," he replied. "But apparently when I get nervous, my thoughts spin into overdrive. So I'll beg your pardon if it seemed like I wasn't hearing you. I loved the sound of every word." He said this last part quietly, and that much had been the truth.

"Nervous about what?" she said.

"Claire, how do you feel about throwing caution to the wind, and instead of trying to think of the right things to say or the right way to say them, we just say them?" He didn't know where these particular words came from, but was glad that at least someone inside was speaking up on his behalf.

There was a pause, and then, "I feel good about it." He could hear the smile formed by her lips.

"I don't know how any of this is supposed to work," Joe said. *That's the understatement of the year,* a committee member snuck in. "And I'm going to use a word fear tells me I ought not. I haven't asked anyone out on a 'date' in a really long time." Fear managed to creep in, and pride forced him to qualify this. "I mean, there have been dates, but they've been set up—"

Before he could exacerbate an impending train wreck, Claire spoke up: "Neither have I."

He laughed. "Okay. Good. I mean— well, I *don't* mean that it's good that you haven't... it's hard to believe a woman as attractive as you hasn't... Oh good god, I'm making a mess of this, aren't I?"

It was her turn to laugh. "Not at all, Joe. We can be awkward together, if that helps. I know I certainly will be. And if it also helps, I already said yes to dinner, last night, when you asked."

The smile that spread on his face threatened to split it in two. "Right. You did. So, I don't know exactly what your schedule is like," (this was at least partially true), "or if you'll need to arrange for a sitter again, and—this being another attempt to speak the things I want to say, rather than thinking of how to say them—I don't know if tonight is too soon, but—"

"It's not. Audrey already said she'd watch the children if you asked."

"Thank heavens for Audrey," Joe said without thinking.

Claire laughed again. "Yes, in many more ways than one." She paused. "Hang on, Joe, wait." Though her tone had become serious, he loved the way his name sounded from her voice.

"Yes?"

"The reporter in me feels I must do my due diligence in asking. You're not a psychopath, or a stalker, or a generalized creep, are you?" Her voice regained a trace of humour in it.

He laughed, albeit nervously. "No. Certainly not intentionally. Not to my knowledge. Never had any complaints." It was the best answer he could come up with. Best to change the subject quickly. "How does six o'clock work?"

"Ooohh, that's pushing another late night in the life of a single mum. But I suppose I can live on the edge, since you're only in town another week." She paused. "I'm kidding, Joe. That works wonderfully."

"Perfect." He felt pent-up air release from his lungs. "I'll pick you up, and in between I promise to make a better plan for dinner than I did for this conversation."

"Sometimes, working without a plan is what works the best," she said.

"Yes…" Joe paused for a moment. "It's certainly working out well lately."

CHAPTER 42
FOLLOWING THE HEART TO THE DOORSTEP

FIVE HOURS. THAT was all Joe had to arrange what felt like the most important first date of his life, in a city where he was a stranger, with a woman he'd known far longer than she'd known him. She had been kidding when she'd said it, but Joe had paused after their call to think, *Am I a stalker? Am I some crazed lunatic or 'generalized creep,' as she put it, for following through with this?*

No. He hadn't asked for any of it. He couldn't even begin to explain how it had all happened, how she'd come to his dreams, how he'd seen through her eyes. When he'd changed his flight destined for San Diego—well, yes, that had been impulsive and reckless. Yet based on finding her, hadn't it been the right decision after all? Hadn't he been meant to find her?

Good lord, I'm sure stalkers say the exact same thing.

No! This was not that. Yes, he was attracted. Yes, he felt a connection. But he had engineered almost none of it. That was evident by the innumerable hours and endless days spent on search and thought that yielded nothing. It was by pure chance he'd seen the bill for Audrey's exhibit while at the theatre—only attending the latter after near coercion by William.

If he was a stalker, he'd certainly done a poor job of it. He hadn't even spotted her in the crowd at the gallery, when she'd apparently been a few feet away. It had taken a turn of his stomach, a mis-stowed billfold, and a literal tap on his shoulder for him to finally find her.

Everything that led him to her had been nudges from somewhere, something, or someone else.

Stop overthinking this, or you're going to think yourself right out of it. You'll be boarding a plane at six p.m. instead of standing at the threshold, saying hello to the most beautiful woman you've ever encountered, who is waiting to spend her evening with you.

Despite the knot in his stomach and the doubts in his head, he followed his heart to her doorstep, and rang the bell promptly at six.

CHAPTER 43
YOU LOOK PERFECT, CLAIRE

Audrey answered the door, flanked by Holly and Ainsley. He recognized them as clear as he would have known one of his nieces or nephews.

In the deep end, we continue to swim, came a comment from within. Probably The Cynic, though Joe had an idea the other members had finally bound his hands and covered his mouth with tape after the night before.

"Joe! How lovely to see you. Right on time, too! How refreshing," Audrey said, reaching for the flowers in his hand. "Ranunculus! How did you know?"

In this particular circumstance, I actually didn't, he thought. He hadn't even known the name. At the florist's he was going to go with can't-miss roses, but when he'd spotted these, something had told him they were the better choice. At no point in any of the dreams had the subject of flowers come up, nor had Claire ever said anything. It just felt right. Before any voice of overthought could wave a flag, he elected to go with the intuition. "I didn't know, they just sort of called to me in the shop."

"Good for you, Joe," Audrey said, sincerity in her voice. "She's going to love them."

"Yes!" Ainsley spoke up with that tiny voice Joe had heard before. "Mummy *loves* ranunculus. Can I take them, Auntie?" She reached little hands skywards toward Audrey, flexing her fingers in a grabbing motion. Holly continued to silently survey Joe.

"Actually," Audrey interjected, "maybe I ought not have been so forward in taking them off your hands, Joe. I should have asked, did you want to give these to her yourself?"

"You must be Ainsley," Joe said, crouching down to greet her. She returned this with a smile. "Your mom told me all about you last night at your auntie's show. Would you *really* like to give them to her?"

"I would *love* to!" Ainsley gushed.

"Then by all means, please do."

Ainsley took the bouquet and ran toward the stairs, the thump of her feet on each step sounding like a tiny jackhammer.

Audrey smiled. "Holly, this is Joe. Joe, this is Holly, Claire's other daughter."

He extended a hand that Claire's middle child accepted in a tentative movement to match the expression on her face. "It's a pleasure to meet you, Holly. Your mother spoke glowingly about you as well."

"Nice to meet you," Holly said, looking away.

"Why don't you come in," Audrey said. "Claire will be just a few minutes. May I offer you some tea, or water, or... what do Canadians like to drink? Please, have a seat," she gestured to the sitting room furniture as she walked toward the adjacent kitchen.

On this front, at least, Joe was relieved. Audrey's

demeanor was not at all what he'd witnessed in dreams; the only flash occurred when David loitered about the night before. What she might have said behind closed doors of Joe and Claire's encounter, he had no idea, but it appeared she'd placed her stamp of approval on this evening's outing. The demeanor was different, but the appearance had been restored to that of his midnight hours: jeans, T-shirt, and a top-knot. And if he wasn't mistaken, some errant plaster. She'd been back to work already. A line about art never being finished popped into his head.

"I'm actually great, Audrey, thank you for offering," Joe said, taking a seat on the sofa. Though his physiology wasn't betraying him on this night with trembling hands or heat along his forehead, he didn't want to risk the nerves he felt making themselves apparent by attempting to hold a glass. He was thirsty, but his mouth felt too cottony to manage a drink at the moment.

"Mummy *loved* them!" a little voice hollered, the stairwell once again punctuated by rapid beats as Ainsley flew down and into the room. She folded her hands behind her back and rocked on her heels. "She told me to tell you she'd be with you *presently*, Mr. Joe," she added with a huge grin, enunciating every syllable in 'presently.'

"Thank you, Ainsley. Your mom tells me you're in Year Two, and that you really like school?"

"I *love* it!" she chimed, performing an impromptu pirouette before dashing from the stairwell to a chair adjacent Joe. *She sure* loves *the word* love, he thought. Ainsley launched into a story about her teacher and classroom, and about the learning stations and building stations and play stations and story stations. Her words coming fast, but clearly not fast enough to satisfy the speed with which she wanted to say them.

Audrey was leaned against the kitchen island, arms folded across her chest, an amused expression on her face. Holly had retreated to the dining table beyond the island and appliances, appearing to be lost in a textbook but having one eye on the page and one on the scene. Jackson was nowhere in view, but that wasn't inconsistent with his presence in the dreams, where he only ever seemed to meander in when his teenaged stomach forced him from his bedroom.

Ainsley continued to recount her school life with equal parts elation and intrigue; she might as well have been describing a primary school day as the pinnacle of drama and suspense. As she spoke, he had a moment to marvel at the intrigue of his own life, and of this very situation. He'd been in this kitchen dozens of times, even sat on this sofa, but via Claire's body. He knew there was a water closet off to the side, parallel to the island Audrey leaned upon. Beyond that were stairs to the basement. He might even be able to name some of the staples found in the refrigerator; on which shelf the milk was placed. It was as though he had stepped onto the set of a favourite television show. The experience was familiar and surreal all the same.

"—but then Mrs. Taylor said that if Jacob wasn't going to share the science kit with me and Sarah that he was going to have to take a break from it on Wednesday, *or maybe even the rest of the week*," Ainsley was saying.

As the youngster built further suspense that never

quite peaked, only increased, they heard steps—slower and quieter than those of earlier—begin to descend the stairs.

Claire had been dressed to the nines when Joe had seen her at the gallery. The sight had knocked him back, after most dream glimpses had her in business apparel or attired as Audrey was now. As she moved along each step and came into view, he saw she was adorned somewhere in-between, a blend of casual and formal. The signature he'd come to learn: quiet and easy elegance.

She paused for a moment halfway down the stairs, in full view now. She looked at Joe and a half-smile quickly formed before darting a glance at Holly, Audrey, and Ainsley—the latter two looking on with something like tempered glee.

"I wasn't sure what to wear," Claire said quietly, looking down and smoothing out her top. "You didn't mention where we were going or what we were doing."

It wouldn't have mattered what she was wearing. She'd stolen his breath and heart once more, and he had the feeling this time she'd taken them for good.

"You look..." he paused, his mind searching for the right, appropriate word to use in the presence of her sister and daughters.

A voice reminded him to put aside thoughts of right or ought or should, and instead let his heart lead the way.

"You look perfect, Claire."

CHAPTER 44
NUTELLA WITH A SPOON

IN WHAT HE was certain elicited a last gasp from prudence, Joe elected to hire Gene again for the evening. The Parliament members that might have had a problem with this were either exhausted from protest, or had gone on strike, exiting the scene altogether. His heart was in charge now, and for once, Joe intended to listen.

Having a driver was a practical decision as well as (he hoped) a romantic one. Of the former, he wasn't about to attempt navigation of the London streets. Of the latter—though he had a moment to fear it could go either way—he thought it might be a pleasant change of custom. Not being interrupted by a waiter during an obvious first date. Fumbling with menus and making decisions on what to eat. Awkward small talk with acquaintances of Claire's they could run into. Joe hoped the presence of the chauffeur—with privacy from the partition they could raise or lower from the back—would help Claire feel comfortable; that this wasn't just a ruse for less than honourable purposes.

Though most sights were closed, Gene would park as close as possible to whatever iconic structure stood

OF DREAMS AND ANGELS

before them. Joe began presenting "An Alternative History of Her Majesty's Royal Kingdom" to Claire, inventing or embellishing facts about this royal residence or that emblematic cathedral. He'd started their journey by saying, "I don't yet know what you like to do for fun, nor how much of the city you're already familiar with," (this much again was true), "and I had no clue how I could compete with the established history of such a place. So I figured I wouldn't even bother, and instead present you with an entirely unfamiliar version. Entirely factual, of course."

Of the Millennium Wheel, newly under construction and beginning to loom large over the Thames, he explained that "Contrary to common belief, this has been the hallowed ground of elaborate amusement park rides for centuries. 'Tis where Sir Joseph and Lady Clairesephine—they of the House of Superfluousness and Royal Lineage of Loquaciousness—had their first courtship, way back in 1498. Back then, the under-construction Half-Millennium Wheel was fabricated entirely of timber and gold. Sir Joseph jimmied their way into the closed-off wheel, where he and Lady Clairesephine snuck into one of the wood capsules—these fashioned from retired stagecoaches of the monarchy. The palace guard pushed the back of each coach to get the wheel in motion. The Ferris wheel industry was in its infancy, after all."

Of Westminster Bridge he purported its actual age predated modern claims by a couple hundred years, fashioned when Sir Joseph—having yet to achieve proficiency beyond canine aquatics—needed a way to cross the

Thames to meet Lady Clairesephine. Big Ben, Joe professed, was constructed merely because Sir Joseph's father, Lord Benjamin—a noted fifteenth century astronomer—spent countless hours and innumerable missed dinners staring at the stars. Lord Ben's wife commissioned the clock's construction along the river where her husband contemplated the cosmos, thus he be never late for family time again.

Joe had procured postcards of the landmarks earlier that afternoon and written the Alternative Histories on the backs. With each stop he'd deliver a mock tour guide address, at times outside the car if parking permitted and the wind subsided. Claire would listen with a grin while she blew on her mittened hands, occasionally asking Joe to elaborate on some particularly fatuous piece of history. At other locales they remained in the vehicle with the partitioned window up; after each "fact" Joe would hand her the card along with another flower from a second bouquet he'd kept in the car. He'd knock on the partition and Gene would roll it down, handing back another "course" of dinner—a collection of some foods Joe knew she liked, and some with which he'd ventured wild guesses.

He knew she was a fiend for tapas or finger foods; he'd observed in dreams that she preferred to nibble throughout the day rather than sit down to full meals. In addition to meats and cheeses and a carefully packaged shrimp cocktail, Joe had asked the hotel kitchen—while promising a generous tip—to pepper the courses with generous amounts of Nutella, delivered in various forms. Nutella on pastry. Nutella on fruit. Nutella straight from the jar with a spoon—which in the end, based on her laughter and delight when he'd handed it to her, seemed to be Claire's favourite mode.

At one point, when Gene passed back diced pineapple with—but of course—more Nutella, she asked Joe how he'd been so spot on with the food selection. He'd shrugged and deflected (hoping colour wouldn't rise in his face), saying something to the tune of "Who doesn't like pineapple or chocolate?"

Thanks to the tight schedule in the afternoon, there had been little opportunity for Joe to agonize over whether she'd enjoy herself or not, whether it would hit the right notes or not. He hadn't felt this kind of anxiousness in longer than he could recall—not a pressure to be perfect, exactly, but a longing for the time spent to be perfect for her. He knew she rarely went out for anything that didn't involve the children or work, rarely treated herself or was treated to. With more time he would have arranged the finest, if he could have. Whatever it took to convey how fortunate he felt to be in this place, in this time, with her.

If her reaction was any indication, Joe was confident he hadn't completely missed the mark, as her laughter—and that smile that could send an endless number of butterflies within him in flight—were far from rare. Unless it was his imagination, after every stop, every ridiculous fact, every tiny tray of food and every flower, she moved ever closer to him, turning into him, open and released. Though he couldn't tell for certain between the twilight sky and muted lamplight through shaded car windows, on a few occasions he thought he saw those eyes he adored misting up along the edges, between the laughs and bites of food and sharing stories of her children or his career or mutual hopes and fears and dreams. He didn't know why, and for the only time since he'd first seen her the night before, he wished he was looking from behind her eyes rather than into them, so he might sense what she was feeling. But it wasn't a sadness he saw, wasn't fear, wasn't pain. Though he didn't have the language for it yet, as his eyes searched hers he could feel an unspoken shorthand forming between them. He knew in this moment it was as though all the cosmos had conspired to contract and fit within the small space they shared, a world made only for two, and for a moment, that tiny universe was perfect.

As she drew closer to him it was almost strange, feeling the energy of connection pass between them externally, after all this time of experiencing life through her eyes. Rather than being a passenger within her sight, within her aura, it was as though their energies were colliding; long dormant and nearly extinguished embers given oxygen to ignite the space between them. He fought every impulse to reach over and take her into his arms, trying to remember that for her, he was still a veritable stranger, someone she'd first glimpsed only twenty-four hours before. No matter the obvious and immediate chemistry—and setting aside his unintentional subterfuge and foreknowledge—he knew that sitting before him was a beautifully strong and brilliant woman, but one who carried a heart heavily bruised and carelessly discarded. Above all things, Joe wanted that heart to feel entirely safe before he proposed to take it in his hands. He only wished he could carry it for her now, as she already carried his.

The only time they physically connected was after a stop at Hamleys on Regent Street. In front of the ornate Christmas display Joe had delivered a soliloquy on the dubious history of the FreeElvesSons, a secret society of defectors from Santa's workshop. These elite toymakers now controlled world governments and markets, all in their ability to mesmerize children and adults alike with displays like the one before them. They'd returned to the car, Claire's cheeks flushed and eyes watering from the cold. She removed her mittens and cupped her hands to her mouth, trying to warm them with breath. Joe reached over and took her hands in his, eliciting sparks he was certain would set the car ablaze, and warmed them with his own breath and touch. It was another moment of unspoken dialogue between their eyes and through their fingers, until—as people in the throes of new connection will do—they'd released and acted as though nothing happened.

Time behaved as time will, whimsical and relative. In contrast to the endless hours Joe trudged these last weeks, their hours together evaporated in mere moments. By ten o'clock, feeling a sense of responsibility to Claire's time (as even with Audrey's help, she still had all the obligations of a regular Monday morning ahead), he'd reluctantly requested that Gene return them to her home.

After Joe opened her car door they made the slow, tentative walk to her front porch, as though the hesitation in their step would slow the passage of time. Claire ascended the stairs leading to her door. Joe followed, remaining on a step below the landing.

"Joe, that was..." Her smile fought to extend to its edges, but a heart taught to distrust kept it at bay. She looked down and held the words. "Thank you for a wonderful evening." As she looked back up, the smile won the struggle between mind and heart.

"It was truly my pleasure, Claire." His smile made no effort to hide. Another moment of silent script passed between them.

Joe looked to the bay window flanking the door, then back to Claire. "I wonder if you might do me the privilege, Claire Langdon, of another evening of your time while I'm here. And, if you like, more dubious facts about the land you call home."

She laughed, snow beginning to blanket her hair. "I would love that, Joe." She looked at her feet again, and for a moment Joe felt as though he was observing the two of them from some place above. In a glimpse as ephemeral as the snow that fell around them, he thought he could see who both of them had been before the world and its heartbreaks armoured their hearts.

"Okay. I'll call you tomorrow. In the meantime, I would offer you a hug goodbye, but I see we've attracted an audience," he said, motioning with his head toward the window. A curtain fluttered and two little eyes disappeared, followed by the sound of muffled giggles from Ainsley and Audrey. Joe and Claire joined the laughter with their own.

"Goodnight, Joe."
"Goodnight, Claire."

CHAPTER 45
LAST FIRST KISS

THE WEEK EVAPORATED, though Joe and Claire tried to hold onto the time like a balloon falling away to the wind. As with their early dialogues, they fell into an easy rhythm through time and space, seeing one another each day while Joe remained in England.

Some of the nights were structured and planned; Joe making reservations for dinner with a museum or movie to follow. On other afternoons (where Claire availed unused holiday time, with Audrey apparently more than happy to assist with the children), their time was spent in coffee shops and bookstores. They passed the hours with endless talk on everything and nothing. It was as though she cast a spell over him; Joe relinquishing reticence when it came to details about his life. Aspirations. Disappointments. Fears. Dreams.

Save for one.

For her part, Claire seemed imbued with the same magic, opening further from that first night in the car. Joe sensed little hesitation, and his ambivalence toward his inside information aside, he knew he'd have a better idea than most if she was holding back—even if that direct connection had been lost since his arrival.

When he'd had a moment to ponder the displaced dreams, it seemed a blessing on several fronts. He didn't know how he would have handled it if she still came to him during this time together, nor would he have been at ease. Not that he'd ever been remotely comfortable, even before confirmation that she was a living, breathing human being. To see through her eyes now would have been too much to process, too much to reconcile. Nevertheless, even with the cosmic connection broken, he was certain he would sense if she wasn't feeling relaxed or safe. He wouldn't have asked to continue seeing her if he had.

As the week progressed they covered a lifetime of subjects both light and meaningful, yet there remained a select few neither spoke of, lest these become real and risk breaking the strands beginning to interweave between them. What would happen Saturday morning, when Joe was scheduled to board his flight home? What came next?

And what was *this*, exactly? Was it merely a week for the ages, a romantic tryst? Bittersweet days removed from time and practicality that both would call from memory in moments of solitude years later? Where the word London would become synonymous with an oasis in which feeling and heart prevailed, but never a place to be revisited, never a time to be recaptured?

Was this just one of those frozen moments in time, where circumstance created the ions between them as much as any actual chemistry or compatibility? Had the finite nature of their encounter thus been responsible for it? Though the evenings were late and the mornings early, propelled by an unwillingness to forfeit more minutes apart, the hours when Joe did sleep were better and deeper than in longer than he could recall. Yet these were the questions, in the liminal state between awareness and sleep, that plied at him.

He knew his answers. He could only hope she might feel the same. He also knew he ought to remain open to the idea she didn't; he wouldn't be the first man in history to mistake friendship, company, and the reluctance to needlessly harm a heart as signs of mutual affection.

As the end of the week drew near, those thoughts encroached the space they shared, dancing around like pockets of carbon monoxide that threatened to choke the air between them. The larger they loomed, the smaller their conversation became, each veering more frequently to the trivial or external. Careers and extended family and long lost history became smoke screens, as though to venture more substantive discourse was to risk confronting the reality of unasked questions, and of the time that had burned down to little more than embers.

For every sentence spoken aloud, dozens more passed wordlessly between their eyes, suggesting Claire shared these thoughts too. Joe could sense the difference between a soft gaze that simply soaked in the moment, and one that questioned, as though by dancing between the irises and peering keenly enough, the thoughts of the other might be revealed. In the earlier part of the week, the way she looked at him had consistently been the first. As the revolutions on the clock became numbered, he'd watched it become more often the last.

Doubt began whispering to him, replacing the hope she shared his desires with a dismay that she might have lost interest, or was too overwhelmed, or had simply not felt the same from the start. By Thursday evening Joe could feel the gates of vulnerability closing, pushed shut by sentinels of fear, and he knew he had to address it all before they clanged shut entirely.

They stood at the entrance to his hotel. They'd come from dinner in Soho with storybook-perfect food and ambiance, but where the air surrounding them became weighted with every passing minute. They'd held hands around the candlelight, yet both found it difficult to hold eye contact—gazes darting to the side, to this painting or that couple, talk drifting from one banality to another.

Outside the hotel doors he interlaced her small fingers with his once more. It was snowing again, the flakes adorning her hair like confetti and softly soaking it through, undoing the styling work from earlier in the day. He noticed as it became damp that her hair began to curl, looking as it had the very first time he'd seen her in the mirror.

Though she brushed at it self-consciously, he pulled her hand back into his. Despite the snow the air was mild, yet he still cupped her hands to his mouth, warming them again with breath. He longed to stand there forever—air being used as an excuse to hold onto her a moment more—rather than give voice to anything that might threaten the end of whatever this was.

"Claire—" he finally managed.

"—Why haven't you kissed me?" she interrupted, pulling her hands away. "Do you not like me, Joe? Have I misunderstood what's been happening this entire week?

Did you hear something or see something you didn't like?"

"Oh, Claire, no... No, that's not it at—"

"—Because I've tried not to get my hopes up too much, I've tried not to read into things too much," she said with increasing cadence, "but am I wrong that there's something going on here, Joe? That there was the beginning of something at the gallery the other night, something that's grown ever since?"

"Claire, no, no, you're not—"

"This wasn't easy for me, Joe. After David left, I looked at those babies and thought 'there's a betrayal here that extends beyond me,' and I just sort of accepted that that would be life now—that *they* would be life now—and I put any notions of romance or heart away. Locked it away, Joe, and fell just short of throwing away the key." Her words were coming in a torrent, nearly colliding with one another.

"Claire—" he reached for her again but she twisted her shoulders away, bundling her hands to her chest. Her hair was soaked now. His stomach was pulled as tight as it had ever been.

"And then you show up and you drop your billfold and I tap your shoulder and you turn and even though you had just vomited you smile like I was the most incredible sight you'd ever seen and something inside of me just sort of... let go, Joe, something just melted... and you give me this beautiful week of presence and kindness and surprises and—it's just been easy, Joe, it's been light, after years of heaviness and hurt..." She paused, as though giving the words a chance to absorb. "And it's all been beautiful, it's all been wonderful, and I wonder where you came from and why I get to be a part of your world for a week. But then the end of every night comes and my stomach goes in knots and my heart flies into my throat, and you just say 'Goodnight, Claire.' And I don't know what that means, and I don't know what to do."

He reached forward, gently placing his hands on her shoulders. This time she didn't turn away, nor did he speak just yet, sensing she needed a moment more.

"Do you not like me, Joe?" Tears ringed the edges of her eyes. "Did you sweep me off my feet just to watch me fall? Because I can't fall again, Joe. Not like that."

He moved his hands to the sides of her face, her hair weaving through his fingers. "That's not it at all, Claire."

"Then *what is it*?" she burst, eyes darting back and forth between his.

"It's that I'm hopeless, Claire. I don't know exactly what any of this is, and I don't know what magic it was that brought me here to you and gave us this beautiful week. I *do* know that it's only been a week, but I also know how I feel. And I know I've been careless with other hearts in the past—enough to know what that means, and what that looks like. Enough to know I dare not be careless with yours." He paused, eyes searching hers, seeing that she expected him to drop the heart she had just begun allowing him to hold.

"I'm hopeless, Claire, and I know now that I'm done. I know that I've fallen for you, but I hadn't known for certain if you felt the same. And I had just been hoping that if I kissed you, it would be the last first kiss of my life."

The tears that held the edges of her eyes let go. He

moved her face to his, and as the December snow fell around them, they fell into each other.

CHAPTER 46
I WANT THE MESS

THEY MADE LOVE throughout the night, bodies weaving into one another as easily as their exchange of words and emotions. When they weren't tangled up in physical expression they remained wrapped around each other, talking the midnight hours away, drifting in and out of sleep, talking some more, connecting evermore.

Daylight eventually found them, as they lay among disheveled sheets in blissful exhaustion. They'd been unable to pull away from one another as they navigated hallways and elevators and doors and furniture on their way to where a week—if not a lifetime—of restrained passion was finally explored, finally released. With the arrival of the morning hour Joe realized Claire hadn't made any calls since they'd crashed into the room so many hours earlier and he panicked, asking if the kids and work were taken care of.

She'd laughed, her body wrapped in a sheet as she lay on her side, propped on an elbow with her head resting on her hand. Hair cascaded down her shoulder, and as Joe looked at her she seemed to shine with a light brighter than the sun fighting through the drapes. Joe couldn't recall ever seeing anyone more beautiful. She assured him Audrey expected this at some point, having nudged Claire that if it felt right not to come home one evening, the obligations of the day would be handled.

They ordered room service for breakfast. A makeshift picnic between them as they sat on the bed in robes, disbelieving the world outside. Their conversation was lighter than the night before; while there wasn't yet clarity on where they were going (apart from Joe's literal trip to the airport in less than twenty-four hours), there was an unspoken understanding of where they found themselves now. For the moment, that was enough.

They passed the daylight as they had the midnight hours, discovering new layers of one another in body and spirit. Claire opened further about her heartbreak at the hands of David. Joe spoke of the scarring from his young love with Rachel and how it had tainted every relationship since. She described her uncertainty about whether the news business was for her anymore, how it hadn't lived up to the ideals of her youth. She thought she might like to write a novel. Move to the country, raise the kids away from the closing walls of an urban and technological world. Joe told her he'd always wanted to spend a year or longer travelling abroad. Learn how to sail. Be a resident of nowhere. She confessed she'd been terrified that even if love found her, she wouldn't know how to love in return. Without caution, without suspicion. He admitted his cynical practice of turning relationships into an island. Somewhere to visit from time to time, but nothing that encroached on the rest of his life.

The earth spun on its axis around them, but as with the rest of the week they felt sheltered in the space of one another. Room service eventually became lunch and lunch became dinner. Daylight faded from the windows as sly as it arrived those many hours before—another reminder that even if this world existed apart from the one outside, it still obeyed the same laws of time, with its unwelcome endings.

She lay with her head on his chest, her fingers running along the lines of his body while the minutes on the clock ran toward a new day—one they had tried to quietly will out of existence. Claire finally broke the silence, giving voice to the unspoken.

"Joe? What happens tomorrow?"

His hands weaved their way through her hair and down along the curve of her back. "Well, I'm going to get on a plane, for now." He shifted so he could see her face. "And then I will find my way back to you, just as I did before."

"Are we being realistic, though?" She moved to create space between them. "No matter what the throes of early romantic notions tell us, are we just being foolish?"

"What do you mean?"

"Well, you're going to go back to your real life, and I'll go back to mine. We'll think about each other probably round-the-clock for the first few days, reliving these hours in our minds, but then life will do what it does best, and get in the way. Absence will make the heart grow yonder, as it were. You'll tell me as you're leaving that you're going to call, you're going to write. And at first you will; I know you will." She sat up now, attempted a smile, reached with a force of will for his hand and interlaced her fingers with his. "I already know you're too good of a man not to, Joe.

"But then you'll have to work late one night or I will, or the time difference will be too awkward to coordinate. And we'll miss a day. And then a day turns into two, and two eventually turns into a week.

"And by then, we're too in-like with each other to want to hurt one another, so we try at first to schedule it, to keep it a priority. Except now it feels forced. Now it feels like something we have to do, instead of wanting to do. And in the meantime the girl that smiles at you while you're at the gym or on the mountain trail makes you wonder if your heart still actually beats on its own, a little bit, and if maybe you weren't really a little confused during that week away in London." She was looking down now, unable to hold his gaze.

He tried interrupting this stream with levity. "Well, that's unlikely, because hiking this time of year in the Rocky Mountains, nobody is smiling. Their faces are too frozen."

She looked up for just a moment and again attempted a smile, but behind it Joe could see the layered pain of years past. "And then maybe one night when we've agreed to talk maybe both of us are just sitting on our sofas half a world apart, hoping the other person *won't* dial the phone—and maybe won't dial it ever again—so we don't have to have the conversation where we're now saying words and phrases like 'it was such a lovely week' and 'you're such a lovely person' and 'maybe if we were closer' and 'we really tried, didn't we?'... and just plodding through such a mess of conversation because while we're heartbroken people, Joe, we're not heart*less*, and we're trying to let each other down gently."

Joe sat up, reaching to take her hands back into his. "And we hang up the phone," Claire continued, "and it's a feeling of relief—if not sorrow—and we hate that what we had now has a black mark on the memory, when we could have just left it as it was, as we are in this hotel room right now: perfect."

He looked awhile into her eyes, absorbing all she had said and wanting to be respectful of it. Not wanting to dismiss. "Claire," he finally managed.

"Yes, Joe?"

"That was probably the most eloquent description of a denouement between two people I've ever heard. You managed to make the lousy sound beautiful." This was enough to bring genuine laughter to both of them.

"I know how badly you've been bruised, Claire. I know you don't want to put yourself at risk of that ever again. And I know the odds are stacked almost exponentially against when there is physical distance.

"But I also know—if I may say it—that that was fear talking, that was the armour guarding a heart. I know because those voices talk to me too. But they aren't the heart itself.

"I've already said this: that I don't know how this works, or how to handle what happens next. All I know is that I want there to *be* a *next*. I don't want this to end today—perfectly. I want us to get *imperfect* with each other."

"It's going to get messy, Joe," she said. He could feel Claire straining against herself, attempting to both pull her hands away while trying to mesh them into his even more.

"I want the mess. I want to know what that looks like and feels like with you," Joe said.

"That's just the infatuation talking, the romance." She forced another smile. "I don't mean that in a cruel way, Joe, because believe me, there's a voice inside that tells me I want the same right now, too. But I don't know if that voice is reasonable. I don't know if it can be trusted."

"Then what's the alternative—that we trust the voice of fear? Of rejection? Of heartbreak?" He turned his own smile now, looked down, brought her hands to his mouth and kissed them.

"Claire, I know your pain. I know your fear. I can't tell you how I know, but I do. I also know that I'm sitting on this bed in this hotel room half a world away from a life where I've tried to plan every moment, manage every risk, take the prescribed path and reach a predetermined destination. And none of it—not its single best moment—has compared to even a minute I've spent with you. Now that I've found you, I'm not going to give that up just so I might be able to say 'At least Claire didn't break my heart.' Because even if you do, I won't have to go to bed at night ever again wondering where you are, or if you were real, or what might have been, or why my— Why the universe brought me to you.

"You can tell me to go, and you can tell me not to call, and if that's truly what your heart—and not all the bricks you were forced to build around it—is saying we should do, I will respect that.

"But if you're tired of carrying those bricks—as I

know I'm tired of carrying mine—then I'm here with you right now, saying I want to dismantle those walls with you. It's going to get messy, sure. We are going to make mistakes. But I would rather get covered in dust and mortar and make those mistakes with you, than make what my heart is telling me would be the biggest mistake of all: to go back to life without you."

A tear she had been resisting broke free, tracing a trail along the side of her face. "I'm scared, Joe. I'm really scared."

"I know," he said.

"And maybe the talk of distance *was* just a ruse, was just fear or armour talking. I am smart enough to know that deep down, past all the disguises of distance or even infidelity, heartbreak so often comes down to just one thing. It wasn't getting cheated on that did the damage, that was just the form it came in. Just like it wouldn't be when you stopped calling that would inflict the actual hurt.

"What I'm really afraid of," she said as more tears released, "what has and what would hurt the most, would be giving my heart to you, and in the end you telling me it wasn't good enough. That I gave you all of me, and you were able to just let go."

"Oh, Claire." He folded her into his arms, her head against his shoulder. She was quiet, but he could feel the catching of her breath, the shoulder of his robe beginning to dampen.

"What if I told you I'm just as afraid of that as you are?" he asked. "And what if we agree to be scared shitless together?" She laughed, pulling back to look at him as he took her face in his hands, kissing her forehead, the tears on her cheeks.

"This is going to sound… well, however it sounds, but you are the woman of my dreams, Claire. The universe brought me to you—sent me across a continent and an ocean to find you, when I hadn't even been looking. I've never, in my entire life, ever, put stock into anything like that before, but when I looked into your eyes for the first time the other night, I knew."

"Knew what?"

"That I was brought here to love you, and I am not going to let that go."

Joe moved his mouth to hers, taking her into his arms. They fell back into the sheets, discovering one another once more.

CHAPTER 47
FAITH, THE ONLY PRACTICAL OPTION

THE GOODBYE AT the airport hadn't been without emotion, but in contrast to Joe's former experience this was imbued with the cautious hope of new lovers, of anticipation of the next meeting.

Claire was curious about the massive hiking pack; Joe skirted the issue with a half-truth that after investing so much in hiking apparel, he hadn't seen the need to further expend on traditional travel ware. She'd offered a laugh and a slight raised eyebrow, accepting the quirk at face value.

It was a reminder for Joe of that which had conveniently faded to the background over the preceding days: the strange magic that had brought them together. It hadn't come close to sitting right with him, the thought of forever avoiding the truth, yet he still hadn't any idea how he would—or could—tell her. For as far-ranging as their conversations had been, nothing so far had broached the paranormal, and in yet another instance of the tightrope tentativeness of early love, he'd been petrified of disturbing the delicate balance.

He knew the crux of her pain was the deception she'd

endured, and it felt irreconcilable to begin their relationship under anything resembling false pretenses—but all at once, what was he supposed to say? *Claire, up until about two months ago my nighttime visions were only ever nonsensical scenes. But then, a few weeks ago, I found myself in your kitchen. With you, your sister, your children. Looking* through *your eyes. That's right—not* in *your eyes, but through them. And then your workplace. And then in the shower...*

Good lord. How insane that would sound, even if it was the absolute truth. There had to be some kind of moral or ethical special clause in this situation, no? That when the truth sounded ludicrous—bordering on delusional—was it then okay to take to the grave? Was this one of those things that would cause more damage by its disclosure than by its omission?

I'm sure David says the same thing to himself about his indiscretions, one of the internal trustees said.

This was quickly becoming the new, maddening train of thought, one that threatened a fall from the clouds on which his heart danced as his plane soared among those beyond the windows. Paradoxical, irreconcilable, hypocritical, ironic—he wasn't sure which of those fit right now, just that none of it fit exactly right. None of it, except for her.

Though it took a tremendous force of will, Joe was able to still the voices of doubt with a single, overarching thought: something had orchestrated this into being. But not him. Not even close.

It wasn't just the dreams, either. It was everything about their encounter. The way her hand fit in his. How their bodies came together in a language as fluent as the words they spoke. The ease and familiarity with which they did speak. These things had been as close to perfection as Joe had ever experienced, no less than the forests and mountains he revered. If this week with Claire *hadn't* been perfection, he would need to abandon hope of ever knowing what was.

In the entirety of his life, if Joe had ever been asked to simply "have faith" in an idea, it would have been tantamount to asking a fish to believe in oxygen outside of water. The language itself wouldn't have absorbed, let alone the concept. Yet here he was, hurtling thirty-five thousand feet above the ground, coming back from a place where he'd discovered a woman to whom he'd been introduced in dreams was not only real, but was becoming the essence of his heart. Though he couldn't begin to comprehend the how or the why, faith seemed like the only practical option.

CHAPTER 48
CLOSING THE DISTANCE

T HE FOLLOWING WEEKS saw the tangible worlds surrounding Joe and Claire evaporate—even if for most of it, half the world kept them apart. In the course of alternating early morning calls for him and late night calls for her, they'd spoken the hours away like teenagers, falling just short of the "you hang up first," "no you hang up" routine. At their age, pride wouldn't permit debasing themselves with the actual words, even if their hearts longed for them to say no better.

In their early phone calls, someone (later on they playfully argued over whom) had eventually located the courage to float the idea of getting together between Christmas and New Year's. Before he knew it, Joe was back on the phone with the airline and hotel making arrangements for another week.

He flew out on Boxing Day, arriving in London the day after, Claire meeting him at Heathrow. *Is there a better feeling than seeing the face of one's affection after walking through the Arrival doors?* he could remember thinking. After a stop at his hotel to check-in—but mostly to check in with one another—they'd gone to her house in Queen's Park.

They had debated how to approach the matter with Claire's children, understanding that in the lifetime of a relationship, three weeks was but a blink. Despite what their hearts had to say in the matter (during one of their sunrise-sunset calls, Claire had said "Soul time feels different than actual time," with Joe in complete agreement), both wanted to tread delicately with Jackson, Ainsley, and in particular, Holly.

Of the elder boy, Joe hadn't conversed beyond a greeting during the previous week in London. After about the third date, Audrey insisted Jack emerge from his bedroom cave and at least say hello. The teen had obliged with a cursory grunt before heading back to his music and video games.

Ainsley remained excited by the new suitor, even if it was unclear what significance post-divorce, grown-up romance held in the world of a six-year-old. As with most children her age, she held greater concern for the universe of friends and playdates and school and Christmas that occupied her days. She seemed to find Joe an amusing curiosity. A new, unwitting ear to listen to the stream-of-consciousness tales her older siblings ignored, and that her mother and aunt—despite best intentions—often only heard with half-awareness. When asked by Audrey what she thought of Joe, Ainsley merely remarked, "He's nice and kind, and he listens to my stories." When asked for her official assessment of the time Joe was spending with her mother, she'd said, "Mummy smiles a lot." That seemed to be enough, by her standards.

Holly continued to be wary, and when Joe showed up with Claire that first Sunday for dinner, she'd retreated to her room. She emerged only when summoned for mealtime, asking to be excused after the main course and declining dessert. Joe second-guessed every interaction, replaying for Claire the limited dialogue between him and Holly. Claire responded by recounting family counselling sessions following David's affair, moving out, recoupling, and blending of houses. Most of Holly's trauma appeared related to that dysregulation, and likely little to do with Joe himself. The therapist had forewarned that most children will rebel at some point against any new partner, forever maintaining their loyalty to the parent, and allegiance (conscious or not) to the original relationship.

Claire spoke of Holly's strained relationship with David. After her ex-husband's emotional grenade-juggling act, all involved sought to downplay the event and avoid outright discussion of the affair. Their reasons for doing so were disparate from one family member to the next, and some succeeded better than others in maintaining decorum and diplomacy (with Joe correctly assuming this was a reference to Audrey). Though Claire was guided by the motive of not outwardly disparaging their father, Holly and Jackson were still old enough to understand what had occurred behind closed doors.

Holly blamed David for the destruction of their home, yet couldn't help her feelings of love and loyalty to him. The concurrent, diametric emotions were impossible to reconcile for a twelve-year-old. Claire surmised that Joe's presence was probably a further reminder of a terminally ill world that had been lanced with upheaval one otherwise unremarkable night at the kitchen table three years ago. Claire assured Joe these factors were likely the nucleus for Holly's reticence, and not to take them on as his own shortcomings or responsibility.

These discussions were fraught with their own reticence; for as open as Joe and Claire had become with one another, some topics were still broached with tentativeness and caution. Spending time around the kids might not have been a factor so soon, had Joe just been a bloke from work or the neighbourhood. It seemed irresponsible for Claire to disappear completely to his hotel during that Christmas break, and just as reckless to start playing at anything resembling house. Joe, for his part, was content to follow Claire's lead on this, having no direct experience of his own.

They decided to proceed delicately, and contented themselves with evenings in his suite after Claire had spent the day with the children. Of their nights alone, they passed the time amid thousands of words both spoken and unsaid. Enwrapped in a million more embraces, some passionate and unrestrained, others delicate and tender. They half-jokingly wondered whether they ought to have done more with the time, taking in more sights (with or without official tour guiding), and providing Joe with a more authentic London experience. He admitted the only experience he wanted was to be in her atmosphere, absorbing every moment, every word, every touch. Claire confessed feeling the same.

He did return to her house for dinner on Thursday, New Year's Eve. It was clear Ainsley had decided to adopt

Joe as a new best friend, leading him upon arrival to her room for introductions to an array of stuffed and plastic friends, insisting he remember the names of each. Holly was slightly less cool this time, and while Joe didn't force any interaction, he'd greeted her with a gentle "It's nice to see you again" and she'd replied with a quiet "You too"—with the three adults privately considering it a small victory. Jackson maintained his indifference, acknowledging Joe with little more than sideways glances and occasional mumbles during the meal. At this, Claire beamed as though they'd just engaged one another in spirited, philosophical discourse. When Jack responded with more than one word to Joe's questions about school and upcoming football tryouts, she had been practically elated.

Audrey appeared to serve as an unofficial ambassador during these encounters. Joe hadn't a clue what he'd done to endear himself to her, thinking she might have been the most significant voice of caution or doubt. Yet she seemed positively pleased with his arrival, even if (in Joe's mind) that was merely from the stark contrast between him and David.

If that contrast afforded Joe time to demonstrate his honourable intentions (if not the clandestine circumstances that brought him here), he would take it. After dessert, while Claire helped Ainsley with bath time and had a private debrief with Holly, Joe stood at the kitchen sink washing dishes as Audrey dried. He ventured small talk, which was cut off almost instantly once listening ears departed the room.

"Joe, I don't imagine I have to give you the talk, do I?" she asked.

"Which talk is that, Audrey?"

"The 'If you hurt my sister, I'm going to hurt *you*' talk." She picked up one of the butter knives in need of drying and waved it in his direction.

"Ahh. No. I don't believe you do."

"I don't know how much Claire has told you, nor what the two of you do in all those midnight hours you've crammed together on these visits—though I do have an active imagination. But she's been hurt before, Joe. Badly, at that. Way more than she's let on, I imagine."

Choosing his words carefully, he said, "I've gotten that sense, yes."

"Claire is my big sister, and through my entire life, a little bit my hero, too—though I'll never tell *her* that. And what David did, and the things she's endured since, well, they nearly broke her apart." Audrey continued drying and stowing dishes away as she spoke.

Joe kept his eyes on the casserole dish he was washing. "She's also the strongest woman I've ever known," Audrey continued, "and it would take more than the likes of David, or any other obstacle thrown her way once he left, to bring her down.

"But—" she pointed a ladle in his direction, flinging soap suds that landed on his cheek. They laughed as he dried it away with an elbow.

"Had to know there was a 'but,'" he said.

"You're damned right there was a 'but,' Joe. I like you. I don't know what it is, and maybe that makes me less of the castle guard I've sought to be ever since that—" she paused, as though attempting to censor herself, "that arsing louse threw a bomb on this entire family. But at all rates, I haven't seen her face look the way it did when I first saw her looking at you, in a *very* long time." Audrey put the ladle away, leaned against the counter and looked out the window over the sink. "That beautiful smile of hers never disappeared. She never allowed it to; would never have allowed David or anything else that kind of power. Especially not when it came to the children.

"But these last years there's always been a hesitation behind it, an unadmitted pain. Even though the smile was formed by her mouth, it was like it had disappeared from her eyes, which is where it really counts."

She turned to face Joe. "But when I walked up to the two of you at the gallery—and after we shooed away that idiot—I saw the smile return to her eyes, even before I saw it on the rest of her face. And though it may have been reckless, in that moment and afterwards, I thought, 'Well that's good enough for me.'

"I can't believe I'm about to say this," she picked up another foam-covered serving spoon and once again held it in front of his face, "but it felt right, you being there. Like you were supposed to have wandered into my little show like a random tourist taking in the London sights on a Saturday night. I could see and sense it by what I saw on my sister's face.

"And I thought, 'I know I promised her—and myself—that I would stand guard against her pain,' and maybe I ought to have been harder on you, or given you the third degree. But after I saw how she looked at you, I thought 'I am not about to stand between her and whatever this is. This shot at what I hope—and God help you, Joe, if you end up proving me wrong..." She waved the spoon, flinging more suds about. "But this shot at what could be a good man, at what could be a return to... Well, a good feeling, anyway.

"So you're just going to have to pardon the lecture, Mr. Riley. If my sister is willing—after everything she's been through—to let you into her heart, then I suppose I'll allow it, too," she winked. "But if you are careless with it... If you... She's just—she's just too good, Joe. She was too good for that man we shall not mention again tonight. She's been too good for the various louts that have come calling ever since we were in primary school. And she's too good, even, for most of us in her life. I'm not speaking ill of myself, nor her friends, and certainly not of the children. But she has a heart that's pure, Joe. I'll never tell her this, but she's the woman I would like to be, if I could ever get out of my own damned way long enough. And I am absolutely petrified that one more failed promise, or one more bad result, or one more drop of her heart is going to break it for good."

Joe continued to listen, though he too had taken his attention away from the dishes and regarded Audrey directly.

"She's sacrificed *every*thing, Joe. And every time we think there's about to be a reprieve, a new chance for her to maybe regain all she gave up when that snake-oil salesman purporting to be Prince Charming swooped in and stole it all away, there's another setback, another sacrifice. And she was just beginning to get to a stable place this last year, when you arrived. So I don't know if that's perfect timing, or horrendously bad." She paused and Joe remained quiet, giving her space to say that which he sensed had been stored up long before he'd ever arrived.

"Well?" she finally broke the silence.

"Well?" he asked in return, breaking into a grin.

"Which is it going to be, Joe? Perfect timing, or are you going to make me regret letting my guard down?"

He considered his words. "Everything about this has been perfect so far, Audrey. That's not me calling Claire perfect—nor myself, that much is certain. But the timing of this, the way it came about..." An internal voice said *Watch it.*

"I'll tell you what, Audrey," Joe said, changing tone.

"I'm listening."

"I believe something led me to Claire. And I've never been the type to ever believe in anything remotely resembling that. I don't know what it is; I won't even pretend to know. But for the first time in my life, I believe I was meant to find someone—for Claire and I to find one another. I don't know what the future holds, and I am not going to predict outcomes I have no control over. I also don't believe that I'm here to rescue her, or fix anything that happened before. As you know, and as you've said, your sister doesn't need rescuing. She's too strong for that."

He fidgeted with the dishcloth for a moment, looked down to gather thoughts that raced within. "But for as long as she affords me the privilege of being let into her heart, I am not going to walk away from that."

Audrey took her own pause. "That's easy to say when things are easy, Joe. But what are you going to do when it's no longer perfect? Because things happen, life happens, and as wonderful as you seem—and as I have an intuition you are—you're not perfect, as you said. As much as I love my sister, I know she's not either. And there is more than just you, or even her, at stake here. There are other lives involved."

Joe regarded her again, searching his heart. "I'm going to choose to believe," he said at last, "that whatever led me to her, will lead us then."

"That's a pretty woo-woo answer for a guy who likes probabilities and numbers and maths."

"If you only knew," he said with a smile.

She considered this. "Well, I guess that's as good an answer as any." She half-squinted, as though sussing him out. "And as woo-woo as it sounds, I do believe that *you* believe it."

"I do."

They heard shuffling behind them; turned to see Claire standing at the foot of the stairs. "What are you two talking so dreadfully about?" she said, with a cautious smile.

"Just you, behind your back," Audrey said without pause. They all broke into a laugh. "I think I like this one, Claire," she added, affecting a dreadful tone. "I think he can come back."

Claire looked at Joe, their eyes closing the distance across the room. "I think he can, too."

CHAPTER 49
WHAT YOU DREAM ABOUT WHEN YOU SLEEP

"MOST PEOPLE HAVE a problem with Mondays," Claire said, "but I'm beginning to loathe Fridays now." They laid in the bed of his hotel room, less than twelve hours away from his return flight to Canada.

After dishes and "The Talk" with Audrey, the adults played board games with the two younger children—Jackson's facial expression suggesting a preference for having his fingernails removed over playing Sorry! with his siblings. They watched New Year's festivities on the television, with Ainsley fighting valiantly to reach midnight. As young children do, she believed the hours following her regular bedtime were filled with mystery, and wanted to witness whatever magic regularly occurred for grownups after eight p.m., perhaps more than her desire to ring in a new year. She'd crashed off and on after ten o'clock, falling asleep against Joe's arm as they played another round of the board game. They'd attempted to shake her awake in time for the countdown, but by then sleep had fully betrayed her intentions and she'd muttered a half-conscious, yet strangely poetic, "What care I, for nineteen ninety-nine?", eliciting laughter from the rest of the family. "Where they get these things, I'll never know," Audrey said as she hiked her niece up the stairs.

Joe and Claire returned to his hotel after the two younger children were settled in bed, unwilling to disturb the delicate ecosystem of the children's home by remaining there overnight, despite the late hour. That, and the lingering matter of David.

Claire's ex had absconded from the island the week before Christmas, taking Miranda and her children to Florida and Disney World. He'd not discussed with Claire the question of whether he'd see his own children over the holiday break, the foregone conclusion of which coming at an inevitable cost borne—as usual—by their mother. Though the children had also acclimated to the unpredictable yet consistent rejection, their tender hearts were unable to distinguish between the pathological behaviour of the self-obsessed, and an outright negation of their entire little lives.

Despite the duplicity, David still managed to occasionally charm his progeny. In a cursory phone call that barely made the bedtime cutoff on Christmas Day, he assured them that their next weekend together would be just as magical as the time he'd bestowed on his de facto foster children. He was due to take Jack, Holly and Ainsley at some point on New Year's Day, and Audrey assured Claire she would handle this hand-off as she had so many others.

Though David hadn't stopped short of leaving his own children behind or arranging for additional time to see them upon his return, he *had* feigned interest via increasing long-distance calls after Ainsley unassumingly relayed news of Joe's arrival. Suddenly there was all manner of urgent discussion with Claire about this school-year issue or that extra-curricular activity. Claire only indulged this on a couple of occasions before asserting that despite David's newfound willingness to expend phone charges in the name of his children, if there was truly a litany of outstanding discussion items, they could arrange a time following his return. At this, he'd point-blank asked if "The Canadian with the Delicate Constitution" would be there. When Claire said no, he'd lost the urgency to hash out the plethora of matters apparently assailing his mind whilst walking The Magic Kingdom.

Claire had been diplomatic with Joe whenever conversation turned to past relationships, and in particular, her marriage. She rarely mentioned David by name and seldom made reference to the infidelity, let alone specific details. She spoke in generalizations and Joe was careful not to pry, prompting her only if he intuited there was something she needed to express but held back out of an unwillingness to malign another human—even one who had so badly betrayed her and her children.

When Joe asked if they ought to be concerned by David's interest, Claire slipped slightly on the diplomatic front, saying, "Oh no. David's harmless, unless his ego is involved. And even then, his retribution arrives simply in the form of wanting to measure phalluses and pee a circle, as you've seen. So all we have to do is make sure we don't give him yet another opportunity to take his pants off."

Claire seemed cognizant (if not a little dejected) that

David's sudden interest had little to do with any lingering feeling for her. She knew it had everything to do with his predilection for women who loved him unequivocally and without end, while he be permitted to pick and choose, come and go. He hadn't chosen Claire, would never choose her again, yet in true narcissistic form couldn't abide by her choosing anyone else.

She elaborated with Joe, saying, "David will be interested in us for a little while, and pretend to make an effort with the kids and me. But when it comes time to expend any *actual* effort, he'll lose interest and refocus on whomever else he likely has on the side now. Probably a sun-kissed Floridian, at the moment. If we should be concerned about anyone, it ought to be Miranda, much as my pain doesn't want me to say that."

Claire remained ambassadorial even on that front; chose to quietly mourn the loss of a friend rather than fixate on the betrayal. If anything, she pitied the woman who was now probably being driven neurotic by David's unceasing and impossible-to-follow web of charm, inattention, focus, absence, affection and indifference.

"I don't want to waste any more of our time talking about any of that," Claire said, her head and arm draped across Joe's chest. "I want to focus on *my man*, for the few hours I have left with him." The way she'd emphasized 'my man' flared warmth in his stomach. "I want to know more, Joe. I can't get enough. Tell me everything. Tell me all your nothings. Your pet peeves. The things that make you laugh until you cry. What you think about when you go hiking. What you dream about when you sleep." At the last, Joe stopped breathing.

"Well," he finally said, "since you asked…"

CHAPTER 50
AMENDING FOR WORDS MISSPOKEN

*Y*OU CHICKENED OUT, the members of Parliament later admonished. *Had a chance to come clean, make it right, and you completely cowed.* Joe wasn't certain that even Uncle Peter wasn't in on the reprimand.

He'd come within seconds of telling Claire, about to open with "Trust me when I say I *know* how crazy this sounds, and I've never experienced anything like this," yet stopped mere moments before the words spilled out. It was as though her eyes could sense something of gravity was about to be said, and she lay there looking at him with bated breath. Newly appointed backbenchers shouted rationalizations like "She'll never believe you!" and "She's going to think you're nuts at best, a deranged stalker at worst!" And the most tenuous of excuses, "She's been hurt so much in the past; this would only injure her further." So instead, on the "since you asked" lead-in, he quickly shifted gears to the topic of her belated Christmas present.

Following their innumerable "When can I see you again" talks after his first trip to London, Joe had called his travel agent to book his return over the Christmas break. When he'd called Claire immediately after to confirm, what he didn't mention was the part where he'd asked the agent to also look into flying Claire out to him during the first two weeks of February.

He'd been asking vague and inconspicuous questions about Claire's vacation time, whether Audrey ever looked after the kids for extended periods, the process of booking time off when one was a member of the media, and so on. He'd peppered those enquiries over several calls, hoping she wouldn't get wise to what he was planning or curious why he was asking. That, and the committee advocating prudence suggested *You ought to see how Christmas goes, first.*

When the nova of time in that last week of December dissipated even quicker than before, he'd been confident Claire would agree to the trip—if not without mild protest over his expenditure. Following the New Year's celebrations, as Claire made the rounds to Holly and Jackson, Joe spilled the beans to Audrey and asked if she would be willing to take up child-rearing full time for two weeks. He insisted the reservations were entirely refundable and she ought not feel obligated, but from the expression on her face Joe knew the answer before she said it aloud.

And so when Claire asked about his everythings and nothings, his thoughts and dreams, he'd at least gone with the thought occupying him lately: two weeks together in the Canadian Rockies, at the Banff Springs Hotel. Hiking, if weather permitted. Plenty of sights, if they wished. Endless hours of connection—at least for a while—within their private world.

Her face lit up at once, and for a moment he was able to forget the internal rebuke from not telling her about the dreams. As quick as the smile spread across her face, she reined it in, saying, "But Joe... this is..." She paused, fidgeting with the blanket between them. "This is a lot, so early. Are you sure about this?"

"Yes. I know you just met me," he said, the wording of this not lost on the committees, "but I know that a month without you is already going to be about twenty-nine days too long. So I made arrangements on my end to hopefully make it as comfortable as possible for you to make arrangements on yours. Is it too soon?"

Another smile quickly formed with the lips he adored, but was just as soon tempered. "No, it's not that. It's just—"

After waiting for her to continue, Joe broke the quiet when she didn't. "It's just what?"

"I don't know how to receive this, Joe. I keep waiting for the other shoe to drop. The last time someone was this nice to me, this thoughtful, it turned out the former was just a façade, and the latter was really just thoughts of himself, covering for all the things he was up to when I wasn't looking.

"I'm trying, so hard, not to let those wounds reopen and affect what's happening between me and you, but it was almost as though every act of 'kindness' before had this bizarre effect of making me feel even *more* unworthy. Because in the beginning, those acts were only in service of what he could take from me. And in the end, what he could take away."

"I'm not David, Claire. I've never been like David, and never will be."

"I know that, Joe. I know you're not, and I know *this* is not *that*. But there are other practical concerns, aren't there? We live entire continents apart. This *will* get hard eventually, if for no other reason than that. You've assured me not to worry, but at some point you will get tired—either of the time, or the money being spent, or the first time my kids get in the way, or the first time I do something that really gets on your nerves. And then it will be all too easy to say, 'Well it was nice, Claire sure is nice, but this distance is too much. Her three kids are too much. Her quirks and peccadillos are too much. I should just settle down with a nice Canadian girl.'"

Joe could feel his heat rising. "This is interesting, how you're taking stock of how you assume I'll feel down the road."

Her tone changed. "Oh comeon, Joe. I'm just being realistic. I'm just being practical. Men and women say a million things when they're in the throes of infatuation, and granted they're—usually, anyway, unless they're certain ex-husbands I know—they're sincere when they say them. I know you think you mean the beautiful things you say and write to me, but in the end those will just be words, Joe, and I can't hold onto words alone. In the end, real life will start again. This has been a beautiful four weeks, a fairytale month I'll never forget, but at some point life will come crashing in again and you'll realize I'm not perfect. You'll remember relationships are far from easy. And you'll want to go back to your ordered, predictable, planned-out life."

"Claire, what is happening—"

"It's easy to say a lot of things right now while *things* are easy. But you haven't seen the hard yet, Joe. I have bad days, like anybody else. I've had bad weeks and bad *months*. I have a bit of a temper. I can get vindictive. There is still so much you don't know about me, nor I about you. I'm a complex human being, Joe, and I'm not just some cautionary tale of a witless girl who married a charming—but very wrong—man, and is therefore 'saved' by some sweeping-in rescuer. That's not how human beings work. I've had challenges in my life that go beyond just some caricature-like story of a husband that couldn't keep it in his pants and fucked about with my best friend." Her use of profanity shocked him; seemed foreign coming from the voice that always played like music to him. "Those things will inevitably show up for us one day, in some form or another.

"Joe, you're a wonderful man. And if this was truly real, if we really had a shot, then I would be the luckiest… But at what point are we going to stop pretending tomorrow doesn't exist? Isn't it better to stop while it's still lovely? Before we've reopened old wounds and ripped open new ones?"

"I don't think it's exactly fair for you to tell me what I want, or what I'm going to want, or what I can or cannot handle. It sounds like those old wounds—"

She sat up on the bed, wrapping a sheet around herself. "I want to believe this is true. I want to believe this beautiful gift you've arranged for me won't come at a cost. That it won't lead to resentment later on. That one day, one of us won't be saying the same things I am now about distance or differences in lifestyle, or that whatever is waiting in the wings for us won't rear its ugly head. So why not say them now? Why wait until it hurts too much?" Her eyes held his in a concentrated gaze. He didn't know whether she felt tentative about the things she'd said, or if she truly believed them.

"Claire—"

"I apologize, Joe." Her tone softened. She adjusted the sheet and looked away from him. "I have this horrible habit when we're together of opening my mouth, and *all* the words come falling out. All of them. The good ones and the bad ones. I don't seem to skimp on any." She attempted a smile, but he could see in her eyes it was pained.

He regarded her for a moment, reeling from the dye she'd cast on what was meant to be a surprise, meant to give them a moment in time to look forward to. The practical side of him knew what she'd said had merit— and were elements he'd already considered, himself—but wondered how much of it was her hurt talking instead of her heart.

Part of him wanted to refute her questions and assertions, point by point. Part of him wanted to shut down and send her away. Yet another part wanted to reach out and take her into his arms.

"Claire." He opted for gravity in his tone that he hoped would be difficult to interrupt.

"Yes, Joe?"

"I know that if we were in a movie right now, we'd have to have a formulaic fight, followed by a requisite period apart. We'd have a sad montage of us going on with our individual lives, yet clearly preoccupied with thought of the other. But are you okay if we just skip all that, right to the part where we realize how much we love each other, and go on, happily ever after?" He paused, while Claire remained silent.

"I'm not naïve, Claire. If anything, I've tried to express how early heartbreak shut me down, walled me off, and informed every decision I've made since about relationships, and every judgment I've made against those in them. You haven't known by seeing it from me, but if you'd known me before, I would have been the last person advocating for a love story. But that was before you came to me, Claire." He caught himself on this last statement. "That was before you tapped me on my shoulder.

"I don't want to have a sad montage where I wonder what might have been, or if you're the one who got away. So you can fight me on this, if you like, if you need to make sure these things are addressed and those fears spoken aloud. I've wondered these things, too. But I'll still be standing right here. I don't need us to fight, or spend time apart, to realize how much I'm in love. Or to question whether or not when those inevitable challenges come, if you're the one I want to have them with."

Her eyes softened. "You're in love with me?"

"Yes. Indelibly. Incontrovertibly. Indubitably. All the ly's." He smiled, and she laughed.

"I'm in love with you, too."

He reached out, touched the sides of her head with his hands. "Then let's hold onto that, and let's build something together based on what we *know* has happened between us, rather than taking it apart based on what *could* happen. There will be challenges, sure. I know there will be. But please, Claire," he pulled her to him, kissed her forehead, then moved his lips to the sides of her face. "Please don't try to convince me of all the ways I won't love you. I already know all the ways I do, and will."

He slid a hand behind her neck, laying her head down on the pillow. They kissed long and slow, as though amending for words misspoken in the past or future. They spoke with their bodies, led by their hearts, and passed another night away as one.

CHAPTER 51
THE INERRANT INEVITABILITY OF TIME

THE FOLLOWING WEEKS were excruciating in their passage of time. Joe was able to stay distracted during working hours by the demands of investment season, while Claire was occupied with the start of a new year—new stories to chase, kids returning to school, extracurriculars back in swing. Their minds remained occupied with one another, however, speaking by phone when they could (burning through endless long-distance cards), and taking up the modern version of love-lettering via their Hotmail accounts.

She told him of stories they were developing at the magazine. Interviews they had lined up and the accompanying background research. Other conversations were filled with trivialities; anything to keep the voice on the other end of the phone. Whether he listened to her describe what she'd cooked for dinner or the latest misadventures on Coronation Street or the challenges and triumphs in the lives of her children—any and all of it pulled him in.

Everything sounded lovelier and more captivating in her voice. He loved the passion he heard. Her view of the world. The way she described each detail of every day as though whatever occupied the hours between sunrise and sunset deserved her unassailable attention. How whether it was the reporters in her stead or the children under her roof or the man in her heart, whomever she was with at that moment was the most important person in the world. He adored that about her, and hoped he could show her that for him, she truly was.

He told her of the twenty-four-hour-a-day nature of his job, and how as a business owner it never quite left him alone. There seemed to be only two exceptions to this: when he was in the mountains, or when he was with her. Even by phone, or in front of a screen filled with words they'd written one another, the rest of the world faded away. He longed to spend more hours of the day in that space, if not all the hours. In an increasing affront to invulnerability he told her these things, and she quietly—if not a bit nervously—told him she wished for the same.

It was as though their hearts were pushing each of them to ask the questions—How do we make this work? How do long-distance relationships work? Do they ever work? When is the right time to take the next step? How will we know? When is it too soon?—but prudence disavowed any direct discussion. There was an unspoken hesitation to do anything that might snuff out the magic of these moments now. Yet in a letter, one might wonder aloud what came next, and in a phone call the other would confess their longing for February to arrive sooner.

In moments of even greater, exposed courage, a wish

would be expressed that one day the trips might not be just a finite, week-or-two space in the calendar. The person hearing or reading this never contradicted what was said or written, usually responding with a woefully inadequate 'me too.' A combination of wounded hearts, broken expectations, experience with or witness to misguided choices of youth that later became anchors in adulthood kept them from adding more words to those conversations. 'Banff' and 'February' became the watchwords that kindled them for now, no matter the unseen paths on which their hearts might lead them.

Time affected its usual, inexplicable pliability; the days and weeks variously expanding and contracting. No matter their longing to speed the hours preceding her arrival or slow the minutes once she did, time also affected its inerrant inevitability, and the morning when her flight number was set to display on the Arrivals screen finally came.

Joe stood at the airport meeting area amongst the flat-capped drivers, bearing flowers in one hand, and his own placard in the other.

The automatic doors parted and for an instant, all the oxygen in the massive airport seemed consumed by everyone else, leaving the dream-crossed lovers without breath as their eyes met. Claire's smile spread as her eyes moved to the flowers and handwritten sign, bearing the words "The Most Beautiful Woman from the Sky."

Joe moved to her with steps bordering on a run, prompting shouts of "Sir you can't—" from scattered voices. She threw her arms around his shoulders as the flowers and sign fell to the polished floor, their mouths meeting with a fervency born of the weeks apart. This was enough to soften the admonishments of even the border guards, and as Joe and Claire's consciousness regained awareness of the world around them, they heard applause. As their faces filled with colour they released their embrace, their inner world complete once more.

CHAPTER 52
LOSING NERVE

Their time was undistracted and calm. The Banff Springs Hotel was a castle away from the demands, a sanctuary amid a beautiful backdrop in which to rewrite the history of their hearts. They walked the corridors of the fabled building, ate late brunches in its various dining rooms, danced in the ballroom to music only they could hear. Claire relished the return to mountains she'd hiked so many years before, when she still believed in love without betrayal, and of souls that might one day find their shelter in another. Joe reveled in revisiting the trails where he once sought solace from the questions that assailed him, paths he walked now alongside a woman in whose heart might be the answers.

Joe's work associates had readily agreed to take up the reins and urged him to turn off his cell phone. They made assurances of having the hotel reach him if there was an issue that could in no way be handled except by him. Which, despite his waning reluctance to hand over control, wouldn't come to pass. In truth, he was feeling ready to begin letting go, at least a little bit. Over these past weeks yet another question had played in his mind: if all these years of planning and preparing weren't leading to some greater aim, some nobler purpose aside from packing it in at age sixty-five and taking lonely guided tours abroad, then what had it all been for?

Back in England, Audrey had been just as willing as Joe's colleagues to handle the day-to-day. In phone calls every couple of Canadian mornings to check in during London evenings, life had carried on mostly without incident. Claire soaked in details of their days from Ainsley (updating on all things school, friends, toys, animals, and random factoids about the universe), Holly (a concise report of homework assignments and friend drama), and Jackson (virtually nothing beyond murmurs of "good" for every answer). On one of these calls, with the day's headlines captured, Audrey took the phone and mentioned an issue with David. Before elaborating, she took an oath from Claire that she wouldn't do anything to curtail the trip, and assured her it was nothing unusual or unexpected.

He had phoned the day prior asking for Claire. When Audrey informed him that she was away on business, saying nothing more, David professed his own need to be out of town during his scheduled custody. He asked if Claire (or Audrey) could keep the kids for the weekend, promising to make it up some other time. This was far from a rare experience: David claiming business abroad every few weeks, consistent only in his vow to compensate for the missed time. These forsaken hours had thus far never been reclaimed. If David was keeping a ledger, it was unclear when he planned to make good on the debt to his children.

In earlier days, after speaking with Claire he'd at least

asked for the children to come to the phone in order to offer his alibis and vacant promises directly. Over time, he'd stopped doing even this much, offering these stories and assurances only to Claire. For a time she'd insisted he continue breaking the news (and subsequent pledges) to the kids himself. Eventually this ceased as well, with Claire recognizing empty vows were worse than no promises at all. Audrey likewise handled this latest reneging accordingly.

Apart from these touchpoints with their regular lives, Joe and Claire's world contracted once more to whatever space they found themselves within. Outsiders such as wait or hotel staff might as well been speaking unintelligible languages whenever they approached to take an order or enquire on any needs. Several days passed with the "Do not Disturb" sign on their suite; the only proof of life coming in the form of room service trays left outside the door.

Joe couldn't drink up enough of her tales of being a youth in London, or of summers in the English countryside. The recounting of a year spent taking the train from one European country to the next. A requisite punk phase (of which he'd demanded photographic evidence during his next trip to see her). A season of embracing social and environmental issues. Not quite bra-burning stuff, but she admitted to what she called "The Patchouli Part of my Life."

Claire likewise soaked up details about his life and upbringing, hearing of his father's serial entrepreneurialism that resulted in several fortunes won and lost. He spoke of his mother's return to postsecondary when her children were in their teens, while still maintaining the books for whatever businesses their father was engaged in. She'd completed her studies with a graduate degree in philosophy, at the top of her class. She'd admitted it had scant practical application, but had lit long-dormant synapses within. Joe had always admired this about her.

Claire laughed at his stories of being coerced into his sister's "all-girl" lip-synching squad, or of innumerable forced teatimes alongside their friends and stuffed animals. She listened to him describe alternating periods of arts and athletics, with Joe showing promise on the baseball diamond. Between the long Canadian winter, three older sisters with their own extracurriculars, a mother balancing work and school, and the feast-or-famine nature of his father's businesses, there had been no real effort to pursue it. As with many children from self-employed families, Joe and his siblings helped out at times with the family business, forming within him the desire to captain his own ship and avoid the maelstroms with which he saw his parents struggle. Thus, school and study, and a subsequent drive to plan, predict, produce.

The lovers lost track of time most of these days in the mountains, the only indication of another turn of the Earth coming from the lengthening or receding light on the hotel walls. They remained orbited around one another, unable, it seemed, to hear sufficient history, to learn enough detail. It felt impossible that their kisses might last long enough, or that the love they made would capture the depth of their desire. It was as though they were trying to gather thirty-some years of life apart, and collect it all into the room they shared or the corridors they walked. Even the outdoor spaces, surrounded by white-capped mountain peaks and soaring spruce trees, seemed an inadequate space for all they longed to hold, as they wandered arm in arm.

"I know this sounds utterly cliché, if not painfully cheesy, but I feel like I've known you longer than these few weeks," Claire said, on their second-to-last night together. They'd relocated from Banff to the Château Lake Louise, near the campground where Claire once worked. They were seated for dinner in the hotel beside windows overlooking the frozen lake. The emerald surface was adorned with ice sculptures lit by coloured floodlights that danced against the night sky.

"I do too," Joe replied. *I only wish I'd started dreaming of you twenty years ago,* he thought. *I would have tried to find you then.*

"I've heard people say things like 'I knew you before I met you,' or even 'I loved you before I met you,' and I always thought it was ridiculous. But somehow—" Her gaze shifted from his eyes to the lake and sculptures below. "Somehow with you, Joe, from that first glimpse in the gallery, I *knew* you already. I can't explain it, and I know it sounds mad, but when I saw you walk in..." She paused again, returning her eyes to his, running a hand through her hair. Even in the candlelight, Joe could see her skin was flushed. "I haven't told you this before—I was too embarrassed to say it aloud, I think—but I actually spotted you before your run to the loo."

Joe let out an awkward laugh. "And *you're* embarrassed about that?"

"Oh my love, my handsome, perfect man," she said,

taking his hand in both of hers. "I didn't say that to have a laugh. I'm *so* glad you ate that bad shrimp, or whatever it was, and made that dash and dropped your cards. It gave me the excuse I needed to talk to you. Because I saw you walk in, Joe, I saw you come through the doors, and I swear to you, it stopped my heart."

He squeezed the small hands holding his, wanting to push the table between them away and move his lips to hers. To make the room surrounding them disappear and be tangled up with no more than threads of linen between them, let alone an ocean of space and time.

"And it wasn't just because of your smashing good looks, that would stop any woman's heart," she said with a flash of a smile, "but it was this feeling..." She paused again, seeking the words befitting an entire shift of a soul.

"It was this feeling that a long search was over," she finally continued. "That in the man I'd just seen come through the gallery doors and brush snow from his shoulders, who glanced around as if he was searching for someone too, while he handed his coat to the attendant... There was somehow this feeling of coming home. I swear to you my heart was screaming up at me from my chest, *'That's him. That is our home.'*"

She released Joe's hand and brought hers over her eyes. "My word. That sounds positively mad, out loud like that. I mean, it's one thing to *think* those things, but it's entirely another to hear them pour out of my mouth. You're never going to believe me any of these times when I tell you *'I'm not normally like this,'* or that I've forever been much more reserved when I speak. All you've ever known is this girl whose words form a torrent when you're around."

"Not at all, Claire." He reached to pull her hand away from her eyes. "I knew you—I *felt* like I knew you before, too. It doesn't sound crazy. It's how I felt as well."

Was it *now* that he was supposed to tell her? As they hung on the words he'd just spoken, his mind raced for the correct ones to say—about the dreams, about his search, about finding her. This seemed like the right segue, the right moment, but still… If Claire had found it mad to share what was otherwise a beautiful expression of her feelings, of a literal moment that had taken place for both of them, how crazy would *he* sound?

"May I tell you our dessert specials, Mr. and Mrs. Riley?" a voice from the side interrupted. Joe felt a breath charge into his lungs. He saw Claire inhale as well, before blushing and looking at the waiter.

"Oh no, we're not—" Claire started to correct.

"If you have anything involving hazelnut chocolate," Joe interjected, "I know this beautiful woman won't need to hear anything further. Barring that, a chocolate lava cake will suffice." Claire laughed, the colour in her face now reflecting the warmth she felt for him, and for this moment.

The waiter smiled as he snapped closed the dessert menus he'd brought to the table. "Two plates, or will you be sharing?"

"We'll share this first one, and see if we need a second plate after that," Claire said, taking Joe's hands in hers once again.

"Very good," the uniformed man said, walking away.

The veil of their private world descended once more. Joe longed for a way to extend time and space beyond the evening and lake surrounding them. To steal extra hours of moonlight before the sun returned to reflect off the frozen water below. He could see in her eyes—and felt, in as close as he had come to those sensations he'd experienced when he'd seen through those beautiful irises—that she longed for the same. No words were exchanged, and Joe lost his nerve to say anything that might shatter the moment.

In time that could have been five or forty-five minutes, the waiter returned with their plate. A base of chocolate melting perfect scoops of vanilla iced cream on top—flanked by single-serve packages of Nutella, normally reserved for the breakfast buffet.

"Enjoy," the attendant said, beaming as though he had crafted the arrangement himself.

"I know we will," Joe said while Claire grinned.

Joe looked on as Claire reached for the silverware with one hand and pushed an errant lock of hair behind her ear with the other. Every movement, every smile, every glance—every strand of hair that refused to stay put—was perfection. He found himself searching for the right words once again, wanting to say nothing and tell her everything at the same time.

He had never been more in love than in that moment.

A glass crashed to the floor, breaking the bliss. In his daydream the sound was at first muted, as though from afar. Joe realized the tumble hadn't occurred off in the distance by some butterfingered waiter. It was Claire's water glass, and though his eyes had observed the scene they hadn't initially absorbed what occurred until after the goblet hit the floor. It landed between the table and window, sending shards and splashes in every direction. His awareness suddenly recalled the sight of her picking up the dessert fork, and somewhere in this unconscious movement executed a million times before, Claire seemed to bobble the utensil, a tremor overcoming her right hand. In the struggle to maintain a hold on the silverware, she'd knocked the glass with the back of her hand, sending it flying over the side.

She looked up at Joe after the shatter broke the quiet between them. Her eyes contained a mixture of embarrassment, and—was it panic? For as much as they felt a knowing that superseded their time together, he was cognizant they were still learning how to interpret certain expressions of body language. She didn't just look self-conscious, she looked worried.

He tried to assuage this with his best, *'It wouldn't matter if you'd just broken wind with the Queen'* smile, reaching for the offending hand. "Claire? Are you okay?"

She reflexively went to pull away from his grasp, but just as quickly acquiesced, grabbing hold with a panicked strength in her small fingers. Her eyes welled with tears.

"Oh babe, it's just a glass, it's nothing at all," he said, as their server approached with a broom and serviettes.

Joe watched Claire swallow hard, which released the tears that had been pooling. "It's not that," she finally choked out.

"Then what is it?" he asked, his tone turning to one of concern.

"Joe..."

CHAPTER 53
THERE'S SOMETHING ELSE I'D RATHER DISCUSS

It began about a year before the marriage ended. The first thing she remembered noticing was the smallest of twitches in her hand. Her thumb would sometimes behave as if it was wired separately from the rest of her fingers, as though it was being tested for current. Her thumb and index finger would clamp up, making it look like she was pinching at an invisible pencil. It was nothing noticeable to anyone else but would drive Claire nutty, particularly if she was handling a literal writing implement.

It was sporadic, and she wrote it off as a side effect from a lifetime of putting pen to paper. A minor irritant she figured would leave as randomly as it arrived. It did go, in a way: it seemed to migrate throughout her body. For several days a muscle in her upper arm would cramp. The next week or month it might be unrelenting stiffness in her legs. There was sudden and unprovoked weakness at times, with routine activities leaving her winded and wondering what she'd done to run herself down.

When she began to notice hesitation in her muscles—as though they were carefully reviewing messages from her nervous system before executing the commands—was when she finally went to see her friend, Dr. Lewiston. By then, whatever was misfiring within was beginning to besiege her on multiple fronts. Tremoring hands, facial twitches, muscle pain and cramping sufficient enough to knock things over or mishandle pens or glasses or silverware. Even her face wouldn't always cooperate: a smile was at times no longer a guaranteed, unconscious thing. Words occasionally slurred from her lips, prompting family and colleagues to ask if perhaps she'd had a glass or two of wine with lunch.

Claire had been petrified. There was a history of neurological conditions in her family, of which she'd so far been spared aside from occasional migraine headaches in youth. It felt like a familial time bomb nonetheless, and with equal parts fear and denial she'd fought her way into the doctor's office.

As with so much else in their marriage, Claire took this on alone. David's improprieties were by this point well known if not overtly discussed, and his presence in the home was becoming the exception rather than the rule. They hardly saw one another—nor in close enough proximity—for him to have taken notice, aside from the dramatics of dropping dinnerware. Of those moments, he'd simply chide her clumsiness, dressing up his cruelties to sound like good-natured ribbing.

Dr. Lewiston was immediately concerned based on Claire's family history, and ordered a battery of tests to coincide with a referral to a neurologist. Though the process became just as much about ruling out other conditions, in the end the diagnosis arrived in the form of Young Onset Parkinson's Disease. It was rare, and there wasn't a specific test to confirm, but many of Claire's symptoms mirrored those of older patients with PD as opposed to Multiple Sclerosis or ALS.

Despite Claire's devastation at what felt like a life sentence, Jacquie assured her that the condition wasn't fatal, and there had been promising advances in treatment over the last few years. They would attempt to manage symptoms with medication, elevating the levels of dopamine in her system. Levels that had fallen from neurons dying off far too early, resulting in the involuntary movements of her body at certain times, or the unresponsiveness of it at others. Complemented by physical therapy, they might be able to mitigate—or at least slow—symptoms that were beginning to interfere with actions she had long taken for granted.

While not the cause—Claire's DNA would take that dubious credit—Dr. Lewiston cautioned that lifestyle factors could exacerbate symptoms. The stress Claire was enduring from an affair and divorce in full view and full flight certainly wasn't helping. Jacquie encouraged her to find healthy mechanisms to manage the strain, and to seek better balance in her schedule. By this time David had already moved out and Audrey came in, equal doses scared and angry. The younger sister managed to be beautifully composed in front of the children, and wildly belligerent in anything to do with David. When it came to Claire's career, Jacquie (though it proved more like pulling teeth than practicing medicine) finally convinced her friend to take a six-week leave of absence, and eventually resume her duties on a reduced timetable, if and when her symptoms stabilized.

The medications worked like a charm early on, apart from side effects Claire could have done without. Nausea and vomiting. Profound fatigue during the day, only to have difficulty staying asleep at night. In the meantime, following the Great Debate concerning time away from work, Claire threw herself headlong into physical therapy, yoga and meditation. After putting Jacquie and Audrey through the paces on why a leave of absence severely offended her sensibilities, she'd finally capitulated and turned her focus to her wellness as though it was a full-time career.

She read books on Buddhism and the power of the mind, and practiced asanas as though preparing to compete in a Yogini Olympics. Jacquie and Audrey observed this with reserved concern, urging temperance. An obsessive focus on anything might still be a flash point for unintended stress, which in turn could place demands on her body to produce responses that were no longer a given. Yet Claire's symptoms remained at bay—had greatly improved, in fact, with an absence of even the slightest tremors or rigidity—and she marked a quiet victory during a time she'd felt under siege.

That had been nearly four years ago, and even with her graduated return to work—where there hadn't been a complete absence of flare-ups—she'd remained stable. There was no way to resuscitate the dying neurons within, yet Dr. Lewiston was hopeful Claire's would be one of the many cases where the rebellion of the body might have been arrested soon enough to allow a normal quality of life. One where she'd see old age, and eventually be tripped up by other factors that seemed to catch all in the end—cancer or heart disease. *You say that with something like* joy *in your voice,* Claire had said to Jacquie during one appointment. *Having one of my best friends with me in the nursing home, where we're complaining about incontinence and bad cholesterol,* will *be a joy for me,* the doctor responded.

"When did it start up again?" Joe finally asked, after she finished recounting this turn of the last few years; one that had thus far gone undetected by him. He wrapped one of the hotel robes around her as she appeared to be shivering (or was it shaking? From worry? From cold? Or from whatever sat on the edge of her nervous system, threatening to attack?). He'd taken her in his arms and whisked her back to the room after the glass had broken, knowing whatever she was about to tell him needn't be said in a public place, even a candlelit one with the nearest couple several tables away. For a time they'd just laid on the bed before she'd said a word, arms and legs wrapped around one another as she wept silently into his shoulder. A million possibilities had run through Joe's mind before she had spoken, wondering what it could be.

"I don't know that it has even 'started' again, because for the most part, everything's been fine. Since the diagnosis, this has just happened every once in awhile. The rigidity or slowness will start somewhere again, or the tremors in my hands will return. I go see the doctors, I go get more tests, and then they up the dose of my medication again, and it calms down. I double-down on the things I do that I hope will keep it at bay, and everything is brilliant for several months again, sometimes longer. But in the last six months—" she brought her face away from his chest and her glassy eyes up to his, "—the flare-ups have been coming more regularly. Like every six to eight weeks. And we just keep upping the dose again. And I keep meditating, keep visualizing, keep trying to pretend it's not there."

She sat up, wiped at the tears pooled in her eyes. "I shouldn't have cried just now, made such a scene in the restaurant." Her tone had hardened. "I'm not worried. This is just part of the package, and I think I was just embarrassed, more than anything."

"Made a scene?" Joe ventured a smile and reached for her hand, tried to pull her back into him. "It was hardly that, my love. You couldn't be undignified even if you tried."

She resisted his reach, continued to speak as though talking to herself. "I'll just keep doing what I'm doing. I'm of the mind that it's the mind itself that carries the most sway in these situations. I know there are biological things here I can't change, but if I believe it's going to get worse, then it almost certainly will. If I believe I will manage, will improve, then that's the start, at least. It's not a guarantee, but if the belief isn't there, not much else has a chance to be."

Joe sat up, took her hands in his. "I hope you'll forgive me if some of the words right now aren't the right ones… I have this completely uncharted feeling where the person I love is hurting, and I don't know how to help." He was looking in her eyes and her gaze returned his, but he could sense her attention was focused elsewhere. "What can I do, Claire? How can I help?"

These last words roused her from wherever she had been, and she released his hands, stood up, and made her way to the washroom. "Nothing, my love. I'm okay. I've managed this before, and I'm going to continue managing it." He followed her to the doorway of the bathroom where she stood at the sink, wiping the makeup from her eyes. She saw him looking at her in the mirror, and appeared to release any remaining preoccupation, turning to him. She flashed a smile, well-practiced from her days of being the one to reassure, even when it was her who needed the assurance. "I'm really okay, Joe. I'm not worried. I don't want *you* to be worried. I was just embarrassed, as I said."

She walked to Joe and took his hands. "Thank you for being sweet. But I'm really okay." She lifted up on her toes, kissed him on the cheek, then moved past him back into the room.

It's like she's trying to outrun me, he thought. She stood at the window overlooking the lake, and the spotlit carvings of polar bears and castles and Inukshuks. Her back was to him, her head tilted to the side as she removed an earring. As often happened whenever he was with her, Joe's thoughts were interrupted by the sight of her, as though seeing her again for the first time. *She's the most beautiful being I've ever seen,* he thought. *Whether I'm looking at her face, running my hands along her skin, hearing the wisdom and wit from her lips, or watching the way her hair falls along her shoulders as she removes an earring, she's the most beautiful woman I've ever known. And for some reason, the universe made* me *the guy to see her in his dreams. The one to find her.*

"Joe? What are you thinking about?" She had turned to look at him and was grinning, the pretense gone from her smile. "You have this funny look on your face, like you were daydreaming." She reached behind her back and fumbled for the zip on her dress.

He walked towards her. "Something like that. I was thinking that I love you." It was his turn to adopt a serious tone. "And I was wondering why you hadn't told me any of this before. I had no idea—it's never come up even once in our conversations."

She moved her hands away from her back, her posture stiffening, that expression of defiance returning to her face. She turned to face the window. "I wasn't trying to be deceptive, Joe. Believe it or not, it doesn't actually cross my mind that often, and when it does, I don't like to give it credence. I feel like if I talk about it any more than I have to, I give it power it doesn't deserve."

Her tone suggested the words she'd chosen were a polite substitute for *I hadn't mentioned it because it's none of your damn business.* Yet her posture softened and she turned back to him, put a hand against his chest, ran her fingers down along the buttons of his shirt. "I wasn't trying to keep anything from you, Joe. You *know* how I feel about that. Everything these last few weeks has just been so—" she turned her head to look back out over the star-draped lake, "—magical, and I didn't want—nor even had the time—to think about much that wasn't the children, my work, or everything that's happened since that beautiful night you walked into the gallery." She grabbed the lapels of his sport coat, lifted up again on her toes, and this time brought her mouth to his.

She lowered back onto her heels, reaching a hand up to his cheek. "I haven't had a flare-up since October, and it went away after the usual course of treatment. So I just haven't thought about it, Joe. That's all. I'm sure there are still plenty of things we haven't told one another—not out of concealment, but simply because it took thirty-some years to find each other. There's a lot of life in there we probably still haven't discussed, even in all our all-nighters." She broke into a grin. "If it makes you feel any better, I suppose I have to give you a 'get out of jail free' card if you've been hanging onto anything." As a knot formed in Joe's chest, he thought he saw a flash of concern before she covered with feigned admonishment. "Unless it's another woman, of course."

"You *are* the woman. The only one."

Tell her. Now.

"Joe?" Her voice interrupted the thought. Her expression had changed again, this time to one Joe didn't need to second-guess. She'd reached back around to the zip on her dress, starting to lower it. "I don't want to talk about this anymore tonight. There's something else I'd rather discuss." She balanced on her tiptoes again, kissing him.

"Is that right?" Joe said, reaching his arms around her, taking the zip and clasps from her hands, leaning in to kiss her fully.

"I love you, Joe," she murmured through connected lips, as they sidestepped away from the windows to the bed. The mattress took them out at the knees and they fell to the side, still wrapped around one another. Claire began to laugh, which never failed to get him going as well.

"I love you, too," he said, once their laughter subsided. They untangled their clothing and tangled into each other, their room alit by the tapestry of stars beyond the window.

CHAPTER 54

IT'S NOT SOON ENOUGH

If the Arrivals area was synonymous with anticipation and bliss, the Departures level was its opposite. They'd stretched their goodbye to the point of admonishment by the airline staff, being told that if they continued their "canoodling," Claire would miss her flight. By their body language, neither would have minded that scenario. One more day. One more hour, even.

During the time in the mountains, they'd taken steps along the path of all long-distance lovers: how, and when, to shorten the space and time between them. They'd done so tentatively at first, neither wanting to risk sounding too eager, too invested. Yet Joe—to complement an increasing retinue of out-of-character acts—admitted he'd begun quiet research on London, along with an overall evaluation of his practice.

The long-term vision had always been to grow to the point where Joe was just the "name on the letterhead," spending his time on client relationships rather than logistics. Absent of his own relationship, he'd been able to prioritize professional expansion. The goal had been to be working as little or often as he desired by his forties, with the business growing at a steady rate with or without him. Thanks to his early efforts, the skills of his team, and his investments outside of the practice, he was well ahead of schedule. The crew was able to steer the ship handily without Joe's physical presence, as evidenced by his spontaneity of late and the ability to take two weeks away during peak investment season.

He'd told Claire early in their courtship of his plan to take a six month sabbatical to hike the Pacific Crest Trail. He lately wondered aloud if perhaps that time might be just as well—if not better—spent roaming the trails of the UK. He also wondered aloud if that time was better spent in this year, instead of the new millennium. He'd begun researching apartments close to her. He'd looked into an international driver's license. He estimated it would take six weeks to get the appropriate wheels in motion, the right bases covered. Thanks to all those years of single-minded focus, of planning and deliberation, he'd determined he could easily take an overdue sojourn starting in April until about October. The summer was typically a slower time anyway, with the couple months before and after spent gearing down and back up again.

And before long, he realized he'd spilled far more information during that particular dinner than he'd ever intended, and searched her face for any hint of reaction.

"I don't know what to say, Joe," she'd begun, as his heart sank.

"It's too much, isn't it?" he'd asked. "It's too soon. I must sound crazy. I must *be* crazy."

"No, it's not that," she'd said, reaching her hand to interlace fingers with his. "It's a couple things, I suppose.

Would this mean you'd be giving up your trip to the coast next year?"

"If I gave that up, it wouldn't be for this reason."

"Because I wouldn't feel great about that. It's one of your dreams."

"You are my dream, Claire."

She blushed and smiled. "You and your *lines*, Joe."

"These are no lines. It's entirely the truth."

"Anyway, that's the first thing. So you'd still be able to make the hike next year?"

"If I wanted to, yes. It wasn't what I planned, but business—and life—has been good to me." His eyes danced between hers. "What's the second thing? It's too early, isn't it? To be that close? I know I should have broached this with you before I started looking into it—I mean, this is probably well-deserved, full-on freak-out material—but I assure you I didn't do anything beyond look into it. Haven't signed anything, haven't made any moves. So if it's too soon I hope you'll feel entirely comfortable telling me."

"Well that's just the thing," she said, moving her hands to his collar and pulling him across the table for a kiss. "It's not soon enough. These six weeks are going to be intolerable."

"Well, let's see what we can do about that, too."

CHAPTER 55
SOMEONE TO SHARE IT WITH

"WHAT'S BEEN GOING on? Have you fallen head over heels for someone, or what?" Dawson said.

The only thing Joe's team knew for certain about their notoriously private leader was that these last months had been markedly different, his predictable patterns becoming unpredictable.

"I mean, we can handle it, you know we can—we were just expecting this for next year, and it's not like you to plan something in such a short window of time." Dawson had that 'give me *something'* look on his face, but Joe wasn't biting—at least not yet. He grinned across his desk at Dawson, sitting in the office in which he'd spent less and less time these past weeks.

Much as it wasn't his style to discuss personal matters any more than it was to plan a six-month sabbatical in six weeks, Joe still felt an irresistible desire to act on yet another cliché of the newly in-love. He wanted to shout it from the rooftops—previously cringe-worthy behavior to a man who looked his younger associate in the eye only months before and declared that "true love never fails."

"I met someone, yes." The smile remained, but Joe attempted to keep his words and tone measured.

"I *knew* it!" Dawson shot up from his chair and paced the office, stopping short of pumping his fists in the air or taking a victory lap. "I knew it! I knew it. I kept telling Karen and Janice that you must have met someone; that even the great, hard-hearted Joe Riley might have actually fallen for someone." He paused. "Sorry, Joe. That makes it sound like we talk about you behind your back as some cynical ol' codger." He winked. "Although you kind of are. Or were."

Joe continued smiling, fiddling with the oft-tinkered-with but never completed Rubik's cube on his desk. Though he wanted to let the words fly, he was enjoying making the younger man pry for them.

"So? Come on, gimme some details. Who is she? Did you meet in London? Is that why the six months away?"

"I want to be cautious, Dawson. It's still early in this thing, and I don't want to have to do what I see others do—I won't name names," Joe said with a wink. "But I want to forego the scenes of spilling my guts only to have to later mop up and rationalize and justify everything said earlier."

"So you're in love? Is that what you're saying?"

Joe smiled.

"I *knew it too!*" Though Dawson had sat back down a moment before, he returned to his feet. *You'd think he was the one in love,* Joe thought.

"Well, I know you're not gonna say anything," Dawson continued, "you're not gonna cough up anything voluntarily, and without the verbal equivalent of a crowbar

I'm not going to get much more out of you. Knowing you, you'll wind up married and we'll only find out one day when you're asking us to prepare your tax documents for you. But I want to tell you," Dawson put his palms on Joe's desk and leaned in, nearly out of breath, "this is good news, man. I am happy for you."

"Thank you, Dawson. I do appreciate that. Though I might have expected this enthusiasm more from Karen or Janice. I thought you were still nursing the broken heart from Kerri."

"Says the man who's been *'nursing a broken heart'* in the form of cynicism and scorn for almost twenty years," Dawson shot back. Just as quickly, his hand shot up to his mouth while his eyes went wide. "Sorry, boss. That was uncalled for."

Joe leveled his eyes at Dawson. "It's all right," he finally said. "I'm sure I've said some things over the past years that were uncalled for as well. You're right. I turned a wound into a scar early on, and it's unfairly tainted everything since."

Dawson sat back down. "You're right, too. I am still licking my wounds from what happened. But it's been worth it."

"Really? You could have fooled me."

"Really. She broke my heart, sure, but in the end that meant I got to know love, for a time. And it was beautiful, even if the ending wasn't."

"That's a hell of an enlightened way to look at it, Dawson."

"Well, I'd rather look at it that way than close off my heart for the next couple decades." He threw out his best

Cheshire-cat grin, though his eyes momentarily darted away from Joe's. "Seriously, man. I'm just really, really happy for you. Love is crazy, sure. It's wild. It's irrational. But I'll be damned if it's not the best thing that ever happens to us, when it happens." He paused, embracing this moment of being the Zen master to the relationship rookie before him.

"I mean, look at the work we do here," Dawson continued, "It's good work, I know that. I'm not saying it's not. It's important. It has value. But have we ever had any of our retirees come in and say that the *'best'* thing that ever happened to them was this planning? Their money? Of coming up with a roadmap and never deviating from it? We know they're grateful, they're certainly happier to be in a position of security than wondering if they're going to run out of money before they run out of life... But that's rarely, if ever, been the underlying motivation that drives most of them."

"Pray tell, young Dawson, what *has* been the motivation?" Joe said, enjoying the moment of letting his associate have *this* moment.

"Love, ol' Joseph. Always love. Family. The person standing beside them at the end of it. The journey. I think we're sent here... and at first, we're separated. At first, we *want* to be separated; to find our own way, to make our own mark. But I think we're sent here not only to find our path, but to find the person we want to walk that path with."

"Wow. Look at Dawson Metzger, waxing poetic about life and love on a Tuesday morning," Joe grinned.

"You can continue to wax cynicism all you want, boss,

but I believe that's when we've come back home—when we find the one we want to walk with. Look at all the old guys and ladies we work with, how distraught they are after the love of their life passes. Think of how many of them pass on within a year of their partners. I can think of at least three. You even said one time that it happened with your grandparents. But in the meantime, the one left living comes here to see us not because they need financial advice, but because they're just trying to pass the hours they would have spent with their best friend."

"Or maybe they're just lonely. They don't know what to do with themselves after becoming so dependent on another human being."

"I'll let that one slide, since I'm guessing your old miserly habits are tough to break," Dawson grinned while shaking his head. "But I can see the truth of it when I look at you these days. And no, I don't believe it's because they're *lonely*, exactly. I mean sure, they miss their person. But I believe it's because they experienced how good life can be when you *find* your person. And they can't wait to get home again."

"That's awfully optimistic for a guy who's had his heart smashed at least—what, twice? three times?—in the last few years."

"That's just the name of the game, Joe. How are you supposed to find that person without putting yourself out there? How are you *ever* supposed to find them by keeping your guard up, by just 'visiting the island,' as you've been fond of saying and doing?" Dawson paused, measuring Joe's reaction. "They're certainly not going to fall out of the sky or arrive on our doorstep, is all I'm saying. Anyway, I hope you've found your home, Joe. It's about time."

Joe let out a laugh. "Are you saying I'm getting old? You're at risk of sounding like my family."

"Not at all. I meant it's about time, in the sense that you have everything else. But you haven't had someone to share it with."

"All right. Fair enough. I'll accept that with a 'thank you.' Now go on, get out of here," he shooed away Dawson with a grin. "We've got a lot of work to do."

The younger man left, and as his thoughts turned to Claire, Joe felt a twinge of fear. He was definitely in that 'out there' place Dawson spoke of, standing with his guard down. What if she didn't feel the same, after a while? What if all the fears she'd voiced—and he'd tried to temper—became reality? What would he do after all this time of trying to find Claire, if he lost her?

CHAPTER 56
STOPPING THE SPIN

Though Dawson certainly intended encouragement and hope, Joe was suddenly plagued by doubt. What on earth was he doing?

Let's replay the tape, the previously-silenced committee members would say. *Yes, you found her. Against all odds, you did. But that wasn't even three months ago.* Only a season before, his life had been progressing along a definitive, mapped-out path, and now he was making moves to drastically shift course. Over a woman he was still getting to know, and who was getting to know him. It was easy to make decisions when things were easy, when passion was plentiful, and there hadn't been enough time to make mistakes.

He'd had such certainty when beginning his plans for abroad; the excitement hadn't left room to imagine anything other than a beautiful outcome. For her part, too, Claire seemed confident—there was less of the reticence or attempts to push him away as there had been those first visits in London. Yet he couldn't help wondering if now, in downtime away from their relationship, if she too was haunted by quiet doubt or fear. Would she feel like he was encroaching on her life? Would he end up feeling like a stranger in a strange land, out of his element and longing for home?

If the Official Opposition of his internal parliament seized the opportunity to move from the backbenches and shout their (not entirely unreasonable) arguments, members of the (for the moment) governing party were quick to raise their own reasoned discourse: this was a temporary move. It wasn't even a move, per se. He wasn't pulling up stakes on his home life and relocating on a complete lark—far from it. Business would continue to run on its own back home, so there wasn't even a financial impact. He'd researched leasing out his condo and had already received vetted applications from potential tenants, thus offsetting the rent on any of the flats he'd been looking at in Claire's neighbourhood.

Officially, he'd still be going to England with the aim of hiking and seeing the neighbouring countries. As they began their dance around the logistics of his stay, Joe wanted to ensure Claire didn't feel an intrusion into what had finally become a fairly ordered life in the aftermath of her marriage. He'd suggested he could spend three or four days of each week going to this location or that, seeing the local sights. He'd return to his flat the other three or four days, where the two of them could spend at least the weekend together. Or at her place, or whatever worked best with her life, which had infinitely more demands than his. He wanted to be able to see her—simply be around her—as much as possible, while balancing her need to work and be present with her children. He wanted to cause the least amount of upheaval to the four lives apart from hers; lives that had witnessed enough chaos these last few years.

In that vein, David continued to renege on visits with the children, citing 'business,' as usual. After the third desertion, though Claire accepted this as a matter of course, Audrey cornered Miranda after spotting her at the local grocer's and demanded to know what was really going on. Miranda burst into tears, at first trying to elude the conversation. After seeing Audrey's contempt change to concern, Miranda became a pool in the breakfast aisle.

Their trip to Florida had been a disaster. David had taken a liking to an actress from one of the interactive theme park dinners, and over the following days while his adopted family queued for rides he would offer to get food or drink, using the time to seek out the ingénue. It took less than a couple days for his charm to take hold, despite the nearly twenty-year age gap between him and the young American. On a day when they were scheduled to go to Universal Studios, David cited food poisoning, complete with his own acting performance. He told them to go on without him, and after they'd safely departed he'd had the Marilyn Monroe wannabe to the hotel for the six hours he knew Miranda and her children would be away.

He'd somehow managed (and subsequently admitted to) seeing the young woman on at least three other occasions during their stay, and since their return had made two trips back to Florida, also citing 'work.' "Plenty of opportunities to secure adverts from resorts trying to attract Brits," he'd claimed. As if those departures weren't enough, he'd arranged an all-expenses-paid trip to London for the actress. It was during this latter liaison where Miranda finally followed through on the gut feeling that had plagued her since Florida. After he'd professed an urgent demand to work through another weekend, even claiming the need to sleep on his office couch, she'd followed him. "I know David has that compulsion to make his job sound like the most brilliant and vital at the entire paper," Miranda said to Audrey, "but I couldn't reason why an ad-man would need to work extra hours at the office like that."

After arranging a sitter for the children and calling his office from a nearby phone booth to make sure he was actually there (he was, at least for that moment), she'd stood across the street from his workplace, shrouded by trees and vehicles. Under an umbrella in the freezing rain, she waited to see if he departed, and for where. David eventually appeared, and in what Audrey knew must have been one of the lowest moments of Miranda's life (though this humiliation in Sainsbury's couldn't be far behind), she'd trailed him to the nearby Ritz Carlton.

He hadn't given any indication of knowing he'd been followed, causing Miranda to consider he might have been there for a legitimate work meeting. Her gut told her otherwise—her *own experience* told her otherwise (the admission of which, Audrey could sense, pained Miranda deeply). Yet for an instant, she'd been overcome by the same impulse that assailed most casualties of infidelity: the overwhelming need to believe it wasn't true.

She'd waited an interminable amount of time in the lobby of the Ritz, sopping wet despite the umbrella, feeling no better than a lost dog escaping the rain. She sat in one of the plush lobby chairs and stared out the window at the blissfully ignorant passersby, a hand over her mouth, tears colliding with the raindrops still on her face, wondering what to possibly do next.

She eventually approached the front desk, doing her best to appear poised. She told the clerk she was Mrs. Bradley, even producing identification, and that she had lost her key somewhere. After endless clacking at the keyboard—a time where Miranda felt oddly like the guilty party—the staffer finally smiled and produced a replacement card. Miranda sheepishly mentioned she'd forgotten the room number, again expecting some kind of morality police to appear and haul her away on several counts of paranoia, but the clerk merely wrote the room number on the key folder and wished her a wonderful stay.

She arrived at the assigned floor, her heart pounding at what felt like three hundred beats per minute, her pulse sonorous in her ears to the point she could scarcely hear anything else. She tiptoed to the room despite the hallway carpet, trying to still her breathing as she leaned an ear to the door, hearing nothing. In a final moment of coalesced anxiety, degradation, suspicion, hope and hopelessness, she'd finally, slowly, swiped the key through the reader. She watched the red light turn to green and heard the locking mechanism shift. She pushed against the door, hoping she was going to suffer merely the humiliation of interrupting David in the middle of a business deal.

"I knew I'd had this coming," Miranda said to Audrey between sobs. "I knew this was the price when you started a relationship from an affair. That this was my penance. But still, Audrey—and I say this *knowing* how much I've hurt and betrayed Claire, you, and the children—still I hoped so desperately that my gut feeling ever since America was false. That a lost sale, and whatever argument that might start between us, would be as bad as it would be."

And there he was, and there *she* was... and fast-forward to these many weeks later, Miranda asked to be spared from recounting those particular details. By then, even Audrey's anger had dissipated; she was certain the devastation Miranda had endured of late was more 'penance' than she deserved. David was the one who deserved far more than he'd yet to receive, and continuing to eviscerate Claire's former best friend wasn't going to change that.

Claire recounted this to Joe, and his first thought was of her children. Wondering what it must be like to have a man in their lives who couldn't be more unambiguous about where his loyalties lay—which happened to be with whomever lay under him for the moment. While Joe hadn't the first clue of the immediate or lasting impact this had, he knew the *last* thing he wanted was to be another source of disruption. He'd mentioned this to Claire during a phone call, and in the absence of body language remained uncertain of her reaction. He didn't know if she'd agreed to be agreeable, or because she also felt it best that Joe maintain distance while being near. He wondered if perhaps this talk of family and upheaval planted a seed of doubt within her, too.

In the face of these unanswered questions, the committee members advocating hope reminded him of the forces that brought them together. Such an improbable joining of two hearts had to mean *something*. The very mechanism that brought Joe and Claire to one another defied rationality, and while these internal proponents weren't inferring he abandon reason altogether, they did suggest that if practicality was the guiding force in human relationships, it would stop the heart long before any couple ever walked down the aisle. If he was supposed to listen to reason alone, he would have never changed his flight destined for California. Would never have seen the playbill for an art show thousands of miles away from his reasoned life. Never felt a tap on his shoulder that changed his life, and his heart, forever.

Yet he remained conflicted and uncertain, and now every action to arrange another detail for his summer across the pond elicited as much anxiety as previously aroused hope. He found himself nervous to talk to Claire, and recalled her fear of one day between calls eventually becoming two—and knew he had to stop the spin before it became any worse.

Joe poked his head out of his office and asked Dawson to prepare a package on Corporate Taxation and Business Overhead Expense insurance. It was time to call William Hollings back in for another appointment.

CHAPTER 57
PEACE IN THE PARADOX

"Do you want my honest opinion?" William asked.

"Of course."

"Yes, telling her about the circumstances under which the two of you met is something that needs to be addressed, one way or another. My general practitioner, novice psychotherapy assessment is that it will eat at you if you don't. But—"

"Knew there was a 'but' coming, even if I have no idea what it's leading to," Joe said with a smile.

"I think your concern about telling her is just window dressing."

"How so?"

William leaned forward on a bony elbow, a smile spreading across his face, alighting the twinkle in his eye. "Joe, let's face it. Relationships are the scariest shit in the world. And you're scared shitless right now."

The profanity startled Joe. "Woah. I wasn't expecting that."

"I know you weren't. I was employing an old trick to

get you out of your head, which is where I suspect you've been spending too much of your time lately."

"That's a fact," Joe sighed. "I feel like the last six months have been a big pendulum-swing from one extreme to the next. I've either been overwhelmed by my mind trying to sort all this out, or by the way I feel about Claire. Especially when I see her, or talk to her."

"Relationships aren't for the faint of heart," William said with a wink. "But that's why they're better suited for that organ, rather than the one between our two ears."

William leaned forward in the leather chair. "Joe, you can grab hold of any one of the excuses you mentioned earlier, and they're all reasonable, they're all relatable. She lives too far away. It's too soon. She has three kids, you have none. You don't even have pets or plants to take care of. She lives in an entirely different country—on an entirely different continent, for crying out loud. You feel unprepared for all of it. This wasn't planned. The circumstances under which you met is the stuff of fantasy, and she has no clue, at least for now." William leaned back, ran a hand across his scalp, sending a shock of grey in myriad directions.

"But again," he continued, "that's all window dressing for the one thing that's really holding you back."

Joe sensed William was waiting for him to respond to the cue. "Which is?" he finally indulged.

"You're afraid she won't love you back. You're afraid you'll fall more than you already have, and there might come a time she won't meet you there."

Joe decided not to pick up this prompt.

William's tone softened a touch. "Joe, I'm not pulling

the ol' 'with age comes wisdom' crap and saying any of this to sound smarmy or sententious. Sometimes I wonder if the only thing age offers is an opportunity to keep making more mistakes, and pile up more regrets. The question—or one of many, I suppose—is what we choose to learn from those mistakes." His eyes glassed over and drifted to the windows.

"I've made a ton," William said softly, turning his attention back to Joe. "And I continue to make them, so on that basis I don't know how qualified I am to say much of anything to you. But I can speak of the regrets I have, and you can feel free to take what you will from it."

"By all means," Joe said.

"Many moons ago, Joseph, I was married. I didn't quite meet my wife in a literal dream like you, but she was my dream woman, I can tell you that much. But in the midst of me playing God with my patients, career, and in every other area of my life, it ended. Maybe those things—the patients, my practice—were just circumstances, however. My 'window dressing,' so to speak. I wonder if my marriage didn't survive because of an unspoken need I had that for every fraction of love I gave Ellie, I demanded she reciprocate at least in equal measure. At *least*."

"How do you mean?"

"I suppose that's just a superfluous way of saying I loved conditionally, Joe. I always loved with an 'if' or 'when' and 'then' attached. *'If'* Ellie does this or that, then I will reciprocate. *'When'* she says this or that, then I will say it back.

"And I learned the really, really hard way that when

there is a 'when,' that isn't love at all, Joe. It merely leads to the inevitable of there being no more 'thens.' One day she'd grown tired of always going first in order for me to react in kind, and then that was it. 'Then' became simply that she'd gone, and I was too late." William's gaze had once more gone out of focus, lost to some point on the horizon.

Joe waited a moment before speaking. "I'll concede I am afraid of what happens next, when I go there. What if we've only worked as a couple so far because of the distance? We don't have time to see one another's imperfections, or be annoyed by idiosyncrasies. What happens when those things emerge?"

"Are you saying you're only willing to love Claire while she's perfect?"

"No, of course not."

"I think you need to be honest there, friend. Everyone says they aren't looking for or expecting perfection, but if that were true the divorce rate wouldn't be fifty percent, or whatever it is. Are you being fully honest about that? Right here and now, in this room, between us gentlemen where you have nothing to lose. Will you love Claire only if she's perfect? Take a moment before you answer."

Joe looked out the window, seeking out the mountains between the skyscrapers. He inhaled deeply, felt his eyes darting as though searching his mind for hidden nooks where deeper truth might reside.

"No," he said finally. "I took a moment as you kindly admonished, William, and looked for what I knew to be honest. Even as that search began, I felt my heart shouting a definitive *'No!'*, but I continued to listen for any voices outside my heart that might suggest otherwise. But I can sense there is a conflict there. Maybe not a conflict, actually, but a fear. Lots of them, really," Joe said with a laugh.

"Fears of what?"

"Of all the things you mentioned, I guess. How will I react the moment we have our first significant conflict? Will I be as magnanimous then as I feel now? Because when I look at my track record, that's never really been true. The moment things have ever become remotely difficult in any relationship, I've been out the door.

"And if I get really honest about it, I suppose the deeper level of truth is I've always had one foot out, anyway."

"Do you think you're doing that here?" William asked.

Joe felt his eyes dancing once more, as though the answer might be in the room somewhere. "No," he finally said again. "If anything, I'm further in than I've ever been. But things have been relatively easy so far. Everything is still so new. We're both loving openly, and—by appearances, at least—unconditionally. But maybe I'm actually as you described, and when things get hard, will I lean in only to the extent that she does? I honestly don't know." Joe leaned back, ran his hands through his hair, rested them behind his head and sighed. "I called this meeting for you to *help*, William, but now I wonder if you're making it worse," he laughed.

"I thought you called this meeting because you wanted to discuss 'over the head insurance,' or whatever your associate called it," William winked.

"You've freaked me right the hell out." Joe turned in

his chair, leaned his elbows on the desk and his head in his hands. "Just like that, the honeymoon phase is already over."

"No, good lord no," William said, straightening up in his chair and leaning toward Joe. "That's horseshit. As someone far wiser than me once said, 'the only meaning something has is the meaning we give it,' or something like that. You can freak yourself out—or even blame me for that—but those are just stories. The 'honeymoon phase' you're in can continue forever, if that's the story you choose to write. But in order to do that, what I'm trying to tell you is you need to be clear about the way you feel, and how you plan to love this woman. Can you do that?"

"I'm entirely clear on how I feel about her."

"Which is?"

Joe laughed. "I'm in love. Head over heels. I thought that was obvious."

"It is, but what isn't clear is if you understand what that means."

"It's my turn to say *'Which is?'*" Joe grinned.

"It means you go first. In all things. No matter what. You make this journey across the ocean, as you're already preparing to do, no matter what your fears tell you. You don't wait for every circumstance in your life to be right. More importantly, you don't wait for all the questions between you and Claire to be answered. You just go.

"You go first on showing her who you are, even if that means you'll be the first one to be imperfect. Because that will create the space for her to be imperfect as well, and that's when you'll *really* start to know and love one another. You don't wait for her to ask before you tell her the things you're afraid of, or the things you're no good at, or the ways in life you've failed. You just give her *you*, and either it's enough or it's not—and if it's the latter, then that has nothing to do with you. There are a million complexities in the realm of human relationships that either make people suited for one another or not. But you don't wait to show her who Joe Riley really is out of fear she might not love what's there. That's loving from a place of 'if' and 'when,' and as I said before, Joe, that isn't love.

"You go first, always. You don't wait. And finally, that means throwing out any sort of a checklist. If—and here's the only time I'm going to bring 'if' or 'when' and 'then' into it—if you really love this woman, then you cast aside any notions you've had about what makes for a perfect relationship, or the right circumstances, or the ideal partner. You don't force Claire to fit into a box, because that isn't how human beings work, and that's a love based out of expectation. All will be well for a time when she seems to fit, but at some point she won't—and the thing that most people are *actually* afraid of will happen: that means you won't fit, either."

William leaned back in the chair, running fingers along the stubble of his chin as though at a beard that wasn't there. "But love has never been about constructing some kind of immovable paradigm and trying to find a person that seems shaped for it. Love is about shaping *yourself* to meld with another human being. I'm not talking about changing the essence of who you are, or bending over backwards to please someone. I'm talking about making a decision to love this woman honestly. To love her fully. Love her for who she is, and let her see who you are. Love her no matter what this relationship throws at you. That's the only way a relationship survives and thrives. Whatever the questions are, whatever the challenges may be, love is always the answer. Without conditions. Without expectations. And where both of you choose to go first, no matter what."

"Wow."

William broke into laughter. "Guess I just threw not just a fastball at you there, but the whole ballgame's worth of pitches."

"No, it was good. It was good. I needed to hear it, I think. Although I'm not sure how both of us are supposed to go first."

"That's one of the many paradoxes of life and love, Joseph. The best I can tell you is to try to find peace in the paradox."

Joe smiled and looked down at his hands folded in his lap. "'*Find peace in the paradox,*'" he repeated, quietly. "I've always treated women as though they were an island in my life—somewhere nice to visit from time to time, but separate from everything else. I've rationalized that with a whole host of excuses: I was too busy building a career, I was watching all the 'mistakes' friends or clients were supposedly making. When it came to anyone I met, I'd tell myself they weren't the 'right' woman, so why would I ever make them a part of the rest of my life?"

"Are you asking me?"

"No, it was rhetorical. I suppose all those things held some validity to an extent, but listening to you speak made me realize a couple of things."

"That you'd like to kick this old man out of your office? That you ought not take advice from an old divorcé?" William flashed his impish grin once more.

"Neither. I realized that that kind of attitude meant those relationships never stood a chance. I realized that although it's been a very long time since I used the word 'love,' it was so very conditional when I *did* use it. 'If' they did this, 'then' I would do that, as you said. And mostly I realized that for the first time, I *don't* feel any of those things: wanting to keep Claire separate from my life, or that business—or anything material—is more important, or that she's not the right person. I'm feeling the opposite, and so as you said earlier, I am scared shitless."

"I wish I could give you a roadmap, Joe, or a plan like you provide. 'Do these things and you're projected to wind up here.' But love defies all that. It forever challenges, and forces us to grow—whether we like it or not," William chuckled. "And it's the scariest thing in the world when you suddenly have something—and more importantly, some*one*—to lose. So I wish I could say 'do this, do that,' in the sense of offering some concrete, measurable actions, but that's not how it works.

"But what do I know; I'm a sixty-eight-year-old man who lost his great love while I was too busy waiting."

"I'd say that means you know a fair bit."

William straightened in his chair again, his expression becoming as dire as Joe had ever seen it. "You go to her, Joe. And you throw everything you have into this. I'm by no means telling you that's a guaranteed recipe for success—if I knew what that was, I'd have written a book on it by now and retired with a much larger portfolio. But

I can tell you what *doesn't* work. Fear. Waiting. Expectation. Anything less than listening to the whispers of your heart.

"You love this woman. You know you do, and it's evident, no matter the timeline. I don't know nearly as much as I wish I did, but I do know you'll be an old man like me someday—far quicker than you can fathom—and if you don't throw everything you have into this, you're going to be sitting across a desk giving some younger buck advice on what *not* to do. A life full of accomplishment, maybe, but a heart full of regret."

"Maybe you ought to write that book after all," Joe said.

William ignored this. "I think we also have to remember what brought you to her in the first place—and the guise under which you began this conversation today. Much as I may have called it 'window dressing' earlier, it plays a big part in this… just not as an excuse for fear."

"How do you mean?"

"I know you've likely turned this over time and again in your mind, but you'd do well to remember what's at work here, no matter how improbable it sounds. You dreamt of a woman whom you'd never met, but turned out to be out there. Despite enormous odds, you managed to find her. I can't even begin to speculate what engineered that, and I don't know that you're ever going to get an explanation. But I do not—even for a second—think that whatever it was that brought you together did it just so you could get your heart broken. If this whole situation doesn't fit the bill for 'meant to be together,' then I don't know what does. Normally that's always just hyperbole, but your story is as close to that statement being built on fact as I've ever known."

"Now that you've mentioned it again—and instead of telling me how scared I am," Joe said with a grin, "can we get back to the part about advice on how to tell her?"

"No."

"No?"

"You're on your own there, son. Because if I was in your shoes, I'd probably crap my shorts thinking about it, too." William burst into laughter.

"Well. That's wonderful. Thank you for that, William." Joe swiveled his chair toward the windows again.

William leaned forward once more. "If I haven't thrown enough cornball at you so far today, then I'll do you one more. Listen to those whispers of your heart that I talked about before. It always knows. It'll give you the words."

"This would be a whole lot better if *you'd* just give me the words. You've given me the words for every other damn thing."

"It might be *easier,* but it wouldn't be better. Just listen. You'll know."

CHAPTER 58
DELICATE DANCE

Joe and Claire continued to talk by phone. For the words they weren't yet brave enough to say out loud, they exchanged via email. Joe did his best to heed William's advice. Claire cautiously moved closer, trying to release her fear that at any moment he'd stop calling, stop writing, stop saying 'I love you.' The weeks passed with tedium; Joe even took to crossing off days in a calendar, keeping a literal count. He'd never been one to do anything of the like, believing it better to stay in the present than daydream about a future unavailable to him. Yet he could hardly wait for a future with her.

There was a brief oasis in the middle of the six weeks where he once again took an airplane to her, and they'd taken up residence in his accustomed accommodations, not even leaving the room during the forty-eight hours he was there. They made love more times than could be counted, and shared more words, feelings, and thoughts than they could possibly recall later. Still, he hadn't found a way to tell her about the dreams. He was finding more reasons to excuse why he shouldn't. Claire held onto a few things as well.

Officially, Joe prepared plans for each week of the six

months ahead: every week another exploration of somewhere new—Scotland, Ireland, France... even as far as the Scandinavian countries part of his family hailed from. All reservations were fully refundable, however, and retained the option to add a companion, should Claire's schedule permit.

Unofficially, Joe's only plan was to be as close to Claire as her life and heart would allow.

David had all but formally relinquished any parental responsibility, his newer life with Miranda in flames as he carried on romancing the American some twenty years his junior. He'd entirely fled his now-fractured family with Claire's former best friend, in addition to the previous one with Claire herself—seemingly unaffected by the distinction that at least in the latter case, the children were his own. Audrey was pushing at Claire to take official steps to remove him from the legal picture entirely. While Claire had always maintained full custody, David possessed enough rights at present to make a mess of things should his whims ever swing around. "Might as well strike while *his* iron is hot," Audrey had said, suggesting he'd be more amenable to signing whatever Claire served in front of him while he was distracted by the aspiring starlet.

Joe continued to insist he not be another unwelcome disruption to her life or those of the children, with Claire insisting he wouldn't be. He wanted to take no part of her life and schedule for granted, however, and for the time being they planned to spend every Thursday evening through Monday morning together, once he'd returned from wherever the weekday adventure had taken him.

In their conversations they continued the delicate dance of the newly in love, but the prevailing feelings were those of anticipation, hope, and the beauty and ineffability of falling further in love. Between the endless hours spent planning logistics for business and pleasure, Joe counted the minutes until their next phone call, until he could hear the voice that elevated his heart rate. Every call, every letter, was a deepening of the imprint they were creating as a new, combined entity. The formation of the home coming to be known as 'Joe & Claire,' where they made new rooms together.

Those were the longest six weeks of his life, waiting to build this new life with her.

CHAPTER 59
THE RULING PARTIES OF LOVE AND HOPE

IT WAS A beautiful spring.

Joe was grateful his reservations for rental cars or train fares or hiking permits were refundable; in those first weeks, they hardly left his flat. Claire took most of his first week in London off from work, and would come to him after the children began school. She'd leave during dinnertime (with Joe occasionally joining her) and returned once Ainsley and Holly were settled, staying overnight and leaving early before the kids awoke. In the weeks following, as Claire reluctantly left for work during the daytime, Joe went about acclimating to his new surroundings. Getting to know the neighbourhoods and shops, the difference between a high street and whatever the others were called, and navigating the tube system. He napped, prolifically and uncharacteristically, as their nights witnessed nearly as many sunrises as twilights. He wasn't sure how Claire managed, but they were both running on the seemingly inexhaustible energy of new love.

There were dinners in upscale restaurants, and Chinese takeaway in bed. Some evenings were spent at the theatre, others at home with a hardly-watched DVD as they cuddled up on the couch. Neither seemed to care about the circumstance; it was enough to breathe the same air, to share the same space. Joe felt a lightness that was unfamiliar, one he was sure he'd never known. He'd never felt more alive.

Their early experiments with having Joe at Claire's house had gone well. Jackson even began to make regular appearances, talking to Joe about hiking; the boy had a neglected interest from the days his father lived under the same roof, taking his son on semi-annual excursions. Jack proffered input on the most "brilliant" places Joe ought to check out during his time abroad. Should he ever get past the London city limits, that was, which had yet to happen more than a couple of occasions since his arrival.

Ainsley readily adopted Joe as her aide-de-camp whenever he was around. If one had asked the young lady whom Joe had come to visit, she likely would have declared Joe *her* guest, available to mingle with other household members only when she was forced to follow such ridiculous parental demands as washing up before dinner or—heaven forbid—go to bed. Of the latter, Joe became her de facto storyteller, Claire having been abruptly removed as that particular dignitary. Ainsley announced that Joe told the stories much better; that his voices were funnier, if for no other reason than his accent. In the hours preceding bedtime, Joe was variously her hide-and-seek partner, teatime socialite (though he barely fit onto the tiny chairs of the tableset in her room), expert fort-builder, or stalwart neighbourhood explorer.

Holly remained lukewarm, though no one expected differently, particularly in the wake of David's latest abandonment. Claire and Audrey attempted to stimulate conversation between the middle child and Joe, but he'd finally taken the grown women aside and suggested that although he was far from the expert, he was content to let any relationship develop on Holly's terms. As the season progressed, so did Holly's monosyllabic dialogue. Claire nearly rejoiced when Holly graduated to compound sentences, including rare questions directed toward Joe. The first time she'd asked him about Canada and the mountains, the three adults beamed. When her trademark scowl was momentarily replaced one evening by a smile—witness to Joe's chronic misfortune in board games, after yet another booting back to the start of Sorry!—they'd nearly fallen out of their chairs.

These weeks were a honeymoon for the two lovers, although at a slower, smoldering pace—the demands of Claire's daily life never taking a moment off. Yet it was enough to know they were never more than a few blocks of distance or a few hours of time away from one another. Joe observed years of hardened, cynical notions falling away; couldn't remember how or why he'd felt them in the first place. There remained only this woman now, who'd swept *him* off his feet simply by who she was. He hoped to do the same for her, whether in the grandest of gestures or smallest of moments, touches, and words between them.

She was the most beautiful woman he'd ever known—in the face, the body, and most acutely in mind and heart—and somehow, she'd been drawn to him after he'd been brought to her. Love had never felt so easy, so effortless, and he hadn't the first clue what he'd done to deserve this. He was quite certain he hadn't done anything, which made holding onto the miracle seem even more important. For whatever trepidation occasionally made its shouts from within, these were easily dampened by the feeling that their love had somehow been ordained, somehow destined. *When one's matchmaker is the stars,* he'd think, *it's not ours to question why or how.* The dissenting internal committee members had either resigned, or been censured by these ruling voices of love and hope.

He knew, long before he'd ever admitted it—even within his own thoughts, let alone out loud to Claire—that he wasn't going back home after the summer. Certainly he'd need to physically return for a time; if he was to heed the whispers that had begun mere weeks into his residency abroad, there would be innumerable phone calls, endless meetings, and mountains of paperwork that would demand time and attention.

But he *knew*, even if it defied every conditioned and ordered thread in his body. Now that he'd found Claire, Joe wasn't about to let her go.

There was only one problem.

CHAPTER 60

WAVERING

In early June, Claire arranged an extended long weekend for her and Joe to go to Scotland, while Audrey looked after the children. Joe wanted to hike a section of The Great Glen Way, with the route holding special interest for her as well. It was the trail she'd hiked in her teens which led to the decision to see more of the world, ultimately leading her to Canada. She hadn't returned to these highlands and was eager to walk the trails alongside her love, seeing the path with a new set of eyes.

They'd left London on Thursday, taking the train. Rail travel was somewhat a rarity in Canada, and Joe wanted to experience this local for-granted mode of transportation as much as possible. The novelty was less for Claire, though she adored watching him look out the window like a little boy, as the countryside rolled past. They arrived in Inverness late afternoon and checked into the famed Culloden House. After adding to their growing history of candlelit dinners in beautiful locales they retreated to the bedroom, making the most of the hours between twilight and an early morning wake-up call.

All had gone well that first day of hiking; they shared

an affinity for stopping whenever something caught their eye, or at waypoints recommended on the maps they carried. Even setting up camp turned into play, as did so much else of their time. Joe had purchased a tent big enough for the two of them, but in his excitement at Claire accompanying him he'd neglected his customary pre-hike preparations—namely, a dry run on setting up their field accommodations. His attention was equally diverted that first night as he worked at raising the tent, watching Claire as she built the fire, the two of them lost in stories of one another, their history, their future together. In his distraction he'd at first constructed a shelter that looked as though it had been painted by one of the cubists: angles and lines askew, the roof jutting out to one side. On his second attempt he'd fared no better, and as they rolled out their mats and sleeping bags the structure collapsed on top of them. Claire burst into the laughter Joe adored, and before fighting their way out of the canvas they'd found each other first, kissing away more of the afternoon in a tangled heap.

On the second day, as they made their way along the high route beside Loch Ness, they'd stopped for a picnic overlooking the water. Earlier that morning Claire had developed a slight drag in her step, which hadn't gone unnoticed by Joe. When he asked, she brushed it off as tightness and fatigue in her leg, professing it was nothing more than the result of years since her last overnight hike.

As they finished packing up from lunch, Joe took a moment to photograph the water and breathe in the mixed scents of the hills, trees, and lake. He heard Claire's voice from behind him. The tone that was always so relaxed and poised was replaced with a wavering he'd heard only once before.

"Joe... Joe, I think I need help."

He turned to her, seeing the turquoise eyes looming with tears. She was sitting at the picnic table, left leg straddled over the bench seat and away from the table, right leg still tucked underneath—her hands grasping her thigh.

"I can't—"

She looked down at her hands, pulling at the pant leg that refused to budge. She looked back up at Joe, and the water at the edge of her eyes spilled over. "I can't move my leg."

CHAPTER 61
WE'LL WALK THIS PART OF THE PATH TOGETHER

No matter what they'd tried, nothing brought back controlled movement. Claire laid on the ground while Joe flexed and stretched her leg. They attempted bearing weight with her arms supported on his shoulders. They elevated her foot on the picnic table bench as the afternoon light cast lengthening sun glitter off the loch behind them.

She had feeling in the leg, but it was scattered and inconsistent. No matter the messages sent by her brain, the couriers in her nervous system apparently abandoned the routes between her hip and toes. After trying all they could think of, Joe took out the map to look for the closest waypoint toward civilization. Toward help.

In contrast to some of his hikes in the Rockies, here they were usually less than an hour away from a road or township. Joe mapped out a trail breaking off from their main route that would take them into the town of Drumnadrochit. According to the scale on the map, it was around five kilometres from their location. Claire urged him to go for help without her, assuring him there was no harm in her continuing to sit and take in the sights. "There are far worse places to be stuck," she said with a nervous smile.

Joe knew—as he had come to learn these past months together—that in all areas of life Claire sought never to be a burden or demand. A lifetime of self-sufficiency coupled with a malignant marriage had steeled that resolve, and this moment now was tantamount to her worst nightmare. Not the loss of control in a leg, but the reliance upon another human being. Upon a partner in a relationship, in particular. He knew that despite the outward show of strength—yet another facet of her heart and mind that he loved—she was likely combating an internal mix of mortification and terror. No matter the words these emotions brought forth from her lips, he wasn't about to leave her.

Joe located a branch in the forest detritus, wrapping one end in layers of his clothing. With this makeshift crutch they began the slow, five kilometre trek into town. Claire was supported on her left side by the branch and working leg, with her right arm wrapped around Joe's shoulder and his arm around her. On their first attempt to move, her right leg dragged behind like driftwood. They hadn't made it more than a few steps before Joe set her down gently and furnished a sling to partially elevate her foot, to avoid catching over exposed roots and rocks.

He left his pack at the picnic table over Claire's continued protests, unable to shoulder it and her at the same time. He listened with a smile to her rationale for prioritizing his goods over her wellbeing, finally saying, "I know your internal committee is suggesting I ought to choose a backpack over you. Or a career. Or a different life. I know it's pushing you to push me to choose those things, before there might come a time where I won't choose you. But I'm telling you, Claire—and I'm going to keep telling you, as long as it takes—that that's not going to happen. Let me love you... and if that means for the moment having you wrapped into me during these steps along the journey, well, I'm definitely going to take it."

She looked at him with eyes that spoke a million words unsaid. He responded with a kiss, availing himself of the advantage of having her tied into him. When their lips parted, he said, "Claire, I know the last thing you want to feel right now is needy, or like a burden. You're neither, nor will you ever be. I know you would walk on your own if you could. But you're my love, and we'll walk this part of the path together."

CHAPTER 62
FREEZING THE MEMORY

They returned to Inverness by car, as it was home to the nearest hospital. Claire argued vehemently against this, saying she would follow up with Dr. Lewiston when they returned to London. She asserted this was no different than flare-ups of the past; that Jacquie would order the usual tests to rule out other causes and conditions, and then up the doses of her levodopa and other therapies.

Joe was hesitant to argue or accede to the idea, asking how she meant to handle the immobility in the meantime. She contended that crutches would be sufficient. He countered that this would likely involve dealing with a medical professional anyway—unless she meant to continue with this most fashionable stick wrapped in his undershorts and shirts. She half-laughed at this, but Joe could read defiance in her expression—not toward him, necessarily, but of the entire situation.

He nearly deferred, thinking she knew how to handle the scenario better than he, asking only how long it usually took before movement returned to her legs. She lowered her head, and when she raised it again Joe saw her defiance laced with surrender. She said that she didn't know, as this was the first time she'd lost full movement. Joe then asked how she wanted to handle it if her left leg went as well, and barely heard her voice when she replied, "We better go now."

At the hospital they ran the battery of tests Claire was accustomed to—bloodwork, urinalysis, and an MRI. Joe and Claire waited in a curtained-off ER bed between tests, reading one another the latest articles of scandal from a copy of The Mirror that Joe found in the gift shoppe. Joe offered his own editorial while recounting the travails of the Spice Girls or Gallagher brothers, providing a stationary edition of the Alternative History he'd curated on their first date. He claimed he was a brother to Noel and Liam, but had been kicked out of the band in the early days due to his unsung (pun fully intended) talents that eclipsed the better-known Oasis kin. When Claire begged him to sing a line or two, he said his days of putting millionaire rock 'n rollers to shame were behind him, to say nothing of the commoner. The indignant smile he received in return came as close to dissolving the stress of the moment as any of his absurdities.

He taught—or at least attempted to teach—Claire how to play gin rummy with a deck of cards he'd also purchased in the shoppe. This quickly devolved as Claire would lay down embellished poker hands instead of the sets and sequences for gin.

Mostly, Joe spent the time between hands of cards or freestyle editorials trying not to look concerned, while searching her eyes and expressions for any hint of what she might be processing. *A dream would be useful right about now,* he caught himself thinking. He knew that at least then he'd have a sense of whether she felt as brave and nonchalant as she looked and spoke. He listened as she told the attending medical staff about her history, composing herself as though this was just another viral infection that would run its course.

In the end Claire was discharged after a few hours much as she'd predicted, with firm instructions to follow up with her physicians at home. This appeared to be another exacerbation of her condition—standard in that it didn't appear to be anything new or different, but concerning with the severity of it. The freezing she'd experienced tended to occur more often in the middle or advanced stages of Parkinson's, and was less common only four years after diagnosis. Not that anything about Claire's situation had ever been conventional.

The hospital provided purpose-built crutches, while the staff commended Joe on his improvised one. He chartered a car and driver back to London so Claire wouldn't need to negotiate train station stairways or platforms, and so he could focus on her without distractions of tannoy announcements or other passengers.

It was in the car that Claire allowed the emotion she'd guarded to finally flow—at first in small streams, and eventually in a quiet flood. She kept apologizing for cutting short his trip, his love for the trails and woods and water. He kept answering that she'd cut short nothing, and it didn't matter where they were, or what they were doing. What mattered was her. It was the first time they'd been able to hike the paths together, to sleep beneath the stars with one another. No matter what had occurred, he was grateful for these things—his gratitude even more that they'd been together when her body refused to rise from the table. He told her that this would be what the trip meant to him, what he would carry in his memory.

The memory would have to be enough.

CHAPTER 63
DOCTOR'S ORDERS

IT WAS A summer meant to begin with new love, new experiences, new memories, new joy. In many ways it was, but as with much of the past year it took a different form from what Joe had planned.

After the episode in the Scottish Highlands, Claire's mobility returned to normal—for a time. She followed up with her doctor and went through the now well-rehearsed routine, continuing to rule out concurrent conditions while adjusting medications and redoubling physical therapies. Dr. Lewiston also advised against further disruptions to routine, advocating for at least a return to regimented days and nights. As a friend she was torn on this front, having not seen Claire this happy in longer than she could recall, but cautioned that too many late nights and disrupted days weren't going to mollify a nervous system already in conflict. Claire, in a moment of innocent fear, asked if her romance had somehow caused this escalation. Jacquie replied that it most assuredly had not. There were still so many unknowns in the treatment of PD, but in the meantime, being in love alongside consistent lifestyle factors certainly wouldn't hurt.

On this subject, the couple was briefly pushed to an

edge. Claire tried to insist Joe didn't need to take this on after taking half a year off, and Joe insisted he hadn't expected—nor even wanted—a flawless, storybook experience. He wanted Claire: time with her, or at least time *near* her, and if that meant predictable routines—well, he was about the last person to find that a hindrance. "This isn't what you signed up for," Claire countered one night as they laid in the darkness of his flat. "I signed up for you, and whatever that means," he'd replied, and for a time, that was enough to pause the conversation.

Claire rarely had the energy to do more than manage the simpler demands of a day. Her stamina had already been in decline from the disease itself, and stooped to new lows while her body coped with adjusted medication and therapies. She tried to shrug off this latest regression and adhere to a normal work-child-exercise-life routine, but by the time she dropped the kids off at school she was already fatigued. An attempt at a full workday compounded with a loss of appetite left Claire scratching at already-depleted reserves by early afternoon. Her attention and focus were scattered, with even the smallest of decisions overwhelming. Yet for whatever internal complaints she might have had, she voiced these to no one.

This attempt at normalcy lasted all of a few days before Audrey placed a covert call to Dr. Lewiston, stopping just shy of demanding that the physician order Claire on sick leave. The doc ordered it anyway, and while this sparked a lively and heated kitchen-island discussion between the two sisters (Joe looking on but staying out), Claire acquiesced almost in relief. She was beyond exhausted, and in what she hoped was merely a physiological adjustment to a new treatment plan, her body was short-circuiting on a regular basis.

Tremors sporadically but frequently assailed her hands, making work of any type difficult. Whether via fatigue or dehydration or just a pure, kicking-while-down side effect, she was now nursing pounding headaches from sunup to sundown. Though the writhing misfires in the rest of her body were occasionally painless, she often had the feeling of being zapped—as though internal messengers were trying to ignite a muscle into movement, only to send sparks off the flint in random directions. There were aches and burning sensations that shifted through her body as if mimicking the weather maps on television. At times, the pain was sharp. At others, a feeling of numbness wracked through muscles and nerves as though they'd been asleep for years, the pins and needles nearly unbearable. Though she desperately fought against it, bed rest became the norm—and the reprieve—during the first couple weeks of forced sick leave.

Audrey was at the ready with the children, but it was Joe who took up this mantle while the kids were still in classes. He'd been practicing driving on the "wrong side of the road" during quiet nights in the London suburbs, and avoided any close scrapes other than his first attempt to make a right turn, where it felt like brushing his teeth with the wrong hand and one eye closed. Audrey accompanied him on the first few drop-offs and pick-ups, but once he'd memorized the routes and routines he'd become the children's de facto chauffeur, much to Ainsley's delight. Jackson and Holly remained largely silent on this transition. Audrey assured Joe that the young man spoke to no one in the morning unless compelled. Of Claire's middle child, Joe respectfully assumed she still viewed him with a healthy dose of suspicion. None of this stopped him during the drives from breaking into Spice Girls hits with Ainsley, however, to the visible chagrin of the older children.

After a couple weeks of routine and the lowest amount of activity Claire would permit herself, there was improvement. The side effects from the medications abated and the freezing and tremors lessened. She'd been able to hold down more food and hold onto the silverware without too much issue. At a follow-up appointment with Dr. Lewiston—Joe at Claire's side, meeting Jacquie for the first time—Claire asserted both her willingness and ability to resume a modified work schedule. A request the physician flatly denied.

"Why are you in such a bloody hurry to return, anyway? You have this devilishly handsome man available to you all day long, and a doctor's note to do something about it," Jacquie said with a smile, throwing up her hands at the same time. "If it takes me writing another doctor's note for a strict program of bedroom activity in order for you to feel better about it, I will, and you can tack it up on your wall. But otherwise, enjoy the time. Take it."

Claire voiced half-hearted objections, less about Jacquie's comment and more toward a body and condition that sought to slow her down. They left the appointment and returned home, and before the kids were back (Audrey assuming pick-up duties on this occasion), Joe and Claire followed doctor's orders.

CHAPTER 64
THE PRIVILEGE OF LOVE

JUNE FADED INTO July, and the school year's end saw the days turn to adventures with the children. A couple hours at first, then an afternoon, and when Claire showed few (or at least manageable) symptoms, full days. Whether at another landmark or oceanfront or city park, Joe resumed his mantle of Dubious Tour Guide, delighting Ainsley with his misbegotten facts, and successfully convincing her of at least half. From the older two, he achieved only requisite eye rolls and groans. Though at times, a small, crooked smile from Holly.

Joe watched each flip of the calendar days with quiet anxiety. His sabbatical was going by in a blink, his Canadian life and career feeling more and more like a dream. There was a weekly conference call with the team back home to keep him informed of any developments. Of which there were none, really; it had been business as usual, and aside from a handful of couples retiring little had transpired above regular client needs. He'd known his team—balanced between Dawson's exuberance and Janice's experience—would be able to handle any demands, and Joe hardly thought of work in the ninety-some days he'd been abroad.

Of his repatriation, he'd refused to give it any more thought than necessary. He found himself unwilling to devote time to anything that would take him away from moments with Claire, collecting these as though deposits into a mental bank account should he ever need memories to draw from. In every shared space was a moment he hadn't known he'd been waiting for these thirty-some years, but now that he was here, Joe didn't care if he held a glance a moment too long, or a smile until she finally asked him what he was grinning about. There never seemed to be an adequate reply; the best he'd mustered was, "I don't know—it's just... You're here." A poet, Joe most certainly was not, but within his heart were written indelible sonnets even when the words remained elusive and unexpressed.

It was the little moments he loved the most. The way Claire dabbed the corners of her mouth with a napkin after they'd devoured a box of takeaway in bed, her movements graceful as though they'd just had dinner in a royal residence. The way he felt her body start to laugh long before he heard it from her lips, as they watched movies while pressed into one another on the couch. The quiet clicking sound her throat made sometimes, as they lay in bed with her head on his chest, safe in silent reflection with one another. *I'm the only man in the world who gets to hear what that sounds like,* he would think.

In those moments, he couldn't compose a better description of what made intimate love so perfect—what the poets and playwrights had long sought to capture.

Except it wasn't found in the grand profession of love from the man on the ground to the girl in the balcony. It was in these moments here. These things no one else got to hear or know. He knew what the soles of her feet felt like when she pressed them up against his under the sheets, trying to find warmth. He knew what she looked like with her hair damp from a shower and cascading along the top of her robe, the secrets of her body just underneath. This was the privilege of love. The honour bestowed only to him.

He didn't know how he was supposed to board a flight departing these things ever again. He knew he couldn't. And so in late July, on what his team thought would be a routine conference call, Joe spoke aloud the idea that had been dancing quietly in his heart for weeks.

CHAPTER 65
ACROSS AN OCEAN TO FIND YOU

THE REPRIEVE WOULDN'T last.

Claire's new treatment regimen worked for a time; she felt balanced and even energetic throughout the summer weeks. With her doctor's cautious assent she'd returned to work on a modified schedule, starting at three hours per day and attempting to build from there. Though she felt conflicted by the desire to enjoy time with Joe and yet return to the passion and drive of her career, what Claire truly sought was a feeling of normalcy. Something to make her feel like a contributing member of society and of her own household.

By August, however, the tremors returned like lightning storms throughout her body, attacking at whim. The episodes were sporadic and severe enough to make any sort of routine unpredictable and even dangerous. Though Joe handled most of the driving, taking her to and from work and navigating excursions with the children, there had been an episode where she'd awoken before the rest of the household and decided—in another act of defiance against her body—to make a quick trip to Starbucks. Although the shop was only blocks away, a tremor that began as she reached for her latte became so violent that by the time she rounded the corner to her home she was driving with one hand, the affected arm useless weight along her side. Upon hearing this at her next appointment, Dr. Lewiston threatened to pull Claire's license should she try driving again before they managed to stabilize her symptoms. The warning was enough, and Claire hadn't attempted further solo voyages—though it wouldn't have mattered.

At the same appointment, Jacquie ordered Claire off work indefinitely, with any return contingent upon stability lasting months or more. She acknowledged Claire's desire to combat whatever was happening with as much normalcy as possible, and though that had ostensibly worked in the past, even Claire had to concede it appeared to be provoking things this time around. "This is a *very* malignant form of Parkinson's," Jacquie had said, cutting short arguments she knew Claire still wanted to make. "Your other physicians and I keep wondering if there's something else going on—if this is something else entirely—but the pathology doesn't conclusively point elsewhere. Apart from the violence of it."

There was a newer surgery making waves in medical journals and neurological circles, but it involved drilling holes into the brain. Neither a cure nor a way to stop the progression of PD, Deep Brain Stimulation was thought to be an alternative only if medication failed to mitigate symptoms. Claire hadn't been deemed a "suitable candidate" due to the limited history of her diagnosis and malevolence of symptoms. Professional conclusions aside, the prospect frightened Jacquie as much as

Claire—at least until there was greater evidence of successful procedures, and there was unequivocal certainty that this wasn't something like ALS or cerebellar ataxia. Unintended consequences from surgery were possible at the best and most benign of times, let alone when dealing with the brain, and the operation could potentially worsen her condition.

One by one, Claire was being robbed of the little pleasures, the for-granted activities of independence. Her daily yoga became a source of stress instead of peace, Claire never knowing when her nerve endings would begin to misfire during a particular pose. There was the embarrassment, too. Her fellow practitioners assured her that it didn't matter, and if anything this was a safe place to be and practice. Still, she'd eventually chosen to withdraw, opting for meditation-only classes if and when her body appeared willing to cooperate.

Along with physical renunciation of the activities and places she loved, Claire seemed to be withdrawing emotionally. Though he'd been at her side for every episode, every building block that was removed from her fundamental physiology, Joe felt like a helpless observer. He was never sure which of his efforts might exasperate her mental state as he walked a thin, indeterminate line of trying to be helpful. She received it all with dignity and gratitude, never doing or saying anything overt to make him second guess his efforts, but he could see the resentment in her eyes. Not toward him, he knew, but in having to rely on anyone for anything.

Time and again she'd said in all but direct words that he should leave. At the peak of a particularly bad stretch where entire limbs had gone unresponsive or misfired so poorly that normal motor function and independent mobility were out, she'd finally been overwhelmed. As Claire laid in her bed all but paralyzed, she told Joe to cut his losses while there was still time.

"Still time for what?" he asked.

"For you to get back to your normal life. For you to leave without guilt. This can't possibly be what you imagined your life turning into when you first boarded that plane to London." Without body language to support the words, her tone was resolute. "This has—or had—been a beautiful year, and I love you so much, Joe, but I think we need to start being realistic here, don't we?"

"What do you mean by that?" He sat on the edge of her bed, putting a hand on a leg that might or might not feel the touch. Whether or not it did, she didn't react.

"Last year we didn't even know the other existed. And now you're here, and it was wonderful—but what exactly do you think is supposed to happen from here? That I'm just going to magically get better, and in the meantime, you're going to—what, collapse your practice back home? We're going to move in together here? We're going to go there? What? What's supposed to happen, Joe?" She turned her head from his toward the bedroom window.

"Claire—"

"We've never really talked about these things," she continued, her eyes still fixed on some point beyond the windowpane. "It seemed like maybe we were both dropping hints about the future before Scotland, but then *that* happened, and we've never talked about it since. So maybe it's just time to be realistic." She met his eyes with hers and put a wavering hand on his knee. "I know you care about me, Joe, and I'm always going to look back on these months as a magical time in my life where you made me feel really loved, really cared for. But don't you think it's time to call this what it is, and we both go the rest of our journeys alone?"

"Are you trying to end things with me, Claire? Because I'm not going—"

"This isn't a pretty or delicate end, Joe, okay?" The tears came now, and her eyes darted from his. "This isn't some movie montage where I get delicately and gracefully sick, and everything is rainbows and roses, and tragic but beautiful. So far it hasn't been completely awful, but it's already been as good as it's going to be, and what happens next won't be pretty."

"Do you think that's what I care—"

"This is *wasting away*, Joe. They call it neurodegenerative disease for a reason. I don't care what Jacquie or the other doctors say at the appointments, about comorbidities or medications or treatments or hope. I know what this is. I can feel it. And nothing about it will be attractive, nothing will be romantic. This is shutting down, with last gasps from parts of my body before they go for good. You don't want any part of that, Joe. You came here for young love and I'm turning into an old woman before your eyes. Worse than that, even—a dead woman, in the body, while my mind is still alive. And as for whatever is left of that, well, I can't guarantee there's going to be much there worth holding onto.

"This won't be romantic scenes of you sitting beside

me at chemo appointments while we still talk about what we'll do if this all gets better. This won't be you holding my hair away from my face before it falls out while I vomit in the night, and me cuddling into you afterward for safety. Not that those things are beautiful either, but there won't be any talk of hopes and dreams here, Joe. One day the talk will cease altogether. Everything will go at some point, save for my eyes, and they've told me I can look forward to problems there, too.

"This is spoon feeds to a mouth that eventually won't be able to close, with a throat that won't be able to swallow. Then diaper changes and catheters and soiled sheets. This is lifting from the bed to the wheelchair and one day not even that. Then it's sponge baths and bedsores. This is a body that will one day look little more than a bag of bones, and that's not what you fell in love with, Joe. This—"

Whatever words she'd intended caught in her throat. Claire inhaled deeply and looked down at the hands she tried to fold in her lap. She'd closed her eyes, and Joe watched helplessly as tears dropped soundlessly onto her blouse. Claire swallowed hard and looked back up at him.

"This is a scene someday of me trying to say 'I love you' but not being able to get that out anymore, and I'm not going to wait for that to happen."

She looked back down at a blanket covering legs that, for now, could still take her from one point to the next. "I want you to go, before that can ever happen," Claire said, her voice barely audible. "I want to still be able to tell you, with my own voice, that I love you. But that also means I have to use that same voice to tell you to leave."

The ticking of a nearby grandfather clock was the only sound in the room. Joe could feel a lump in his throat threatening to choke away the air. The truth of everything she'd just said had become undeniable. A part of him had mused these things ever since the first reprieve failed and relapse ensued, but some internal mercy had prohibited the thoughts from rising to the surface. Joe wondered if this was the first scenario in his life that he *hadn't* tried to predict and plan, the first time he'd knowingly kept his head in the sand. The weight of what it could mean had been too much to bear.

"That will be enough," he finally said, his voice sounding as though invisible cords were pulling tension around his throat.

"What will be enough?"

"Your eyes. You said before that everything will go except your eyes. And that will be enough. More than enough. They were the first part of you I saw, the first thing I fell in love with. We both know the eyes always say far more than our mouths ever do, and as long as I can still see yours looking back at mine, I'll know. And it will be enough. Because even then, it wasn't just your eyes I fell in love with. It wasn't your body—though I certainly have no complaints there," he said, forcing a smile in the hope of seeing one from her as well. "It was the soul behind the eyes, the heart within the body. That's what I fell in love with, and that's what I'll never stop being in love with, no matter what happens to the rest."

She reached for him as though his shoulders were a life raft in waters that threatened to drown her within this room. She sobbed quietly, the only indication of it in the tremble he felt against his body.

"But how do you know?" she finally said, pulling away from his body to search his eyes. "How do you know? You've never experienced this before. You've never been with someone whose body suffocated them from the outside in. In the grand scale of our lives, we barely know one another, we've barely been a part of the other's life.

"I'm not going to get better, Joe. Do you understand that? It was always going to be a case of arresting this as well as we could for as long as we could, but it's looking like we can't even do that, anymore. I'm not going to get better. How do you know it will be enough? How do you know you'll still love me?"

"I know, baby, I just know. I can't explain how, or why, and I know the part we've been together has been just a blink compared to the time we were apart. But I was meant to find you. I *know* I was." He stood up, pacing the space along the foot of her bed.

"That's all well and good for a movie or a love story," Claire interrupted. "I believe we were meant to find one another for a time, too. But I don't think you're being realistic about how things are now, and how they're going to be. You're going to want to leave, and I'm trying to make that easier for you."

Joe could feel the colour rising in his face, his heart rate increasing. "Why do you keep trying to tell *me* what *I* want? Why do you keep trying to tell me all the ways I'm not going to love you, or not show up for you? You've done that since the beginning, and it didn't sit very well the first time, and it's definitely not sitting well now."

"Because one of us has to be realistic, Joe, and it certainly hasn't been you." The volume in her voice had elevated, the closest either one had ever come to shouting at the other. She caught herself quickly. "I don't think you're understanding the promises you're making. They're sweet, Joe, they really are, and you are too. The sweetest man I've ever known."

"Don't patronize me, okay?" He grappled to restrain his own volume as quickly as she had. "You don't understand what's happened here."

Her expression ran a gamut, first of surprise when he'd snapped back at her, then of wounding, then of confusion. She took a breath. "What do you mean, I 'don't understand?'"

His blood was still up, and the words escaped before he'd considered them. "I was sent to find you."

She searched his eyes, trying to decipher if he was being funny, serious, ludicrous, or something else entirely. "You're right. I'm not understanding, Joe."

"I was supposed to find you. Something brought you to me, and told me to find you." He was still pacing, not looking at her, sounding like a man possessed.

She pulled the blankets away and stood, the effort taking three times longer than it would have a year before. She caught him mid-stride and put a quavering hand against his cheek. "Joe, honey, I felt the same way. You know I did. Or do. The moment I saw you I felt like I already knew you. I'm not condescending, Joe, because I felt—I feel—those things too. And these are the beautiful things people feel and say to each other when they've fallen in love. I know you mean it, and it means the world to me that you do. I'm not trying to talk you out of loving me—"

"Yes you are."

"Okay. Maybe I am. That's fair. Because I'm afraid, Joe, and you know I have been from the beginning. I've had no evidence in my life that a man will stick around when life changes, and that was *before* I had a body that was shutting down. I didn't want to get hurt even before that happened, when I was still living with the wounds that you might not find me good enough, or would leave when something—when someone—better came along. How do you imagine I feel now?"

She waited for him to respond, and when he didn't—his eyes darting back and forth between hers—she continued. "Joe, you've put your life on pause for me. It's been such a beautiful gift. *You* have been such a beautiful gift." Earlier tears she'd suppressed welled up again. "If the universe has decided I'm now on borrowed time, I at least have that to carry with me. That I was loved—truly loved—and that I was enough.

"But that also has to *be* enough. I can't ask you to do more than that."

"Is that all love is?" he finally said. "Sticking around when things are going well?"

She let go of him and went back to the bed. "That's not what I was saying at all, and you know it."

"No, I don't know it. I don't know what you *are* saying. 'Thanks for the romance, but now it's time for you to leave'?"

"In so many words, maybe."

"How the hell am I supposed to feel about that? Even

though you're asking *me* to go, it's really you that's leaving, that's giving up on us. Just because you don't want me to see you suffer. You can dress that up all you like to make it sound noble and selfless, or that you're being realistic, or sparing me pain... but the reality is you're trying to spare *yourself* pain, while asking me to walk away from the love of my life. Have you even considered how that makes me feel?

"I'm standing here, right now, saying that I'll keep standing here, no matter what. That I *want* to be here. That I *need* to be here. That I'm *supposed* to be here. I don't know what more I'm supposed to do. And still, you insist on trying to make your prophesy of 'all men leave' come true, because of your bullshit reasons for needing it to be true. But I'm not going."

She reeled on him. "*YOU HAVE NO IDEA WHAT YOU'RE SAYING! You have this little, schoolboy crush, and this fancy that you're supposed to ride in and save the girl, but that* is not *what's happening here, Joe!*"

He felt as though she'd slapped him. "I'm going to pretend you didn't just say that."

"No! That's exactly the problem! We need to stop pretending this is more than it actually is."

"But it *is* more than you've ever realized."

"*How?* Tell me how. Since you seem to know so much, Joe, tell me *exactly* how you know."

This can't get any worse, he thought. *The worst that can happen is she thinks I'm crazy, shows me the door, and asks me never to see her again—and she's already doing all the above.*

He reached for her hands, having to pry them loose

from the tight cross she'd made over her chest. She fought his grasp for a moment, then acquiesced. He pulled her to the edge of the bed, where they sat down.

"There's something I need to tell you," he said. "I've been wanting to tell you for awhile, but I didn't know how. And then for a time I told myself it didn't matter. But maybe it matters now more than ever."

Her eyes made a frantic search of his, Joe guessed in an effort to decipher what could be coming next, or perhaps in trying to decide if she should force him out before she could be wounded further.

Before she could say anything, he said, "We didn't meet by accident, that night in the gallery. I had come across the ocean to find you."

CHAPTER 66

YOU WON'T HAVE TO, BECAUSE YOU HAVE A PICTURE

H E BEGAN BY describing the first dream: how he'd been in her kitchen, unable to make sense of words or sights. How he'd seen through her eyes—literally—with the experience so disconcerting that he'd been overcome with nausea and violently awoken. How the first visions were out of focus, and sounds felt like cathedral bells within his skull. And how, after the dreams persisted, he'd come to the feeling that she was a real person, somewhere in the world, living life parallel to him.

Joe told her of the 'remedies' he'd tried: sleeping pills, physician visits, meditation, psychologist visits, binaural beats, psychic readings, and of William—erstwhile doctor turned client, turned confidante, turned co-conspirator on the journey overseas. He told Claire how the dreams permeated nearly every moment of his waking and sleeping hours. How she'd been with him long before that first touch in the gallery, before first words were ever exchanged. How what began as confused meanderings of his subconscious (or so he had thought) made a quantum shift in not only his understanding of life and the universe, but in his heart and spirit. He told her of how he'd nearly given up, and were it not for a theatre production and a flyer for Audrey's show, he might have come within twenty-four hours and a stone's throw of finding the love of his life, only to turn back.

Claire's expression yielded almost nothing during Joe's avalanche of words. He assumed the traces of reaction he did see contained bemusement at best, outright rejection at worst. The less she said the more he pressed forth, defying all he'd learned about sales by throwing his proverbial cards on the table. He told her of the first time he'd seen her face, and though he hadn't recognized it then, how he'd begun to fall in that moment. When an eyebrow betrayed her stone expression by raising slightly, he'd been quick to qualify that at no point had he seen anything improper, nor anything he didn't believe he was meant to. One of his thoughts suggested she might have been more indignant at the shower-time intrusion, had she not thought the claim so ludicrous.

As they sat on the bed he reached for her hands, saying, "You haven't said a word, my love. You've barely reacted. I know this all probably sounds crazy."

She pulled her hands away and stuffed them under the bedding. "You *think* it sounds crazy, Joe?"

"Okay—I *know* it sounds crazy. But it's the absolute truth."

Claire remained silent. "I wouldn't lie about this," Joe continued. "Believe me, I was the last person this kind of thing ever happened to. I was the least likely candidate. Let alone to act on it, or speak of it aloud. But here I am.

Here we are." He paused, looking for any sign of feedback. "Say something, please, Claire."

She shifted—not without strain—and cleared her throat. "I don't have even the slightest clue of how I'm supposed to react to this, Joe."

"I know. It's wild. For thirty-eight years of my life things went in one almost undeviating direction, in every regard. Those dreams flipped everything on its head."

"Is this just some desperate ploy, Joe? And if it is, you certainly take the cake for the most originality, if not the most lunacy." She caught the look in his eyes and pivoted. "I'm sorry to say that, but this really is... something else." She began moving as though meaning to stand. *Probably to get up and get the hell away from me,* Joe thought.

"If you only had an idea of how crazy it feels to tell you—if you could only see through *my* eyes and feel my thoughts—then you'd know I was telling the truth," he said.

"So you've been spying on me, is that what you're saying? Not only have you been some kind of cosmic stalker, but you've been able to read my thoughts too? Joe, even if I could wrap my head around this and find some way to *try* to believe you, what of that? Am I supposed to feel chuffed that you'd been watching me for months before we met, that you knew all these intimate things about me... and furthermore, that you've kept all of it from me until now? What am I supposed to do with this, Joe?"

"No, no—I wasn't able to *read* your thoughts, I could just *feel* them, if that makes sense."

"No, it doesn't, but oh! That makes it *so* much better." *She's never been sarcastic with me before,* Joe thought.

He put his arms on her shoulders, the two of them standing now. She was clearly heading for the door. "Claire, baby, this is *me*. I'm the same guy you've known all this time. Think about it—why would I make something like this up? Why—of all the desperate ploys I could try—would I go with something that sounds this unbelievable?"

"You've got me there," Claire said, moving her shoulders away from his arms and brushing past him.

"Claire—"

She reached the bedroom door and opened it, standing to the side like an usher showing him the way out. "Joe, I think you need to leave."

"Claire, comeon, this is—"

"No. Please stop." Though her expression was stoic, as she cast her eyes downward he saw that they had begun to mist over. "I have no idea what this is," she said quietly, "but it's too much. I can't deal with this on top of everything else." She returned her eyes to his and swallowed hard. "I want you to go."

"Claire..." For the first time in his life Joe felt a compulsion to kneel. To beg, if he had to. He fought the impulse but took a moment to wonder how and why everything about their lives had begun to unravel. He looked into the eyes of the only woman he'd ever truly loved, and couldn't make sense of how she looked at him now like a stranger. An unwelcome one, at that.

She looked back down at the floor. "Please leave," she said, gesturing toward the hallway.

Joe's mind raced for words that might lead her to believe him, that might mend everything that had frayed in the last hour. He wished he had known her since they were children. He wished they had more history than what didn't even amount to a year. If they did, she would know he was telling the truth, incredible though it sounded.

He wished he could show her his heart, and then she would know. Not just the truth of what had brought them together but what would keep them as one, no matter the future, no matter the cost. Those things felt impossible now, as did any words that could salvage an entire world that had fallen apart in less than an instant.

If he wasn't mistaken, he could feel the heart he longed to show her come apart in his chest.

Joe reached for the coat he'd tossed on the corner of the bed. *This can't be how it ends,* he thought. *Whether she believes it or not we were led to each other, and whatever did that couldn't have meant for us to end this way.* He inhaled a neglected breath, glancing at her dresser beside the doorway. He looked at the frames along the top, pictures of Claire and the children. And the newest addition, a photo of her and Joe from their hike in Scotland. The two of them smiling, wrapped into one another without a thread of space between them. That moment felt more like a dream now than any that had led him here.

He looked at Claire as she kept her face turned from his. She was unmoving, her chest the only part of her body betraying a rare stillness as it hitched with stifled breaths. Joe took another breath of his own and began the steps between his body and hers, leading to the hallway beyond, and to a world outside that would no longer hold the two of them together.

As he passed her body he didn't know whether to pause, to touch a hand to her arm, to hold her one last time, or simply leave her alone. Long dormant committee members shouted for him to stop, to wrap her in his arms and say, *No, I'm not leaving, I'm staying here until we make sense of this and then I'm staying forever after.* He decided to respect the space her body seemed to be asking for. To give room for the part of her heart that must have been breaking, too.

Joe reached the stairwell at the end of the hall when he heard a sudden breath behind him. "I'm sure going to miss your face," Claire said, her voice broken.

He stopped, trying to gather himself before looking back. He forced a smile, hoping the tears welling in his eyes wouldn't show. He looked to her, his breath and words arrested as they had been from the first moment he'd seen her, and any moment she had come into view since. His attempt at a smile fell, and though he willed it back into place he looked downward. He knew if he held her gaze a moment longer the torrent behind his eyes would release, and the heart that continued beating for now—if only to keep him on his feet—would cease altogether.

"You won't have to miss my face, because you have a picture now," he finally choked out. He turned toward the stairs and started to descend.

"I beg your pardon?" he heard Claire say, after she tried to swallow the lump overtaking her throat.

He looked up from the stairwell, seeing her through

the railing. Though fibers within his chest tore apart quicker than he could contain and threatened to drop him where he stood, he forced himself to look at her, to try and capture this last glance. "I said, 'You won't have to miss my face, because you have a picture.'"

He feigned a last smile.

"I love you, Claire."

Joe descended the remaining steps and walked out into the London rain.

CHAPTER 67
MAYBE THIS WAS ALL A DREAM

He made the walk from her house to his flat. What normally took less than ten minutes seemed to stretch twice that through the rain. Joe felt as though he was trudging through mud.

He was sufficiently nestled in the shock of the moment to be buffered from its implications. He could sense the waves of emotion that would undoubtedly hit him later, but for now he felt almost numb. His mind raced. Certainly, one would get a 'do-over,' would have a second chance after such an abrupt end? This couldn't possibly be the way their great love came to a close. Yet some part of him—a reemergence of Uncle Peter and his unwavering pragmatism, perhaps—told him he ought to prepare for it. The moment when he'd paused to look at the face he loved might very well have been the last.

That thought unleashed the deluge, and as he ascended the stairs to his flat he felt the strength go out of his legs. He paused between steps, holding the rail, giving serious consideration to unraveling then and there. He might have, were it not for the possibility of being seen by one of the neighbours he hardly knew. This thought forced him to redouble his grip on the railing and lift legs that felt like dead weight. Somehow he made it to his door, fumbling with the lock and handle. By force of will he made it to his bedroom where he collapsed on the bed, still clad in his rain-soaked clothing. He felt at home neither in this place nor in his body. He could hardly breathe.

His mind spiraled within a cacophony of conflicting thoughts. What should he do now? Begin packing up? Make arrangements to go home? Call the office? Call his landlord? Stay and wait a day or two? Call the person he wanted to speak with the most? Run back over there in the hope this had all been its own, vivid dream? Maybe she would open the door with her gorgeous, wide smile, and there'd be no evidence of the conversation they'd just had. Maybe her body would be healed, too.

The more he sought a plan to handle this, the less his mind seemed able to grab onto any one thing, flitting from one dichotomous thought to the next. What he really longed for now was sleep, though it was the middle of the afternoon. Sixteen hours of unbroken, dreamless sleep. The best he managed was to kick off his shoes.

After an indeterminate amount of time, his mind having raced the world over but his body moving not an inch, he looked at the clock beside the bed. He rose and went to the small office within the flat. He sat at the desk, picked up the phone and dialed.

He lost count of the tones by about the eighth ring, but eventually heard the click of a receiver. There were further sounds of fumbling before Joe heard a voice on the other end. He finally heard a muffled "Hello?"

"I need your help," Joe said.

CHAPTER 68

IF FAITH IS A FLOWER

There was a knock at the door, and Joe stood from the sofa with a start. His shoulders fell when he opened the door and saw the lone figure standing there. He had hoped she would be with him.

William shook out the rain from his umbrella and offered a tentative smile. Joe wasn't sure how to read it. William moved past him into the hallway, kicking off his shoes.

"Well?" Joe finally asked, as William removed his overcoat.

"May I sit? I know that walk probably doesn't trouble a young buck like yourself, but for an older guy, I just need a breath."

Joe realized he'd been holding his own, and breathed in while William sat on the sofa. The older man removed his glasses and dried the rain droplets with his shirt.

Two days earlier, Joe had woken William with a desperate phone call. The bookstore proprietor boarded the earliest flight he could find, the same red-eye route Joe was so familiar with. The younger man rented a car and met William at Heathrow, and after attempts to mitigate jetlag, the plan had been for the retired doc to go to Claire's door earlier this afternoon. Joe had barely slept these last days either, exhausted with anticipation and feeling his patience strained as William took time getting comfortable.

"William. I'm dying here."

The older man raised his glasses toward the overhead light, checking for remaining water spots or smudges. Satisfied, he wrapped the wire temple tips around his ears and settled the pads atop the bridge of his nose. He cleared his throat as his eyes pulled focus on Joe.

"Well, let me start by saying I'm surprised I even made it past the entryway. Audrey was far less cordial than she was at the gallery. She's a feisty one," William said.

"That she is."

"I had to answer about eight thousand questions just from her—while parrying several threats to call the authorities or jackbooted thugs, whatever it might take to get me to leave—before I even saw or spoke with Claire."

Joe felt his impatience surging. "But you *did* see her? You did talk to her?"

"I did, yes."

"William, you're killing me here."

"I apologize, but I'm trying to find the words to describe what was the most surreal conversation I've ever had. Which is saying something, after these last months."

"Just tell me what happened. Doctor's notes. High level."

"She's furious. She's doubtful. She's scared, and still doesn't know exactly what to make of any of it. Her body and health are failing, and this almost feels like the thing that puts her ability to cope over the top. It's too bizarre, and in the midst of it, she's fending with a broken heart along with her breaking body. Quite simply, she's overwhelmed right now, Joseph.

"But..." William paused.

"But what?"

"But she's open."

"What does that mean?"

"It took all my powers of persuasion, and while I think there's not an insignificant part of her that remains wildly skeptical, I also think, in the end, more of her believed me than not. Her sister, too."

"What did you say?"

"It's difficult to recall exact details now—believe me, my adrenaline was running as though *I* was the man fighting for love—though that may have been the jet-lag..." William's eyes drifted to the rain-streaked windows.

"William, please."

"Yes." His attention snapped back. "Anyway, though I can't remember an exact transcript of all that was said, I simply started from the beginning. Often the easiest thing to do.

"I told her—them, really—about how you and I met. Your wandering into the store on a random day, no history between us. Of course, by discussing the store I felt the need to qualify and give a bit of my own background, lest they think I was some kook you hired—and I'm not entirely certain *some* part of them doesn't still believe that. I explained that the first time we spoke you were only a handful of dreams in, knowing nothing about

Claire or the family beyond what you'd seen, and you and I took the tack of deciphering the meaning behind it all as opposed to any notion she might be a real, living, breathing human being. I handed her your journal, and told her I even encouraged the additional entries documenting everything that led up to the dreams.

"I spoke about our relationship outside the visions. How I'd become your client, and putting the dreams aside, my experience of you was largely one of deduction and logic. That while you never struck me as anything other than perfectly sensible during that first conversation in the store, our experience of working together confirmed it. And as the dreams progressed, I observed an ordinary man thrust into an extraordinary situation through no machinations of his own, and you responded as sensibly as any human being would.

"I described how my medical practice was general family medicine and I didn't specialize in conditions of the mind, however I did see everything under the sun with my patients. With the store, I've continued to see all sorts of psychological archetypes. And nothing you ever said or did suggested a man who had taken leave of his faculties."

"How did they react to that? Was it still the two of them?" Joe asked.

"Oh it was most definitely the two of them; Audrey wasn't about to leave her sister's side. Again, I think the reaction was mostly skepticism, but there was also enough seed of doubt to keep the figurative and literal door open. Either this is the most senseless hoax perpetrated by a nearly middle-aged and certainly senior-aged man they've ever encountered, or there's some glimmer of truth in it. At best, I think Claire *wants* to believe you, and at worst, I think she might think—and I know this sounds patronizing—that at least *you* believe the things that you told her."

"Where do things stand now?"

"She said she needed to sit on it. It was a lot to absorb, Joe, as I'm sure you can imagine."

William rubbed at a chin flecked with grey stubble that never appeared to be shaved, but never grew longer, either. "One could think that with running the store I might have lost touch, a little bit. Head in the clouds, that sort of thing. But I think you know that's not the case, Joe, in spite of all I've heard across the counter over the years. It's actually been in large part due to *your* experience that I've been opened up like never before.

"But the point is, I still understand how it is for most people. There are no burning bushes, no angels on high—that we can hear, anyway—no parting of the seas. Most people go their entire lives without any experience of the paranormal. In truth, I don't think most people *want* that experience. So it's hard to hear, let alone believe in something that hits so close to home. It changes everything we think we know about this world.

"Faith and belief are one thing, but an event that bridges the gap of *evidence*... well, that's a whole other kettle of fish." William again stroked at an absent beard.

"Faith is in fact the rationale—or even the excuse—for our normal lack of evidence," he continued. "We're told that's what constitutes *true* faith: a belief or trust in the things for which we have no proof. So we get accustomed to that, we even get comfortable with it. We still long for God—or whatever it is that's out there, whatever it was that sent those visions of Claire to you—to settle the burden of proof. But around the same time we let go of our fear of monsters under the bed, we let go of that expectation—of that hope, even—that we'll ever have a direct experience of the divine. Or of anything that extends beyond our day-to-day understanding of the way things work, really.

"So I think when something like this happens, it confounds our ability to reconcile. It's the thing we want the most, and yet our innate need to understand, to rationalize, to conceptualize, to compartmentalize… these things balk. We don't want to be duped. We don't want to admit our hope only to discover we were set up."

"William," said Joe, "this is profound, and I appreciate it, I really do. But metaphysics aside, what did she say? Where did you leave it? You said she needed to sit on it…"

"Yes, she does, and I was trying to offer some solace as to why."

"It is helpful, I'm not disputing that. I'm just—though I hate to use the word—desperate to know what to do next."

"What you do next is give her more time to absorb this, and if I dare suggest, be grateful she's at least willing to do that. The National Health Service wasn't called to come after either of us, and for her part, she's having to engage in exactly that kind of faith I spoke about. *You* have the proof, even if you don't understand it, because *you* experienced the dreams. She has nearly nothing. She has a guy who showed up out of nowhere, swept her off her feet, and now she has a life that's falling apart and in the midst of it gets told by that same guy that she came to him in a vision. That he's effectively been spying on her without the credentials of MI6.

"All she has, if she's willing to grab onto it, is faith. And if faith is a flower, then time is its water, and trust is its sunshine. If the latter is lacking for the moment, you can at least give her the former."

"Wow, William. You've really outdone yourself with that one," Joe replied, his tone absent of derision. "I worry that we don't have a lot of the former, though, either."

"I worry about that too. I hadn't seen her since December, and only the once, but the change is... surprising."

Joe ran his hands through his hair, stood up with an audible exhale, and walked to the window. "So what do I do now? Tell me what to do, William. You're saying to wait... does that mean she's going to call at some point? Does that mean I go to her, eventually?"

"It means that you, too, need to grab onto that dirty F-word as well, I'm afraid. Faith, Joseph."

Joe laughed, though there was no mirth in it. "That feels difficult, when there's so much on the line. The love of my life. Wasted time. Finite time."

William stood and joined him at the window. "I'm not trying to tell you that you shouldn't feel exactly the way you do now. If I could go back in time to that place where the love of *my* life began slipping through my fingers, I'd do whatever I could to hold on, too.

"What I am trying to suggest, however—because if nothing else, it's all you *can* hold onto right now—is that for one more time, you have faith in the thing that brought you here. We've spoken about it before, but it bears repeating. Do you think that whatever it was that brought you two together would then sabotage the whole thing?"

"Maybe it wasn't the *thing* that sabotaged it, though. Maybe it was us. Maybe it was me."

William considered this. "Maybe. And maybe your fear is telling you it would have been easier not to tell her."

"Well it's certainly difficult *not* to believe that right now. She was trying to tell me to leave before that, yeah, but this made it a whole lot easier to show me the door."

"But what if—maybe—part of the story of Joe and Claire involved telling her? What if there's a reason she needed to know, beyond just simple honesty?"

"I don't know, William. I really don't. Again, I appreciate this, but I need to put away the bigger-picture questions right now. I just need to know what to do next."

"That's what I'm trying to tell you, but I can appreciate that you need a written prescription with a schedule. So for now, tough as this is to hear, you wait. At least for today. Give her the time she asked for. She promised me she wouldn't leave things hanging."

"Promised how?"

"She said that although me showing up to corroborate your story helped, it still wasn't what was giving her pause."

"What was?"

"Something you said as you were leaving, apparently."

"What did I say?"

"I can't remember the exact wording, but something about how she told you she was going to miss you, and you said that she wouldn't need to, because she had a picture. It didn't make much sense to me—if anything it sounded passive-aggressive—but she said she'd been thinking about it ever since. I wanted to get more detail, but she mentioned it while she and Audrey were showing *me* the door. Claire looked exhausted, like it would probably involve her last ounces of strength just to return to a chair or bed, so I didn't want to press. She told me that part, then said she would call—me, at least. Didn't want for me to have made this long trip just to be stranded in silence."

"I forgot I even said it," Joe said, his eyes dancing as he looked at the old man.

"What did it mean?"

"Ainsley said it, in one of the dreams. Claire had picked her up from school, and she was chattering away in the backseat while Claire drove. I missed a lot of what the two of them said, as I was looking for clues to where they were. Ainsley handed Claire an envelope with her school pictures in it, and Claire gushed while the car was stopped. A few minutes later she said something like, 'I'm so glad to see you, I really missed your face,' and Ainsley replied, 'Well now you won't have to miss it, because you have a picture.' It was cute and Claire laughed, and I've just remembered it ever since.

"It's something Claire says sometimes: 'I missed your face.' When she asked me to leave, I was walking out of the bedroom and my eye caught the photos on her dresser—ones of her and the kids, the kids on their own, including that school photo of Ainsley, and a picture of the two of us. So when Claire said it to me, I replied with Ainsley's words, almost automatically."

"Had the two of you ever talked about that before? Had she told you that story?"

"Not that I recall."

"Well there you go," William said, a huge grin spreading across his face.

"There I go how?"

"It isn't proof, by any means. But between that and your journal, it couldn't have hurt. It's insider information. It's not a burning bush, sure. It's not irrefutable. But it's something, and it just might be enough."

CHAPTER 69

THE HEART OF THE ONE WHO HELPED YOU FIND YOUR OWN

Chess games, card games, and rented VHS tapes filled the hours, if not the void of uncertainty pervading the apartment. William procured a selection of films not widely distributed in North America, proclaiming the superior artistry of British cinema compared to its Hollywood counterpart. The movies proved more entertaining for the old man, spared as he was from the distraction of acute heartbreak. Joe spent most of the time looking in the direction of the telephone.

"What do I do if she doesn't call?" he finally blurted during a screening of *Her Majesty, Mrs. Brown*.

William's gaze peeled from the television, having been enrapt with the performance of Judi Dench. "She will. She said she would."

"Yes but what if she doesn't?"

"She will." William was hunting between the chesterfield cushions for the remote.

"William."

The older man paused the video. "Joe, I know you know Claire far better than I do, but—and please forgive any unintended immodesty here—I usually get a good read on people. Came with the job—old and new, I suppose. She doesn't strike me as the kind of person to say something like that and not follow through, no matter how strange the situation. Just keep the faith, Joseph."

Joe buried his head in his hands. *"Oh for crying out loud. What the hell would you know about it?"* he muttered.

"Pardon? I didn't quite catch that one," William replied, ready to unpause the tape.

Joe turned to face him. "I said, *'What the hell would you know about it?'*"

"Excuse me?"

"For the love of god." Joe leaned toward the older man as though by adjusting his posture he could improve the acoustics in the living room. "I said *'What the—'*"

"Oh I fully heard the words you said. What I didn't understand, is that while I appreciate you're struggling—"

"You're damned right I'm struggling!" Joe stood, walked toward the window. "I don't even know what I'm still doing here. I don't know what the point was of me being here in the first place. And I certainly don't know what *you're* doing here."

"*You* called *me*, Joe, if you need that reminder."

"I did, but I called you to *help*, William. Not to have you come litter up my apartment with takeout boxes and blare the TV twenty-four-seven, and offer occasional pithy platitudes between bites and films." He turned to face the older man, daggers in his eyes. "*She hasn't called, William. It's been days.* You keep saying she will, and you wrap that assurance up in increasing inanities about the beauty and complexity of relationships, but what on earth do you know about it, really?"

Joe turned back to the window. "By your own admission, you lost the only love you've apparently had, so what would you know about it, anyway? How do I know that all the 'advice' you're giving isn't doomed to make things worse?"

"Hey. Asshole." The sound of the weathered voice prompted a start from Joe. William had risen from the couch and was standing directly behind him.

"Once again, I know you're struggling," William said, his tone stern, yet gentle. "I know, because in this one respect at least, I've been where you are now—wondering how things went wrong, and if it's too late to fix it. In my case, it certainly was.

"But regardless of how you're feeling, you're going to take a seat instead of taking it out on me." The mirth returned to William's eyes. "And by the smell of it, you're going to take a shower when this conversation is done."

Joe sat back down, propping his forehead on hands that splayed through disheveled hair.

"Do you know who the 'Kemp' was, in 'Kemp's Books & Wares?'" William asked.

"You said it was an 'old friend' or something like that, who got sick. You were the executor," Joe muttered.

"All true, though 'friend' might be both an understated and generous term. Ellie Kemp was my wife."

Joe lifted his head, his eyes regarding the old man

through spread fingers. "Why did you tell me she was just a friend?"

"Well, because by the end, that's all I could claim—and even then, maybe from her perspective that term was a bit of a stretch." William feigned a smile, shifting on the sofa that seemed to engulf his slumped shoulders. "And besides, it's generally not first-conversation appropriate when someone wanders into the store."

"First-conversation appropriate? I had just told you I was dreaming through the eyes of a woman I'd never met," Joe said with a sardonic laugh.

"Perhaps, but what was I supposed to say? 'Don't be shy about your dreams, son, and about what you feel in your heart. The old man you see before you used to be a young man who traded his heart for ambition, and in the end went from medicine to the mystical in what's probably been some misguided attempt to keep that love alive. To assuage the guilt at breaking both our hearts by choosing career over her.'" He forced another smile. "What does that make me? Probably a cliché, at best."

Joe adjusted his tone. "I don't know about that, William. I haven't met too many people who gave up their life's work for love, even if it was lost love."

The old man chuckled. "Before all this, I don't get the impression you met many people who were much more to you than the Gross Income line on their tax return." He raised his hands in defense. "I don't mean to trade insults with you, Joe."

"It's okay. You're probably right. And I apologize, for before. I am truly grateful that you're here."

The doc cleared his throat. "I know the last thing you

probably need or want right now is a sad-sack tale of regret from an old man, so I'll spare you the gorier details that have probably been universal to tales of lost love since humans first waded out of the oceans. Ellie asked me to choose her. Not choose her *instead* of medicine, but to be certain that my career was a means to an end—that end being us, and all that an 'us' entails." His eyes had begun to glass over, and William turned his gaze to the world outside.

"She wasn't asking for much—and it certainly wasn't an ultimatum—but she just wanted *something*. Something that might let her know she was chosen, she was worthy, she was everything I hoped to find in another human being. She asked me to choose her, Joe, and I didn't. I said—if not in so many words—that she could wait. *We* could wait. I argued that I just needed to get things off the ground, and there would be time for us later.

"She told me that later is never guaranteed, there is only now, and if I couldn't bring some level of dedication to us in the way I brought it to external pursuits, then what was the 'later' I was expecting to come home to? One where she'd still be sitting around? A life unlived? Waiting for a day when the door would open and I'd walk through and say, 'Okay, I took care of everything else first, and now I finally have time for you?' I didn't realize that if I had taken care of *us* first, the rest would have taken care of itself.

"I did open the door one day—far too late as always—and she was gone. She left a note saying she missed her lover and best friend, but she missed herself just as much while putting her life on hold waiting for a sign. Any sign that might suggest my favourite part of the day wasn't when I left in the morning, but when I got to come back home to her. She said she felt deeply that there had to be more than this—pursuit in the name of prestige, and a house full of things but empty of a soul—and so she was heading out into the world to reclaim hers. She said she hoped one day I would join her there.

"But I never did. Pride got in my way far too severely for far too long. I made our divorce difficult. I derided her attempts to 'find herself' and open the store. I hoped for its failure; that one day I'd come home and she would be back, having found only an avalanche of unpaid bills. I wanted her to be wrong. I wanted her to pay for abandoning us. I couldn't get over the idea that she could have gotten over me.

"I paid in full for that way of thinking, Joseph. I'm still paying for it." As William returned his eyes to Joe's, the younger man saw the cobalt blue irises buoyed upon a wave of emotion that the older man fought to restrain.

"You asked 'what the hell I knew about it,'" William continued, "and maybe you're right, I don't know much about what makes love work. Turns out what I know about practicing love is commensurate to what I know about the practice of science: figuring out what doesn't work. What isn't true.

"Ellie was the most beautiful woman I've ever known, Joe, in any possible way that description fits. And she was too good, Joe, she wouldn't give in to the resentment or pettiness or games. She was true to her word that she would find something more and would wait for me there—while not waiting around—but I never showed. Oh, I turned up physically, at times, arriving at her little store to park my Porsche out in front and flash my matching cufflinks and offer unsolicited updates about how I had accepted this board appointment or been published in that journal. She only ever smiled." William attempted his own smile at this, the rise of his cheek pushing a drop from his eye.

"I guess I thought that if I showed up at her door enough times, and paraded all that she was missing out on, she'd find her way back to *my* door. She just smiled, Joe. And one day, too many years later, she did walk through the *clinic* door. And though the smile was still there, I knew in a heartbeat that something was wrong. She certainly wasn't there to capitulate to what I thought I wanted. It was almost as though she was saying—although I know this would never have been her heart—'Okay show me. Prove that the life you traded me for is powerful enough to fix this.'"

William spoke barely above a whisper now. "And I couldn't, Joe. I threw everything I had into saving her—every therapy, every specialist, every waking hour I could find to the study of oncology—and still I couldn't. She still went, and I'm scared she left without knowing how much I loved her, or how much I missed her, or how I spent every night even before she got sick coming home from work knowing that no matter how many people I healed it wouldn't matter, because I had hurt her heart."

The tears fell freely now. "And you're not supposed to break the heart of the one who helped you find your own."

A silence engulfed the room. William eventually broke the quiet with a clear of his throat. "Anyway. I'm sure it's entirely cliché for me to say to you that I don't want you to make the same mistakes. Do I have selfish intent for being here? Maybe. Is it to fill your fridge with takeaway boxes and rack up late charges on videos from the newsstand? No. Is it because I see in you a man I used to be, and the chance for you not to turn into the man I am now? Probably. And perhaps that's entirely wrong, Joseph. Perhaps I have no right to be here, even if you asked. I know that you mending things with Claire won't bring Ellie back to me, or atone for my mistakes. I know it's unfair to hope that a piece of my heart will heal if the two of you heal yours.

"I know I ought not tell you that when I lay my head down at night, though I don't dream through Ellie's eyes—wherever she is—I do hope she can see through mine, and sees what's happening here. And I probably shouldn't say this either, Joe, but I *know* she does. I don't 'know' it in the way I know certain physics equations or prescription contraindications. But something tells me that she sees me. She sees my heart now. She sees you, and Claire, and this situation. And the same thing that tells me that, tells me that Claire will call."

Joe cleared his throat, swallowing the lump that had formed. "Maybe Claire just said she would because she was trying to get rid of you."

"Maybe, but I doubt it. Try to remember how much she had on her plate already, *before* you tossed that little grenade on the situation. Her body is deteriorating. She has three children, where on one end is a bundle of energy still of a really dependent age, and on the other, a teenager moving from one hormonal crisis to another. In the middle, one who longs to grow up by tomorrow without having to relinquish the childhood of yesterday. And they're all on summer break. Their father has fled to the US to pursue his version of the American dream: a young lover who doesn't ask too many questions.

"She's staring down some heavy, heavy possible outcomes here, Joe, and in the meantime she's trying to get herself in and out of bed without help. And she knows there's a chance that won't last."

"I know," Joe said quietly. "I guess that's part of why I brought it up in the first place. The easiest thing she could do right now, as it pertains to the two of us, would be to simply never pick up that phone again. So I'm really asking you; I do want your advice. What do I do if that's what she decides? How long do I wait until I accept this for what it is, and make my way back home?"

William considered this for a moment, fighting the drift of his eyes back to the screen and Dame Judi. At last he said, "I have an idea."

CHAPTER 70
JUST LISTEN

"**I'M REALLY BAD** at this kind of thing," Joe said.

"Just sit and listen. Not to what you hear here," William pointed a bony finger at the center of his forehead, "but to what you hear *here*." He moved the finger to the middle of his chest. "Call it cornball if you like, but if you do that, it's impossible to go wrong. I'm not saying she's going to automatically swoon and take you back, but *you'll* know. You'll have said what needed to be said, and left it up to fate after that. Which is all you can do."

Joe shook his head.

"What?" William asked. "Too over the top, even for me?" he said with a wink.

"No. It's not that. It's just... sometimes I'm just... *overwhelmed,* I guess is the word. Sitting here, right now, trying to find the words for the woman I've fallen in love with. Hoping to find them as fast as she might be falling *out* of love with me. Hoping to say the right thing so she knows I'm telling the truth. Knows that this really was the stuff of dreams. That I was the man lucky enough for this to have happened to, and that I was even luckier to have found her."

"See? You don't have a problem with the words." William put a hand on Joe's shoulder. "Remember: just listen. Turn off the noise you're hearing between your two ears, and then *really* listen. Whatever it is you hear will be enough."

CHAPTER 71
WRITTEN ON MY HEART LONG BEFORE YOU WROTE YOUR NUMBER

August 31, 1999

My love,

I don't know how to do this. I'm not sure how to find the right words, to say the right combination of things that will make you believe, that will bring you back to me. I feel like never before, in all of human history, has so much been riding on the ink that passes through a pen onto the paper below.

I want to be poetic. I want to sweep you off your feet with these words. I want you to feel safe, and protected, and I want you to know my love is true. And I have no idea how to convey that, aside from the inadequate words I've already written. But I've been told that if I listen to my heart, it will provide the way. I desperately hope that's true.

I'm not going to try to convince you that what happened is the truth. It is, but believe me when I say I know how improbable it sounds, and how impossible it must feel to hear it. I wish I could find a way to just show you, like some magic film trick where someone touches the hand of another, and they suddenly see their memories and feelings. But I can't, so I'll focus on what I can convey to you.

I think I fell in love with your eyes, first. The first time I ever saw them, they took my breath away—cliché though that may sound. It's true. I stopped breathing for a moment, and didn't realize it until I took in a breath however much time later. I'd never seen eyes like yours before—the way they seemed to glow with a colour that was almost translucent. See? I'm not great at this kind of stuff. I write that, and it feels too cheesy. But all at once it's true. It's what I fell in love with first.

More than what I saw *in* your eyes, I think I was starting to fall in love with what I saw *behind* them. I didn't know enough yet to know exactly what you were going through, but I recognized—in that wordless narrative the eyes convey—that there was unbelievable strength. Resolve. Patience. Humility. I was looking at the most beautiful woman I had ever seen, reflected in that mirror, but perhaps what I loved the most is that I knew *she* didn't know it—she was too modest for that. I saw character. I saw intelligence and determination. And just as it took me a moment to notice the breaths I hadn't been taking, it took even longer to realize my heart had seemingly stopped, too, before it began beating again with a rhythm I'd never felt before. It was as though it had just recognized itself in another. I don't know how to explain that any better than anything else in this letter, but that's how it felt. That's what happened.

I fell in love with your laugh. The way it slowly builds, how I can see it so often in your body before I can hear it. I fell in love with the way you look at your children. How when they talk to you, your attention moves solely to them, like whatever they have to say is the most important, breaking news you've ever heard in your life. More than that, I love that it's not just a front you're putting on. The things they tell you *are* the most important thing you've ever heard in your life.

I love the way you weave through life with grace and composure. And then I love how when you're overcome, the words just spill forth, flowing in a deluge you can't seem to help. Despite some of the difficult conversations we've had, or that I've watched you have, I've always loved it. Those are the times where I feel like I can hear the words your heart would say if it had the ability to speak all on its own.

You have the most beautiful heart I've ever known, Claire, and of all that I love, I know it's what I love the most. And for a brief time, for whatever reason, I've been the man who was permitted the honour of residing there with you. It has been the most beautiful time of my life, and my greatest gift. To think that it might be over now is a thought I can hardly bear, though I must.

I think the worst part of when two hearts come undone is our inability to know, in those last moments, that they *are* the last moments. If I had known the last time I kissed you was going to be our last kiss, I would have lingered a moment longer. I would have remembered every touch, every movement of our lips. I would have held you closer, and stayed in that embrace an extra minute. I would have tried to let you know with my body everything I felt in my heart. And if you could have known it, could have felt it somehow, maybe we would have never let go.

At the beginning of this letter I said I didn't know how to do this. I meant the writing, of course, but more than that I don't know how I'm supposed to let you go. These have been indescribably painful days, where my wounded heart has tried to tell me that the old line about "better to have loved and lost" is an old lie. But I know, even in the midst of this hurt, that it isn't. To have loved you has been my greatest privilege, and I would have held that honour the rest of our lives. I know that, now. I think I knew it from the first moment.

I wish I could see or sense what you've been feeling and thinking these last days. I wish I could see *you*. More than anything, I wish I could show you what I believe was written on my heart long before you wrote your number on the card I dropped that led to your tap on my shoulder.

I don't know what happens next. I don't know if this will be the last time any sort of words are passed between us, and as I read over them now I still fear they're not enough. But I want you to know, Claire, beyond any shred of doubt, that *you* were enough. I know you've lived a life where that has been called into question far too many times by men even more foolish than me, but I hope you know you were everything I ever wanted, and more than I knew I needed. More than I knew to hope for. You have been the great love of my life, and I'll be forever grateful to the stars that sent me to find you.

Your love,

Joe

CHAPTER 72
CALLING HOME

IT TOOK SOME time, but Claire eventually called. After Joe had agonized over the wording at least a half-dozen times, he'd sealed his letter and left it in the hands of fate. Or in William's literal, withered hands, at least: the good doctor delivering it to Claire's mailbox and playing a septuagenarian version of door dash—ringing and taking off in a not-too-swift shuffle.

"What I couldn't answer," Claire said later, "was *why* you would make something like that up." And although it hadn't served as the most unassailable piece of evidence when Joe quoted Ainsley about the photo, it cast enough doubt for Claire to wonder.

Beyond Joe's burden of proof, there was a piece Claire had been holding onto as well. She admitted experiencing her own strange phenomena around the time of Joe's dreams: she'd felt as though she was being watched. Not in a disconcerting way, exactly, but as though an energy had attached itself to her spirit and was along for the ride from time to time. She told him of a tingling she'd felt at the back of her neck, writing it off as a transient quirk of her condition. She mentioned how Dr. Lewiston had asked her to journal any symptoms along with their accompanying life events. When Claire compared Joe's diary to her own, she realized the warmth she'd felt at the base of her hairline coincided with the timeline of the dreams. And how strangely, the feeling had left after they'd met.

Knowing this feeling might have been Joe, she'd decided during their anguished period apart to choose that there must have been a reason for all of it, even if neither of them understood what that could be. If what he'd said was true, he hadn't chosen the experience any more than she, and in the end, it had brought them together. It had created that sense of knowing and familiarity, of two souls finally meeting and seeing their reflection in one another.

Claire determined that for all the knowledge of human existence one isn't afforded, of all the mysteries one is compelled to accept, she'd accepted far worse than finding the love of her life. She couldn't initially say why she'd fought to reject this gift, but in the end, she knew the answer. It was one thing for her body to reject itself; realms of physiology and DNA mapped out from the moment of her creation, and over which neither she nor even the forces of medicine and science had any control. But with Joe, and with love, there was the fragile dance of revealing the spirit forged over a limited lifetime. The heart with its set of beliefs, desires, hurts and hopes. To have those things rejected was not merely an affront to biology through genetic coding gone wrong. It was an affront to the essence of what made her human. The gift of a great and perfect love suddenly rescinded was a thought too devastating, a loss too irrevocable.

She recounted to Joe her experience with her parents, of losing first one and then the other, and how if there might be any merit in physical death, it was perhaps the finality of it. The knowledge that the person was never coming back. *Couldn't* come back. But when it came to the death of a relationship, the infinitely more impossible element to accept was that the person was still out there. That they could have stayed, but did not. That they might come back, but would not.

To lose her body, and perhaps her life, was enough to endure. But to lose her heart in the process, abjured by another, would be a loss to eclipse the rest. Her fears told her not to let that happen, so while her body continued to betray her, she'd permitted her words to do the same to her heart when she'd asked him to leave. He'd simply made the process easier by giving those fears something to cling onto. She'd known he was telling the truth—could see it in his eyes, hear it in his tone, feel it in that invisible field of energy that enveloped the two of them anytime they were near. But his admission led something inside of her to shout, "This! This is the thing," and gave her uncertainty the reason it needed to insist that he leave.

Her fear had needed something—*anything*—to grasp upon, because just as she'd known the truth of his desperate admission, she'd also known the truth of his heart when it came to what frightened her most. She knew he wasn't going to leave, despite her physical descent. She even knew he'd begun making arrangements regarding home and work. Though he hadn't said these things aloud—Claire knew Joe would never present a plan without first preparing the data—she'd seen notes on the desk in his apartment, or the way his eyes danced with an "I'm up to something" gleam whenever anyone mentioned his life across the ocean.

What Claire *didn't* know was how to accept it. To have faith that this man would stay. That he would continue to love. These ideas stretched the bounds of her comprehension as much as any designs of the ethereal. Men left, when things became difficult. Apart from her father, that had been her experience, and the world didn't make men like her father anymore.

Yet here stood a man with every reason to go, and still he remained. Though she hadn't the first notion how to understand this, let alone receive it, she had seen the certainty in her lover's eyes. And she knew that to ask him to leave was to ask him to forsake the place he truly called home.

Her heart.

Fate had brought him there, and she knew now that he would never leave.

CHAPTER 73
AN IDEA TOO PAINFUL TO BROACH

THE WEEKS PROGRESSED as did the deepening of their bond, the intertwining of their spirits. For as much as Joe and Claire longed for the means to slow or halt time altogether, life progressed as well. Their relationship now without question, Joe briefly returned to Canada in September to settle matters at home. He put his involvement in his practice on indefinite hiatus, arranging for another senior advisor in his office to nominally take over while Dawson, Janice, and Karen maintained the day-to-day.

The part he didn't mention to his team was the research he'd done into permanent relocation. His company had offices throughout the world, including London. Though the licensing and technical details differed, the practice of financial planning did not, and he'd begun to envision building from the ground-up again. For the moment that would wait, however, to be revisited if and when Claire's health stabilized. He was struck by the ease in which he'd let go of his attachment to work, to progress, to achievement; these cornerstones of his old life feeling trivial measured against life with Claire.

The renter he'd found for his condo was more than happy to extend their lease agreement, this time signing on for a year in the perfectly located, tastefully furnished inner-city apartment. Across the pond his current landlord mirrored the enthusiasm, content to have Joe sign on for another six months. The owner pressed for a longer commitment, pleased to have a mature tenant who kept the place immaculate. Joe wanted flexibility, however, hoping to spend less time in the space and more in the house a few blocks away as time went on.

The two lovers spoke about Joe spending more time at Claire's, but continued to want the children to set the pace. As had been the trend, Ainsley likely would have delighted in the decision, pleased to have a permanent board game teammate and teatime companion. Jackson maintained his practiced indifference, with the implicit condition that nothing affect his social time or status. Holly's demeanor suggested ambivalence, though out of the three children she seemed most in tune with Claire's deteriorating condition, most aware of the reality that came with it.

The days were spent with Joe at the house until Claire was ready for sleep, at which time he'd walk beneath the London stars back to his flat. The evening was the most difficult time to pull themselves apart, after passing the bedtime hours side by side with endless talk or books read aloud to one another. Yet they'd arrived at the reluctant conclusion that for the moment, this arrangement seemed best. Having the children wake to find Joe wandering the house with disheveled hair and clothes from the day before still seemed too much of a disruption to their delicate ecosystem. They were dealing with enough, the lovers agreed, without adding that particular energy to the mix.

Their father had officially relinquished all titles that summer: parent, husband, employee, resident of England. He was largely incommunicado with both families, the only recent update coming from Miranda in another awkward encounter with Audrey. David had apparently taken the young actress globetrotting to places like Ibiza and Peru, his young paramour more than eager to assist in burning through family savings he was halving now for the second time.

With David's characteristic disregard for the wake left behind, Claire assumed further roles in her portfolio of responsibilities to the children. Psychologist and mediator, trying to help their young minds and hearts grapple with the literal and emotional abandonment. Barrister as well, knowing there was a potential perfect storm on the horizon. With her declining abilities and David's flight, she'd been forced to consider what might happen if her condition didn't improve. Though he tried to abstain from venturing his opinion unless asked, Joe gently seconded Audrey's persistent advice that Claire retain a lawyer.

On the physical front, most days Claire was still ambulatory, if not without aid. She remarked that the thing she missed most was the previously unknown delight of moving without having to plan it first. Unless her legs felt particularly stable, she walked with a cane to mitigate sudden freezing or buckling. Some of the more harrowing scenes occurred when Claire shuffled from one spot to another, and with her stooped upper body would almost appear to launch into a headfirst, impromptu run as she lost control over her gait, nearly crashing into walls or furniture. Everyone feared a fall but it seemed too soon, too criminal to relinquish the freedom of mobility, of simply getting from one place to the next. Joe quietly installed supports around the home, hanging railing on both sides of the stairs, and placing smaller grab bars throughout hallways and rooms.

Most days Claire elected for a bath, in part for the reduced likelihood of a fall, and for the comfort of the weightlessness in water. For this reprieve she usually required Joe's help to get her safely in and out of the tub. He was more than happy to oblige, often getting into the suds with her, where they'd pass more hours in the secret world of inside humour and shared shorthand and intertwined hearts. Most baths had them emerging incalculable time later with their bodies pruned, leading to Joe applying lotion on Claire's skin and massaging her spent body underneath. And when opportunity allowed, when her body was able to give and receive, they made love into the night. It seemed some sensations were immune to the slow theft of feeling.

As the London cityscape painted itself in the colours of fall, Joe and Claire spent increasing time in doctor's visits and hospital hallways. Aids like the cane (good days) or a walker (bad days) still felt foreign to all of them, as though this was some kind of car accident that would mend. When Dr. Lewiston recommended a wheelchair for the worst days, after watching her friend struggle to the point of exhaustion, Claire replied, "I've lost so much already, I'm just not prepared to lose one more thing. If it takes ten minutes to move ten steps then so be it, but I want to take those steps with my own two feet while I still can."

More than once, Joe needed to carry her from the main floor to her bedroom, the two of them knowing no external device would get her from one level to the next. The first time, as she'd wrapped her arms around his shoulders and looked in his eyes, her expression seemed to say, "Sorry about this, I'll be better soon." Over time she'd simply folded into him, her head upon his shoulder, taking in his strength.

When it came to the children Audrey had assumed most tactical duties, imposing discipline on her night owl schedule, but apparently not to the detriment of her art. Since the success of her show the previous fall she'd held a handful of exhibitions since, and a flattering piece in ArtReview brought almost more commissions than she could handle. Though it had taken some adjustment to find the muse while the children were at school, it nonetheless had worked out in the form of increasing requests and consistent referrals from the London elite. On days or evenings when inspiration was boundless she'd call from her apartment out back, and barring medical appointments that couldn't be modified, Joe and Claire found a way to accommodate the spur of creativity.

Audrey had even found time to begin a relationship with a publicist she'd met at one of her exhibitions. Daniel served as her own shelter in this season of storm, and they appeared to work well together, his steady hand complementing her bohemian spirit. On afternoons where Audrey was in flow with her art, he too had stepped up and taken on tasks like school shuttling or cooking dinner—Daniel being the lone member of the burgeoning crew with any flair in the kitchen.

All worked to foster whatever disrupted the children's lives the least. This may have amounted to little more than holding them within the eye of the hurricane, but for Claire, and for now, that was enough. If the worst she could be accused of was a bit of coddling during this time, she would accept that.

Ainsley maintained her default of wonderful oblivion, or so it appeared. For every adjustment made with Claire or to the home—walking aids, hand bars, or the eventual relocation of Claire's bedroom to the office on the main floor—these seemed more like new discoveries and adventures to the young girl. She'd insisted on "sleeping over" with Claire that first night on the main level, saying it would help her Mum not be frightened in the new room. She helped steer the walker in lockstep with her mother, or happily ran errands asking Joe or Audrey for refills of tea, or lent her tiny arms when Claire needed help moving from one spot to another.

On occasion Ainsley let slip questions that hinted at musings underneath. During one of the remaining dinners where Claire could still keep herself upright in a regular chair, or manage food and drink on her own, Ainsley had watched her closely. In the middle of collective teasing toward Jack regarding a high school love interest, Ainsley blurted out, "Are you going to die, Mummy?"

As the conversation and laughter ceased, Claire forced a smile and said, "What makes you say that, honey?"

"Are you dying right now? Is that why your body can't do things anymore? Sarah at school said you're dying."

Though she had considered the question more times than she cared to recall—and had begun making arrangements for that eventuality—the question of how, and when, and what to tell the children had been territory remaining off-limits within Claire's mind. An idea too painful to broach.

"Your Mum's body is just being *really* silly, Ainsley," Audrey interjected. "We've talked about that, darling, and your Mum is trying many things to get her muscles to behave again."

"But she's getting worse."

"Honey," Claire reached a vibrating hand toward Ainsley. "I... I don't... I'm right here, baby," she finally said. "That's all we ever have, is just the day we're living, the time we have right now." She attempted another smile.

"Yes but what about *later?*" Ainsley replied.

Holly stood and ran for the stairs.

CHAPTER 74
I THOUGHT WE WOULD, TOO

"Why don't you want to talk about this, Holly?"

Claire's middle child had refused to speak with anyone—in any meaningful way, at least—for days following her flight from the dinner table. On an evening when Claire's legs were cooperating, Joe guided her up the stairwell for the latest attempt to breach Holly's defenses. At Claire's quiet request, Joe lingered in the hall within earshot of Holly's room.

"What is there to talk about?" Holly snapped back at Claire.

"Anything. Everything. Whatever you'd like to say, honey."

"You say that but it's bullshit," Holly said, cursing for the first time Claire could ever recall.

"Woah, language, please." Claire reached a hand to her daughter. Holly refused it, hugging her knees to her chest.

"If we can talk about anything and everything, then why can't we be honest about the fact you're dying?"

"I didn't realize we were being dishonest about it," Claire said.

"The other night when Ainsley started asking you about it, you shrugged it off like nothing was happening. Or that if we would just think positive enough, everything will be sunshine and rainbows. But we both know it's not." Holly buried her head into her folded arms.

Claire shifted toward her daughter, enveloping her in an unsteady hug. She considered her words.

"It's not that I want to shrug it off, love. I can't really shrug anymore, anyway, unless it's by accident—and then I do it several times a day," Claire said with a smile. Holly looked up with a teary-eyed glare. "Okay not funny. Real talk now, okay?" She searched Holly's eyes, and the preteen finally nodded.

"We don't know for sure that I'm dying," Claire went on. "Parkinson's itself isn't fatal, and although things are progressing faster than we'd like, the doctors and I keep trying—and keep hoping—that we'll find the right combination of things to slow whatever's happening, or figure out if there is anything else going on.

"My job is mostly the hope part. And that can be far from easy. So when Ainsley asked about it the other night, I was trying to rally hope. Not just for her, or for you and your brother, but for me, as well. I need all the hope I can get, okay?"

Holly gave a tearful nod.

"But you're right, my love. And I don't know how to say this without my heart breaking a little more than it already has, but there is a possibility my body will keep shutting down."

"A *possibility?*" Holly's voice erupted.

Claire lowered her tone to offset her daughter's. "A

strong possibility. There may come a time that after my outer body has stopped working, the inner parts will as well. I won't be able to eat on my own anymore—chew my food or swallow. I might not be able to speak."

"You're already having trouble speaking," Holly choked out between sobs, her voice muffled as she pressed it into Claire's chest.

"I know. And I think that breaks my heart the most. The idea I might not be able to tell you how much I love you." Tears began welling in Claire's own eyes. It seemed this part of her physiology functioned without hindrance, yet she welcomed any outward expressions of emotion for however long they remained. She cleared her throat to speak and shifted back to regard Holly directly. "So it's not that I want to pretend, or that I'm not willing to talk about these things. I always will with you, Holly. With Ainsley too, with your brother, with everyone. I just want to make sure we spend at least as much time talking about the good things as well, okay?" Claire could feel her strength—physical and emotional—draining quickly, like watching a petrol needle descend on a steep incline. She didn't want to lose all composure in front of her daughter.

"Okay," Holly finally agreed.

"We're going to keep fighting, and keep hoping, and most of all, keep loving, okay?" Claire said while nodding, hoping to prompt the same reaction from Holly despite the tears that flowed from both of them. Holly nodded back, unable to speak, burying her head into her mother once more. They laid down together on the child-sized mattress, their bodies quietly heaving.

When he hadn't heard any sound after several minutes, Joe peeked his head around the door. Holly had fallen asleep in Claire's arms, and Claire mouthed *I'll sleep here.* Joe nodded and went to the main floor bedroom to grab pillows and blankets, returning upstairs to set up a makeshift campsite in the hallway in case Claire needed him in the night. More often than not these days, she did.

Though she took the following night "off," needing to recover from the physical and emotional drain, Claire made a similar approach with Jackson two nights later. Joe guided her downstairs to Jack's basement lair, knocking at the door over the sound of Oasis blaring within. *I don't even have to tell my hand to knock anymore,* she joked with Joe. *I just hold my arm up against the door and it takes care of itself.* They both tried to laugh, but it was stifled; the emotion from the looming conversation charging to the surface. When the music lowered, Joe assisted her to Jack's bed before taking his post in the outer hallway.

"I've just started acting like I'm already an orphan," was Jack's opening salvo, after Claire had settled.

"My god, Jack, that's awful," Claire responded. She'd expected some sort of jaded reaction to her question of how he was *really* doing, but as was often the case with adolescents, she still managed to be surprised.

As was also the case with boys his age, Jack knew that he'd hurt his mum, not having considered the impact of his words whenever he'd rehearsed them earlier in his head. His pained and practiced veneer dropped, and it was he who made the first move of physical connection, putting his hand on her forearm. "I'm sorry, Mum. I didn't mean that to hurt you, really. I guess I just mean that I've tried to... I dunno... prepare myself, d'you know?"

"I understand."

"What will happen if you—" He stopped to consider his words. "—If you don't get better?" Claire could see the softening of his expression, the toddler he'd once been behind the body and face now somehow more like a man's. She saw the fear behind his eyes framed by an expression that reminded her of their earliest years together, despite the acne dotting his cheeks and mop of hair hanging in his eyes.

"Well, I've been waiting for the right time to tell you and your sisters this, but I guess this is as good a time as any—at least with you. Are you sure you're okay to talk about this?" Claire asked.

"I'm *sixteen* now, Mum, I can more than handle it," Jack said. Claire smiled, before mollifying her expression.

"When your father—" It was Claire's turn to consider the wording. She nearly laughed to herself at the mind's ability to go vacant despite internally rehearsed conversations. "When your father decided to go to the States, and when things started to take a turn with me..." She swallowed hard. "I had to spend a lot of time thinking about what would be best for you and your sisters. It wasn't easy, believe me."

"Did you ever think about asking *us* what would be best for us?" Jack buried his head into arms crossed over his knees.

"Yes of course, my love. Nothing has been set in stone yet, but we're getting there. I had to talk to a lawyer anyway because of my condition, for power of attorney and advanced directives. So at the same time I discussed all of that with Auntie Audrey, I talked to her about you children."

"What about Dad?"

Claire took a moment to inhale, to summon the right words once more. "I've tried to talk to your father. And I want you to remember that deep down, I think there's still a wonderful man in there. I loved him once, and in a certain sort of way, I always will. He gave me you, after all." She reached up to run a hand through Jack's mop of hair.

"But what? You're gonna say 'but.'"

"But he hasn't exactly said he'd step in if something should happen. He definitely hasn't said it any time I've managed to get ahold of him, which hasn't been for weeks now. His actions haven't suggested it, either." Jack looked down, hiding his eyes. "I'm so sorry, honey," Claire continued. "It has nothing to do with you or your sisters. It's just something your father is going through right now."

"Doesn't he care about what *we're* going through?" Jack erupted. "And you could say it's 'just something he's going through' if this was just lately, but he hasn't cared for years."

"Jack, I want you to remember that no matter what happens, this has nothing to do with you."

"You said that already. And it doesn't feel that way. He doesn't give a bloody damn about us, and now you're leaving us too."

Claire felt like a knife had plunged through her chest.

"No matter what happens," she said softly, "you will be taken care of. I've made sure of it. You are loved, so deeply, by so many people."

"Just not by the ones who matter."

"Jack—"

His head shot up from his arms, and Claire saw rivulets lining his face in every direction. With his tears he looked now only like the little boy she had held before anyone else. His first cries, first words, first steps all flashed through her mind. She couldn't move, couldn't breathe, and for a moment didn't know if it was the situation or her body. It seemed impossible that their time might be limited. She had planned for a lifetime; had expected to see him hold *his* firstborn, hear about *his* child's first moments.

"I didn't mean that either, Mum. You've loved us—and me—like mad, even when we've made it hard for you."

"I know you didn't mean it, sweetheart." Claire reached for Jack, longed to cradle him as she had when he was a fraction of her size, before becoming the young man who towered over her now. She still cradled him as well as she could manage, feeling his body acquiesce as it had when he was an infant. "This is an impossibly hard time. I always thought we'd have more time."

Claire caught herself; tried to steel her expression as quickly as possible. Joe, in the outer hall, didn't fare nearly as well, the emotion overcoming him. He couldn't fathom what this was like for her.

As if picking up the thought, Claire said, "I can only imagine what this is like for you, Jack, and I am so, so sorry." They wept together, Jack balled up in her arms, his tears soaking her shirt. Joe quietly released his grief in the hall.

He couldn't help the next thought that came.
I thought we'd have more time, too.

CHAPTER 75
BREATHING

IT WAS NEARLY impossible not to curse the gods, or the universe, or *the* God—whatever was out there—for what was happening now. Joe managed the days with relative success, keeping his emotions in check. At night, as Claire slept and he lay holding her quivering body—with even these involuntary movements occurring less and less, as though part of an overall, unrelenting shutdown—the grief overtook him like the shadows, and he longed to lash out. To find whoever had arranged this cosmic screwup and have words, ask questions, demand a reversal. Not of their meeting, not even of the dreams, but of watching the love of his life held captive in the prison of a malfunctioning body.

For a time he'd begun to feel like an overheated vessel without a relief valve. Entire days and nights were now spent at her side, one day blurring into the next. Neither of them had had a full night's rest in longer than they could recall. Like so much of the situation now, circumstances compelled Joe's de facto moving in without discussion or fanfare; it had merely been the most practical solution when Claire began needing consistent assistance in the night. With Audrey taking point on the children,

Joe remained on guard for his love, though the fight was overwhelming.

Joe did have somewhat of an outlet in William. Following the lover's brief separation, the older man returned to Canada, keeping touch with Joe in what had become weekly phone calls between the unlikely friends. After several weeks of listening to Joe recount Claire's rapid deterioration, William had appeared one afternoon on the doorstep unannounced, stating he knew both Joe and Claire would have fought the suggestion had he mentioned it in advance. Though unexpected, the sight of the little old man was welcomed by everyone in the home, even if they hadn't known how to receive or thank him.

He took up an unofficial role as Claire's aide, carrying out the treatment plan prescribed by Dr. Lewiston (and to his quiet delight, conferring with the active physician whenever she asked his advice). With Joe effectively moved into Claire's house, William took up residence in the rented flat, professing enjoyment of his "exotic, overseas retirement." He'd put the store up for sale after his previous visit, telling Joe that after all their talk of love and loss, he believed Ellie wouldn't have wanted him to sit around forever mourning what might have been, and would have wanted him to get back into the world. If that meant England for the third time this year, then so be it. "Besides," the elder man said with his trademark wink, "I knew you'd be calling any day saying we ought to 'review my plan' again, so I figured I'd just make it easy and come to you."

Joe wondered if William was really there for the emotional health of all involved. A source of mirth for the family, a confidant for Claire, an outlet for Joe, and an amusing oddity for the children. Ainsley, for one, took pleasure in dressing William in a ratty bathrobe to substitute for the absent physician's overcoat, and provided him with a plastic stethoscope, headlamp and thermometer from a toy medical kit purchased sometime over the years. She delighted even further in directing the retired doc on how to properly care for her mother.

William seemed to have an innate instinct for collective decompression. On some occasions, that took the form of a night on the recliner outside Claire's makeshift bedroom, so Joe could make an attempt at undisturbed sleep in her old bedroom on the second floor. At other times, William would announce a field trip with the children for dinner and a movie, in order to give the adults a quiet evening. He'd even become proficient in driving on the wrong side of the road to assist with errands and transport.

On one of the nights where he read Claire to sleep with Dickens ("When in London," he'd averred), William had issued "Doctor's orders" and sent Joe upstairs to bed. Though he usually put up a cursory fight with the older man when it came to these shifts, Joe knew he ought to engage in a modicum of self-care in order to bring his best to Claire. Yet no matter the tremors, despite the shallow dips into slumber, and even in spite of the occasionally soiled sheets, Joe found it difficult to sleep without being at her side.

When the hours passed without a minute of reprieve, Joe finally dressed, descended the stairs, and passed the recliner where William lay sleeping. Joe took a moment to look at Claire as she lay in the stillness, then made his way into the London night. He walked to the nearby park, hoping open air would at least provide the illusion of being able to breathe easier. Sitting on a bench, with no one in sight at two in the morning, he cried out.

"WHY DID YOU DO THIS TO US?" The sound of his voice surprised him, louder than he'd expected, broken between the words and yet the words colliding with one another. The dam around his eyes broke. His voice had startled the unseen city wildlife; birds fluttered in the trees amidst the shadows.

He leaned forward, elbows on his knees and face in his hands. The open air hadn't helped; his lungs felt squeezed, every breath stifled. He fought the emotion, for reasons he wasn't certain. There was no one around, and months of mounting anguish had stacked upon one another, begging to be released. Yet he fought it anyway, constricting his chest and throat further. His eyes were burning. He took his hands away from his face and balled them into fists, quietly beating them against the bench.

He threw his head back to the stars, and though quieter this time, asked with the same anguished urgency, *"What was the point of this? Why did you bring me to her, just to watch her go?"* The grief overwhelmed him, and in some measure of mercy his chest, throat, eyes—every area of constrained muscle—released. For the first time he could ever recall, he cried freely.

As the conflict within his body let go, so did it leave his mind. Joe welcomed the deluge of emotion that was for once not met with attempts to rationalize or scrutinize or philosophize. His heart—perhaps even his soul—

was breaking in a new, entirely different way, and he had no desire to stop it, to curtail or protect. He'd found the love of his life and now he was losing her, and he would make no effort to feel anything but devastated. For a brief moment, in these weeks shrouded by uncertainty and strife and fear, he felt entirely present to his experience. For a moment, he felt released.

When the raw emotion began to ease and the outer world made itself known to his consciousness once more, he leaned forward again, wiping away the water on his face and taking in a breath. Each inhalation felt new and unprecedented, as though he hadn't taken millions before.

"I don't know if I can do this," he finally said, his voice raw. Though he held muted hope for a reply, none came.

"I don't know if I have the *strength* to do this." The physical strain threatened to return while the internal committee emerged from a prolonged recess: *What are you talking about*—you *don't know if* you *have the strength? Look at what* she's *going through. You've got it easy by comparison, friend.*

"But I don't know how I'm supposed to watch her die." Everything constricted once more, and he was gone again to minutes without thought, only feeling.

He sat without conception of time, vacillating between inner and outer dialogue, questions and rebuttals, denials and capitulation. He couldn't reconcile anything, every moment before this one feeling surreal. It was as though a targeted tide of amnesia was creeping up the shoreline of his memory, making it impossible to remember how he'd arrived here. At this place, at this time, with the entirety of his heart and life crumbling around him.

He expected to wake at any moment, to be back in his condo in Canada, all of this some wildly elaborate dream with reality just another Thursday with clients and calculations and certainty and calm. Somewhere in these past weeks he'd been enveloped by a numbness, likely intended to counteract the feeling of exposed nerve endings. It had caused the whole situation to feel entirely unreal, shielding him from emotion but also any thought of how to confront it.

"Just tell me what to do," he finally managed when his throat had released. "You brought me here, you brought me to her, just tell me what to do. Tell me how to be strong. Tell me how to keep loving her, knowing that I'm losing her." New tears welled but the rest of his body remained wilted, as though too weary to tense up once more. "Whatever it is, I'll do it. I just need to know what to do."

Joe listened to the interminable stillness, hoping again for some reply. Any reply. He couldn't have said what he was looking for exactly, short of an angel or lightning flash to cut the dark with unmistakable direction. Neither came. He listened, and all he heard was the hum of incandescent lights and the steady sound of crickets.

Joe didn't know whether to curse or collapse. To rail against the cosmos that had abandoned him, or lay in resignation on the bench beneath him. He felt an exhaustion at the level of the soul, a weariness unlike any he'd ever known. He laid on his side against the hard wooden slats, his consciousness reduced to a desperate plea for sleep, for a reprieve that might last even a moment.

He drifted, and she came to him. Or he went to her. He'd nearly forgotten the feeling, let alone the language to describe it. He was looking through her eyes, and not only was his own movement paralyzed, he could sense the entirety of her body was as well.

And she couldn't breathe.

CHAPTER 76
I COULD FEEL YOU HERE

"I DON'T CARE what anybody says, I'm not leaving your side ever again," Joe whispered from his edge of the bed. William flanked the other, assessing vital signs and bumbling about in the quiet, practiced way of the professional. Audrey and Daniel stood bleary-eyed at the door, Audrey having twice intercepted children woken from the commotion.

Claire's throat had simply failed to reflexively swallow in what amounted to less than a flicker of a moment, an action the rest of the household performed hundreds of times a day without a trace of awareness. This led to a blockage which nearly led to aspiration, and her eyes had shot open when her physiology detected its inability to take in a cleansing breath.

As with so much else about her pathology, this happened in a quiet yet internally violent scene within the darkened bedroom. Her brain screamed various commands to clear the airway, sit upright, pound her chest, turn on a light, call for help—all of these orders unheeded. When Joe had burst through the door William was still sound asleep, as was the rest of the silent house. Joe found her wide-eyed and at the edge of consciousness; even in the street-lit room he could see the pallor in her face tinged with an ominous shade of blue. He'd yelled for William while straightening Claire upright from the concave position her body had contorted into.

The old doc bounded up from the recliner and activated dormant but not forgotten emergency reflexes. With a gentle hand contrasting the tumult of the moment, he cleared her airway with the suction machine (procured weeks earlier "just in case"), and applied oxygen. After an excruciating fit of coughs and spasms, Claire wheezed in a desperate breath that seemed to reverberate through the house. The rest of the family—bursting in after Joe radioed Audrey with one of the walkie-talkies kept on the bedside table—all breathed in at the same time, unaware they'd been holding their own oxygen at bay. When Claire eventually spoke, her words punctuated by shallow gasps, the shoulders in the room relaxed as well. She said, "I figured if I had to be awake in the middle of the night, I might as well have company." It took a moment, but the group finally allowed themselves a nervous laugh.

When the adrenaline subsided and the family members departed for their bedrooms, satisfied she was stable, Joe climbed into the bed and wrapped his arms around Claire. As they kissed, she whispered, "I knew you'd come."

"What do you mean, my love?" he whispered back.

Claire reached up and touched the back of her neck.

"I could feel you here," she said, smiling before the exhaustion took both of them.

This latest complication prompted Dr. Lewiston to decree it "was time," during the next house call. In spite of best efforts from the group to attend to Claire's deteriorating state, and despite Jacquie's own misgivings about a potential move, the attending physician wanted Claire under round-the-clock supervision. While there would be further tests to confirm or correct, Dr. Lewiston (and Dr. Hollings, though he respectfully deferred to the practicing physician) was quite certain of what these would reveal. The slow shutdown that had begun at the periphery of Claire's nervous system was most likely closing in on her, making internal functions of vital physiology difficult, if not eventually impossible.

These things could be mitigated to an extent with intervention, but this would require constant oversight. In the meantime, Jacquie said, the family had their own care to consider. While they had done a beyond-admirable job thus far, there could only be so many sleepless nights and close calls before the toll was too great, impacting not only the wellbeing of the individuals involved, but Claire herself. She needed consistent—and to a degree, dispassionate—care, from people who if they were up nights, were wide awake and being paid to do so.

Throughout the discussion, Claire shifted glances between the doctor and Joe. Though the rest of her physical expression was so often curtailed by the contortion of muscles that now acted of their own accord, her eyes remained bright and alive. In those irises, Joe could still glean all the information he ever needed.

"No," he finally said, interrupting a side discussion between Audrey and Jacquie concerning potential interventions.

Dr. Lewiston turned to him. "'No' what?"

"She doesn't want to go. We don't want her to go."

The doctor turned her eyes to Claire. "Luv, I know you don't. I know none of you do. But as gently as I can say this, your condition has forced our hand, and stopped being about what any of us wanted long ago."

Claire tried to speak, and after her vocal chords failed to produce more than the first half of a WH-word in several attempts, she looked to Joe. He took a cloth and gently dabbed the side of her mouth before turning to face the doctor again. "We'll get her the care she needs here," he said. "We'll hire homecare in day and evening shifts, or three eight-hour shifts. Whatever the protocol is. We'll get the equipment needed for monitoring and—" his voice choked at the last, "—whatever else might be necessary. William's here, and he's assured me it isn't charity, now that he's drawing a retirement income." Joe flashed an imitation of William's trademark wink-and-grin at the older man, who nodded and grinned in return.

"We'll get a housekeeper," Joe continued, looking back at Jacquie. "A cook. Someone to do the laundry. Whatever it takes. I promise we'll take care of ourselves, but only to make us better at taking care of her." He turned back to look into the eyes that had never stopped drawing him in, and reached a hand up to the face that held them.

"Claire's benefits only go so far," Jacquie said. "And while it's outside my purview, even if she has the resources..." Dr. Lewiston trailed off, searching for the words. Joe saved her from having to find them.

"It will be taken care of." He hadn't broken the gaze he shared with Claire, and his tone halted further discussion. Claire managed a single nod, while her eyes filled.

"I love you," he whispered to her.

Her mouth formed the words without sound. *I love you too.*

CHAPTER 77
ABLE TO SAY THE ONLY THING THAT EVER MATTERED

As autumn transitioned to winter, Joe watched the passing of the season with bemusement. *Is this meant to be a metaphor?* he thought, during one of his daily walks in the park across the street. These sojourns were usually solo, Joe always wishing Claire could be with him to have a glimpse that extended beyond the front window. To walk beneath the beautiful but bittersweet surrender of the leaves.

Occasionally, when the temperature was warm and her body was stable, they made the painstaking effort to get her dressed and into the wheelchair. They'd navigate the park pathways together and soak in as many minutes—sometimes hours—as her body would permit. Her face always expressed a longing for more, but Joe would watch for the telltale glint of weariness behind her eyes, and feign his own need to go back inside for whatever trivial reason he could muster.

The worst part of the decline was the unevenness of it. Most days were part of an unforgivable, unrelenting downward trajectory, but there were scattered reprieves. Afternoons where the words formed easily and they could recapture the patter from their earliest moments. *How I long for those tidal waves of words and emotion,* Joe would often think, *where I could barely get a word in. I wouldn't try to interrupt anymore. I'd just sit and listen to her forever.*

Most of their communication remained unspoken and through the eyes, and on most days, that was enough. On luckier days, there was deliberate and voluntary touch, where her hand could grasp back with only mild tremor, or her mouth could move in flow with his as they kissed. Joe tried to accept these gifts for what they were, but it was an impossible endeavour not to remember what was, not to wonder what might have been.

The only caesura from those thoughts was the irreconcilable reminder that these moments too, would eventually be a memory. That one day, he would long for these days as well.

Remaining too long in that thought also broke his heart.

It was on a particularly good day, however, after they'd walked through Queen's Park with the leaves crunching beneath them and a rare blue sky above, a picnic beside the pond, and feeling that obeyed Claire's commands as her mouth met his, that—before he'd even had time to consider the words—Joe said, "Would you marry me?"

Even in his days of entrenched bachelorhood, some element of him knew that though it might be a dormant part of his heart, there was nevertheless a longing for a great love story. For a beautiful soul to intertwine with.

For a love that would outlast their time. In that period of unadmitted desire, had he been asked to venture a prediction Joe might have conjured visions of a grand proposal. The peak of a mountain at sunset, helicopter flying in with a photographer to catch the moment, flutes of champagne to commemorate the occasion afterward. Perhaps a surprise encounter on a busy street in a much-loved locale, him on bended knee, ring in upraised hand, letting the world around them know he'd found the love of his life, and to her his life was pledged. He might have imagined these things. Might have tried to force such a moment to perfection.

But this was the life he'd been gifted instead, the woman who had captured his soul. And though her body was bent in ways that were unnatural and cruel, though they were losing the words and means of connection by the day and sometimes by the hour, their roots continued to wrap around one another, deepening their touch in ways that fingers interlaced or even a kiss prolonged could not. He'd found a love he hadn't been looking for in a woman he might never have met, and he wanted her to know that for him, that love would remain eternal.

So on an otherwise unremarkable Tuesday, in the middle of a park where life around them affirmed its impermanence, and as he sat upon dried grass that clung to his jeans and she in a chair that seemed an affront to a basic human right, and while the wind raised pink blooms on their cheeks and provoked ceaseless sniffles from their noses, Joe shifted to one knee, adjusted the hood around Claire's head, dabbed her nose with a mittened hand, and voiced what he'd heard his heart say to him long ago:

"Will you marry me, Claire Langdon? Will you let me love you forever, no matter how long forever is?"

There was no crowd, no helicopter, no photos or champagne to record or commemorate. There were random passersby whose gazes remained oblivious to the surroundings as they rushed from one appointment to another. There was a wind that occasionally and unceremoniously whipped the impending winter through the park and chilled its visitors. There were squirrels that broke the silences as they scampered across the leaf-covered greenspaces. There were juice boxes and bent plastic straws and applesauce cups and spoons he'd guided to her lips. There was only this.

But it didn't matter, because as with every moment they ever shared, there was only Joe and Claire. There was only this world made for two. And she was able to say the only thing that had ever mattered.

"Yes."

CHAPTER 78
THIS DREAM COME TRUE

It was an intimate affair, yet even if circumstances hadn't necessitated a close-knit gathering, the lovers imagined that would have remained their choice. Though their love felt like one for the ages, it hadn't needed a display. What had always mattered was what passed in the space between them. The words, when they were there. The touch, when it was possible. The world that existed when their eyes met. That was what would remain, after the vows and rings were exchanged, the toasts made and the cake eaten.

Joe and Claire had found their indelible match in one another and no matter what life might take away in time beyond, it had given them this moment. It was this they celebrated on a rainy Saturday in December before the new millennium. A connection that transcended notions of time and space. Their love could only ever be theirs alone, and neither passing seasons nor new millennia nor faltering health would diminish it.

Furniture had been displaced from the living room and an arch was constructed by Audrey, who'd delighted in using her artistry for turning the home-turned-homecare space into one of romance and matrimony. For days leading up to the event the rest of the family was banished from the area while Audrey was "in flow" with her vision of Claire's wishes. She went as far as to hide the area from view with plastic sheeting, feeling as all artists do about a work in progress. When the space was finally revealed, she'd left everyone stunned by the transformation of a sitting room into a mountain and forest retreat. Surrounded by sculptures of trees and snow-capped peaks, and aglow in lights glimmering like stars, for an afternoon and evening they were transported from a space that had lately resembled a hospice more than a home. For a time, life was as it had been, sowed with possibility of what could be.

The wedding party consisted of William, Daniel, and Jackson as groomsmen. Audrey, Holly, and Ainsley stood as bridesmaids, with Ainsley also self-appointing to roles of ring bearer, emcee, flower girl, choreographer, and general wedding director. There was no aisle, exactly, nor did Claire move down one, but that wasn't going to stop the young girl from spreading petals everywhere. Jacquie Lewiston officiated, having taken on the scramble of procuring the appropriate licenses and authority to do so. The red-headed, bouffant-haired Lucille from yoga served as dressmaker, spending the first couple of weeks following Joe's proposal pouring over bridal magazines and finding a style Claire liked before sewing the dress herself. Her unceasing enthusiasm extended to the food service, as she assisted Daniel in the kitchen and ensured no plate or glass went empty that day.

The gentlemen took over much of the tactical work,

tending to this or that errand, fetching more supplies as needed by Audrey, moving furniture as decreed by the bridal party, or tending to the feast to follow. The entire event had become a collective effort, a grouped force of will to carry out a beautiful day while time and circumstance allowed. Even Jackson occasionally emerged from his den to assist with decorating or gathering supplies, sometimes spending hours in conversation with Joe or William about hiking or finance or sport or medicine or philosophy—finding, as teenagers do, footholds in the experiences of others to make sense of his own standing in the world.

For a time, the adult sisters debated (verbally for Audrey, gestures for Claire) whether to use Claire's wheelchair for the ceremony. In the end, much as the decision pained, they'd elected to roll Claire's medical bed into the living room. She hadn't been able to sit upright of her own volition for a couple of weeks, but this too was taken with a stiff upper lip; Audrey had simply decorated the inclined bed to match the rest of the room before they'd rolled it under the archway.

I can't believe this is my life, was the thought in Joe's mind as they gathered. It echoed with tones of profound gratitude and wondrous disbelief at a personal fortune that had nothing to do with money, rates of return, planning, or even ability. He looked at his bride and saw not the mechanical bed dressed to look like anything but, nor the IV lines and monitors disguised in foliage. He saw a love—he saw a woman—who had changed everything. His fundamental understanding of the purpose of life.

His reason for being on this earth. His notions of true love and what was possible in the heart of man.

He saw the eyes that had captured his heart from the first glance, and the soul that endured behind them. It wouldn't have mattered what she was wearing, or if she was standing, or whether her body was what it had once been. It remained the body, the heart, the soul and the eyes of the only woman he had ever truly, fully loved. And on this Saturday, in a converted living room a world away from a life he'd once believed was everything, she was the most beautiful woman he'd ever seen. *She* was everything.

If little else about the celebration was routine, neither were the vows they shared. As it seemed they must, they'd composed their own; Joe once again agonizing over his ability to express words worthy of her, and Claire, long unable to write—and now speak—her own. In addition to art direction and event management, Audrey had been at her side for this endeavour as well, painstakingly capturing Claire's words each day over the previous weeks. Sometimes a mere sentence or two per day, other times an entire paragraph. In certain moments Audrey could merely guess at what Claire was trying to articulate, hearing fragments of speech that had devolved into drawn-out vowel sounds and stuttered consonants. Without feeding words to the older sister she adored, Audrey would ask "Are you trying to say...?", and wait for Claire's agreement or dissent. In the end, after Audrey read back a draft written over endless hours and polished for the dozenth time, Claire's eyes were alight. She'd nodded, slowly clenching a fist as though to say, "We've got it. It's perfect." At this, the sisters had burst into tears, holding onto one another long after.

Joe went first, reading her the letter he'd revised right up until forty-five minutes before the appointed hour. And for the first time that day, he took his eyes away from hers. He knew from the lump that squeezed his throat and the sting he felt at the corners of his eyes that if he looked up, the words would cease altogether and tears would mar the page. He wanted to be present to the moment, to convey with his tone everything the language might not. Yet as he began speaking he knew that as with so much else about their love, he'd simply have to accept what was, and hope she knew he'd yearned to give her all she deserved. When he finished and looked up, his weren't the only tears that had fallen. No one in the room had held on.

In lieu of being in the wedding party and to complement her role as officiant, Claire had asked Jacquie to read her letter to Joe. After taking a moment for composure and a sip of water that felt like sand, the best-friend turned-physician tried to read. The grains in her throat persisted, worsening after the first sentence, becoming impossible after the next. She looked to Audrey, who shook her head emphatically, spilling her own tears over. Jacquie was about to hand the letter to William, when a voice piped up.

"I'll read it, Mum," Holly said.

December 11, 1999

My dearest Joe, my great love,

When you found me, the smile that you saw and the warmth that I gave belied a brokenness within that seemed to have fused with the body without. I was healthy then, by outside appearance, but there were wounds marked with scars that had taken on a permanence I not only accepted, but allowed to crowd out the thought—or even hope—that life, and love, and the bonds of trust could somehow be different, somehow be true and honourable. I had stopped permitting myself the belief that love between two people could ever be what books or films promised. I had my babies, and I had my little life, and though it was wounded I had what remained of my heart. I made a promise to myself to safeguard those things for whatever time might remain. I promised not to let anyone in, ever again, and to work on believing that I, of myself, was enough.

And it worked! I did the work. I made peace with myself and the experiences that shaped (or misshaped) the woman within. I was blessed with children that were wonderful and kind, family and friends selfless and understanding. And even when my body threatened to buckle, I knew that it was possible to live with the broken pieces and remain intact. But there was still a quiet sadness, a silent mourning. For all the things that had gone right in my life I tried to tell myself I could live with the one thing gone wrong: that I had missed the chance to hold a heart that had searched for my own. That even though I knew I was good enough for me, I grieved the chance to know I might be enough for another, and they might know they were enough for me.

I don't know why life was created that way, why we search for that. Believe me, I don't have the first clue of the reason for most of what occurs in life. Maybe we invented it, with our books and movies. But when there's a longing in a human heart, the idea that someone, somewhere, might be looking for this exact one, seeking to love it as its very own... while that's sometimes the quietest voice within, it's the one most impossible to ignore.

So there you were, in a city not your own, on a night you hadn't planned, in a place you hadn't yet dreamed, and when I looked into your eyes and saw the way they looked at me, my heart knew. That yours had been looking. That mine was the one it wanted to find. And I knew I was home.

Joe, there isn't enough paper in the world, and we both know there will not be enough time, for me to ever properly tell you how much I love you, or the gift you've given me with your love. You have healed what I thought was irrevocably broken. You have made a year outlast a lifetime.

And though the body that holds it is falling apart, the heart within is whole. You've given me more than I felt I had a right to hope for, and in return, I make these vows, I give you this heart, and I offer you whatever time we have left. And for once I don't question if those things are enough, because from our very first moment you've never let me doubt they were.

If being loved by you has been my greatest gift, then loving you has been my greatest honour. Thank you for asking me to be your wife. Thank you for always looking at me the way you did that very first night. Thank you for holding me up and holding me close while my body let go. One day, when the words have entirely left, and even when the body has gone with them, know that I've done my best to hold you up as well, and speak those things that can only be expressed in a love like ours.

Thank you for the gift of knowing true love exists, and that the world I leave has men like you. That my children will be safe; that their dreams are possible too. That I can let go, without needing anything more. Thank you for holding my heart. Thank you for being my last first kiss. Thank you for finding me.

And to whomever I owe this to, thank you for this dream come true.

Yours in love, now and always,
Claire

CHAPTER 79
FORCE OF NATURE

Claire died eight weeks later.

There had been no obvious moment, no grand denouement where they'd known she was going, where she'd said her goodbyes and passed in the arms of her loved ones. In the days and weeks prior it appeared different systems would start and fail on different days, some in glaring displays where Claire struggled and strained, others in quiet surrender, like a candle flame reaching the end of its wick. On the last night, many had snuffed out at once.

Later, her passing would be attributed to complications from pneumonia, with her body simply too ill-equipped to fight back. But in the end, of all the messages that went undelivered from her brain to her body, those that told her lungs to continue rising and falling simply stopped sending. The monitors in the bedroom had shrieked, and though Joe woke within mere moments of the last breath Claire ever took, he knew she was gone. Not because the machines told him so, but because of what he saw when he looked at her face. For the first time since the night of their wedding, she looked at peace.

Months earlier, when Claire prepared her will and

advanced directives, in among the far too many difficult conversations she was forced to endure she'd finally indicated a wish for no extraordinary acts. If there was an inadvertent emergency—another choking episode, say—she'd assented to intervention. Yet if her fundamental biology could no longer sustain life of its own accord, she made it clear she would let her body let go.

During one of the endless appointments at Jacquie's office before Claire was housebound, the physician had delicately broached the subjects of feeding tubes and resuscitation measures. With emotion hidden from her face and tone, Claire had asked, "Can you make me better? Am I ever going to get better?" With far too much emotion visible in her eyes and voice, Jacquie had replied that she could not, and Claire would not.

It seemed wanton and strange to make such determinations at any age, let alone one where children remained. Yet if this was when her physical self had chosen to concede its function, Claire couldn't imagine years of a mind that willed but a body that would not. It was an excruciating choice, Claire unable to comprehend not having decades more with her loved ones. But the malevolence of her condition had forced these considerations, and the ultimate, impossible decision.

Though she had never shown it, Joe knew her scrawled signature on the directive had been a knife through her heart. An admission she would never know how her children looked or sounded as adults. Would not see their aspirations evolve or their dreams attained. Would not know the other side of parenthood, of having adult relationships that moved her role closer to confidante or friend. She knew she would never care for any of her babies should their own genetic code turn against them.

Joe wondered, though this too was never spoken aloud, if these admissions had weakened her resolve and accelerated her decline. She could never be faulted if they had; barring a miracle, her body was never going to improve, would rarely remain stable, would most often worsen. Any artificial prolonging of her life would merely underscore the heartbreaking reality that while she might witness Jack come home from his first day of work, or help Holly with university applications, or know whether Ainsley was as free-spirited a teenager as she was a child, in the end it would still be borrowed time, and would only get her heart-wrenchingly closer to moments still stolen away.

Maybe it had been easier to accept that the time she had now—and her loved ones as they were in these moments—would be the last she would know. Maybe that was easier to make peace with, rather than hoping for a future that might or might not be taken away, might or might not be better or worse. Perhaps it was a bittersweet gift, under the circumstances, to know that life had reached its own measure of perfection in the children she'd raised, the family she'd drawn closer to, the man she'd loved and who loved her deeply in return.

And so it was, while the monitors continued to scream as though giving voice to the howling of his heart within, that Joe stood at Claire's side, struggling to honour the last request she'd ever made.

William had flown into the room flanked by that evening's nurse, the old man having fallen asleep on the couch after watching a movie with the children. As Joe held Claire's hand and pushed the hair away from her face, the doctor confirmed what the machines had made clear. There was no need for words, and after brief eye contact and a nearly imperceptible nod, William and the nurse turned off the monitors, backed out of the room, and closed the door.

Joe stood in the silence, afraid any movement would buckle him.

When breath finally insisted, he broke to his knees, burying his head into her side. The grief assailed him with avarice, reaching beyond the deepest places of instinct and emotion. He'd known the moment was imminent; had spent many a night contemplating the loaded knowledge of a loved one nearing the end. But cognitive preparation had been no match for this moment of *real* loss, blooming across his consciousness now like dye bleeding on linen. His understanding became visceral and irrevocable, knowing as he gripped her hand that she would not return the touch. Her eyes would not open to look into his.

The last words—or at least as close to words as they'd been—came after he'd held a straw to her mouth for a sip of water, asked if he could get her anything else before bed, kissed her forehead goodnight and whispered 'I love you,' and her mouth returned the parts of those words it still could. This was the last record, the last moment he would ever say anything to her when she would still hear him, the last time her eyes would convey what her voice would not.

All of that was over now. Claire was gone, and no remedy of science nor force of nature would bring her back to the body that had carried and then destroyed her.

Joe felt like he too might never breathe again.

CHAPTER 80
ADRIFT

THERE WAS A service a week later, allowing time for family and friends abroad to make arrangements. For Joe, the days before and after formed a void, an interminable blackness shrouding every motion he made, every thought he had, every hour he trudged through. To have asked him years later the events of the first months of the new millennium—where he went, whom he spoke with, what transpired—he couldn't have said, these things painted over in his memory with gray brushstrokes that blended with the pain beneath. The agony that remained had been more than enough; a remembrance of a time where although she would never leave his heart, Claire had left his life.

He remained in England, the thought of leaving too painful, the act of staying illuminating his grief. As he'd only ever known London as he'd known it with Claire, every place was a memory of her. Yet it was what he had left to hold onto, and he clung tighter than he knew was healthy. He visited the sights they'd seen on their first date, remembered the conversations they'd had, tried to feel the touch they'd shared. He walked the park that had become the limit of their world in the only autumn they would ever know. To leave these places, and the memories that felt as immediate as the moments in which they'd lived them, would have entrenched the loss with a finality he wasn't willing to accept.

He'd retreated to his flat the day she passed, having no clue how to spend the night in the house he'd been with her, despite the family's offer to stay. He came during the days to clean and restore the space to a normal family home, removing artifacts of the sickness that had pervaded their lives. They returned Claire's bedroom to life before bed rails and grab bars, and the main floor office to a mode beyond makeshift hospice. Though the family members had little use for a workspace, the sanitized and generic look detracted from the other reminders they couldn't avoid.

William remained in the apartment and visited the home with Joe during these weeks of slow recalibration, leaving for Canada only when excuses to touch up another coat of paint or colour another picture book or watch another football match had been exhausted. He'd offered to continue paying half the rent on the flat with money he knew neither of them needed, and when the younger man politely declined, William recognized the time had arrived for Joe to process in solitude. In his many years of practice and his own years of love and loss, the old man knew there came a point on the path of sorrow that needed to be walked alone. And thus with a threat to make a fourth overnight flight if Joe failed to keep their weekly phone calls, William left the younger man to take his next steps.

Where this path was meant to lead him, Joe hadn't any

idea. He didn't need to get back to work. Didn't need to return home. Didn't need to be anywhere. At times some element of the job or family would call his attention back, sometimes even instilling a willingness to press forward. Yet these moments were fleeting, and led to subsequent fallouts that exceeded the conviction with which they began.

Though it was an ongoing argument with instinct, he'd determined not to remain housebound for any longer than a few days at a time. Yet as the seasons changed, Joe recognized his lengthening hiking trips for what they really were: an avenue of escape rather than a path of repose. He saw more of Europe than he'd ever imagined, lost in unfamiliar languages and undiscovered mountain ranges, where the words he heard meant nothing to him and the sights he saw carried no memories.

He longed for someone to tell him the timeline. To let him know when he might reemerge above the surface and take a new breath for the one he'd been holding since Claire exhaled her last. He could work with that. Buy and hold, as went the enduring edict of his old life. Wait for the moment of maturity. He'd been good at it, known how to do it, known how to lead others to do it for themselves.

If someone could tell him these things, he'd know whether to worry about the part of him that held on. That longed for her return, for a reversal of everything gone wrong. That didn't know how to live a life he'd come to believe he would live in union with her. He knew these things were an impossibility, and yet no one could tell him how to negate those voices of his heart and soul. In all the assurances about time and its ability to reconcile, no one could tell him what to do next. No one *knew* what came next.

He'd tried, during resupply trips to London between backcountry treks, to visit with Audrey and the children. It felt wrong to simply exit their lives after the lines of distinction had dissolved so rapidly that previous fall. It felt like a negation of those relationships, which felt like a negation of Claire herself. The afternoons or evenings in their home were always pleasant, if not without an undertone of sadness. For Joe, their faces were a bittersweet memorial. For them, his presence was a healing reminder. Proof beyond their own lives that Claire's life lived on in one who had been there by choice, compelled by love, and within whose heart her memory endured.

They invited Joe for dinners and board games, movies and museums, even short trips away to Center Parcs. None of these occasions felt forced, no invitations made from pity or obligation. Though devastated by Claire's absence, the children had responded with a certain pliability. Audrey told Joe they seemed better than adults at having a blowout if a blowout was required, creating space for the immediacy of their grief. In other moments they appeared to harmonize with their mourning rather than avoid it, asking for foods Claire loved to savour or writing stories she would have been proud of, these things done in celebration as much as sorrow.

While the legal transition of Claire's passing felt like a tectonic shift for Audrey, for the children—at least on the surface—all remained as it had been before. Claire's assets were left in trust to the kids with their aunt as executor, which meant little change to daily life as they continued on in the same home and same schools, amid the same friends and routines.

In addition to arranging her estate, Claire's lawyer had petitioned on her behalf for sole parental rights. They'd managed to serve David with the paperwork during a rare trip back to the UK, after he returned to collect possessions from Miranda's home—an "anonymous" phone call made from that residence to Claire's, tipping off his arrival. David hadn't contested, already awash in legal action from his latest separation, while trying to relocate to the US and marry (presumably to secure a green card from) the Floridian actress.

Claire had been prepared for a fight, if for no reasons other than David's inexhaustible ego and compulsion to attain the upper hand. But there had been none. He'd even called the house after signing off, speaking with Claire while she'd still been able. The conversation had been calm, surprisingly conciliatory. He'd made no excuses nor attempted any gaslighting. He said he'd tried to learn to live with his abject failure as a father and a husband. He surmised that the best way to amend these transgressions might be to subject Claire and the kids to them no further.

Claire toed a line of diplomacy in this conversation, at once furious and taken aback. She told him it wasn't too late with his children, suggesting that if he really wanted to make amends, it might take the form of living action. He said he wished for that, but knew he was too reckless, too self-absorbed. He said he would maintain communication, try to see them whenever he was in the UK, but suggested it was better not to build expectation until he knew he could follow through.

Unable to argue the logic and still wishing to tear out his throat through the phone, Claire reminded him of the inevitability of time. He couldn't suddenly wish to be a father when Ainsley was seventeen and recapture the seven-year-old she was today. David countered that the woman Ainsley would become might stand a chance if he didn't destroy hope with the little girl she was now. He'd ended the call by saying, "I know what I am, Claire. And I'm sorry."

Throughout all of this, Joe had walked a cautious line between support and uncertainty. He hadn't quite known where to step while Claire was still alive, and that path seemed even more shrouded now. He'd come to love the children in his own way, to feel a part of their lives, and they a part of his. He admired the traits that made them unique and the blend of characteristics that bound them as siblings. He saw Claire in all three, in mannerism, appearance, and spirit. He'd felt a connection he'd never quite experienced, a glimpse of how it might feel to have children of his own.

He'd watched as Claire tried to guide them, to build them up while letting them find their place in the world. He'd known there was nothing they ever did, nor could ever do, to cause her affection to become guarded or conditional. He'd understood that love was pure when the heart couldn't be broken by unmet need or expectation. And yet his heart broke now, a little more, at the sight of them. He drifted between wanting to be there all the time and not at all.

Beyond his grief and uncertainty, the most maddening element for Joe was the irreconcilability. A part of him couldn't imagine having never known Claire. Even the thought sent a twinge through his chest. And yet there it was, sometimes as loud or louder than any other thought at all: what if he had never met her? Joe could try to tell himself that without her, his life might have been a banal pursuit of the inane. A life lived only in numbers and probabilities, from nine to five and cradle to grave, devoid of any meaning. But at what cost had he thrown away his carefully crafted mechanisms that—shallow or not—had kept him safe, kept him stable, kept his mind at ease? Now he felt like an island unto himself, absconded from any sense of home, any feeling of solid ground.

No. This was *worse* than being an island. He was adrift, pushed by irregular and irrational tides that moved him in every direction, and therefore none at all.

Without her, there would not have been this.

There would not be this pain.

Though it felt like damning her as well, he damned the dreams that had brought him to Claire, only to take her away.

CHAPTER 81
SHE WAS HOME

"Can you pass the yorkies, please, Mr. Riley?"

Ainsley was dressed in a costume mashup of Belle's yellow ball gown from Beauty and the Beast, and Jessie's hat and vest from Toy Story. The gown portion of the ensemble was apparently responsible for affecting proper decorum while requesting additional servings.

Joe looked up with eyes that had glazed over while staring into the gravy boat, feigned a smile, and passed the plate to the young lady. He'd been assigned the role of Woody for this otherwise normal summer Saturday lunch, donning a cardboard cowboy hat that persisted in falling into his eyes. He couldn't very well remove it however, having been made by the young cowgirl-belle-of-the-ball herself.

"Say 'To Infinity and Beyond!' again!" Ainsley coaxed.

"You know Woody doesn't say that, right? Buzz does?" Joe replied.

Ainsley burst into a giggle. "Say 'Buzz does' again!"

"Buzz does."

This time the laughter was contagious, at first infecting Audrey and Daniel across the table, then spreading through to Holly. It even caught Jack when Ainsley snorted, causing a spray of milk to depart one of her nostrils. By then, even Joe was not immune. Her little laugh was reminiscent of her mother's, along with the tiny, barely detectable snort. It would always get him going when Claire had done it, and for once, this reminder wasn't accompanied by a tidal wave of grief.

"To infinity, AND BEYOND!" Joe suddenly bellowed. Ainsley erupted in a shriek, followed by a rolling giggle that bent her over at the side, one hand on her tummy, the other covering her nose and mouth. Milk was everywhere.

It had been a good day.

Joe had been considering talking to Audrey about lessening these visits. Dinners that in those first weeks were nearly every day, then twice a week in the spring. Now only Saturdays or Sundays. The standing invitation had remained, but what had been at first an equitable tradeoff between heartwarming and heart-wrenching was now squarely the latter. Save for rare exceptions, like these days of laughter and milk through the nose, board games afterward (with Joe's losing streak untarnished), and capped by a movie on the couch.

He'd been cleaning up while the children readied for bed, washing dishes when Audrey walked over with a drying towel.

"How are you doing, Joe?"

The question surprised him. As a fellow recipient of that impossible query, they had implicitly agreed not to trouble the other with it. The shock of her asking it now pushed out of his mind any pre-planned prose of half-formed reasons why he ought not come around anymore.

"You know, after six months, you'd think I'd have taken *some* time to formulate some kind of canned response to that, but—" He cleared his throat, felt the familiar squeeze coming on.

"I don't have the first idea how to answer that question, Audrey."

She picked up a plate and began drying. "I do. In general I have two replies, depending on my mood. 'Sod off,' or if I'm feeling particularly magnanimous, I'll say, 'Shall I show you the inside of your arsehole, so you'll have an idea?' Both seem to work rather effectively."

Joe let out a choked laugh, and busied himself with scouring a casserole dish.

"Kidding aside—though I'm not kidding about those canned replies, as you called them—I do think I have an idea of how you can answer that. At least with us," Audrey said.

"Which is?" Joe kept his eyes down.

"The truth, whatever that looks like. If you're pissed, then be pissed. If you're sad, be sad. If you're numb, well then you're numb. And if you just need to tell someone to sod off—well, you can safely do that here. Not to the children, of course. You know what I mean."

Joe let out another stifled laugh. "Of course."

Audrey leaned over the sink, pushing herself into his peripheral vision. "Joe. Seriously. I'm getting a little worried about you, and I get decidedly uncomfortable when I worry about other people." She turned his shoulder in order to face him directly. "Are you okay? You don't look well. You kept rubbing your neck and shoulders during dinner, and you're starting to look like an insomniatic skeleton with hypertension for complexion."

The last comment elicited a full, unrestrained laugh. Joe had a moment to reflect that a record had likely been broken: the smiles and laughter of the day surpassing those of the last months combined.

"I'm okay," he said, when the laughter subsided. "That's probably the best word for it, actually. Just had some kind of a headache earlier, and overall I'm not getting a lot of rest. Nothing a good night of sleep won't fix, I'm sure."

"Okay. I'm going to accept that for now, and I'm going to take that sponge—that you're not making great work with, by the way, with those listless little circles on the pan—and I'll finish up the dishes here. You're going to head home, on the condition that you go straight to bed and sleep round-the-clock if you have to. Deal?"

"That's just the thing though, Audrey." He felt the tightening again, the squeeze from his chest up through his throat, towards his head and eyes. He swallowed hard.

"What's that?"

"*She* was home."

"I know she was, Joe. I know."

CHAPTER 82
A FULL HEART

"Joe."

He tried to turn his head.

"Joe, wake up."

The feeling was of straining to become conscious while fifty feet underwater. He could hear the muted sounds of the surface and see its refracted lights, but when he opened his eyes it seemed too far away. The blackness around him and the fatigue he felt were too much to swim against. He closed his eyes again.

The last thing he could remember was an almost out-of-body experience of losing composure. Rather than going to bed per Audrey's orders, a voice had told him to start packing up his flat. To close down this torment and flee to anywhere that wasn't this place. This island. He recalled a vague scene of watching himself thrash around the apartment, strewing papers and clothing and books and perhaps even dishes—whatever his agony could grab hold of—in every direction.

The despair he'd felt after William turned off the machines, the tidal sweep of emotion that dissolved his corporeal self and left him a curled up vibration of torment beside her bed, the otherworldly cries he let loose in the blankets covering her vacant body, cries that then snuffed out like an inferno exhausting the oxygen in the room... These things returned after *his* body seemingly breached, having reached its lifelong limit of sorrow, exploding like a backdraft.

He couldn't recall what time he had capitulated, whether night or day, or the transition of one to the other. He remembered only a fatigue that had withered and worn through every strand of his body, finally leading to collapse somewhere in the apartment—perhaps on his bed, perhaps the sofa, perhaps even the floor. Something was trying to pull him away from the winter's sleep that had overtaken him, and whatever strength he had left tried to fight it.

"Open your eyes, Joe." The voice again, muffled and distant.

He tried to propel himself further underwater, to quell the sound completely.

"I'm here, my love."

This voice now unmistakable, now undeniable, as though having cut the space between sound and reception in a nanosecond, speaking directly into his ear.

He opened his eyes and began wading toward a picture that was at once clear and muddled. He saw several places and none specifically. There was Claire's kitchen blending with their hotel room at Culloden House. The park across the street merged with their trail in Scotland. The Château Lake Louise fused with the art gallery. He was standing in each of these places and yet none at all, the confusion momentarily distracting him from the voice he'd heard.

"Joe. My love."

He turned his head toward the sound. His chest immediately hitched, a sudden inhale coming in slips while he fought for an unbroken stream of air. Joe's eyes welled instantly, threatening to obscure the sight before him.

It was her.

It was Claire.

"How is this—" he finally managed, his voice trembling and on the edge of control. "How did— where are—" He looked around again, though the motion was involuntary; he hadn't wanted to move his gaze lest his shift in focus cause her to vanish.

"Oh Claire," he finally said, turning back to her. He attempted more but his throat bound against the words. A tear let go of his right eye, dissolving the hold against the rest.

She smiled, and lifted a hand to his face. He felt her warmth, though it wasn't direct. It was the subdued sensation he'd felt in only one other circumstance. "I love you so much," she said, pulling him in. He broke.

"I've missed you so much. So, so, much," he heaved into her shoulder, as he felt one of her arms wrapped around his back and a hand in his hair. Her touch was strong, stable. She felt healthy. Unwavering. Unbroken.

"I've missed you too, my love." She stepped back to look at him, and wiped away his tears. Her smile was constant. His eyes searched hers. A realization dawned, and he nearly pulled away in reflex.

"Am I dreaming this? Are you a dream?"

OF DREAMS AND ANGELS

She leaned forward to kiss his cheek. "You are dreaming, my love, but I am not a dream."

"No," he said, pulling away. "I can't do this. This can't just be a dream." The tenuous restraint he'd affected let go once again. "It's too hard without you, Claire. I don't want to do this life without you."

"I didn't want that either, honey."

"Don't tell me you're here just to tell me that it's going to be okay, all right? Don't tell me that. Don't tell me that there's some reason for this, or give me some rationale why I should be okay and move on." He could hear internal dialogue shouting at him not to waste this moment, not to be angry at her—though it had never been her he was angry with—and that this moment might end any second, his anguish might make her disappear.

"I won't, Joe." She reached a hand to his cheek again. "I just wanted to tell you that I love you."

"I don't understand, Claire. Help me understand. Why did they send me to you in the first place? Why are you here now? Why did they do this, only to take us away from each other?" His eyes searched hers again, swept as always into the ocean green. "I don't understand," he repeated, "and I don't know what to do."

"You've been asking yourself, 'What was the point?'" She lifted his hand and kissed the back of it. "You've been torturing yourself with why, and what to do next."

Joe nodded, his throat too clenched to reply.

"And I'm going to honour your request not to tell you it's okay." She smiled, and lifted his hand to her cheek, touching it against the side of her face. God, how he had missed her touch. "But is it okay if I tell you *part* of the why?" she asked.

He nodded again. Internal voices admonished him for not having greater control, but he was helpless in her presence. He always had been.

"I'm not going to lie, Joseph Riley. In the endless hours toward the end—but hours that still could never have been enough—when I went through my own existential crises, I often asked why. Not the 'why me' part of having a disease, or of dying young, though I asked those things plenty of times too. But why us? Why this? Why the 'giveth, only to take away' bollocks?" She said this with another grin, the one she'd disarmed him with time and again.

"I don't think I could have been given any answer during that time that would have made things easier, Joe. That would have taken away the pain I felt every time I looked in your eyes and wondered if it was the last time. That would have made it okay those times that you kissed me, and I couldn't kiss you back." She leaned forward and gently touched her mouth to his. "And no answer would have ever made it okay after I couldn't tell you I loved you anymore."

Joe shook his head and swallowed hard. "I always knew, Claire, I always felt it. Always saw it in your eyes."

"I know, but that seemed like the cruelest twist of fate. To finally find love, and then not be able to say it any longer. It helps my heart to know you still felt it, though."

Joe could feel himself losing hold again. "Can I stay here with you, Claire? I don't want to go back. There's nothing out there for me anymore."

"Oh my love, but there is."

He shook his head again, releasing further tears. "Don't *tell me that,* Claire, I don't *want that.* All I want is you."

"I know, honey. I want that too. But I also want you to know what would have happened if we hadn't met. And, difficult as it has been, impossible as it feels, if we hadn't parted."

His stomach twisted, her eyes the only thing keeping him steady. He wanted to tear apart the mosaic of memory floating around them. To search behind the shroud for someone who would answer for this.

She kissed him again, pulling his attention back to her. "My body started letting go of itself, silently, long before the dreams that brought you to me. And it would have, whether you'd found me or not." She nodded at him, and he reluctantly returned the gesture.

"If you hadn't seen me, if you hadn't found me, I would have ended these days with a mostly beautiful life, and my beautiful children, but with the idea that this world was nothing but an unending stream of unmet hopes and unrealistic dreams. I couldn't have looked my kids in the eye at the end and earnestly told them it was a really good life, that it was okay to hope, okay to dream. You changed that, Joe. You changed *me.*

"I tried to tell you that before I left, and I think maybe you even believed it for a time. But your pain has consumed you. It has made you forget. You forget why the pain exists in the first place. You look at our love as the cost, and pain as the reward for finding each other. And that can't be why our love existed, Joe. It can't be something that drives you further underground. There's a world out there that still needs you. There are some things still left for you to do.

"I am so, so sorry you're hurting. And please know I never wanted to leave you. But when I was called home, I got to go with a full heart. That's more than a lot of people get, and it was more than I hoped for.

"A lot of people want to change the world, Joe." She pulled him close, her mouth next to his ear. "I never needed to, and I don't think you did, either. But still, you changed *mine*. My entire world. My whole heart. You made me believe in love again, and while it may not have healed my body—these vessels of ours are going to go one way or another, some day or another—it healed my heart. It made me believe."

She moved back to face him once more. He held her tighter, afraid to let go. "Will I see you again?" he finally asked, afraid the question itself would make this—whatever it was—finite, unavailable, never to happen again.

"You can see me anytime you want to, Joe."

"How?"

"There are three babies who love you, a family that got to see what love looks like—though it didn't look the way most of us are used to. You can see me in them. And they get to remember pieces of me in you. You changed their world, too.

"You can see me in these places that move around us, right now. You can remember that for a time, you took these spaces available to the whole world and made them just for me. A world where I was the most important.

Most beautiful. Most loved. Not just *felt* like I was, Joe. I *know* that I was.

"And you can even find me in dreams." She kissed him once more.

"But I hope I can be permitted one last wish, Joe, one last request—which is a lot to ask, I know." She flashed a grin once more. "That's not what I want for you. We can see each other here, but the dreams were never about giving you a place to escape. They were about showing you what's possible.

"I want you to live your life, Joe. I don't mean living out the days just to get to the nights, in the hope we'll see each other again. I spent my entire life with a crenellated heart because of loss, and mourning what might have been. In that last year, you helped me take that armour down, helped show *me* what is possible.

"I'll be with you always, as long as you don't lose sight of that. I'll be with you, even though you can't see it. If you look without using your eyes, you'll feel it."

"Wait—" Joe reached up, touched a hand to the nape of his neck. "Dinner... I thought I was getting a headache... The back of my head—was that you?"

Claire smiled.

He pulled her into him and kissed her, remembering the night under London rain when their lips met for the first time.

When they released, he could read her eyes as if he had been looking through them.

"This feels like goodbye," he choked.

"We already said goodbye. Maybe not the way you

imagined, but then, when was anything about our love according to plan?" She smiled, kissed him once more.

"It was a beautiful dream, Joe. And now it's time to wake up."

CHAPTER 83
HERE TO SEE IT

JUNE 2001

JOE STOOD AT the ridge and looked toward the horizon, saw the Loch alight with flickering yellows and reds from the setting sun. Another day's hike would do it; a day spent to recapture days that never were. If she couldn't be there in body he would take her there in spirit, and go beyond that last step taken on the trail together.

He would have given her the world, and though there hadn't been time to see it with her, he'd make good on his promise, somehow.

"Joe? Sorry to bother, but I think I have the kindling ready. I didn't mean to startle you."

"You didn't startle me at all, just got lost in thought," Joe replied, throwing an arm around Jack's shoulder. "And you're *never* bothering me, okay? Let's go see how you did. Perfectly, I'm sure."

They walked from the ridge to the campsite chosen "by committee"—equal votes allotted to the plush animals in Ainsley's backpack, over protests from the older children. The girls (mostly Holly, while Ainsley and the stuffies supervised) had set up their tent without Joe's assistance, despite only a few practice runs in the backyard. Jackson had constructed his own with proficiency rivaling Joe's lifetime of experience. The young man was a natural, it seemed.

For Joe, he would sleep under the stars, and wonder where she was among them.

"When do we get to have the marshmallows and chocolate?" Ainsley asked, as the gentlemen inspected Jack's kindling arrangement.

"We call them 'S'mores,' and you get to have them after your brother lights this expert campfire setup. And *after* you've had a healthy dinner of roasted hotdogs, too."

"Why are they called 'S'mores' again?"

"Because once you've had one, you're gonna want to have *S-MORE!*" Joe said, scooping her up and spinning her around, her giggles echoing off the rocks and trees.

As the glow on their faces transitioned from sunset to dancing campfire light, Joe watched the children revel in their nutritionally irresponsible dinners and desserts. Maybe food *was* for fun, after all.

He listened as each recounted stories of the closing school year, of favourite teachers and boring studies, of last year's friendships faded and this year's begun anew. He laughed as they grappled with the chocolate and marshmallow sandwiches, witnessing first bites taken and toothless grins appearing around bits of cookie stuck to their teeth. He heard their plans, their stories, their hopes, their disappointments. Their dreams. He saw Claire in all of it, in every word and gesture.

A voice interrupted these thoughts, pulling him back to the world within the firelight.

"Thank you for today, Joe."

"Oh, you're very welcome, Holly."

"Thank you, Joe!", "Yes, thank you," added the others. Joe smiled and looked into the fire.

"And for everything else," Holly said, quieter this time.

Joe looked back up, the water in his eyes blurring his sight. Before emotion could threaten further, he stood to grab another log for the fire. "Thank *you*. I really should be thanking the three of you, for letting me drag you out into the wilderness." This was met with more toothy grins. "Ainsley, what did the weather printout say for tomorrow?"

The youngest girl cleared her marshmallow-laden throat and affected her best reporting voice. "It said, 'Partly cloudy with thirties-chances of rain.'"

"Perfect," Joe grinned. He'd had the weather charts memorized for days, but used any excuse to hear her say 'thirties-' or 'forties-chances' when recounting the probability of precipitation.

It's the little moments, he thought.

The kids reached for their roasting sticks, at first with hesitation and then delight as Joe sanctioned the move by passing around more marshmallows and chocolate. He excused himself as they indulged another small pleasure he'd once known but long forgotten.

He walked back toward the ridge, to a place he'd once stood with her.

"Are you there?" he whispered.

He heard only the sounds of the forest, of the campfire

crackling behind him, of a burst of distant laughter from the three children.

"I know. It's silly," he said, looking down, pushing leaves and rocks around with his boot. "I didn't actually expect to see or hear you, but I still catch myself thinking that we'll come around a corner or over a ridge and you'll be there, smiling, waiting for us."

Joe took a breath and looked over his shoulder to the campfire, then back to the darkened earth beneath his feet.

"I remember you every day, Claire."

He pinched the sides of his eyes, took in a breath, and looked up toward the silhouetted lake.

"I know you asked me to keep going. Not to spend all my time trying to find you again. And I've tried to do that, even though I wonder where you went. I try to honour what we had by seeing it in every part of my life." Another sound of laughter turned him back toward the firelight.

"I just sometimes wish that you were still here to see it too."

He stepped toward the campfire but stopped short. A smile began to cross his face.

Joe reached up and touched the back of his neck.

AUTHOR'S NOTE

WHEN I WAS eleven-years-old, my maternal grandmother passed away after a brief, yet violent struggle with a neurodegenerative condition. Officially, she had been diagnosed with Parkinson's Disease, however in the years since her passing, my mother—a healthcare professional with a lifetime spent working in hospitals, and specifically in palliative care—never came across or even heard of another case as aggressive. The period between Grandma's diagnosis and death was less than five years.

The line from the story, "This is a *very* malignant form of Parkinson's," was an actual statement made by one of her physicians, and we wondered both then and now if there had been a concurrent condition, or if it was something else altogether. Grandma died before we could find out for certain. It was the early 90's, and some of the options available today were either unknown or untested then. It cannot be understated that Parkinson's Disease itself is not fatal, as additional quotes from the book assert, and it would do well to reiterate that fact here.

I did not set out to write a book about PD or neurodegenerative disease, nor is *Of Dreams and Angels* solely a story about either. Stephen King, in his memoir *On Writing,* describes how many stories can be framed as a

"What if?" question. When the tale within these covers first knocked on the door of my imagination, it arrived simply in that form: What if a man began to dream through the eyes of a woman he'd never met, yet actually existed? That was it. That's all I started with, that's all I knew. As my good ol' unbeknownst-to-him mentor Steve might also tell you, everything that happened from there was what was revealed as I set out to answer that question.

Again, no part of me began with the intent of recounting the tragedy of an active mind trapped by a deteriorating body. Nor did I deliberately intend to memorialize a loved one by ensuring part of her untold story appeared somewhere, though I am grateful it will. I just kept showing up to the keyboard, after that *What if* question popped into my head from wherever it is that stories come from. And as many a writer can attest, the book gave *me* the answers, and not the other way around.

What I *have* intended to do is my utmost not to mischaracterize neurodegenerative conditions, nor those who are affected by them. Young Onset Parkinson's Disease is rare, with statistics estimating that between 2-10% of the overall PD population is under the age of 40. Those living with Parkinson's typically have a similar life expectancy to those without. In fact, when my grandmother received her diagnosis, my mom remembers an initial feeling of relief that it wasn't a condition known to be life-threatening.

At the same time, I have endeavoured not to mischaracterize or downplay a real-life occurrence in our family, nor the woman it happened to. Claire is not my grandmother; Claire is who she told me she is. What I do know for certain about her, my grandmother, my mother (who bore witness to Grandma's story), and my wife (who inspired much of Claire's personality), is that they're all beautifully strong individuals. Wonderfully complex. Impossible to relegate or limit. Generous with their hearts, and courageous with their lives. These were the stories I really tried to tell.

My conscious memories of my grandmother and her condition are woefully inadequate, and come more in the form of feeling than specific details. As such, I've had to rely on the memories, research, and expertise of others. To those individuals, I owe a huge debt of gratitude. For the places within the story where I got it right, the credit belongs to them. Any mistakes are entirely my own.

Of Dreams and Angels is a story about possibility, faith, and healing our hearts within despite our challenges without. Neurodegenerative disease is part of that story, just as it is part of the story of my family. Yet it is not the defining theme here any more than it was of my grandmother's life, nor of the lives of those who face these challenges every day. I hope I have honoured her. I hope I have honoured the courageous individuals and families that contend with these conditions. For whatever ways my depiction of Claire may have been inadequate, I do hope you still feel seen. I hope you feel incredibly loved.

Thank you for being here, dear reader. Thank you for your time.

—Jared Morrison
Alberta, Canada, March 9, 2021

ACKNOWLEDGEMENTS

Stephen King once said that "Writing is a lonely job." And yet the art of turning what began as a single thought from the cosmos into the book you hold in your hands is nothing short of a village raising a child of the imagination. To everyone who helped make *Of Dreams* a reality, either directly or through the part you have played in my life, you have my ineffable and humble gratitude. With a debut novel, that ends up being a sizable list, but every person here walked some part of the path with me, either via a single step in the form of an encouraging word, or for endless miles, in the form of their presence in my life. This book would not exist without each and every step. I will inevitability and unintentionally end up forgetting names here, so please accept my earnest apologies in advance, and know that it's a writer's curse to read their work later on and see all the things (or people) that are missing.

To my first readers, Brenda, Sherry and Sonja. I handed you a mass of uncurated, stream-of-consciousness prose, and you helped me find the poetry. Your feedback was invaluable and helped me shape this story into what it needed to be. I know you're enjoying retirement, but you did too well of a job and I'm sorry to say that you're hired for life.

OF DREAMS AND ANGELS

To Rose, who said those fateful words to me several years ago—"Do you ever write?"—and suggested I put pen to paper to make sense of the world. I would have never arrived here if you hadn't encouraged me to start there.

To Ken, who handed me that little token and said, "This may be a little weird, but it's just meant to be a reminder to never stop writing." It wasn't weird, Ken. And I did stop for a little while, after I had tried to *be* the story, instead of letting the stories come through me. But your gift sat waiting on the desk until I was ready, and has sat beside me every day since.

To Ashley Santoro and Phillip Gessert, who brought their individual design talents to creating the most beautiful book I've ever seen. Thank you both for working so diligently with the Love of my Life to manifest the perfect visual representation of this labour of love. It was one of those things where I couldn't possibly have articulated what I was hoping for, but once I saw all of it, I knew it was exactly right. Which is just about perfect for a love story.

To the incredible Instagram community. Some of you have been reading along since the beginning, before I knew anything more about the woman in Joe's dreams than he did. Your support has meant the world to me. When I started the @jaredwrites account, it was after hearing one of those little internal voices saying, "Your job is to put the words out there, and let the universe handle the rest." Well, the universe connected me with you, and for that alone I shall remain eternally grateful, let alone for the beautiful poetry, prose, and books you've brought into my life. To Abbie, Abby, Aimee, Alex, Alexandra, Alix, Alicia, Alycia, Allister, Ama, Amanda, Amber, Amelie, Amy, Anastasia, Andrea, Angel, Angela, Ann, Anna, Anni, Antoine, Antonio, Autumn, Bay, Beau, Becca, Bekka, Berly, Bethany, Brandi, Brandy, Bree, Brittany, Bronagh, Brooklyn, Brooklynn, Caroline, Carrie, Casey, Cass, CC, Celeste, Chance, Cheryl, Christina, Christine, Christopher, CJ, Clare, Cortny, Courtney, Craig, Daisy, Daleen, Danni, Danielle, Darren, Dave, Davyne, Deanna, Debasmita, Dee, Denise, Dev, Devin, Dolores, Drew, DS, Dusty, Elena, Elle, Ellie, Elliot, Emanuelle, Emily, Eve, Fatima, Gabi, GG, Gillian, Glenda, Greta, Gretchen, Hawksley, Ian, Ignacio, Iris, Jai, Jakki, James, Jasmina, Jaycee, Jean-Philippe, Jen, Jenn, Jennifer, Jess, Jessi, Jillian, Jocelyn, Jon, Jordyn, Joy, Julian, Julie, Karen, Kari, Kate, Kathleen, Katie, Katina, Keekee, Kelly, Kellie, Kristina, Kristi, Kyli, Lanie, Laura, Lauren, Leanne, Leigh, Lindsay, Lindsey, Lisa, Louie, Louise, Luisa, Madeline, Mateja, Matthew, Melissa, Mert, Michael, Michelle, MJ, Nadia, Natalie, Natascha, Nicole, Nicholas, Nikki, Odile, Pam, Paul, Pearl, Penny, Pooja, Rachel, Raisa, Raiza, Rajat, Realf, Rebekah, Riley, Rob, Robin, Rolly, Rosie, Rowan, Ryne, Samson, Sandra, Sanella, Sara, Sarah, Savitri, Serene, Seyda, Shanna, Shannon, Sharmeen, Sinead, SK, Somi, Sonny, Sophie, Stacey, Stacie, Stella, Steph, Stephanie, Sue, Susannah, Suze, Tanya, Tara, Tash, Tasha, Taylor, Tiffany, Tilly, Todd, Tori, Tracie, Tricia, Valerie, Vanessa, Victoria, Wali, Wendy, Wrenn, Zee, and for the many more whose names I don't know (you fun little anonymous creators, you!), or connected with after this book went to print, thank you

OF DREAMS AND ANGELS

for giving a home to the words. Never stop sharing *your* words, your art, your books, your reviews, and your creative gifts with the world.

To Jonny, Kiki, Sansinski, Uncle Mark, Shootsy, Pam, Gavin, Brandie, Scotty Prime (yes, I have now immortalized that ridiculous nickname in a book—you're welcome), Doug, Josh, Jack, Rick and Bill. Thank you for always being in my corner, despite the many of those I managed to back myself into over the years. Thank you for saying more than "That's nice," when I mentioned something as vulnerable as having written a book, and for listening when I felt safe to say more because of your encouragement. I am grateful for our friendship. I am grateful for who you are.

To Stephen King. I hadn't the first clue I would write a novel when I sat down to read *On Writing*. I hadn't even read any works of fiction for about twenty years at that point. But your words helped me find my way back to the wonderful world of the imagination, back to the world of dreams, and eventually back to my own words and the endless fossils of stories still waiting to be unearthed. I wouldn't have written this book had it not been for you, which I realize is a backhanded compliment if you ever happen to read it and decide to include it in your next edition as a worthier example of what *not* to do. Either way, thank you for helping me to find my words, and thank you for your lifetime of giving yours to the world. Long days and pleasant nights.

To Mom and Dad. Where do I even begin? Thank you for being the first people I knew I could call, no matter how many calls you'd taken before then that a parent shouldn't have to. Thank you for showing me what unconditional love really looks like. Thank you for always telling me to go after my dreams. Thank you for buying me *On Writing,* Mama, before I had much more than a few dollar store journals as writing credits. Thank you to both of you for leading by example in so many areas of life that I'm only beginning to understand and appreciate now. Thanks for always crying openly, Dad, so that I never feel embarrassed when I do, like right now as I write this. Thank you for never giving up. I was about to write, "I love you more than you'll ever know," but I've learned through having my own children that it's the other way around, so instead I'll say that I love you more than I'll ever know how to express. As I write this in the present, I can see your faces as you read it in the future (Stephen King also said that writing is telepathy). And I'll bet your faces look a lot like mine. Which means we all need some tissues and a big hug.

To Kelsey. I can't begin to tell you how lucky I feel that we're getting to know one another now, in the way we never did as kids. I used to blame our relative unfamiliarity (is that a play on words or what?) on our minor age gap, but I know now of some other things that are true beyond a difference in years. And rather than launch into an unhelpful catalogue of regret, perhaps it's better to say that if I was able to do some things (of many) over again, I would be more present, I would work harder to celebrate you, and be grateful for our time together. And while I can't go back to do so with the fiery little spirit with whom I shared a childhood home, I can endeavour to be present with and celebrate the incredible, brilliant, kind, talented, courageous, and fiery big spirit you are today. I am so, so in awe of you, Kelsey Ann. I love you. I love your family. I love getting to know who you are now, and I can't wait to see you again.

To Aidan and Avery. I thought I had a glimmer of what love felt like before you came into my life. Now I know that without you, I never would have had a clue. You are the greatest joy of my life. Just as I wrote above about not knowing how to express my feelings properly to the rest of our family, that's magnified about tenfold here.

Aidan, I have never met a purer soul than you. I love your inquisitiveness. I love your empathy. I love your intellect. I love your drive and discipline. I love your view of the world, and the way you've taken such amazing initiative to find your place in it. I am impressed and amazed by you. And I couldn't feel prouder or luckier to call you my son. Go forth always in the direction of your dreams. Don't ever let anyone tell you that you can't (though many will try), and definitely don't allow their words to stop you. Your strength of character is beyond measure, and you will get there if you believe. You've changed my world, and you will change the rest of it, too. I love you.

Avery, you are the funniest, kindest, strongest, most brilliant young person I know. I love hearing about your experience of life, your thoughts, your dreams, your disappointments, your wishes. I love your creativity. Your perceptiveness. Your curiosity. Your ingenuity. I'm so excited to see the person you are becoming, while I love and enjoy every second of who you are now. I am so inspired by watching you assert your worth, protect your boundaries, and stake your claim on the world. You know who you are, and who you are is nothing short of amazing. You are going to do incredible things, Avery Grace, and being your Dad has been one of the greatest gifts of my entire life. I love you.

To Erin. Oh no. I'm in trouble already, trying to write this. Where did Mom and Dad go with the tissues?

This book wouldn't exist without you. I don't mean the physical pages held within that beautiful cover you helped bring to life—although you've rendered me speechless with your efforts to make sure people will one day hold this story in their hands. But the story wouldn't be there if you hadn't said yes that first time I asked to hold *your* hand, or if you hadn't been willing to let me hold your heart, clumsy as I was with it at first.

You are the most beautiful human being I have ever known, Erin. Part of what makes you that way is you've no idea how incredible you are, though I would give anything for you to be able to see yourself through my eyes. You're brilliant. You're strong. You're uncompromising in your commitment to lead with love. You've written an amazing book that is changing an exponential number of lives, just as the Get the Hell Out of Debt program already had before you put it into written form. Not just because it's hilarious, intelligent, insightful, honest yet kind (though you're the best at all these things), but because you've always led with your heart, and your heart has led you to serve, and the world is infinitely better because of it.

You've opened my heart in a way I never knew possible. You've unlocked within me things I didn't even know were there. If someone would have told me a few years ago I'd be writing love stories, I would have thought it ridiculous. And it would have been, had I not met you.

I feel exactly like Joe, in that I read back over these words and I know they're not enough. They never could be, when one's life has been changed, their soul renewed, their heart healed, by the woman who came to them in dreams. An entire novel isn't enough, but for whatever it's worth, every word within was for you.

ABOUT THE AUTHOR

Jared Morrison is... oh who are we kidding. Most authors end up writing their own bios, and most of us hate doing it. So why stand on ceremony with the third-person talk? No "Royal We" around here.

I'm a lover of words, writing love stories. *Of Dreams and Angels* is my debut novel, inspired in part by a dream I had that led me to the love of my life. I'm currently (as of Sunday, March 14th, 2021, 4:46 p.m., anyway) working on my second novel entitled, *If You Leave,* about a man who wakes up eight years in the past, in his old house, in his old marriage. It's the moment right before life goes sideways, and he's offered the chance to avoid the mistakes of his past. The catch? Back in the present, he's met the love of *his* life. Which direction will he choose? Ooohhh sounds intriguing, yes? If you and I were texting right now, I would insert a winky-face emoji here. Perhaps an "LOL." Kidding. I type that bugger right out.

I'm married to the gorgeous, inimitable Erin Skye Kelly, author of the bestselling Get the Hell Out of Debt. We have four amazing children, and we live near the Canadian Rocky Mountains. Which is lovely, but after innumerable Canadian winters, we're ready for sand and sun. We get quite a kick out of this thing called life, and we're grateful to be here. We're grateful you're here too.

Stay up to date with us at www.jaredmorrison.ca